ELEPHANT SAFARI

ELEPHANT SAFARI

A MBUNO & PERO THRILLER

Peter Riva

OPEN ROAD
INTEGRATED MEDIA
NEW YORK

ISBN: 978-1-5040-8539-7

This edition published in 2024 by Open Road Integrated Media, Inc.
180 Maiden Lane
New York, NY 10038
www.openroadmedia.com

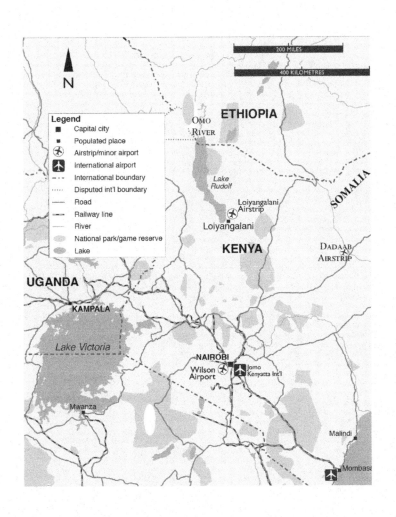

ELEPHANT SAFARI

CHAPTER 1

FROM LAKE RUDOLF, GOING NORTH ALONG THE OMO RIVER

On the third day of their walking and taping safari, tracking a migrating family herd of twelve elephants, tracker Mbuno suddenly knew something was very wrong. He motioned over to his kindred brother, documentary producer Pero Baltazar, but it was Nancy Breiton, camerawoman, who caught Mbuno's hand signal. She tugged at Pero's sleeve and pointed to Mbuno who was waving with flat palm downward. Both Pero and Nancy dropped low into a crouch.

Mbuno Waliangulu, East Africa's premier safari guide, had learned elephants from his father, and his father had learned from his father, on down the ages into a distant Kenyan past. There was nothing that the experienced, fit, and slim Mbuno, an elder of the tribe Liangulu, knew better than elephants. For over a decade, Pero—and more recently Nancy—had learned to trust Mbuno with their lives, just as he trusted them.

Pero smacked a mosquito, for the tenth time that day, as it fed off his forearm, leaving a smear of blood behind. Tsetse fly extermination had become an almost unconscious reaction for Pero and Nancy since day one. Mbuno seemed largely immune.

With several Emmys behind him, Pero was otherwise reveling in their walking safari. Fit, tall, and still well built for his middle age, Pero had been encouraged by his German-born wife, Susanna, and Mbuno's wife, Niamba, to reconnect with the East Africa Pero loved so well. Pero had put up a strong defense.

Susanna, however, was more direct, knowing Pero wouldn't want to leave his pregnant wife behind. "Quatsch. You! Go take a walking safari with your brother Mbuno; go somewhere he and you have never been. When you are less stressed, mein dummer Mann, come back to us." Niamba merely patted Pero's hand, squinting her eyes to reinforce Susanna's command. Mbuno, standing behind his wife, shrugged as much to warn Pero not to disobey Niamba, a powerful *liabon*, or witch doctor, as to obey Susanna.

Pero could never indulge himself without purpose, so, resigned, he arranged for Nancy Breiton to hand-video a walking safari. They would follow elephants, north from his favorite hotel in Loiyangalani on Lake Rudolf, in northern Kenya. Since he left his wife behind three days ago, the walk had been peaceful, and it seemed to Pero like stepping back in time—a time of over a century ago.

As he might in a more primitive Africa one hundred years past, at that moment, three days in, Mbuno sensed, more than heard, elephants in distress somewhere east of their position in dense forest.

For days, Pero and the thirtysomething, fit, talented Nancy had been following and taping Mbuno, who led them on the trail of a small family herd of migrating elephants—the subject of their documentary *A Walk with Elephants*. Pero had presold the show to a cable channel in the States. Mbuno had initially felt uneasy being on camera, but Pero had convinced him that only Mbuno's oneness with nature and the elephants would win the viewers over. "People don't relate to elephants, they can't really understand them. But you, a human, that they can understand, so seeing how you react will teach them to care as well."

Mbuno had agreed, "Ndiyo." Yes. "People must understand before there are no ndovu left." A traditionalist, Mbuno used the old Swahili word for elephant and not the more modern *tembo*.

The three of them had set off across the arid desert landscape of northern Kenya into Ethiopia. They followed the meandering Omo River at the top of Lake Rudolf where the typical northern Kenya forest held tight, awaiting the annual monsoon rains, the ground underneath dusty and parched. Dotted across the landscape were the low bushes and trees Pero and Mbuno were familiar with near Lake Rudolf: cordia with bright yellow fruit, the low fan-shaped acacia with white fuzz-ball flowers awaiting the rainy season, and, the most majestic, the sycamore fig bearing fruit later in the season but always providing umbrella shade for animals and tribespeople alike.

By the third day, the landscape had changed completely. Gone were the more common shrubby trees, replaced by trees along the Omo River digging their roots into the water table. Mahogany trees and the open-branched, tall Senegal mellifera and the short and squat thorny acacia blackthorn. The *Tapura fischeri*, also known as the leafberry tree, usually had edible fruit at the base of each leaf cluster. The leafberry was a favorite of monkeys and locals alike.

Although fit and adventuresome, Nancy had finally gotten used to walking and taping for hours, then all day, always watching Mbuno leading their threesome. Nancy was glad of the small camera's stability lens, which helped her get less vibration. The ground was uneven and capturing the visual flow was increasingly hard.

Ahead, Mbuno's lithe torso twisted and swayed to allow his legs to keep a steady, determined rhythm. Pero knew that unlike either him or Nancy, Mbuno used his feet to measure the soil underfoot, advising of hidden animal holes, soft earth, and changing terrain. Once he started tracking, Mbuno was never in a hurry. To hurry was to risk faltering. To keep a good pace was to arrive. Mbuno measured all of life in easy strides. Being one with the land, he had once explained to an impatient safari client tapping his watch, "No, bwana, a watch does not tell the time of the land, only the time of the sky." In the wild, Mbuno kept pace with nature.

Pero had always relied on Mbuno to keep them safe on safari—a safari he, Pero, always carefully managed and organized. What they were taping now had never been attempted before. They were walking a few dozen yards behind the wild elephants, tagging along on perhaps a two-week migration north into Ethiopian marshlands. Every step they took was farther and farther into a realm where Land Rovers struggle, where man seldom went and, above all, where elephants journeyed to find food and water in times of drought—before the annual rains brought abundance.

Even in the dry season, the swarms of tsetse flies were alarming. Nancy, especially, sprayed her DEET repellent constantly. Spraying the underside of her baseball cap visor kept the mosquitoes away from her eyes and face, especially as she was concentrating on taping.

Out here, alone except for the elephants and sporadic animals watching their passing with anxiety, the pace of the land kept Mbuno's internal clock, set his stride, determined his day, and enveloped him in the oneness that was becoming rarer. Away from civilization, Mbuno often thought, *This is a good day.* At night, around a fire, Mbuno explained to his friends that he wasn't referring to the weather or prospects for adventure. He always considered the speak of the land: the voices of the trees, bushes, ponds, reeds, birds, and *nyama*—game. They all spoke to him, all the time. Sometimes he heard their reflected sentiments clearly, other days dimly. In times of silence, the warning of danger was palpable. He carefully explained that for him, everything in the wild had a different *jini*, a spirit, a jini he could actually feel. These shared spirits held his soul, shared their essence on his skin, controlled his life's urges, and tingled in palpable rhythms along his spine.

However, for Mbuno, as was clear to Pero and Nancy, the closest other beings he understood were the elephants. Mbuno was, more than anything else, a tribesman of the greatest of all African elephant-hunting tribes, the millennia-old tribe called Liangulu. He was, and always would be Waliangulu, meaning of the Liangulu tribe. In decades past, not modern times, hunting the greatest of all beasts, the elephant, took the greatest skill. The meat provided food for the tribe, the hide provided clothing, the hairs were woven into jewelry and used as sewing thread. The bones were carved by neighboring tribes into tools. None of the animal was wasted. Even the ivory had found a use in ceremonial staffs of office and, in the last two hundred years, was traded for grain or commodities the Waliangulu could not otherwise afford, like cloth or soap. Now, all too aware of the ways of the East African governments, Mbuno knew that the time of the wild elephants was passing. His home region in Kenya was turning into a tourist zoo. Mbuno had, long ago, ceased hunting elephants, preferring instead to take out clients with cameras.

On their foot safari transiting into Ethiopia, Pero and Nancy were acutely aware that they were, perhaps, the first documentary people to follow elephants on a northerly migration from the top of Lake Rudolf, following the rust-colored Omo River, deeper into Ethiopia, a country still at war with itself, its tribes and, not least, plagued by criminal gangs, the *shufti*. In the largely lawless and impoverished southern Ethiopian frontier, shufti pillaged anything for quick cash. It was Pero's hope that their documentary would shed some light on this millennial-old elephant migration route and help preserve its importance to all life in the region.

Pero had gone along with his wife's urging. She suggested this particular taping safari would be a return to normal life, to one he loved: being in nature, in the wild, away from the political and governmental forces that had sculpted his life over the previous few years. Once a part-time volunteer runner for the State Department and CIA, events had conspired to involve him deeply in terrorist dangers—dangers he then asked his companions to help him thwart three times. Pero paced his mental words in rhythm with the steps being taken, *As the French say, jamais deux sans trois . . . never two without three.* Three world terrorist events had been combated. Pero and his team were the victors. Governments across the globe were reluctantly grateful. Pero felt only relief it was all over. The CIA and State Department had fired him for the risks he had taken the last time, rescuing kidnapped schoolgirls from Boko Haram. Privately, to himself, he admitted being terrified at the geopolitical risks he'd had to take, the dangers he had subjected others to. His wife, Susanna, whom he met only two years before, understood his relief at being fired but refused to allow him to be gloomy over their success. Pregnant with their first child, she had stayed behind at their favorite lodge on Lake Rudolf, the Oasis Lodge run by an irascible German named Wolfgang Deschler.

Adjusting his heavy backpack, Pero remembered he had relied on Mbuno's clear rationale for all that had transpired in the last events, then recalled that everything usually unfolded with Mbuno having to save the day. However slowly, this return to nature was curing Pero's doubts of who he was—a film and television producer—and why, indeed, he thought perhaps it was time to put aside the events of the past . . . *Mbuno's right— furahifu-goba—all's well that ends well. I may have been fired by the US government, but at least I don't have to look back.*

Nancy gripped a small state-of-the-art digital camera tightly. For her part, she needed this expedition. She needed to commune with real wildlife, with beautiful flora and fauna, too, trusting Mbuno to reattach her to the natural world. Her night-mares had not stopped, nightmares of the terrified Boko Haram girls she'd helped rescue and a terrorist guard who'd been killed, with her knife if not her hand. Instinctively, her left hand went to the same knife hilt for reassurance. Walking steadily, she watched Mbuno through the camera lens with her right eye, keeping her left open for branches and possible threats. She was fairly sure, being with these two men, that she was safe, but their past adventure just months ago had exposed her to the reality of the continent's dangers. However successful they'd been, she calculated that luck had played a large part. *Perhaps less with Mbuno and Pero*, she thought, *but luck nonetheless.*

On their third day, in the afternoon, an hour before Mbuno made them crouch, they'd picked up the pace, stepping between tall clumps of kangaroo grass. In the dry season, the flopping of Mbuno's crepe-soled safari shoes made more dust than bare feet would have. The telltale puffs of pink dust drifted off to his left, which was all right; he wasn't evading a predator. Nancy used the puffs of dust on the video to showcase his relentless walking rhythm. Mbuno's senses were keen. His pace always appeared determined but unhurried, sending a message of defiance to any predator looking for a quick meal. He appeared, simply, resolute in manner and pace; just another creature onward bound.

What none of them had enjoyed, so far on this walk, were, again, the mosquitoes. The Omo River is famous for three man-killers: hippos, crocs, and malaria tsetse fly mosquitoes. If the tsetse fly got you, and you had not taken your prophylactics, then within a day the chills and raging fever would begin. Oh, sure, Pero knew, it comes on weak, but by the time you're into your sixth day, you feel like dying . . . and possibly could. Before the walk, Mbuno had talked to the Rendille tribesmen at the top of Lake Rudolf and asked what they used to prevent the tsetse fly attacks. They gave Mbuno the fruit of the leafberry tree to crush and smear on his skin. Mbuno had made sure Pero and Nancy did the same even though they doubted the berry's efficacy.

Even with that, all three took the prophylactic pills that the ex–white hunter Tone Bowman of Flamingo Tours had insisted they take with them. "You don't want malaria from that region," he warned. "It's nasty, truly nasty." Fortunately, that form of malaria, once contracted, wasn't as deadly as cerebral malaria, which had become more prevalent in parts of Central America. That malaria had a two- to three-day survival factor. The malaria of East Africa could be deadly, but you had weeks to take the cure.

As the day wore on, the three found the going slower. Here there were more young trees, especially ant acacias with their especially sharp thorns. Outside of any Kenyan national park, the wait-a-minute bushes had not been purposefully burned out here as they had been in Kenya's national parks, so Mbuno twisted this way and that, avoiding the cat claw–shaped thorns.

If you struggled, they held you fast. Elephants could plow through, their hides impervious to the thorns, but once the pachyderms were past, the bushes simply sprang back upright to trap the next oncomers.

Soon they spotted four elegant antelope standing under an especially large ficus tree whose trunk was easily four feet in diameter. The tan, long-necked relations of the giraffe called gerenuk were congregated in a sparse group under shade trees. Fleet of foot, and always ready to bolt, the foursome, with ears erect, watched the human trio's movement northward.

Mbuno stepped a bit higher over a cotton bush seedling, careful not to dislodge a yet-to-open seed pod.

The gerenuk took fright and leaped away to safety. Their dash raised a flock of mourning doves and caused a scurry of ground squirrels into their holes. In the wild, one animal served as watchman for all.

There were fewer animals now, outside any protected reserve, especially as their migration routes throughout East Africa had been altered by wire fences. Mbuno was concerned that lookout animals' warning calls, heeded by all animals including the scout, might also be fewer.

Across their path, a copse of sedum growing at the bases of touching tall Commiphora bushes blocked their way. Sedum groves were the preferred hiding places for spitting cobra, so Mbuno retraced their steps and turned east. He worked them past the thorny barrier, planning to turn back in a semicircle toward the elephants' route.

All this bush lore Mbuno knew both by experience and ingrained habit. He did not mind the added obstacles, the miles of thornbushes he picked his way through, nor the cover grasses with their seeded heads that could implant tiny seeds into the skin of your ankles, germinating into festering sores for weeks to come. He'd dealt with these aspects of the wilderness since he was born, they were second nature to him. But he also knew that what wildlife remained was more desperate, more determined to survive, especially at the end of the dry season. All this increased the danger to him and his safari charges. Taping him or not, Pero and Nancy were his responsibility.

By coincidence, Pero was thinking exactly the same about Mbuno and Nancy. Pero wondered if this tracking documentary was safe enough. He noticed that Nancy, small video camera in right hand, repeatedly checked the knife in her belt with her left, in between smacking mosquitoes.

That morning, Mbuno had stopped and focused on one euphorbia tree the elephants had marched past. The branches held no monkeys, nor flocks of birds, nor vultures. All around the clearing surrounding the trunk, the bushes resounded to the call of a solitary superb starling, its red breast flashing as it hopped from branch to branch.

Its piping was a constant warning that could only spell danger, perhaps in the form of a leopard, possibly with a fresh kill carried up into the branches. Leopards were strong, ferocious loners, and, mostly, unpredictable. Or perhaps a large python was up the tree, ready to drop on its dinner. The speak of the wild was strong that day, Mbuno trusted it; so, without Western curiosity or a backward glance, he gave the tree a wide berth and followed a more faint trail, perhaps a miniature antelope trail, a dik-dik's pathway, in between grass clumps into a forest alongside and closer to the river. In the way of a hunter leaving almost no trace, Mbuno's feet kept single file, motioning to Nancy and Pero at the rear to do the same as they all entered the green density. After they left the euphorbia tree safely behind, Mbuno regained the elephants' trail, his internal compass righting his route automatically.

He slowed their pace to allow time to reconnect his senses with this forested land. It was new to him. He had never been this far north and certainly not into Ethiopia. Of course, the nonborder between Kenya and Ethiopia meant nothing to him or wildlife. It was simply that, as a paid scout, he had never been asked to take a group into Ethiopia.

Mbuno was constantly amazed at how very different the land could be from place to place, even though often just a day's or a week's walk apart. Experts he had taken on safari were quick to identify some birds as being of only one species, whereas Mbuno could tell which ones came from which valley, only miles apart. Most were different mutations to his practiced eye. When he learned to read adult books during a hospital stay after a spitting cobra incident, a friend in Nairobi gave him Darwin's *On the Origin of Species*. It struck him as difficult to read for something so obvious. Why Darwin needed island birds way out in the ocean to teach him these truths puzzled Mbuno. Mbuno knew he could show Darwin four hidden valleys near Ngorongoro Crater, each containing a different species of lion, from black manes, to orange ones, to yellow, to almost none, like the ones down in Tsavo near his homeland.

As Mbuno led Pero and Nancy into the forest ahead, he spotted an especially wide umbrella acacia tree the elephants had just passed in the distance, its silver shiny leaves lightly mirroring the breeze, with a termite mound underneath. At almost six feet high, the termite mound formed a tower, now slightly higher than Mbuno's five foot three. He motioned to Nancy to videotape the mound. With Mbuno's back in frame, Nancy could see that something . . . no, some larger things, were moving around the termite mound.

Pero saw the shapes and grew anxious. What if they were baboons? Baboon troops were always to be avoided. Strong and determined, with large teeth, they could be lethal. He knew they sometimes attacked termite mounds. He hoped the apes' focus would be on an insect meal.

Mbuno urged them closer to within fifty yards. The larger shapes they saw seemed to hop between the grass clumps around the termite mound. Nancy zoomed in to see through the shimmering heat that the ground around the termite mound also was moving, seething as if alive. Mbuno realized what they were witnessing. His father had taught him how termite nymphs emerge from their nest, their wings still wet, ready to disperse across the land and start colonies elsewhere. Flightless and vulnerable, they must spread their wings to dry in order to escape. In a mass hatching, for a very short while, tens of thousands could be flightless—prisoners by evolution and design—a seething carpet of one-inch bugs.

All around, not baboons, but large golden eagles, looking like overgrown chickens, were pecking at the fluid, brown carpet and hopping from place to place. The two men watched and Nancy filmed the eagles' feast. *Food for the eagles*, Mbuno thought, *only a few nymphs will escape. But a few is all that's needed to start new termite colonies.* Then he wondered, *How do they know, all these eagles who never fly together, how do they know to come here, at this moment, to this place?*

Mbuno enjoyed the question, savoring it like a piece of candy. He knew the truth, if not the answer. It was simply the way or what the *mzungus*, the Europeans, the white man, chose to call Nature. So he sat on his haunches in the shade of a stunted cedar bush and observed. It was a rare sight for any person to see twenty or so eagles acting like chickens. When the real rains came, the eagles, like all predators, would go hungry, their prey able to redisperse and hide over a renewed green vast land instead of staying condensed in the open around water holes and riverbanks. The hatching termites were a last feast before a time of hunger.

After a little while, time enough for the flies to hover incessantly over their sweat-stained khaki shirts, Mbuno chanted a farewell, "Eat well now, my friends, for there will be much rain this year." He had said it aloud in Swahili, but softly. A golden eagle raised its head, fixed him in its yellow-eyed stare, tilted its head in an unmistakable but unasked question, and then resumed pecking.

Mbuno started a detour to avoid disturbing the eagles' feast. He guided the three of them around a fan-shaped leafberry tree, looked up at the monkeys playing in the shade of its canopy, which Nancy quickly filmed, and mapped his semicircular route in his mind's eye, that they might start again on his route to follow the migration. The termite mound remained out of sight, as Mbuno intended.

As Pero stepped over a rotting log, his foot slipped and he muttered, "Damn." A solitary bushbuck, watching their passing, leaped away at his voiced comment.

And then it happened. The land speak became especially demanding, overwhelming Mbuno's thoughts. A tiny elephant shrew scurried across his shoe, looked up, and darted off. Under that unfamiliar forest canopy, Mbuno was frozen stock-still. Then he crouched along with Pero and Nancy. He cleared his mind and opened his senses. Indeed, the land urgently whispered to him and it said, *More elephants here, now, danger.* Crouching, he listened intently, palm flat on the ground sensing for vibration, eyes scanning the thick bushes and trees for signs of movement. Any trees that swayed when there was no wind, or birds that erupted from thornbushes, could point to where an elephant hid from the afternoon's sun. A faint tremble in the earth on his palm told him the elephants were near, but way off the track they were following, off to the east. He wondered, *A second herd?*

He knew the sunny time of day was when elephants could be economical in the heat. They stayed in the shade, moved very little, listened, alert to danger, waiting for the cooling late-afternoon breeze to coax them back into feeding and movement. Here, under the trees, there would be plenty of shade and camouflage for a herd. Unusually, Mbuno still did not know where they were. To get a more sensitive reading, he knelt and rested his cheekbone on the packed earth. Yes, the tremble was there, faint, off to the east away from the herd they were following, but there. But its rhythms repeated, *Something is wrong.*

Decades ago, Mbuno had stalked and hunted elephants in forests. He did so all his teenage life. He knew the soil, knew how much the recent rain would affect the vibrations, and what the distances were. His brain calculated subconsciously; he was sure the new herd was less than four hundred yards away. He smiled in admiration even as he realized this could not be part of the herd they had been following—it was too far east. Still, it had to be a disciplined herd to make no sound, no flop of ears, no squeal or mew of *mtoto*—baby. Either they were a frightened herd under a very strong leader or they were a local herd, used to the place, and its sounds, and easily prepared for fight or flight if discovered.

And yet, that day, something made him hesitate. The land speak was clear, something was definitely not right. Dropping to his belly onto the forest floor, Mbuno motioned to Pero and Nancy to say put, stay low, and then crawling, inched closer, following the tremor with his palm and stopping to check with his cheekbone. A little right, closer, then a little left. He was aware that his sweaty safari clothing would give him away, so when he was sure the slight wind was coming at him, bringing their scent, blowing his away, he silently stripped almost bare except for his shoes—stuffing his clothing in the hollow of a ficus tree—and rolled in the earth. Immediately, as odor often does, his memories were triggered of the days spent with his father, on his stomach in the dirt, following a herd just such as these. If they charged, there was nowhere to hide. Back home, the Commiphora and giant baobab trees might slow them down but even there, trees would be no refuge for a lone unarmed man. The smaller ficus and leafberry trees of this forest along with thornbushes and spiny forest acacia trees would be insignificant to an angry bull or cow. The trick was not to let them know he was there and if they did, to present no threat. Smelling like the earth helped. He crept closer, yard by yard.

Taking the hunting posture of his tribe, Mbuno knew he had to determine what was wrong with the herd. They could be under threat by local hunters or, worse, were wounded and leaving a blood trail for hyenas and jackals to follow. Wounded elephants were always dangerous, trampling villages and villagers in their desperate anger. To safeguard Pero and Nancy, he needed to assess the danger, and that meant getting closer than a normal man would dare.

All Liangulu hunters knew the skills of approaching, soundlessly, downwind of a herd. The Liangulu had perfected it over the millennia, ever since they'd moved to the banks of the Tsavo River. The Waliangulu—the people of the Liangulu tribe—traditionally hunted the elephant with longbow and arrow, with quick-acting poison tips made by the recipe shown to them by the gods on the side of what was now called Mount Kilimanjaro—the three peaks of snow. The Waliangulu hunters had quickly learned they could not safely get near the young, tender meat. Function follows practice, so thereafter the young were never their target. To hunt the young was dishonorable, and the gods would not be pleased. Their target was the almost senile five-ton old bull or old matriarch. They waited patiently to watch how the elephant challenged them. If he, or she, moved swiftly, youthfully, the hunters would run—if they could. Oh yes, Mbuno knew, even though the arrows could kill anything they hit, young and old elephants alike, if the challenge was swift and fierce, it meant the herd was safe, protected behind a virile leader to be respected, not culled. So the Waliangulu hunters would walk on, perhaps for days, until they would come across a herd where the leader merely bellowed a warning or did a foot stomp and ear flapping. If the ears went back, a charge was coming. If they did not, the leader was old, undoubtedly sterile, and needed to be culled. That one would be their target and tribal salvation.

A younger bull or cow would then assume natural leadership. In this way, the Liangulu were part of the elephant herd's health, part of the pattern of nature. Mbuno remembered a safari client from Texas exclaiming, "We do the same thing on the ranch, put the old bull or cow in the freezer."

However, in modern Kenya and most of East Africa, elephants were dying out; Mbuno knew this and lamented. His chest ached for them. Gone were the innumerable small herds of his youth, mostly replaced by farms, settlements, human sprawl, and tourist attractions. What elephants remained had their age-old pathways and migration routes blocked, stopped, fenced, and constantly monitored. White men came and collared them, watched them on scopes, darted them, sampled them, and even shot them when they became a nuisance to farmers with cash. What elephants modern man did not manage in parks were easy prey for poachers. The days of the Liangulu hunter were over. Mbuno knew this, accepted this, and did not mind even half as much as he mourned the passing of the realm of the elephant.

All of Africa had once been the realm of the elephant. As the largest beast, immune to the normal prey and hunter battles going on all around, the elephant set the pace of the land, fertilized the forests, cropped the prairies, and paved the migration routes that all the migratory species followed. In times of drought, elephants' superior intelligence showed where water could be found and they even taught man to dig in dry riverbeds for a boundary layer of precious liquid. They created mudholes for mud baths to keep the insects at bay, used also by Cape buffalo and rhino. Over the millennia, they brushed aside acacia thorns and baobab saplings with equal ease, creating the open plains. And, in time, Africa's rhythm resounded to the beat of their feet and their migratory timekeeping. Without the elephants ruling the land, the land fell into the discordant rhythm of the upright apes and began to fracture. Mbuno had known the last best years of the elephants' realm and, sadly, was now witnessing the fall of Africa's harnessing stability. Without the elephants to freely roam, the balance of nature would be broken, herds would grow to enormous size in protected parks and, outside that protection, devoid of traditional hunters, herds could be led by weak leaders who would fail to protect them from ivory hunters. Mbuno had heard this had happened before. At the end of the slave and ivory trade in 1911, there were fewer elephants than now and the herds were only brought back from extinction by white hunters—led by Teddy Roosevelt—using farm and ranch husbandry methods—culling every senile cow and bull. Young, vibrant herds repopulated the migration routes. But now the elephants and Mbuno's tribal way of life were both threatened once again.

Mbuno looked back to make sure Pero and Nancy were crouched, waiting a few hundred yards away as he instructed.

He then inched closer to the worrying herd, prone again, a sharp stone rolling under his hip painfully. He dared not move quickly, the bush above him would vibrate. He stopped any forward movement as he spotted feet, the small gray feet of a baby elephant, a mtoto.

One foot had an encircling, red, puss-oozing sore. Behind the mtoto's feet stood the mother. Mbuno could see the way the weight was shifting on both mother and child that the mother was soothing the young one who would be in pain. *Silent pain, the sign of a strong herd leader. Or a very frightened herd, one that is being hunted.* The mtoto's sore had been caused by a wire snare that had probably dropped off. Mbuno had seen this far too often. Now Mbuno felt compelled to do something, not just observe. It was now a matter of honor, duty, and common ancestry, not to mention his responsibility for the safety of his safari charges.

Mbuno's mind made decisions quickly. In the bush, life and death were often just moments apart. Soundlessly, moving no bush or twig, he retreated the way he had come, donned his pants only, and set himself into a running crouch. It was his usual hunter's pace, swift, determined, and ready for a change in direction. Circling the place where he knew the herd to be, he stayed four hundred yards away at least. Starting downwind and determinedly coming full half circle until he announced his presence to their sensitive noses, he tested their resolve. When he was sure they had smelled him, he knew there was real danger here because there was no charge, no bellowing threat, no foot stomp. The elephants could smell that he was only one man and also that he was a man of the bush. As Mbuno had feared, they clearly had a more dangerous enemy threat nearby, for they did not give themselves away. He continued his crouching circling run, sweating from adrenaline and the jini of the hunt. For he was hunting, but not elephant.

When he was three-quarters the way around his circle, Mbuno sensed and then, diving behind a fallen log on his stomach, saw the men just outside the forest's edge. One was sitting on a pickup truck's hood, and two stood in the flatbed. They wore no uniform. The man sitting was dressed as an Arab with a face scarf and camouflage trousers and bush shirt. He had binoculars but no gun. And two standing tribesmen looked like Pokot, Mbuno thought—northern, violent Maasai cousins. Hunters, not cattlemen. The two tribesmen had black rifles with yellow wood stocks and foregrips. Mbuno knew AK-47s when he saw them. Mbuno had seen these types of poachers before. They snared a baby and, in its squeals, it attracted the herd; close and closer until the slaughter would be efficient, deadly, machine gun rapid.

Standing behind a tree trunk on tiptoe, peeking out, Mbuno saw the *panga*—machete—on the flatbed tailgate, unsheathed, its twelve-inch blade glistening, freshly sharpened. The back of the truck held two freshly drawn tusks, the brown blood still not yet black. The herd had been running and not just because of the mtoto.

Mbuno did not hesitate, did not reason, did not moralize. In the bush, the law of the land was kill or be killed. These men had killed, wasted the life of elephant, wanted to slaughter the rest, and were dishonorable. He saw them as little more than *wanyama*—vermin—to be stopped. Without altering his run, he circled behind the pickup and approached them from behind, soundlessly, before the men could even know he was coming.

The panga was indeed sharp. Mbuno scrambled onto the truck and reached to grab the blade. The first Pokot warrior started to raise his rifle just as Mbuno slashed upward. The blade bit deep, upward, just below the ear. On the downswing, Mbuno grazed the arm of the second Pokot, struggling with the safety catch of his weapon. The AK-47 fired one shot into the dirt at Mbuno's feet and rose to point at Mbuno's chest. The second swing of the blade ended the man's life. Mbuno jumped down from the truck. The Arab ran at him, a silver glimmering dagger drawn, but he was no match for a seasoned bushman in a fight to the death.

Hearing the shot, Pero ran to assist his friend. When he reached the end of the forest, the fight was over. Seeing Mbuno alive, he approached without words. Nancy followed a few moments later also keeping quiet and not yet taping.

CHAPTER 2

MTOTO FIRST AID

Mbuno and Pero shallowly buried the two native men using the truck's shovel in the silty sand. In Pokot tradition, Mbuno placed them facedown for dishonor, never to look to the heavens. To honor them would have been, in his tribe's ethic, to dishonor the elephant they had killed. Likewise, he asked Pero to help him strip the Arab of clothing. Mbuno instructed Nancy and Pero they were going to leave him naked to the jackals and vultures. Mbuno knew that Arabs hated to be left exposed in death and hoped this one's spirit was in agony.

Nancy turned away in disgust, not at the fate of the poacher, but at the brutality of death she had witnessed in the past few months in Africa. As a missionary in Nigeria, she had seen the quick tempo of brutality, but their recent rescue of the kidnapped girls in Tanzania had resulted in too many corpses and wounds. Nancy had agreed to the foot safari as a way to return to a more spiritual communion with nature. Standing there, her back turned from the two men stripping the corpse and leaving it for the scavengers, Nancy realized that the isolation afforded by her so-called civilized life was, in reality, simply hiding. She stiffened her spine and turned, resolved to toughen up as her brother used to tell her when she skinned her knee. Using a professional voice, "When you boys are through," she said, "let's concentrate on what I can film here. Okay?"

Pero agreed. Mbuno collected the man's clothing and everything that had fallen clear of the corpse—dagger, money, and binoculars—and placed it all in the truck, motioning to Pero to go through the contents.

The guns, AK-47s, had been easy to disable. Mbuno had learned that trick some years ago. Bent barrels could never be fired again, so he leaned them against a tire and stomped each one, hard. The bullets and firing pins he threw into the dense wait-a-minute thornbushes. He knew all this noise and activity could spook the herd, but they should also calm shortly as he heard no trumpeting. He was sure they were a strong herd; they had already proved themselves to him. Their honor was now his to uphold. And they needed all his attention now, before they angered, turned rogue, and were culled by the authorities. Waliangulu honor and elephant honor were inexorably intertwined.

As Nancy motioned to Mbuno, seeking permission to start taping, he nodded and she only filmed him in close-up as he placed the bent AK-47s on the hood of the pickup. He placed three hats on the front bench seat. The ivory was a prize for some other man to claim. As a Waliangulu, Mbuno only saw ivory as barter. This barter was tainted; he wanted no part of it.

Still angry at the carnage and disgusted with poachers generally, Nancy ran the camera over the flatbed, zooming in on the ivory stumps and blood. When Mbuno was clear of the shot, she filmed the truck, concentrating on the bent rifles in a wide shot.

The sounds of Mbuno's attack and the stifled scream of the

dying men had indeed spooked the herd. There were squeals and stomach rumblings now—calls elephants made to one another. Mbuno knew he needed to get the herd moving. Disregarding Nancy, who was still taping, he went back into his crouching run, not back the way he had come, but getting upwind of the herd instead. He used his scent and the smell of fresh human blood on the ground to frighten them away from him and the truck, back toward the river.

Nancy turned to film Mbuno's run. Pero pushed Nancy's hand with the camera down and shook his head. "Watch Mbuno, follow but not closely. I'll check out the truck and look for permits and papers."

Nancy responded, "Okay, Pero, but let me finish. The empty truck and the tusks—I need a close-up—it'll be proof of the dangers for elephants. And I need a reverse angle." Pero nodded in agreement.

As soon as Nancy had filmed less than thirty seconds, Pero told her to follow Mbuno. "But stay behind, well behind." Pero unloaded his backpack and took out his small Leica digital camera. He reached into the truck bed and rummaged through the Arab's clothing. He pulled out any documents he found and added those to papers he found stuffed into the glove compartment. His camera, on silent mode, made no sound as he took multiple shots. In searching the camouflage trouser pockets as well as the many pockets of the Arab's bush shirt, Pero extracted permits issued to a Somali named Abdul Abdukhad, several notes of Ethiopian birr currency, and, raising his eyebrows at the discovery, a wad of notes in Somali shillings. Pero counted fifty notes with the usual three camels and three goats on the 5,000-shilling notes. To himself, he muttered, "About fifty bucks," and shook his head. He was puzzled. He now had no doubt that the Arab was Somali, not Ethiopian. What was a Somali smuggler, a shufti, doing this far southwest in Ethiopia? The man's identity papers showed no Ethiopian entry stamp. Pero's still camera clicked away.

On the floor of the truck, a black pencil shape peeked out from under the front passenger seat. Pero leaned in and pulled. A beat-up walkie-talkie, with the manufacturer's name Yaesu, was attached, not to a pencil, but to a black antenna. The power was off, the Cyrillic buttons meaning nothing to Pero. On the back was a taped-on label with what he assumed were VHF frequencies. Held with a rubber band was a folded typed paper Pero could not read. Arabic scroll was not easily learned, although he had tried over the years.

There was no time to waste. He stuffed everything he found into his backpack, hoisted it, adjusted the straps, and set off at a trot to catch up to Nancy.

As the herd crashed through the forest, Mbuno followed along with Pero and Nancy catching up, maybe fifty yards behind. When they passed Mbuno's clothing hiding place, he donned his shirt and pack. The smell of his sweat-stained shirt would drive the elephants faster, he knew. Nancy and Pero came up to him and whispered questions. He held up his hand. "There may be more hunters, we must move the elephants. Stay back, back." Nancy was proud her camera captured the urgency in his expression and voice.

Over the next hour, Mbuno urged the herd left and right, at first listening to their bellows and the now-scared mtoto's squeals, foot painful beyond doubt. Eventually, the guide's smell let the elephants know it was he, the one they had sensed before; for elephants never forgot a human's smell. Then, when he tried to turn them toward the river once again, heading due west, the elder bull came back out to challenge him. Mbuno dropped to his stomach.

Pero and Nancy stopped and kept back, frightened. A

four- or five-ton elephant challenge is terrifying. Keeping two hundred yards behind, neither had ever seen—let alone filmed—anything like it. The bull halted, making not a sound, trunk raised like a periscope, sensing for other danger, finding none. Mbuno slowly rose and advanced ten feet, and waited, whistling very softly, then making a strange burping and humming sound. The bull shook his head and turned back into the herd of adults. So Mbuno continued to press them, guiding them from the rear. The bull seemed to understand. The bull moved to the head of the herd, now leading in the direction Mbuno was urging from behind, paralleling the river upstream, northward. The pace quickened, but the mtoto still lagged behind with her mother's trunk pulling her on, sometimes almost lifting her. For hour after hour, they slowly trudged ahead, Mbuno whistling, the bull leading, listening.

Swapping memory chips in the camera, Nancy whispered to Pero, "Where's he taking them?"

Pero was out of breath. "My guess is he will follow the river, about four miles ahead across the water, into the Mago National Park, which connects to the Omo National Park. They should be safer there under the park rangers' care."

As a sixtysomething-year-old, a most experienced safari guide, an ex-hunter, and an ex-guide for Hemingway, Holden, Peck, the Aga Khan, Prince Philip, and decades of celebrities, royalty, and artists, Mbuno was acutely aware that fences, especially Kenya's national park fences, offered a small degree of safety for wildlife. In most cases, the Kenya fences' barbed wire tops faced outward, not inward. Once inside and safe, animals had little intention of leaving. Keeping out humans was the primary goal of most national parks in East Africa. Mbuno knew these elephants needed what safety the Mago and Omo National

Parks could afford them. For once, he just hoped there would be dreaded fences and also rangers ready to open the gates.

Two hours later, the elephants left the forest cover. On the very bank of the Omo River, they paused, unsure where to go. They knew the little man was urging them onward, northward. Pero surmised that Mbuno's fear of another poaching gang nearby was now unlikely—the terrain had become too rough and boggy on the bank of the river for a vehicle. Pero approached and asked Mbuno to pause, "I need to get our bearings, brother." Pero took out a small GPS unit, took a reading, and unfolded the map from his breast pocket. "I think we're here, about one mile to go before there's shallow rapids where we can cross into the park." He spread open the map on the ground. "But I can't see where any ranger station is, or the park headquarters."

Mbuno looked back at the forest edge. Seeing a suitable nearly fallen-over nyangatom tree that the elephants had brushed aside, he climbed as high as he could. Placing his hand above his eyes to shield the sun from the west, he could see what Pero meant by rapids. The normally rust-brown, slow river, was way ahead, rippling in the afternoon light. He called down, "It will be not so deep. We will cross there."

Nancy asked Pero for another chip for the camera. Pero asked if the batteries were holding out and Nancy responded with a nod, pointing over her shoulder at the solar panel. A thin feed wire was clipped to her shoulder strap, taped to her right forearm, and connected to the minicam. Pero took a waterproof case out of his backpack, extracted a new chip, and swapped it with the one Nancy took from the camera. Nancy turned the camera back on and said, "Day three, chip twelve, afternoon, Omo River, chasing elephants," and she panned the scene before them. "I'm ready."

Mbuno nodded and set off walking directly toward the herd. Nancy filmed on and off, acting as camerawomen and director. Pero had planned this shoot knowing the editing would be complex and had to follow an in-your-face documentary visual style.

As Mbuno approached the elephant leader, it spun and stomped a foot, a clear warning. Mbuno commenced the strange belching-humming sound and Pero saw the bull lean his head to the side inquisitively. Mbuno walked straight into the herd and out the other side. The bull followed and then trotted with intent directly at Mbuno but stopped when Mbuno was not chased away.

Resigned to a novel experience, the intelligent elephant followed the strange little man and led the herd at Mbuno's pace toward the rapids.

It is a mistake to say elephants are not afraid of water. Water can be treacherous, can contain quicksand, strong currents, and boulders being pushed by the force of water. Rapids are not, usually, a place elephants prefer to venture. Mbuno was determined to cross there. When he reached the rapids, he could see they were only feet deep and because the rainy season had not yet arrived, moving slowly enough for humans to cross safely. Mbuno looked back at Pero to check they were okay. Pero gestured with a thumbs-up while Nancy kept taping.

Mbuno stood knee-deep in the water and turned, stomach humming as his father had taught him. Elephants make rumbling sounds, talking to one another over large distances. Mbuno's rumblings could not be called loud, but they were identifiable as elephant talk and, at the very least, it gave the bull confidence that this small, upright ape was trying to speak. But enter the water, no, that wasn't the bull's preference.

Mbuno knew a secret of all elephants. He had learned it decades ago and had seen it manifest at Jane Goodall's rehab center near Mount Kenya. Jane Goodall grew bananas for war refugee chimpanzees. However, no matter how she tried with giant electric fencing, her banana plantings could not be protected from elephants who simply adored bananas.

Mbuno still carried his lunch, a ripe, warm banana.

Walking back into the herd, Mbuno cut the banana in half—peel and all—and offered it to the mtoto, first letting the mama smell what he carried. The mtoto took the banana greedily and immediately wanted more. Mbuno waved the other half in front of the baby and encouraged it to follow. Once in the water, knee height, Mbuno shared the remnant, saving one strip of the skin for the bull, who showed interest in the fruit but no desire to get his feet wet in the rapids. The banana won him over. Mbuno let him have the peel and immediately proceeded to cross the rapids. The herd followed. About halfway across, the water came up to Mbuno's waist, so he plodded on, making his belching humming sounds. But this time, the elephants, having understood they were crossing, caught up to him and passed him, bumping him and causing him to stumble into deeper water. The mama of the mtoto picked him up with her trunk and, treating him like a baby, nudged him on.

Pero, mouth agape, started to laugh. Nancy backhanded Pero, adding, "Shush!"

On the far shore, Mbuno decided north had to be deeper into the park territory, if indeed they were in the park by then. The elephant herd followed, sometimes a trunk probed Mbuno's pants, pockets, and small satchel in case there were more bananas.

Watching them, Pero smiled, thinking, *They like bananas as much as Mbuno likes honey*. Throughout their adventures together, Pero and every crew member had come to know that Mbuno's one weakness was honey, especially honey on toast.

Pero was carrying three more bananas and wondered how he was going to remind Mbuno when they crested a small hill and came upon a Suri village of maybe thirty huts arranged in a large semicircle, the open end facing the river. Beyond the village were green fields, laid to crops mostly, and a few goats tethered to clear weeds. Pero could see the villagers were busy with chores.

The sight of an elephant herd approaching their small village, especially one led by a non-Suri man in Western clothing, caused immediate alarm. Mbuno halted the herd simply by squatting and refusing to budge, even when the bull elephant nudged him.

The Suri women hurriedly gathered up children and ran into their clay huts. The huts reminded Pero of tan mushrooms in design, each with a small, tilted straw hat. The men grabbed their thin, tan fighting sticks, some six feet long, and prepared to repulse the intruders. Although Mbuno had never been to a Suri village before, he had met Suri men from time to time near Lake Rudolf in northern Kenya. The men were always elaborately decorated with white chalk markings, almost like zebra stripes, and also had extensive ceremonial scarring causing their skins to look rippled in places. The greater the warrior, he knew, the more elaborate the scarring. Such skin decoration was not uncommon among peoples all along the African Rift Valley. What worried Mbuno more was the reputation of the Suri warriors with their sticks. With their sticks, called *donga*, they were fierce fighters.

Mbuno's other problem was that he didn't speak Suri. He remembered the two men he had met long ago had spoken broken Swahili and now Mbuno hoped someone here would be able to understand. "Mimi ni rafiki." I am a friend. Sitting there, he called it out loudly, twice, "Mimi ni rafiki. Mimi ni kulinda tembo . . . tembo, ndovu." I am protecting elephants. He got no response. So he yelled "Swahili!" A teenage boy ran into one of the huts and emerged dragging a frightened teen girl. He pulled her to the front of the tribespeople, to the elder with the longest white egret feathers arranged in his hair, clearly their leader.

Prodded by the elder there, she said, "Naongea Swahili." I am speaking Swahili. Mbuno stood, opened his arms, and turned all the way around to show he was unarmed and repeated his message. She translated for the elder who spoke to her.

Mbuno had difficulty understanding the girl. Already of age to be wed, the girl already had all her bottom teeth removed and her lower lip had been stretched with a clay disc about three inches in diameter. Mbuno knew this tradition existed, but thought it unnecessary, and he was certainly sure his wife, a liabon—tribal medicine woman, would not allow Liangulu girls to alter their features that way. But the girl's enlarged, pierced lip along with no lower teeth did make her Swahili hard to understand.

When she shouted out the chief's words, Mbuno had to ask her to repeat everything, to make sure he understood. Her high-pitched voice barely carried up the hill, "Tembo kutembea juu ya mazao . . ." Elephant walk on crops. "Haruhusiwi hapa." Not allowed here. The "h's" were particularly hard to understand.

Mbuno needed to know, "Wapi Hifadhi mgambo? Mago Park au Omo Park mgambo?" Where is the ranger? Mago Park or Omo Park ranger?

The girl translated and the elder pointed upriver and spoke. The girl translated, "Kutembea wa siku moja." A walk of one day.

Mbuno thanked them, shouted, "Sisi kwenda—mbali" (We go—away), and, recommencing his humming, he stood and marched directly at the men, the elephants again following. Mbuno waved the tribespeople aside back to their village, pointing where he was going, along the river, upstream, but not, evidently, anywhere near their crops. The warriors seemed to accept Mbuno's confidence. Every man gave a small head nod and pounded their donga on the ground followed by a hard clash with the warrior's stick nearest them. Effectively, they made a fierce show of a fighting barrier to protect the village.

As Mbuno and the herd walked, some Suri called back toward their village huts, calling out families. By this time, the children of the village had already overcome fear and allowed natural curiosity full rein. They gathered in groups, laughing and pointing. It reminded Pero, following along, waving in friendship as he passed, of a circus coming through town back in the States, maybe a hundred years ago. Nancy smiled and waved but mostly kept secretly taping the Suri village and villagers. Pero admired her documentary good sense but secretly registered the disdain and perhaps anger on the faces of the Suri elders at the two white people following the herd. Pero wondered if the Suri's reputation for attacking tourists, especially the "hated white man" that Victorian explorer Richard Burton had written about, still prevailed.

Once they left the village, Pero took the occasion to skirt around the herd, ran up to Mbuno, and handed him three bananas. Mbuno kept up his belch humming and only nodded. Pero scurried off to the left, waited, and took up his rear station next to Nancy again.

Nancy spoke quietly but was eager to know, "What's that strange sound he's making? It sounds like he's belching and humming at the same time."

"Mbuno's father taught him the basic language of elephants, and he's trying to imitate their stomach rumblings."

"You're kidding!" She picked up the camera again and trained it on the herd. "It seems to work, but I can't hear their responses."

"Lower frequency, their rumbling carries for miles. His is for local ears only, but I think the elephants are smart enough to know he's trying to speak their language. I've seen him do this before. Always amazing. Don't know how long he can keep it up though . . ."

What bothered Pero was simple: How were they supposed to march at the current pace for another day? The relevance of the Somali papers in his backpack weighed on his subconscious, finding no room—yet—for more active consideration. To Pero, the Suri were dangerous or could be. The elephant were dangerous and might be. And, never least, where the heck was the park entrance?

The Omo River meandered. Not the Blue Nile of torrents and cascades found in northern Ethiopia nor the wide expanse of the White Nile in southern Sudan, here the headwaters of one of the region's greatest rivers was waiting patiently to regain strength. When the rains came in the mountains of central Ethiopia, usually for thirty days straight, the lakes would fill, burst, and then the river would roar, yell, overrun its banks, flooding thousands of square miles, and declare its full potential. For now, it wandered, waiting to awaken.

The Suri villagers had understood Mbuno's question. With their village on the boundary of the Mago and Omo Parks, the Suri were often protected from their enemy tribe, the Nyangatom, by the park rangers and local police. The Suri were mostly a peaceful, aloof, agricultural people and wanted to remain that way. For the local Ethiopian park rangers, most likely political appointees from the capital Addis Ababa, having friendly tribespeople on the southern end of their responsibility made their jobs easier.

But now, the Suri also had a mission to fulfill as part of their bargain with the park rangers. They needed to get word that someone was coming into the park and that there were two mzungus in tow. The Suri were the eyes and ears for the park's southern border. The fittest young men, two of them, were chosen to convey a message that the man leading the elephants to the park rangers would take a day to arrive walking along the river accompanied by two mzungus. The chief knew that the direct path to the park headquarters was a three-hour straight run, and he sent the young men on their way, knowing they would arrive before the light faded and jackals, hyenas, and other predators could cause the young warriors problems.

A half mile along the river, when the herd had skirted the village and nearest crops, Mbuno saw they were developing another problem; the forest had disappeared completely on this side of the river and Mbuno wondered what the elephants would get to eat. An hour later, the elephants solved the problem.

"The thing about ndovu, my brother, is that they are not all the same. These elephant are not as big as the Tsavo elephant." Mbuno was explaining to Pero and Nancy as they relaxed on a clump of soft grass alongside a marshy oxbow lake. Immediately after the elephant had spotted the still water—which allowed bamboo shoots and pampas grass to grow quickly—the herd had waded into the shallow water and began feeding. Pero saw that they were quite discerning, using their trunks to pick out the youngest, smallest bamboo shoots and consume the three-foot plant, roots and all. The mtoto took the opportunity to suckle its mother. With binoculars, Pero was close enough to see that the mtoto's wound, just underwater, was surrounded by a roiling of small silvery fish. He pointed it out to Nancy.

Zooming a close-up with the handheld minicam, Nancy held up her left hand for silence. The call of river birds, coupled with what could easily be interpreted as contented stomach rumbling by the herd was caught on camera. She lowered the lens, "I know what's happening. I went to a pedicure place in San Francisco last year. You put your feet in this tropical fish tank and the tiny fish eat all the dead and calloused skin off your feet."

Mbuno borrowed the binoculars and looked closer. "It is as you say. This is first aid." He sat back, adding, "I learned first aid three years ago. It is very good. Now I will have to tell Niamba"—he meant his wife—"about this."

Pero wanted Mbuno to finish talking about their elephants. "You were saying about different elephant types? Something special about this herd?"

It was like a late afternoon get-together, comfortable talk with no hurry. Pero didn't want to discuss the papers he had recovered yet. Now was the time to concentrate on where they were, what they were doing, and, importantly, what they were going to do. Pero was apprehensive this close to the bank of the Omo River, a sanctuary for some of Africa's largest and most voracious crocs. On top of that, Pero had spotted a hippo's ears in the oxbow lake that submerged when the elephants went in.

Quietly, enjoying the respite from the strains of the day, Mbuno regaled them with tales of the twelve different types of elephant he had met and seen, from desert elephants to high-altitude jungle elephants that lived with the mountain gorilla and rhinos. "They are all different. Different sizes, colors, and the ears are larger or smaller. Some can swim, some can stand on hind legs to feed on trees the giraffe like very much. Always they must kukabiliana . . ." He paused, searching for the right English word. "Ah, yes, change to live."

Pero knew what he meant, evolve. But Nancy was enthralled. "I thought all elephants in Africa were the same."

"La, la." No, no. "A different place makes a big difference." Mbuno pronounced *big* the way most East Africans do, "beeg." He looked down at the bubbling water caused by the feeding small fish. "It is like all of East Africa I have been to, a small distance makes many changes."

Pero nodded, explaining to Nancy that the cichlids of Lake Tanganyika were vastly different in color, temperament, and breeding cycles to their closest relatives in Lake Kivu. "Even though a river connects the two. Nature always fills a vacuum and sets the local needs as a priority—making the same species develop differently." He turned to face Mbuno and said, "Yet these elephant can hear you and follow? If they're different . . ." He left the question hanging.

Mbuno shrugged. "We may never know. I am so very glad they trust." He stood and looked around. "We will stay here for the night. If the herd moves, we wake and move also." He asked Pero to break out supplies.

So near water, Pero was sure they could filter the water they needed. He took out the Katadyn filter and gave it to Nancy who walked off a dozen yards, upriver, to find cleaner water than the oxbow lake. Then he took out three MREs—meals ready to eat from US military suppliers—along with the zip-up sleeping bags. Made only of webbed ultrathin Mylar-coated Kevlar, all three bags took up less than a third of his pack. When they had decided to undertake this trek with the migrating elephants, Pero had these flown over, along with the MREs, to sustain them when, and if, they weren't staying with villagers along the way. Three hundred miles is a long way and Pero worried about having enough MREs in case the villages became more scarce or uninviting. Remembering the looks on the Suri faces at the sight of Pero and Nancy, Pero had to ask, "The Suri do not like strangers, especially white men. Are we safe here?"

Mbuno sensed this worry was real, but confidently explained, "From now on, when we leave elephants in the park, we will walk from one village on the other side"—he pointed across the Omo River—"away from the Suri on this side, to the next village. Then you will see the pathways in the forest . . ." He looked back across the river. "When we go back over there, it will be all right."

Not that he wanted to doubt Mbuno, but Pero knew enough about East Africa to know that already the Suri village was telling all neighboring villages—and probably the park rangers—that strangers were on a walking safari with elephants. Pero frowned but thought, *Trust him, he knows what's best.* Pero looked across the water too. "Where do you think our first herd is now? Have we lost them?" Mbuno shook his head. Pero didn't know if that meant Mbuno didn't know or was confirming they were not lost.

Nancy came back with water and asked, "Lost what?"

Before Pero could explain, Mbuno stopped speculation and simply said, "We eat and sleep now. These ndovu will eat and sleep where they are—until they want to go. We must be ready."

Pero had hoped, as the day faded, to discuss the papers and go through them with Nancy and Mbuno, but as Nancy looked to the west seeing the sun just beginning to sink below the westernmost mountaintops, Pero could see she was fatigued. *Hell, I am too,* he thought.

Nancy grabbed an MRE, drank some water, and settled down to try and enjoy the end of a long, weird day, saying forcibly, "That's enough excitement for one day. Time to zip up." She wasn't just talking about the sleeping bag. Pero, too, checked the sun's descent. At the equator, the sun sets very quickly. Within minutes they would be in pitch black until the moon came up. He hoped the elephants would wait until then. Soon, still chewing the peanut butter–flavored MRE, Pero felt himself nodding off, allowing the exhaustion to take hold. He hoped he'd have time tomorrow to discuss the paperwork he had recovered from the poachers' truck. It was the last thought he remembered before being awakened in the middle of the night.

Mbuno had his hand over Pero's mouth. He whispered in his ear. "It is a car, it comes slowly." The moon was up in the east, a quarter moon only, but there were no clouds.

Pero looked around and saw the headlights, still maybe a mile or more off, upriver from the oxbow lake, inching its way down the riverbank toward them. The dim yellow car lights seemed to wobble, jump up and down, then side to side. *The going must be rough*, he thought, *and slow*. Pero asked Mbuno, who was waking Nancy, "Mbuno, brother, should we take cover? These could be more shufti." Pero looked about. There was no forest to hide in, the water would be treacherous, and the oxbow lake papyrus reeds and bamboo were too small to hide in without risking deeper water.

Mbuno, rolling up his sleeping bag, indicated to Nancy and Pero to do the same. Pero busied himself stuffing the backpack.

Mbuno's eyes were fixed on the vehicle. Then he tilted his head and listened. After a few brief moments, he said, "It is a Land Rover, diesel, not shufti." Like the poachers, most bandits preferred flatbed small Nissan, older Datsun, or especially Toyota trucks—none new, and all burned *petrol*—gasoline. Diesels were too expensive for the shufti. "It may be park rangers."

Whoever it was, it seemed they had the good sense not to drive up to the calm elephants, their gray freshly washed hides clearly visible in the moonlight. Stopping a half mile from the oxbow lake, a door opened, headlights extinguished, and as the door was closed, Pero was pleased it was not slammed. Pero turned to Nancy and asked, "Ready?" She showed Pero the camera already in hand. From her breast pocket she extracted a piece of electrical tape and tore off a small piece. She covered the telltale red light. No one would know she was taping. Pero turned, in the moonlight, to ask Mbuno, "Mbuno?" He was gone.

Nancy and Pero waited. There was little they could do. To advance toward the car might awaken the slumbering elephants. To sit still invited a surprise attack. For a nervous ten minutes, Pero and Nancy strained their eyes in the moonlight hoping to see anything, any movement that would warn them of danger. Suddenly, off to their left coming over a small rise, Mbuno came quickly in a crouch. He patted Nancy's arm reassuringly.

"It is all right. It is the park ranger. He was worried there were tourists out on foot. It is very dangerous here to be on foot; there are many hippo on land at night he said. Yes, I told him, the ndovu protect us." Elephant and hippo were not friends so hippos stay away from elephant herds. "He was most puzzled. He wants me to bring you to the Land Rover . . ." Then he added, with a bit of a chuckle, "And he wants to rescue you."

Pero wondered if it was a good idea. "Are you sure he is a park ranger?"

"Ndiyo, he has a badge and a ranger uniform." Mbuno looked at Nancy and Pero. "I think we can leave the ndovu here and go with him. The ndovu will wake and move upriver, I am sure; it is where they normally go in the migration. They are feeding, they will not go very fast." It was, after all, the migration time of year, before the rains came, that had inspired their safari in the first place. "Come . . . ready?" Pero and Nancy nodded and grabbed gear. Pero quickly commanded his companions not to reveal the fate of the poachers. Even in the dark, he could sense their understanding.

The three made their way up the small rise and down into a small vale. Mbuno turned north and led the way in the moonlight. After a while, he whistled imitating a starling. A whistle answered and the interior light of the Land Rover came back on. The engine started.

Standing between the headlights was a young man, perhaps thirty years old, revolver and holster on his right side, green uniform with the words *African Parks Network* embroidered in white thread on his shirt. "I am Ranger Akale Hassan, the ranger for Mago National Park and Omo National Park. It is most dangerous to be out without a vehicle."

Pero stepped forward. "I'm Pero Baltazar, and this is Nancy Breiton, both Americans. You've met Mbuno Waliangulu, our guide. Thank you for coming out at this hour to check on us."

Akale Hassan looked taken aback. "I am rescuing you."

Pero pretended to be surprised. "Oh, we really had no idea. Well, thank you so much, but the elephants were protecting us and we them, so we are fine."

Akale was having none of it. "You must come with me . . ." Pero knew they would have to, papers needed inspecting, a small bribe probably, a small lecture, business as usual. Akale continued, "I will need to inspect permits and write a report. The villagers—the Suri tribe you disturbed—are most angry at your trespassing. They want birr for the crops they say you destroyed . . ."

Nancy started to protest, but Mbuno put his hand on her arm. Pero, assuming the role of expedition leader, responded, "Of course, we are happy to help you in any way we can. I have colleagues at the Walta Information Center in Addis who will be very pleased to hear of your efficiency and care for the region." Akale's mouth opened and shut. Pero continued, "Shall we go? Sooner we help you out, sooner we can resume our safari." Pero opened the Land Rover passenger door, ushered Nancy in, and followed. "Mbuno, you sit up front with Mr. Hassan." When they started off, making a U-turn in the soft earth, Pero leaned over and whispered to Nancy, "The Walta Information Center controls the funds for the African Parks Network in Ethiopia. There are huge corruption and tribal issues. I looked it all up before we came. It'll be all right."

CHAPTER 3

4,068 SQUARE KILOMETERS AND NOT A HOPE IN SIGHT

Following the Land Rover's tracks, once they left the unbeaten path and found a less rough track, Akale decided to slip into his tourist guide mode. "It is most fortunate you did not have difficulties with the Suri. They do not like tourist demands." Nancy asked what demands. "Special ceremonies, mock donga fighting, photography all the time. Tourists pay money, but they do not like tourists. We help arrange these tourist parties." He said "parties" like it was a bad word, then emphasized, "Addis insists." He meant his bosses in the capital. Now talkative, Akale was in full swing, "And it makes their enemy, the Nyangatom, jealous that the Suri make money. Tourist cameras prefer lip discs and body scars to necklaces."

Negotiating a steep decline and a sharp bend at the bottom kept Akale momentarily quiet. Pero explained to Mbuno and Nancy, "The Suri women put in those lip discs, like few other tribes on earth. The Nyangatom women, maybe twenty miles away here, wear more and more necklaces around their neck, very much like the Benin tribes of West Africa. Each necklace elongates the neck a quarter inch or more but also holds the head in position for their whole life. The result is very stretched necks. Without the necklaces, their heads would flop and they would die. For some reason, the Nyangatom and the Suri hate each other."

"Āwo tikikili nehi ∷," Akale responded. No one understood, so he repeated, "Yes, you are right," then respectfully added, "Mr. Aleka."

Once before, Pero had been called *Mr. Aleka* by a cabdriver in Addis Ababa who thankfully translated it as "boss." More used to the Swahili equivalent, bwana, Pero explained the meaning to Mbuno and Nancy. Searching his memory, he slowly said, "Ā-mes-egin-alehu." Thank you. "I am sorry I do not speak Amharic, but your English is excellent." Changing the subject, Pero asked, "How much farther?"

"About five minutes to my bēti, my hut, you can stay there tonight. My English was taught at the Bridge School of English. My father is a banker and wanted me to work with the park services. But that was before all the troubles." Akale surely meant the famines but probably also meant the wars with Eritrea and Somalia. "And then the African Parks Network took over here, to rescue all the parks, but they have no soldiers to stop poaching. I work for them but I cannot stop the poaching."

As the headlights caught white-painted rocks lining the ranger's driveway, Pero asked, "Are you having many problems with elephant poaching?"

"Āwo." Yes. "My bosses say we've lost twenty thousand elephants, all the rhinos, and most of the Nubian giraffes and all the Grévy zebras. Before the fighting, the troubles"—so clearly he also meant the Somali and Eritrea wars—"there were many NGOs here from the UN to help protect, but they all left."

Pero could not be sure, from Akale's tone, if he felt regret at the slaughter or was simply resigned to something that had preceded his time as the park ranger.

Akale paused, slowed the Land Rover, tuned to face Pero, and said, somewhat miserably, "Now, it is just me and twelve men for the whole park." His worry was unmistakable.

Immediately Pero understood what could be Akale's other worry. If anything had happened to Nancy, Mbuno, and Pero, the little funding Akale received would have been cut. Any deaths of visitors cut tourist traffic and cut park budgets. To Pero's dismay, neither the Mago nor Omo park had any barbed wire fencing, no park gates, just Akale and twelve locals who would be, more or less, grossly underpaid and open to bribery by poachers. The same situation had repeated itself all across Africa, east and west, north and south.

As the Land Rover stopped and Akale welcomed them to his whitewashed home, Pero, Nancy, and Mbuno alighted into the darkness, each acutely aware that their foot safari had evolved into a trek both more dangerous than planned and Pero thought had better be kept secret now more than ever. Anyone celebrating the elephant, as opposed to the politically endorsed tribal tourism, might become a quick target for poaching gangs profiting from the lack of protection in and around the park. Not quite sure how to navigate the politics yet, Pero knew Akale would, perhaps in the morning, want to know why they were on foot.

Not sure of Akale's poaching involvement—if any—silence afforded the team's safety at least for a night's sleep. Of course, preparing, as they settled on camp beds outside on the bēti's wide veranda, Pero tried to mentally concoct a plausible story for their foot safari following the elephants. Meanwhile, the weight of the Somali's papers in his backpack and the shots he took with his camera constantly invaded his thoughts. At last, supremely fatigued, he slept. Nightmares followed.

Pero woke before sunrise, his head doing calculations on where they were. Omo National Park was half the size of Yellowstone National Park, Mago National Park roughly a quarter of that. Yellowstone had over seven hundred park rangers, not to mention all the surrounding police forces. These two huge Ethiopian areas of national park had one man for each three hundred square kilometers—and that's assuming a twenty-four-hour shift, seven days a week. In reality, it meant each man, on shift rotation, had to cover almost a thousand square kilometers—3,861 square miles—larger than greater New York City and surrounding boroughs. It occurred to Pero that the key to any questioning that he was sure to come from Akale at first light was to find some way to convince him to allow them to champion the ranger's efforts. Pero searched for a way to convince him that Pero could indeed bring reinforcements if needed. *I wonder if he has a radio that works?*

As soon as Pero stood, Mbuno, already dressed and ready, carefully woke Nancy. The sun broke the horizon and the layout of the bēti and the carefully maintained grounds came into focus. Taking the four steps down from the veranda to the packed earth, Pero saw there was a water trough with fresh water, probably from a well or captured rainwater. Pero, Nancy, and Mbuno washed their faces and said little. Mbuno looked at Pero in the way the two old friends had of communicating without words and Pero nodded. Mbuno understood Pero had to calculate an angle to avoid trouble. If Akale suspected they had killed poachers, he would call in the police—if he had a way to call anyone.

Akale's footsteps on the wooden hall floor of his bēti caused them all to turn, look up, and face the entrance. The screened front door opened and Akale emerged, stretching, and said, "Inidēti āderiki . . . good morning." He was smiling, content to see that the trio were awake and waiting for his emergence. "There is a toilet over there." He pointed to his left, to a small wooden outhouse. "And I see you have found our water. It is good." He stretched slowly, showing he was at ease and, along with the revolver at his hip, his body language said he was taking control. "When you are ready, I invite you to my home, to have breakfast. You like?" Pero said they would and thanked him. Akale went back inside.

Pero checked Mbuno's and Nancy's expressions, seeing that they also understood the one-upmanship game being played. Pero said, "Ladies first with the restroom . . ." and Nancy started walking.

Mbuno ran ahead of her. "I check first for snakes." He quickly checked the rudimentary outhouse and held the door open for her. "It is clear." Coming back to Pero, he asked, "You have a plan?"

Pero nodded. "Look around. No other staff visible. Only the one vehicle and it's in bad shape. He needs help, he needs money, he needs us. We can and will help him, as long as he is not part of the poaching. We have to find out." Pero paused. "Until we are sure of him, he must not find out we are taping the elephant migration." Pero tapped his backpack with his toe. "Another issue. I have papers here, from the truck, which we need to review." Mbuno looked concerned. Nancy emerged from the outhouse. "We'll discuss all this later. For now, I need to settle some dust, and have some food"—the smell of fresh bread baking had reached them. To them both he added, "And probe Akale's loyalties. Once we know where he stands, we can make our decisions together. Agreed?" Mbuno nodded.

Nancy immediately agreed. "Yup, pays to be careful."

Two minutes later, the three climbed the steps onto the veranda, opened the screened door, and announced their presence. Akale called from the back for them to come through. They passed a study on the right and a bedroom with a hammock strung for sleeping. Pero looked up and saw half the ceiling was missing, the rafters covered in cobwebs. Pero could see the millions of holes left by termites. Down the narrow hallway they found the kitchen. Two women wearing full-length white cotton dresses, with netela shawls with embroidered crosses— were laying out plates of fresh mango slices, a wooden chopping board with steaming freshly cut bread, and three bowls of cornmeal, piping hot. The netela dresses' crosses were Coptic in origin. Pero sensed that the two women were from the north where the most ancient Christianity was still celebrated—the Coptic Ethiopian Orthodox Church.

Akale invited everyone to sit, including Mbuno—which Pero took as a good sign—and then proceeded to say a Christian prayer before the meal started. *Qurs*, breakfast in Amharic, is traditionally eaten by Coptic households in rotation. First, the men eat, and then the women. Pero watched Akale's expression, and that of the two women serving, as a diplomatic Nancy asked, "May I eat with you?"

After a brief discussion, Akale dismissing the objections of the two women, he told Nancy she was welcome. He understood Western customs. Pero knew that the ranger's upbringing in Addis Ababa must have been upper class, exposed to more Western ways. Nancy, on the other hand, once again amazed Pero with her understanding of different cultures. Sensing his curiosity, Nancy quickly said, "Remember I was a missionary in Nigeria. It's the same." Decades ago her Christian work in Nigeria had given Nancy an understanding few others from America could have.

Akale's two women, however, clearly did not approve. Pero asked Akale if these women were his relations, or perhaps a wife? Akale laughed. "Inē iyasitemariku yaluti ye'āgoti lijoch." He said it in Amharic, clearly wanting the two to understand. "They are my cousins, I am teaching them." He finished chewing a piece of bread. "I did not want them here, but my family insisted. They are not used to modern ways." He turned to the two, "Titehi mehēdi tichilalehi ።." They left and Pero assumed he told them to leave them. The questioning was surely about to begin.

Pero wanted to take quick control of that conversation, so he asked, "How may we help you? Clearly, you are undermanned, underfunded, and underappreciated. Anyone who can drive in the pitch black of night, find us without disturbing the elephants that were near us, and then welcomes us to safety in his own bēti—this is a man operating with a level of experience and excellence who deserves better. So how can we help?"

Akale put his knife and mango down. His eyes narrowed and his brow wrinkled. "Why do you think I need help?"

"Need help? No. Deserve help? Yes. We have contacts, resources, and people with budgets. Not for corrupt politicians in Addis or Nairobi, but for people in the bush who are capable."

Again Akale paused. It could be a trap. If he said he needed anything, it could be a political nightmare for him if his bosses in Addis heard he was asking for or getting outside help. If he refused help, these *nech'i sewi*—white men—could report him anyway. He needed to turn the conversation around, and quickly. "What are you doing in Ethiopia, here in my park?"

"We're on safari, foot safari. We have permits."

"Given by who?"

Pero looked him in the eye and dropped a bombshell. "Meles Zenawi." He paused. "Personally."

Akale stood and leaned on the table facing Pero, clearly angry. "That cannot be. Show me now." It was a demand, calling Pero's bluff. The problem was that Pero wasn't bluffing. From his left breast pocket, he pulled a plastic bag surrounding his US passport and a folded letter from the ex-minister of the interior, Meles Zenawi, who recently had become prime minister. He handed the letter over to Akale. Seeing the embossed stationery and the signature, Akale flopped back onto his chair even as he read the words aloud, "I have granted my good friends Pero Baltazar, Nancy Breiton, and Mbuno Waliangulu the uninterrupted pleasure of a walking safari near the Omo River for as long as they like . . ." He stopped reading aloud but continued to read the Amharic commands that insisted to all who would read the letter that they allow and assist Pero's safari in any way possible. Akale looked defeated.

Pero knew there could only be a few reasons Akale should feel that way. These foreigners could be here to catch him as part of a poaching ring or he could be blamed for not stopping the poaching ring. Or maybe it was simply that he was a bad park ranger. No matter how he looked at it, Akale might feel Pero would tell Minister Zenawi that he had to go. Pero decided to press for a response, "Akale, tell me now. What have you done that has you so very worried?"

Akale was visibly shrinking, hands on thighs, body leaning forward, head bowed. The interrogation was on the other foot and he felt trapped and lost. Shaking his head back and forth, like a child denying he did anything wrong, he rambled, "I did not know how to stop them. I do not have permission to stop them. I do not have the army help they promised, it is not my fault, I tried . . ."

Mbuno asked, "Stop? Who?"

Akal's lips were moistened, and words tumbled out, spilling

everything he knew, "The Somalis who come every year at this time before the rains when the migration brings animals from Kenya. I have asked for guns, the army, and even police, but no one comes. No one cares. Soon there will be no park to guard. And the Suri—all the tribes around and in the park—none of them respect the park. I tell them it belongs to all Ethiopia, our country. They see it as theirs and that I am in the way. The APN . . ." He pointed at his shirt's embroidery letters, *African Parks Network*. He was almost tearful now. "The APN do not help anymore and they have warned me they will abandon the park very soon."

Pero had read that the postfamine situation, coupled with the Eritrea and Somali wars had split the county into antitourism and protourism. Here, then, was firsthand proof of how the system was breaking down. And there was no doubt that the wildlife—all of it—would get slaughtered for bush meat and ivory as the two sides collided. People say culture wars have no real effect. Pero knew that assumption was dead wrong and he was witnessing the proof there at breakfast in this ranger's bēti and in those elephants Mbuno had rescued.

Pero asked Akale to let the three of them talk in private for a moment. Akale, feeling powerless, left the kitchen. Quickly, Pero conferred with Mbuno about Akale. Mbuno, an expert in animal behavior, likened Akale to the buffalo, "He is like the nyati, very stubborn, wants peace and quiet life. The nyati is happy grazing but now must run or fight. Akale does not yet know which one." Mbuno patted Pero's arm. "You must help him." Nancy agreed. Pero called out for Akale to come back.

"Akale, may I ask you some more questions?" Akale, sitting, nodded, his head down. "Good. The two ladies, your cousins, can you get them home quickly?" Akale's head came up—he wasn't being reprimanded; it was a relief. He said he could, so Pero asked, "How soon?"

"Joshua, my other cousin works here, he can drive them today."

Pero noticed he did not ask why or question Pero's intent. "Good, now before we do that, I have an important question. How many Somali gangs are in the park or near the park, do you know?"

"I do not know. One came last week with a truck with many Pokot who had rifles. Only one got out of the truck; other Somali may be in the truck. It was getting dark and I could not see. The Somali showed me he had a permit for meat."

"To hunt? From whom? Did you recognize a name?" Suddenly, Akale again looked terrified. Pero recognized the symptoms. When you utter the name of someone way up the corrupt pecking order, it usually meant you were going to be under threat as a risk. And that suspicion could lead to inter-rogation. And, in a country struggling to find its way through a half century of corruption and violence, interrogation was often permanent, deadly. Pero quickly added, "Sorry, it is okay, Akale. It doesn't matter for now, I get the picture."

Leaning forward, eyes focused only on Akale, Mbuno inter-jected, saying, "Many Pokot means many poaching teams."

Akale looked at Mbuno. "How do you know?" Then he shook his head as if to apologize for even asking.

Nancy, voicing what was going through Pero's and Mbuno's heads, said, "Here we go again." She sounded resigned yet determined. Pero asked her if she was all right. Nancy nodded, adding, without any self-pity, "Fate plays a hell of a strange hand out here."

Mbuno patted her arm as a father would. Pero admired Nancy, thinking, *Remarkably strong, always amazes me.* He continued, looking at Akale, "Okay, Akale, we need your help and then we'll help you more than you can know. What we've seen and witnessed a day ago will already bring these Somali back to visit you." Akale leaped to his feet. "Yes, already there was poaching and . . ." Pero paused, looking briefly at Mbuno and Nancy for visual permission, receiving it he continued, "And a Somali and two Pokot will not be returning home."

Akale's head came up, eyes focused on something distant, and he appeared resignedly decisive. "My cousins must leave." It was clear he understood why their departure was critical now. Somali shufti were known to take women captives for a few days and then discard them to the hyenas. Terror was a weapon of choice for shufti. "They are not safe."

"Yes, that is why. Can you also leave? Do you have a radio to report a poaching gang? Can you do such a thing?"

With too many questions to answer, Akale stumbled into a rambling thought pattern again, "I wanted a radio, they said I should have a radio, the director promised I would have one last year, Igiz'ābiḥēri āyiwedenyimi." He sat down suddenly, held his head in his hands. "No, no, no . . . God doesn't love me . . . but I cannot leave them alone."

"Who? Who would you leave alone?" Mbuno asked.

"My men. They keep the tribes from fighting, try and keep the animals safe." He raised his eyes, then said with passion and some pride creeping into his voice, "We have three hundred and six species of animals here; I have studied them, they are important. If they go, the park closes, everything will be lost. I was train-ed, many months I was train-ed. It is my job." He said it with sincerity.

Pero explained he wanted to help Akale fulfill his mission, his job, but the danger was here, now, already on his doorstep. If Akale did not want to flee home, if he wanted to stay and fight for the park, Pero, Mbuno, and Nancy could help. But, and Pero stressed this, Akale had to understand there would be dangers and he had a right to leave, even taking all his twelve men with him. Pero exaggerated, "We could continue our foot safari, say nothing to anyone here, and when we get back, to our base, to Addis, we will tell Prime Minister Meles Zenawi what a great job you are doing and that you need more resources."

Akale looked pleased and started to say he agreed . . . Pero cut him off, "But, Akale, remember, already one of the Somali and a few Pokot attacked a herd, the herd you saw us near, and they killed the leader, took the tusks. About a day's walk from here, downriver, on the west side, there's a flatbed truck with tusks and guns. No sign of the poachers, just papers I retrieved from the truck."

"Where are they?" The ranger meant the poachers. He furtively looked about the room, as if they would be listening. His body language was close to flight.

"Akale, be calm, assume they are no longer. If they abandoned their truck and weapons, they must be gone." Pero's meaning was clear, they were dead. He continued, "But their friends will try and find them and anyone who might know why they disappeared." Pero had already surmised that the Somalis, having visited Akale as the only local authority, could now assume he had information of the missing men's whereabouts. The Somali leader would not care if Akale knew or not; they would presume he did and if Akale did not have information, he and everyone near him could be silenced—a meat license is not a poaching license. Collecting meat, however illegally, meant the origin of the animal must always be concealed. Somali shufti were, in all regards, terrorists, aligned with al-Shabaab—a well-organized, deadly force not to be underestimated.

Pero's words landed on Akale with impact. Either Akale had to flee, now, immediately, or stay and fight. And all his team too. His face showed the anxiety over the dilemma he was in.

He pulled the revolver from its holster and laid it on the table. "I only have four bullets." It was a pathetic admission of how underequipped he and the APN service were.

Mbuno said, "It is a decision you must make." Mbuno was telling Akale that he, and only he, could decide to flee or stay. Perfectly assessed as a Cape buffalo, the man before them looked left and right, wondering if there was a safe way out.

Slowly, Akale realized that there was none. The Somalis knew who he was, where he was, and would come asking, demanding. And because they knew who he was, he had to stay and fight. Akale was educated, he could think, not simply react. He looked from face to face before him, assessing Pero, Nancy, and Mbuno's worth as allies. His evaluation finally presented itself as a hard response, "We fight together, yes or no?"

"Ndiyo," responded Mbuno slapping his hands flat on the table. He looked at Nancy who simply pulled her knife from its sheath and also placed it on the table. Mbuno knew Pero already had decided. Brothers have a bond of trust and common morals.

Pero placed his hands, palms down, next to Mbuno's. Pero took count of the situation they were presented with. "One poaching gang is stopped, there is at least one other and perhaps a master, a leader we've not seen yet." Akale nodded. "And if they are taking the nyama, the meat, there must be a truck with refrigeration. Did you see anything like that?"

"Yes, the truck they came in had a metal box on top that was making a noise like a fan."

Pero thought, then said, "That could be a reefer, a refrigeration unit. Okay. Now, we need to get help from the villages. The Suri will not want poachers. Will they help, will any tribe?"

"If their village is attacked, maybe, but they are not hunters, not trackers." He held up a fist, raising one finger at a time, "The Mursi are shepherds, Kara fishers, Kwegu farmers; Bodi,

Mursi, and Suri have cattle, and the Hamar and their Maza also have cattle but they are too far away." He thought for a moment, lowered his now open hand, then added, "The Nyangatom are fierce fighters, like the Suri, but they do not care about the park. But the Kwegu, yes, the Kwegu are also hunters; maybe they will help protect the wild animals?" It struck Pero as a forlorn hope, accentuated when Akale added, "But they are three days away."

The sound of an approaching vehicle made Akale jump up and put his revolver back in its holster. A beat-up, old Toyota station wagon came to the back door and three men, all with well-worn APN shirts, came up the back steps and entered the kitchen. Seeing the three visitors at the table, the first man inside asked Akale, "Inezïhi sewochi inemani nachewi?" Who are these people? The man's tone was nervous. His words came out too quickly to be any part of a greeting.

Akale responded with a command, "Zimi beli Joshua ∷ Bek'iribu inegirihalehu ∷." Stay quiet, Joshua, I will tell you soon. Akale then turned to Mbuno, Pero, and Nancy, explaining, "These are my men; this is my cousin Joshua. I told them to be quiet and wait." He paused then went on, "What should I tell them?"

Pero asked the men, "Do any of you speak English or Swahili?

They looked at one another and the last man to enter said, "Kiswahili? Naongea kidogo." Mbuno nodded at the man, urging him on. "Mimi ni mgambo." I am a park ranger.

Mbuno asked, "Je, gari ina petroli nyingi?" Does the car have much petrol? The man nodded. Mbuno turned to Pero. "That car is ready, it has gas."

Pero motioned for Akale to follow him down the hallway to the front of the bēti, asking Nancy to follow him as well. As they left the kitchen, he could hear Mbuno asking questions about the roads, the coming rains, and distance in time to drive to Addis.

Pero did not want to assume the men could not understand English. He had no way of knowing if any of the other park employees were in the pay of the shufti. *Probably not*, he thought, *but let's take no chances*. He asked Akale, "Are these the men who can take your cousins to Addis?" Akale nodded. "Good. And how many other men are nearby? How soon can the rest of your men get here?"

Akale explained that except for these three, the rest of the rangers under his supervision were way west and north where the park is very barren. They were there keeping the tribes from fighting and grazing too many cattle. Pero asked if the poachers would go to those other regions of the park. Akale thought not. "They want the migration elephant; that is along the Omo River." Pero thought this logical as did Nancy.

Nancy suggested, "Pity we don't have aerial surveillance . . ." Pero knew she was referring to the CIA's capability of satellite and drone look-down. Pero's old job was rearing its head. Fired by the CIA as he was, Nancy's comment made him wonder if he could extract one more favor from Washington.

Suddenly shaking his head, to dispel any such notion, Pero remembered that there was no way to contact anyone anyway. He said to Nancy, "No radio, no phone, let's forget that."

She added, skeptically, "For now . . ." Smiling, she added, "You'll find a way."

Pero frowned at her. Turning to Akale, "Do you trust these three men to take your cousins to Addis?" Akale said he did, but he asked if the men's wives could go too. Pero felt stupid. Of course, they would each have family with them. This was a faraway posting and family had to accompany the men. Pero agreed with Akale that they should all go. "Now, Akale, do you have pen and paper inside? I need to write a letter for the men to take to Meles Zenawi. It will be secret. Can we trust them?"

The fact that the prime minister would get a letter from a man staying at his bēti gave Akale confidence and increased respect for Pero. Using the honorific, he responded, "Mr. Aleka Pero, I will make sure they will do as you say. When do you want them to leave?" After a brief discussion, it was agreed that the men and his cousins and all the wives would bundle together possessions, pack the station wagon, including the roof rack, and leave before noon. Reentering the bēti, Akale ran ahead to the small study and came back with Omo National Park stationery and a Bic pen. The end was well chewed but Pero assumed it still worked. Akale said he would give instructions and went back to the kitchen.

Moments later, Mbuno joined Nancy and Pero. "The men are afraid, and they will do what Akale is telling them. But they know something is very wrong. They do not ask questions." Mbuno looked at Pero intently. "It is good you send them all away; they know more than they have told Akale, their boss. I will tell you later."

"Can they be trusted?" Pero had to know.

Mbuno shook his head. "They will do as he is telling them, but do not tell secrets to them."

Pero was staring down at the piece of paper. He knew he had to give Meles Zenawi instruction, instruction no one else would understand. Like many East African leaders, Meles Zenawi had been fully briefed on Pero's previous CIA exploits in Kenya and Tanzania. As part of the Organization of African Unity, the prime minister of Ethiopia relied on AFRICOM, the USA's Central African Command, and their covert actions against terrorism. Pero's and Mbuno's heroism was well known to him. It was why he gave permission for the foot safari.

Sitting at Akale's ranger's desk, Pero wrote:

Prime Minister Zenawi, greetings from your good friends at the
ranger station in the Omo National Park. I have a favor to ask, one
you may want to enjoy as well. Please call this number 202-654-0002
and ask Charles, he's sort of my uncle, to have a look-down at where
we are. There are many interesting animals here and many interesting
people, some, sadly, from the same tribes we got to know in Kenya
a few years ago at a Christian ceremony. It is upsetting that Charles
cannot come and join us here to make new acquaintances. I am sure
he will tell you how valuable meeting these new acquaintances would
be for your work. Too.

He finished off the letter with warm regards and thanks for all
the minister's kind support. He showed it to Nancy. She laughed
a little. "Charles . . . come and join us?" That's going to make
your CIA man Lewis really angry with you." Seeing Pero didn't
care, she shrugged as he handed the letter to Mbuno.

Mbuno read the letter carefully and added, "Not just
acquaintances, but magaidi acquaintances . . . this is a word
they can find but no Somali would know." Pero knew the word,
it was Swahili for terrorist. Pero added the letters carefully
above the line. Then he folded the note and opened a drawer
and found an envelope. He addressed it to the minister at
Menelik Palace in Addis Ababa. Then he wrote, in bold letters,
PRIVATE and URGENT.

As he tapped the letter on his knuckles walking back to the
kitchen, Pero doubted it could ever get through.

As soon as the three men left in the station wagon to collect
their families and belongings, Akale, Mbuno, Nancy, and Pero
pored over Pero's map on the kitchen table. Akale knew his park

and surrounding region well. Akale asked them to wait, went to the study and lifted down the official park map from the wall, and returned to the kitchen table. Side by side, the two maps were in a different scale, but the places they had walked on safari and where they found the elephants were well known to Akale. "It is a good forest for the elephants, there is much shade."

Mbuno had warmed to Akale. Seeing Akale genuinely respected the animals of the region, especially the elephant herd migrating north before the rains and then south after, Mbuno found hope that their mission to save the one herd and stop the poachers could be successful. Akale, for his part, quickly understood that Mbuno was a revered elder who understood elephants. When Nancy told the story of Mbuno walking with the elephants across the river, Akale was dumbstruck and his admiration for Mbuno solidified.

It was Nancy who interrupted the bonding. "Guys, I need to know. Are we taping or not?" Pero had expected the question. For starters, Nancy was a professional and documenting this antipoaching discussion, maps, men agreeing that the poachers' activities should be opposed—all this made for great television. And on top of her professionalism, Pero knew that Nancy would also be right to film in case everything went wrong. At least they would have video evidence.

Mbuno looked at Akale and said, "She has a camera. I want her to use it." Akale immediately agreed.

By this time, Pero was sure of Akale. He turned to Nancy and said, "Play the video—the reverse long shot of the truck, with Mbuno driving the herd." Nancy's eyebrows went up as if to ask if Pero was sure. "I'm sure. We have to test resolve." Pero was in his producer's mode, assessing participants, testing boundaries, and capabilities—all elements of a successful production under adverse conditions. And if there was one thing Pero was sure of, the conditions would get worse. Shufti, especially al-Shabaab Somali shufti, were organized, military-trained, and determined. Pero's only hope of getting his companions out of their predicament was either to avoid contact or be prepared. Making sure Akale knew what they were capable of could give him the confidence to be a reliable member of the team or scatter his resolve and want to flee. Either way, Pero would know where they stood.

It took Nancy only moments to swap chips and fast-forward to the sequence Pero had asked for. Akale leaned over the table to see the tiny screen close up. "T'emenijawochi! Yech'ineti mekīnawi!" Pero asked him for English. "I see guns and a truck, the truck you said." The video showed the contents of the back of the truck, the drying blood covered in buzzing flies. "Kifati ፣ isu kifu newi ።" He looked up at Mbuno. "This is bad spirit."

Pero asked, "You mean evil? Like hell?"

Akale shook his head, "Be'inezīya sewochi wisit'i nefisi yelemi ፣ igizī'ābiḥēri yelemi." He crossed himself and mumbled a prayer. Ready to explain, he responded, "Who does this has no soul, there is no God in those men." Pausing to cross himself again, he continued, "They are not men of God who do this. God will punish them."

Nancy muttered, "God already did . . ." Pero shot her a glance.

Mbuno patted Akale on the back to calm him. "We can stop them, when we know where they are. When we know where they are going." He pointed to the map and asked Akale which way the truck had gone when it left the ranger's home.

Akale traced his finger along the map to the river and then turned north. "There is a narrow valley here . . ." He indicated the place on Pero's map as well as to the side of the park's map, just outside of the park's boundary. "I have no authority there, but the Suri tell me bad men have a camp there last year."

Mbuno said, "Then that is where we must go. First, we must find the elephants." He turned to Nancy. "We will follow them and you can film."

Nancy nodded and mumbled, "Pied Piper of the elephants . . ." Pero laughed and Mbuno, not fully understanding, gave a small chuckle. Akale was mystified. Nancy explained, "Mbuno walks with the elephants and plays his burping sounds to them, like elephant music. It's weird . . ." She smiled. "But really cool."

The sound of the returning Toyota station wagon caused Akale to call out to his female cousins. He went to join and help them. Soon, the two women, each carrying a large bundle of cloth undoubtedly containing their possessions, came back through the kitchen. They looked distressed as Akale hurried them along. Pero could not understand the words, but the gestures and inquisitiveness of their tone told him they were frightened at having to leave in a hurry and wondered why Akale wasn't coming with them. Finally, he said, "Yibek'ali. Tihēdalehi." And they were quiet as they climbed into the back, onto the bench seat shared with two other women. In the very back of the car in the luggage area was one of the APN rangers and a woman. He held and comforted her; presumably she was his wife. The roof of the Toyota was a web of string, baling wire, and bungee cords holding down bundles similar to the cousins' belongings. The two APN rangers tied the new bundles down and got into the front seats. The springs of the old car sagged further, the ones at the rear were already on the stops. Through the open window, Akale and his cousin Joshua gripped forearms, in a gesture of farewell. Akale gave him last-minute instructions and money for the journey . . . the words *petrol* and *Ganada* were clear. Finally, Akale told them to go, and do not stop until they reach Addis Ababa.

As an afterthought, Akale asked, "Debidabēwi ālewoti?"

Joshua reached under his shirt and pulled Pero's envelope from his trouser waistband. He waved it to show it was safe, then tucked it back in. He said something Pero could not catch and the Toyota started off on the way to Addis Ababa, yet seemed to be heading south.

CHAPTER 4

MAPENZI YA MUNGU YATIMIZWE— GOD'S WILL BE DONE

Back in the kitchen, looking over the maps, Pero said to Mbuno, "That's about six hundred kilometers. If the roads are dry to Labuko here off to the southeast, then they will head for Key Afer and then Ganada, from there on it is highway to Addis. They should make Ganada tonight. If not, tomorrow anyway. Say two to three days to Addis."

He thought, *Hell, even if they get the letter through, we'll never know anyway. Suddenly, I do not feel so smart taking this foot safari without my satellite phone.* Pero looked at Nancy, knowing she was thinking the same thing. "Yeah, sorry, Nancy."

Nancy could not let that go unchallenged. "Look, it was a walking safari. There were no reports of poachers, no reports of any dangers. We all wanted the same thing. For you and me, it was a return to the foot safaris of old. To relive the real safari experience." She looked at Mbuno. "For you, it was to see a place you had not been before . . ."

"With my brother," Mbuno added.

Nancy agreed. "Okay, there's that too. We all needed this change from our time in Tanzania, to go back to the old ways, to the real East Africa."

Pero shook his head. "We should have known better. There is no East Africa of old anymore. It was a dream to follow a foot safari, an unrealistic dream."

Nancy laughed. "But the TV will be good!" She patted Pero on the shoulder. "Look, we're here. Those people are safely on their way. If we can move with the elephants north and somehow keep them safe, the taping will be good, the walk will be an adventure, and, with any luck, we'll never see another poacher." To keep morale up, Pero agreed. Mbuno gave him a stern look. Mbuno knew that taking the elephants north was heading them toward the narrow gap Akale had shown them on the map. Walking to the edge of the park jurisdiction, after a huge bend in the river, where the poachers were said to have an encampment, was heading toward danger, not away from it.

Mbuno looked again at Pero, expecting him to explain the next steps. It is what their partnership was built on: Pero was the decision maker and Mbuno was the interpreter of wildlife and man of action when necessary. Pero was deep in thought. He turned away from the kitchen table and went down the hall to the front porch. There, sitting on the top step, his brow creased, he planned eventualities. It's what producers do. Mbuno and Nancy left him alone. Akale looked on wondering why Mbuno and Nancy were so silent, letting Pero leave them.

Pero's dilemma was that they could turn south, walk three days back to safety. That would abandon Akale and, almost certainly, the shufti would catch up to them, or worse. Offense is the best defense, he thought, then, Whoever thought that up must have been thinking of an easier decision. Weighing up the risks, and taking responsibility, Pero put his producer's mind to work.

A half hour later, Pero stood and pronounced to himself, "We have to get around them, disappear, so then the element of surprise will be ours and not theirs chasing us south." Marching back to the kitchen table, Pero laid out his plan, using his finger on the map. "We'll meet up with the elephants—Mbuno, do you think they will still be where we left them?"

Mbuno closed his eyes for a moment, then said, "Bamboo is a favorite food."

"Okay, let's hope. Then we'll take them back across the river. We'll head in the general direction of Labuko, see? Just north of Labuko, before turning west again and coming down into the narrows after this curve, you see it?" He pointed to a spot on the map. "Here. We'll be above the encampment, above the narrows."

Mbuno asked incredulously, "Do we bring the ndovu with us?"

Pero needed to know. "Can you? Can you get them to go into the Mago?" He pointed at a section of the map.

"Is it flat?" Mbuno was wondering if there were hills or perhaps rocks.

Akale looked from Pero's map to his official park map. Almost speaking to himself, "Yelemi ⵝ yihi kewenizu daricha kefi yale newi ⵝ gini t'efit'afa maleti yichalali ꞉꞉." He looked at Mbuno who was waiting for a translation, "Sorry. No, this is a little higher than the river . . ." He ran his finger over the eastern side of the Omo River banks toward the horn of the Mago Park. "Yes, higher, but almost flat. There are bushes, and small trees in the valley and very large trees on the hillsides, and grass still, here everywhere." He ran his finger deeper into Mago Park. "But here it gets higher, there is a valley here"—his finger paused—"that goes up, up, to here . . ." His finger stopped.

"Then it is mountain cliff this way"—his finger pointed east— "but before, the way back to the river follows a tributary . . ." His finger traced a loop back west to the Omo. "Joining here." His finger was planted on the Omo River again. All four looked at the spot he indicated. It was clear the spot was above, north, of where he had pointed out the shufti encampment was in the narrows. Akale smiled, pleased he was able to trace a possible route.

Pero explained that getting the elephants off to the east into the Mago Park might be enough to protect them, but the elephants would, he was sure, want to go back to their primordial migration route alongside the Omo River, and then right into the encampment and the poachers. Mbuno agreed. "It is very possible, yes. It is possible I cannot stop them."

"But can you get them to follow to the valley Akale says is here?" He pointed to the spot, north of Labuko that Akale had indicated was a valley going uphill.

"Akale, is there water? Is there food for them to follow?" Mbuno paused. "What nyama, what animals live there?"

Akale knew his park animals well. "Giraffe and lesser kudu, Cape buffalo and Grévy's zebra with the giant eland. In the valley higher up here"—he pointed to a spot on the map—"topi and oryx. And lion. There are no cheetahs in the valley but there are lions."

"No ndovu, elephants?"

"Yelemi." No.

Mbuno looked at Pero. "If there is food for the buffalo and giraffe, the elephants will eat. They will follow if I have bananas . . ." Akale looked shocked. Mbuno asked him, "Do you have bananas?"

"Zīhi yelemiln" (not here), "In the dukka" (shop), "In Key Afer they have bananas."

Nancy interrupted, "Guys, listen, you're talking about taking elephants to a place they've never been. Hell, taking is the wrong word. Leading? Bribing with bananas? Is this possible? And anyway, then what? As Mbuno says, they will simply want to return to their migration route, right?"

"Nancy," Pero answered, "the reason we take them into the Mago, deeper than they may have been before, is to delay their march north. Then, we continue to go around"—he swung a finger around Mago Park past the small habitat called Labuko— "and, as the shufti await elephant to migrate from the south along the river, we can come down to the river north of their position. If we get there safely, the elephants can turn north, avoiding the shufti."

Akale asked, "And what would we do then?"

Pero was firm. "Find a way to stop the shufti—after the elephant are safe." He took a deep breath. "Look, if East Africa is no longer the same, then it is because of people like this. They are the enemy—of the animals, of the culture, of life. Somali, probably al-Shabaab . . . such a deadly force in Ethiopia is bad for the whole region. If they gain a foothold here, they will not leave. It'll be like the Taliban in Afghanistan or that new enemy the Isis in Iraq. Ethiopia deserves better; all of East Africa deserves better."

Mbuno asked, "Can you make the call?"

Pero knew what Mbuno meant. Nancy did too. To deal with the shufti would require military and CIA support. Pero responded, "Yes, when, if, we reach a phone. Meantime, I have this . . ." He reached into his backpack and extracted the Russian walkie-talkie taken from the truck. "It's VHF only, line of sight, but maybe we can listen in."

Mbuno put his hand on Pero's arm. "Ni mapenzi ya Mungu." It is God's will.

In the 1960s, Mbuno had been involved in the Troubles in Kenya when the Mau Mau rebellion sought terror to overthrow the British rulers. Acting as a scout for the British forces, it was his job to track down and stop Mau Mau marauders intent on butchery of white settlers and non-Kikuyu tribespeople. Those were nights of terror and Mbuno's skills as a tracker and hunter were tested for months on end. Here, assessing Pero's plan to lead the elephants past a shufti encampment, the shufti well armed and well trained by Somali terrorists, most likely al-Shabaab, Mbuno was faced with a sense of déjà vu. Decades before when he was younger and desperate to save lives, over wooden kitchen tables such as this, he came to see the need to eliminate the Mau Mau warriors before they killed again and again. He took no pleasure in the memory; it was simply kill or be killed, protect life where he could against indiscriminate slaughter of women and children.

The problem facing Mbuno this day was complicated. He had an affinity for the elephants. They were, in a spiritual sense, his extended family, part of his tribe's symbiotic relationship with what Westerners called nature. He knew all this; his jini tingled with the urge to protect the elephants. He assessed the cause and effect of Pero's plan and knew what was required—to safeguard the elephants' traditional migratory route, the shufti must be stopped. Pero was right about that, Mbuno agreed. What he did not want to voice was how to stop them. He looked at Pero and saw, in his brother's eyes, the same calm determination and anger that here, once again, they would have to act for the greater good. Mbuno needed to be clear. "You want to stop them, yes?"

Pero responded, "Ndiyo."

"As before?" Mbuno referred to the many killings they had been forced to commit in the past.

"Ndiyo. If it comes to that. It all depends on who I can reach."

Mbuno nodded. To Akale, Pero said, "Take the Land Rover now and go to Key Afer with Nancy, buy bananas, as many as you can." Pero handed all the money he had to Nancy.

Nancy said, "I'll film the shopping for continuity." Pero nodded.

Mbuno asked Akale, "Walking to the Suri, how long? Straight not along the river?" Mbuno had correctly assessed that the Suri runners had told Akale where they were with the elephant long before that first nightfall.

Akale was puzzled by the speed of their planning, but he responded immediately, infected by an ability to join the team's effort, saying they could drop Mbuno and Pero off on the way and pick them up on the way back. Pero didn't ask why they were going to the Suri.

Within ten minutes, backpack stuffed with maps and material along with some food, the Land Rover departed the bēti and inched its way along the rutted road toward the river and then on to the Suri village. Once they reached the small straw-topped huts, Akale beeped the horn and men came out with their donga fighting sticks menacingly. Pero and Mbuno got out and Mbuno told Akale to leave. Nancy was taping from an open window. Still offering to help, Akale was hushed and again asked to hurry away. He did, much to the puzzlement of the Suri men. His parting words were, "I can be back in three hours."

As the tires' dust settled, Mbuno sat on the ground, cross-legged. Pero copied him. The Suri men kept their distance, calling back for someone. The little girl who spoke Swahili was pushed forward, given words to translate, and then she asked what the two men wanted.

Mbuno responded, "Mimi haja ya kuzungumza na daktari wako laibon." I need to speak to your doctor, the laiboni.

Laiboni was the Swahili word for medicine man or, in the case of Mbuno's powerful wife, Niamba, medicine woman.

His body painted with fresh white chalk lines resembling zebra stripes laid over half-inch raised scars, the chief came forward and, mimicking the peaceful pose of Mbuno and Pero, sat across from them crossing his legs. Warriors formed a semi-circle around their chief, standing, leaning on their fighting sticks. The chief leaned forward, showing his teeth to make sure his message of potential violence was still clear. He placed his donga across his lap and, using his right hand, he ran his fingers across the many scars on his torso and left biceps—a form of bragging. Rippled and knotted, his scars were impressive marks of passage into manhood and, later, bravery. The continuing message was clear—this was a man not to be trifled with, lied to, or opposed.

In response, without words, Mbuno took out his small knife from its leather sheath. From the ground, he picked up a piece of wood a quarter of an inch thick and deftly swiped his blade through the wood, cutting it cleanly. He returned the blade to its sheath and sat patiently, waiting. The chief gave one of his warriors a command and the man ran off. The translating girl was told to stand next to the chief, which she did nervously. He spoke, she translated.

Although standing nearer this time, her lip plate and missing bottom teeth still made her Swahili difficult to understand. Sometimes Mbuno had to ask her to repeat what she said, and each time the chief grew angry the girl was perhaps not speaking Swahili properly. As the villager chosen to attend school, her role was clear: to be the tribe's translator to the modern world. Back and forth the conversation haltingly proceeded. For ten or more minutes, the men exchanged names of tribes, origins, status. It was clear the chief originally thought Pero was the leader and had been surprised that a white man was taking orders from an African, especially a small, not scarred, elderly African. In the way of tribal authority, however, bit by bit the chief came to understand that before him sat a *mzee*, an elder of another tribe. When he learned that the Liangulu tribe had a woman liabon, and that woman was this mzee's wife, Mbuno's status became clear. Finally, the chief asked the all-important question, man-to-man, "Have you killed?" He did not mean animals.

Mbuno's response proved difficult for the girl to translate. She asked questions, and Mbuno patiently explained. The chief got impatient and demanded she tell him all Mbuno was saying. She told him that Mbuno had not answered killed properly because he had said he only killed vermin and she had said the chief meant killed a man and Mbuno had explained and insisted he said exactly that, he had killed vermin. She explained that Mbuno wasn't properly answering. She had told Mbuno that the chief knows that vermin are animals and not men, but Mbuno had insisted vermin was what he meant.

The chief held up his hand, silencing her. He suddenly understood perfectly. He leaned across to Mbuno and extended his right arm. Mbuno reached forward and clasped the man's forearm.

The chief called for the tribe's doctor to advance. The ring of warriors around the chief opened and an old man, perhaps sixty or more years, walked hesitatingly forward. The chief patted the ground next to him and the doctor sat. The girl said, her lip plate flopping up and down, "Mkuu wetu anataka kuuliza nini unataka." Our chief wants you to ask what it is you want.

"I will ask the enkidong." The enkidong was a foretelling device also used by Mbuno's wife and many tribes in East Africa. Often made from a large squash gourd, it was decorated and filled with an odd assortment of chosen pebbles—even a few chips of glass. In the hands of a practiced liabon, the contents of the gourd were spilled onto a shaved hide decorated with symbols and designs. Niamba, Mbuno's wife, would move this stone or that bit of bone and pronounce likely events and possibilities. Pero had seen Mbuno's wife's capabilities and witnessed the outcome of her accurate predictions that, as recent events in Tanzania had proven, were critical to their success in rescuing the Nigerian girls kidnapped by Boko Haram mercenaries.

In asking for an enkidong, Mbuno knew that the spiritual ancestry of many East African tribes could form an instant bond. Here, sitting before the Suri people, was a nontribesman asking for predictions, the very spiritual connection, from another tribe. No greater honor could be shown or requested. The chief spoke to the liabon, changing the sound of the word *enkidong* with a click sound at the end. The liabon called over his shoulder and moments later a young man, whom Pero assumed was his apprentice, came running with a rolled-up hide and a two-foot elongated squash gourd, green on the outside with white painted stripes.

The girl translated, "What do you want to know?"

Mbuno asked her to tell the liabon a story. He began, "Mimi ni wawindaji wa ndovu. Sio tena." I am a hunter of elephant. No longer.

She asked, "Ndovu?"

Pero responded, "He means tembo."

"Aiah, ndovu inamaanisha tembo." She nodded. Aha, ndovu means elephant.

Mbuno waved a hand for silence, forcing her to listen. "Tembo ni Afrika. Inafanya Afrika. Hakuna tembo? Hakuna Afrika." Elephant is Africa. It makes Africa. No elephant. No Africa.

The girl translated. The chief and all the warriors agreed, some stamping their donga on the ground in approval. Pero was amazed. These Suri people were not hunters, they did not hunt elephants, elephants raided their crops, and surely they should hate the elephants. And yet, here they were agreeing. Pero thought, *If only all those conservation groups could understand that the real people of East Africa understand the elephant's importance to the land. Tribes are not the problem but Westernizing tribes changed all that perspective . . .*

Mbuno continued, taking his time as the girl was carefully translating, mimicking Mbuno's hand gestures as well, "Watu wabaya wanakuja hapa na kuua tembo. Watu wabaya wataua nchi yenu." Bad men come here and kill elephant. Bad men will kill your land.

The chief was readily agreeing, head bobbing up and down.

Mbuno continued, "Swali langu . . ." My question . . . and Mbuno looked at the liabon, "Je, Suri anaenda kutusaidia kuwazuia?" Are the Suri going to help us stop them?

The chief realized that Mbuno's question was directed as much to the Suri people as to the liabon for divination with his enkidong. Feeling trapped, listening to the murmurs of his warriors behind him, he angrily commanded them to be quiet, stopped the liabon from casting the stones, and looked Mbuno in the eye. The girl translated his words, trying to copy the chief's hissed words carefully and slowly, "And if we don't?"

"Tutakuacha bila wewe, bila ya heshima ya watu wa Suri kulinda nchi yao." We will stop them without you, without the honor of the Suri people protecting their own land.

Pero understood enough Swahili to see what Mbuno had set up and felt the need to add more leverage when Mbuno looked at him with a quick eyebrow raised. Pero said, "I will bring soldiers when necessary."

Mbuno translated to Swahili, using the word *askari* instead of the military soldiers Pero meant. Pero knew askari meant anything from a guard to a local policeman. So he added, "Not askari, but military soldiers." Mbuno nodded and retranslated the English.

When the girl heard, "Wanajeshi wa kijeshi," and translated, the chief and all the warriors became agitated. One poked Pero with his donga as a threat until the chief told him to stop. It was clear that any relationship the tribe had with soldiers had not been a welcome one. Mbuno asked why and the chief explained that soldiers had come in the past years, soldiers from far away. They came with guns and wanted the Suri's food and women. They stopped them after a battle. Mbuno wanted to know how many men had died. The chief admitted that six of his tribe had passed. Mbuno asked if any of the soldiers had been killed. The chief shook his head. It was clearly a matter of shame.

Mbuno told the girl to translate one sentence at a time, carefully. She nodded. "They were not soldiers because they had guns. They were vermin. They are the vermin we want to stop. Three passed away"—he pointed behind him and past the river—"the other day. They are passed and will not go to heaven."

"You know this? They had guns?" The chief was eager to know.

"I know this, they had guns. They were not soldiers. They were bad men from two tribes. Two were Pokot . . ." At this the chief and many of the warriors spat on the ground. "And one was Somali." Mbuno looked at Pero who understood and extracted the papers he had retrieved from the poachers' truck. He showed the picture permit to the chief, who called out for his men to look, each peering over his shoulder. To a man, they affirmed that this was one of the supposed soldiers they had been raided by.

The chief asked, "Can you show me where this body is?"

Mbuno responded carefully, "I can show you where he passed. He was left naked for scavengers. Vermin eaten by vermin."

This greatly pleased the chief. "And the Pokot?"

"They are there, in the ground, looking down." Hearing this translation, the men visibly recoiled. To be buried facedown was to never see the afterlife, to be dishonored as many East African cultures believed. When their shock dissipated, the warriors talked among themselves, clearly happy that retribution had been served.

The chief, although pleased, said, "Three. There are many more."

"Ndiyo," Mbuno admitted. "We only saw three, three that are no more."

The chief looked at Pero and asked, "Why do you want to bring more soldiers?"

Mbuno waved him off explaining again that the three were not soldiers because they had guns, they were vermin and not soldiers. Slowly, he explained matters that any Westerner would have known, that real soldiers have a uniform and are protectors and that in Ethiopia, there are real soldiers fighting the Somali terrorists even now. They fight for all in Ethiopia, the very land the Suri reside in. If the Suri are in danger, the protectors will come.

For Pero, Mbuno's simple explanation was an affirmation of the beauty of East Africa. Here, within a few days' drive of the capital were a people who had no concept of the nation of Ethiopia . . . and yet, there was a name that might please or displease them. So Pero asked, "Do you remember Haile Selassie?" Mbuno translated.

The warriors had no idea who that was, but the liabon did. "Our revered father Tafari Makonnen, you call Haile Selassie, died when I was already a man." He meant past the age of thirteen. The mention of Tafari Makonnen also had an effect on the older warriors who knew who the legendary figure was. The liabon said, "Tafari Makonnen loved the Suri."

Pero was relieved. "I come from a people who revered Haile Selassie. The vermin whom Mbuno speaks of hated Haile Selassie and fought him." He let that sink in. "The men in Addis Ababa today fight in the name of Haile Selassie to protect all people and tribes of Ethiopia, this land where the Suri live."

The chief asked, "The soldiers you want to bring, are they Haile Selassie's men?" He meant of the same tribe. Pero nodded. The chief was pleased. "Then we must await their arrival to fight the . . ." He paused, using the word carefully, "vermin." He looked at the liabon and issued a command. The hide was unfurled, releasing a strong billy goat musk. Carefully orientated to the sun, the enkidong was shaken, tipped up, and the stones and a few animal bones spilled onto the hide.

For several moments, the liabon removed this or that stone, turned or removed a few bones, then sat back on his haunches, eyelids fluttering, and proclaimed his reading to the chief. The girl was told not to translate. The chief needed to ponder. The reading was confusing to the chief. Pero and Mbuno knew the reading was sacrosanct—no one but the liabon could interpret the reading—and that the chief's eventual decision needed to comply, in a sense, with that reading. Abruptly, the chief rose and summoned several of the older warriors away from the gathering. The remaining warriors closed ranks, blocking Pero and Mbuno. They awaited the chief's return.

Pero was nervous. The reading could have said that Mbuno and Pero would get them all killed. Until Pero knew how big the Somali force was, he had no idea who would prevail. And to make matters worse, Pero really could not guarantee that he could summon an army, even if the CIA wanted to listen to him ever again. And his relationship with the prime minister—while aware of Pero and Mbuno's success in Tanzania and Kenya at thwarting terrorists—was friendly but hardly close enough to ask for military intervention to stop a bunch of poachers.

Mbuno, on the other hand, had watched the enkidong carefully. He knew the importance of some of the symbols, those denoting death in many East African cultures, and he assumed that the bones represented weakness as they did when Niamba used them. Many bones had been removed as irrelevant, a good sign. And the death symbols? Only two stones rolled to those symbols, the rest formed a straight line across the blue wavy line down the middle that Mbuno took to mean the Omo River. The two stones that had rolled to the death symbols were the only stones that were black—often the color of enemies when Niamba used them. Mbuno was optimistic.

He had reason to be. When the chief returned with the elder warriors, Mbuno was pulled to his feet and warmly welcomed, as was Pero. Ushered forward, they were taken by a woman to the chief's hut, and, once seated inside, dried fruit and nuts were presented along with chipped-enamel metal cups filled with warm goat's milk, the cream drops floating on top.

The chief and the young girl translator entered, and the woman escort, clearly the chief's wife, left the hut. After welcoming Pero and Mbuno to his home, the chief got straight down to business. First, he wanted to know how many Mbuno had in his army. Mbuno told him the truth. The chief knew Akale, remembered he had a gun, and yet was not impressed. He explained that the bad soldiers who had raided their village were many. Pero asked, "How many were Pokot and how many were not Pokot?" The chief said the Pokot were many in number, but there were only three who were not Pokot. One of the ones who had raided the village was in the picture Pero had shown. Pero said to Mbuno, "So, only two others . . ."

Mbuno agreed that was likely, remembering the two black stones, but reminded Pero that there was an encampment that could have many more. The chief remembered the elephants and asked why Mbuno had brought them. He never asked how Mbuno had arranged to have the elephants follow him, but from the tone in his voice, it was clear he was slightly frightened by Mbuno's seeming magic control of the beasts. Mbuno told the story of the mtoto and how the bad men snared the baby to bring the adults for them to slaughter. At this, the chief and the girl translating cried out in horror. A warrior quickly entered thinking his chief could be in danger. The chief ordered him out of the hut. The chief did not understand why anyone would do this and kept repeating the words for why. The girl translated each time. "Sababu? Sababu? Sababu?" There was no sane answer Mbuno or Pero could give. Even to them, an explanation would seem crazier than the act itself. The meat and hide would be wasted, the structure of the wild broken all for what?

A few dollars for . . . Pero thought, *A few dollars? No, a lot of dollars . . .* He suddenly saw the connection. He turned to Mbuno. "I need to read his permit carefully, there is a clue as to why." He rummaged in the backpack and pulled out all the papers and the money. He looked at each scrap, each item carefully. Then he spotted a dreaded symbol: بابشلا on the backside—an Arabic translation—of the permit. He tapped the Arabic calligraphy. His brow creased with worry. He turned the permit over and reread the front. In Somali, instead of Arabic, was a translation of the name and company the man worked for. The people who were financing and running the Somali "meat" operation were the Dhalinyarada Shirkad. He could not know what Dhalinyarada was. Shirkad he knew. It was a generic name for a corporation. The customs clearance agents he always used for film and video equipment was a Swiss company called Schenker, and their translation into Somali was printed alongside six other languages on their stationery for all the permits of his gear arriving through customs. For business into and out of Mogadishu in Somalia, Schenker Shirkad was their corporate name. But Dhalinyarada meant nothing until he saw that Arabic calligraphy: الشباب‎ It was a unique signature meaning "The Youth"—pronounced al-Shabaab in Arabic. Pero knew it well. Al-Shabaab sympathizers daubed buildings and rail cars in Nairobi with graffiti calligraphy. It was, for Pero, unmistakable.

Pero said softly to Mbuno, showing him the calligraphy, "See this, remember the people we fought in Nairobi?" Mbuno looked stern. Pero confirmed it, "Yes, the same. Their meat permit is issued to the same organization masquerading as a company, a corporation."

Mbuno took the permit and showed it to the girl and told her who these non-Pokot people were. Mbuno made sure to stress that these were deadly Muslim fighters. He could not expect the girl to understand the word *terrorist*. When she had finished explaining to the chief, the chief had a question, "Do they want us to become Muslims?"

Pero assumed the Suri were not Copts, orthodox or otherwise. He had seen no crosses or other symbols as were common among Ethiopians who worshiped that ancient Christianity. But they were not Muslims, either . . . Pero had seen baby warthogs in a pen beyond the huts.

Mbuno explained the Somali bad men were not here to make anyone Muslim. They were here to take ivory and only ivory to sell for money to buy more guns and force tribes, like the Suri, under their control. In time, yes, they would expect captured tribesmen to become Muslim. To which the chief responded,

"Never!" Then he talked for a few moments about their gods and the power of life all around, how a few Somali bad men cannot beat their gods.

Pero and Mbuno both felt he was right. The Suri and neighboring tribes would fight to the death if necessary if asked to give up their culture. Death was exactly what al-Shabaab and their kin, ISIS and al-Qaida, had in mind if people resisted. Envisioning these brave men with their donga, set against AK-47s and modern weaponry, Pero had no doubt the bloodbath would be swift and lethal. Pero hoped Mbuno had more inspiring insight for the Suri.

He did. Mbuno put the palms of his hands on the earthen floor of the hut. "I feel the vibration of the land. The land wants the Suri to be safe. To be safe the Suri must chase the bad men away now, before more bad men come, more guns come and the Suri tribe will be lost."

The chief agreed. In his growing anger, not forgetting the warriors who had already perished, he bravely said, "If my men perish in battle, they will die for the Suri and the land will be reborn Suri." It was as brave a sentiment Pero had ever heard, even if the translation came haltingly from the lisping disc lips of a girl speaking halting Swahili.

To celebrate the Suri commitment and solidify their collaboration, the chief clapped his hands for his wife to reenter. He spoke quickly and she turned, bent double, and exited the low doorway, pushing the hide flap aside. The men sat and talked, Mbuno drawing a map with his knife tip on the earthen floor. Here was the river, then the place where the truck can be found, where he walked with the elephants, and so on. Pero sat quietly, waiting.

More food arrived, dried meat strips, *probably goat*, Pero thought, along with slices of squash well toasted on one side to be eaten like watermelon at a church picnic. Pero relished the flavor, the woodsmoke adding depth to the flesh. The small seeds the chief handed over, indicating they were to be eaten, reminded Pero of sunflower seeds, only twice as large. Pero crunched his way through two or three before he noticed that Mbuno and the chief spat out the hulls. The seed hulls were salty and Pero had enjoyed them, smiling to the chief, he said, "Napenda chumvi, ladha nzuri." I like salt, good taste. The girl translated. The chief answered and her translation, which Mbuno had to translate back for Pero was that he, too, liked the salt, but he sucked it off, as the seeds were too much like wood. The chief, laughing, then made a motion with his left hand at his bottom and Pero got the idea. The roughage could prove hard to pass. All three men bonded in laughter.

During the meal break, Mbuno finished explaining to the chief where he wanted to walk the elephant—away from the poachers' camp and trap. And he wanted the Suri men to accompany them, to protect the elephants. Using his knife, he traced the path as he had using Akale's map to show leading them to the mountain valley before the actual mountain. Mbuno explained that he was worried the elephant may not want to follow away from the river and here he needed the Suri's help to turn them inland, away from the migratory route. The chief pondered, asking if Mbuno's magic would make them follow. Mbuno said he could make them follow, especially if the Suri warriors made a wall. The chief agreed, saying Mbuno's magic was strong, and he had faith. To Pero, it seemed as if the chief was already committed to Mbuno's plan.

For another hour, the two men discussed plans, the use of the donga sticks, the use of bananas, and, especially, the need to move quickly. News of the bananas, the chief found amusing. The girl struggled to keep up, many sentences needing to be explained and reexplained. Pero's lack of fluent Swahili made him lose most of the details, trusting Mbuno to set a plan in place. He asked the chief's permission to leave the hut. It was granted, the chief telling a warrior to escort Pero to what the chief assumed was a bathroom call.

As Pero exited the hut, a dozen or more warriors were gathered awaiting their chief's command. One warrior took Pero's hand and walked him off, up the slope. They marched inland a few hundred yards, over a small hill, and the warrior pointed to a group of bushes. Pero settled some dust and quickly returned. He looked over the Suri village. From where he was, Pero could see that the village was made up of over sixty huts. Many had thorn-fenced areas with goats or, in a few cases, baby warthogs, raised as livestock. Guinea hens ran everywhere, along with children playing games and often practicing with smaller versions of donga fighting sticks. Unlike Maasai encampments, called *manyattas*, there was no outer perimeter of gathered wait-a-minute and four-inch thornbushes surrounding the bomas or huts. It was clear to Pero that the Suri did not have to fend off lions as did the Maasai. He wondered, though, how they coped with jackals, hyenas, and the ever-present packs of Ethiopian wild dogs. Pero tried to imitate the sound of the dogs yipping. The warrior looked puzzled but understood. Pero waved his arm to encompass the village and gave a quizzical look to indicate the full question. The warrior simply took his donga stick and slashed through the air with a speed and dexterity that made Pero understand immediately. Hit with a stick traveling that fast, there was no doubt that the dogs and most likely all wild animals understood this was a place not to trifle with.

It also told Pero something he needed to know. With a necessary nighttime watch routine, several of the warriors would be on night rotation. He motioned that he wanted to return to the chief's hut. Once inside he apologized and asked to speak to Mbuno. He quickly explained that the Suri had a night watch. Mbuno's eyebrows rose and he understood the significance immediately. "I was asking how many men he could spare to accompany us and the elephants. I will make sure we take men for both the day and the night."

CHAPTER 5

SURI TO THE RESCUE

Mbuno and the girl talked, she translated, and the chief responded. The chief had an idea that Mbuno readily accepted. The chief called to three men who appeared through the hide curtain that served as the door. He gave them instructions, pointing to the earth map on the floor. All three understood the instructions and left. Pero followed to see what they were up to.

All three went in different directions, calling ahead in haste. They gathered in three small groups and the warriors received their orders. Immediately, two of the groups made hand gestures that Pero thought looked similar to paper, scissors, rock challenges. The men who won ran off at a pace to the huts. Pero squatted, waiting. Soon, six men emerged and formed a squad, dongas in hand. As they had emerged from their huts, their wives had daubed more white stripes on bare skin. The six men looked at one another, formed up, and trotted off toward the river, turning north when they reached the bank.

Pero went back inside the chief's hut, addressing Mbuno respectfully, "Six warriors have left, well armed and decorated, heading upriver. Where are they going?"

Mbuno pointed to the map, upstream. "A place to cross, perhaps at night."

"Ah, the night watch. Okay got it. There are two other groups, now getting ready . . ."

"One, also numbering six men, is to protect the march, walking with us. One, another six, will find the ndovu herd, then they will return here to protect the village." Mbuno asked the girl a question, and the chief heard the question and responded. Mbuno told Pero, "The second group have already left, he says, to find the elephant."

Pero thought it was a sensible plan. At that moment, the sound of an approaching diesel made Pero leave the hut and look off downriver. "It's Akale's Land Rover, I think."

Picking his way over the rutted surface, Akale pulled up and stopped, staying close to the river. Nancy got out and called to Pero. "We got every banana they had, the back's full. We can't carry that many . . ." She turned to Mbuno. "But you asked for them!"

Mbuno went over to the Land Rover and peered inside the rear windows. There were six full banana bunches, still on stems. Mbuno called the chief and the girl over to look inside. He explained the bananas and, after a while, asked the chief if he could lend a few men to carry them. The chief said no, emphatically no. Mbuno started to ask again, not sure the girl had translated properly. The response was, "It is not man's job."

The chief called his wife over and explained. The rear door of the Land Rover was opened and a bunch lifted out. His wife hefted it and said something. She called over to several women who ran into their huts and emerged with large cloth wraps.

At the Land Rover, she placed a bunch in the cloth, tied a knot using diagonally opposite tips, and put the bunch on a woman's back with the knot on her forehead. The woman seemed to think it was portable enough. The chief's wife moved the knot to a shoulder and the cloth wrap under the opposite arm, positioning the bananas on the small of the woman's back. They seemed to agree that was the most comfortable. Immediately five other women came with their cloth squares and the chief's wife loaded them up.

Standing by the Land Rover, the six women with their banana parcels on their backs, and six men with their donga sticks at the ready, Pero felt they presented quite a task force. He looked over at Mbuno and Nancy who seemed equally pleased. That was until Pero realized that the girl could not accompany them. He turned to Akale and asked, "Do you speak any Suri?"

Akale said he had been working on it and could speak a few phrases and words. He guessed why Pero posed the question and asked the chief if his Suri could be understood. The chief seemed to think it was okay, flapping a hand to show it wasn't exactly perfect. Pero turned to the girl and Mbuno, "We need to teach important words to Akale and us." The girl and Mbuno went off together along with Akale to make a list of words. Pero overheard the Swahili word for "danger"—hatari—and left them to it.

Pero and Nancy compared notes on what had happened over the past hours. Nancy had something important to tell Pero, in private, and wondered how they could slip away. Everyone was milling about, around the Land Rover, waiting. Women with their banana packages squatted, banana wrap by their feet, the Suri warriors standing patiently, chatting excitedly away anticipating the beginning of an adventure. Pero looked at Nancy and suggested they get in the Land Rover. Together, on the back seat, they could hear the people talking but were fairly sure their words, chosen carefully, would not be understood.

"First," Nancy said, "I confirmed Joshua and the other rangers and women passed through and presumably are on their way safely. The dukka manager said they stopped for food." Pero was pleased to hear that they got away. "Now, there was a phone, you know, at one of the markets. Not the dukka where we bought bananas, but a fish market; I was on my own." Pero wondered why the fish market was important. Nancy anticipated his puzzlement. "Fish has to be ordered from the dock, top of Lake Rudolf. That's why they have a phone." Pero nodded. "The line was down, it only works before seven in the morning when the night generator is still working in town. I gave them money and a number to call . . ."

"Which number?"

"Tone Bowman's." Anthony Bowman was Kenya's oldest and most respected tour outfitter. He was also Mbuno's employer and friend, as well as Pero's supplier for decades. "I had to think of a simple message they could read one word at a time. They didn't speak English but they spoke Swahili. You know my Swahili's not good . . ." Again Pero nodded. "I used that new word he wanted to put in the message, majangili." Poachers.

"Good choice. Tone knows that word well."

"And then these words: Tu-nataka msaada (we want help), Omo River, simu Lewis (call Lewis), Tuna vijana (The youth are here). You told me after Tanzania what al-Shabaab meant, so I used that, the Youth. And then just one word, 'satellite.' The guy wrote it down and promised he would call first thing tomorrow."

Pero was impressed, congratulating her on her choice of words. He repeated the message, "Poachers, we want help, Omo River, call Lewis, the Youth are here, and satellite." Pero chuckled. "That ought to make Tone nervous and curious at the same time. And knowing what we went through in Tanzania, he'll get on the phone to Washington pronto." Pero had a sudden thought that Tone would probably also call Susanna, his wife, who was staying at the Oasis Lodge on Lake Rudolf, awaiting Pero's return alone. "This was supposed to be a ten-day break, maybe two weeks, without incident. Susanna will not be happy if she finds out."

Nancy agreed, but responded, "Yeah, so what? She knows what you have done before, knows you weren't intending to find problems here. She'll also lean on Lewis at the CIA, right? That is, if she's worried."

Pero thought it possible. What CIA Director Lewis said when Pero was fired rang in his memory, "Stay out of trouble. We will not, I repeat not, be coming to your rescue . . . for any reason." The word any had been stressed. Pero hadn't told Susanna or Tone any of that.

Mbuno tapped on the Land Rover window. Pero opened the door. It was time to get going. Mbuno explained, "We will drive the women along the river to the place we left the ndovu. The men will follow." To Pero, it made sense to unite there, where the elephant had been. The tracks would be fresh enough if the elephant had moved on. If they had, the six Suri warriors who were scouting ahead would have information.

Pero asked Mbuno to make sure the chief told the women to ride in the Land Rover and that it would take them to the last place Pero's group left the elephants. Mbuno told the girl and the chief refused. A small argument ensued between the girl and the chief. The chief won, naturally. The girl explained to Mbuno, "Suri wala wapanda katika Land Rover." Suri do not ride in Land Rover. Mbuno understood the inflection. The chief meant never ride in cars.

Pero felt foolish. It was well known that the Suri rejected any modernization. Many had tried to "uplift" the Suri—evangelists, doctors, mercenaries, well-meaning charities—all thought the life and ways of the Suri were primitive and therefore needed improvement to help the Suri live happier more productive lives. The Suri thought otherwise. They tolerated the tourists with their clicking cameras, their need of demonstrations of body painting and mock donga fighting. They saw the zebra-painted minivans come and go. Along with those vehicles there came the charity negotiators, well-meaning people who offered modern tools, even shoes. All were either taken and discarded later in secret or simply refused. Pero turned to Akale and apologized for suggesting the ride to the chief. Translation made, the chief looked at Pero and smiled, teeth covered, showing he meant it as a friendly response.

Pero asked Mbuno if they, too, should walk. Mbuno said that was a good idea. Akale agreed, taking the Land Rover's keys and putting them under the driver's seat. "Ready?" he asked and the translation tree passed it on to the chief who pointed his donga upriver and said, "Sisi," which everyone took to mean yes. And so the procession commenced, Mbuno and six warriors leading the way, followed by the six women with banana bundles, followed by Akale, Pero, and Nancy. The chief waved them off. Pero turned and said, "Thank you! Asante sana!" The translator waved.

Three hours later, they reached the oxbow lake. A warrior stood patiently waiting. He explained to Akale that the elephants were moments ahead, and the five men kept pace behind. As they set off, the sole warrior joined the ranks. The women made smaller strides but kept pace.

Nancy had resumed taping. All along their walk, she took

shots, wide panoramas, and, when she could, close-ups of the women and warriors. For her, this was the adventure of a lifetime, the real Africa, real tribesmen and tribeswomen. The beauty of these people startled her, dispelling Western conceptions.

Pero felt the strength of these men, so nearly naked, their bodies terribly, ritually, scarred, covered in white chalk daubing, hair festooned with egret feathers, as they set a rhythm in their pace, each footfall matching the others' and dongas held in the ready position. Without guns, knives, or other weapons, Pero still sensed their fighting spirit and ability. Men who move in a troop as one body were always a formidable force. It lifted his spirits.

The Omo River meanders near the two parks and, rounding a bend, they came upon the five other warriors. The men made the international sign for silence, motioning that the elephants were close, around the next bend. Mbuno told Akale to tell them to wait. He reached into a woman's bundle and took four bananas. Then Mbuno set off on his hunting run, keeping low to the ground.

Mbuno knew the herd would recognize him if, and only if, they were not already frightened. He had to observe them first, then tempt them with bananas. He needn't have worried. They were downwind of Mbuno and knew who was approaching. The mother ndovu and mtoto came out to greet him and, on offering the mtoto a banana, stood swaying side to side, stomach rumbling contentedly. The new leader, who had been promoted after the killing of the largest of their herd, flapped his ears showing impatience. Mbuno threw him a banana, and another one to the mother of the mtoto. Then he sat by the water, looking upstream, wondering where they could cross.

It had occurred to Mbuno that the elephants were not wary or afraid of the Suri when he had walked them past the village. The

Suri had not killed them. Yes, probably they had been thwacked with the donga to get them out of the squash gardens over the years, but such a hit to an elephant would be as a mosquito bite to a human. The elephant learned the Suri did not want to eat them, but they also learned the Suri were animals of the land, not machines. Mbuno realized that the Suri hatred of modern devices fitted their pastoral and peaceful existence within nature. He was sure the elephants would tolerate the warriors—providing they and their donga kept their distance.

Mbuno returned to the warriors and women and explained, which Akale translated, "We will walk with the ndovu. I will lead them to the next river crossing . . ."

Akale translated a warrior's interruption, "He says it is around the bend after this one, it is shallow."

Mbuno continued, "Good." He pointed to the original six men who had advanced upriver. "They need to go around the elephants, cross the river, and wait. We will camp there, on the other side." Akale translated, drawing in the dirt, and six men took off at a trot, skirting the elephants by several hundred yards, making as little sound as possible. Mbuno turned to Pero and asked, "The map?"

Pero pulled it from the backpack and spread it on a flat rock. "We're here, as best I can tell." Akale agreed. "If the crossing is around the bend after the next, maybe a mile away now, then the turning point away from the river will be only a half mile farther." Again Akale agreed. Mbuno said that was what he guessed and why he wanted to stop for the night after they crossed the river. Pero put the map away, as Akale and Nancy also discussed and agreed with the plan. The remaining six warriors seemed pleased to take Mbuno's guidance.

It was time to move the elephants. Mbuno took one bundle from one of the women and slung it over his head, adjusting the knot, bringing the banana stalk to rest on his back just above his waist. He set off following the first six warriors, again skirting the elephants. Pero motioned for the rest to follow him and get closer to the herd, but not too fast or too far, which might spook the animals. Everyone seemed to understand.

Soon, waiting patiently, they had eyes on the herd, maybe two hundred yards ahead. Pero motioned everyone to squat down to look less threatening. Some of the elephants at the rear of the herd looked back nervously, ears flapping.

Suddenly, the whole herd spun to face away from Pero's group. They started to move. They weren't running, but it was clear they had purpose and went away from Pero and the women and the warriors. Nancy was peering through the camera's finder and exclaimed, "It's Mbuno; he's laying a trail of bananas and leading them on. I'm on full zoom, and we'll have to fix sound later, this is incredible." She was clearly happy. Akale explained to the Suri men and women who understood but were amazed.

Now the whole circus was moving. Pero and the group had to keep pace. Around the first bend they went. They approached the second. Pero could just see the dancing wavelets, indicating a shallows for crossing. Since the bend in the river allowed Pero to see Mbuno way ahead, he watched and Nancy filmed. Mbuno dropping bananas until none were left except what he had in his hands. He advanced into the water, the shallow reaching only to his knees. He waved the bananas at the herd.

Elephant never forget. They had trusted this little man before crossing the river. They did not hesitate as he thought they might. Suddenly, the elephant were gleefully entering the water, bumping Mbuno, trunks taking the last bananas he held.

The elephant crossed to the other side and the leader looked back at the humans now standing on the opposite bank. He let out a trumpeting sound that Pero thought, and later Nancy agreed, sounded like a taunt: "The water's fine, I dare you!"

Mbuno had walked the rest of the shallows inside the herd. On the opposite bank, he walked a hundred yards farther on and sat. The mother of the mtoto nudged him to move. He refused. The mtoto came up and searched Mbuno's body for more treats. Mbuno paid them no attention. He waved at Pero, waving him over.

Nancy was taping when the Akale and the Suri men and women crossed. The men took up station on the outside of the women, protecting them if necessary from crocodiles known to be some of the fiercest in Africa. When the women were safely on the other side, they turned away from the herd, walked a hundred yards downstream, and sat, waiting for Pero and Nancy.

Pero pointed to the bushes behind the Suri men and women and there emerged the first six Suri warriors, well camouflaged, to join their tribal gathering. Nancy filmed. Then she and Pero crossed the two hundred yards, aware that the shallows could hardly stop a big croc from a rapid attack. Pero stepped on something that moved and he caught a glimpse of a big catfish powering away. It sent shivers up his spine.

Before they regained the opposite side, Pero refilled their water bottles with clear running water. Rejoining the tribespeople, Pero and Nancy stayed a little ways apart so Nancy could film.

Mbuno called for more bananas. Pero, Akale, and six warriors took a bundle to perhaps twenty yards from Mbuno who ambled over. The herd followed. Pero, Akale, and the warriors withdrew. Mbuno called out, "Here we stay, we sleep. Tomorrow we turn them into the valley."

Pero knew Mbuno would sleep with the herd. He had to. Elephants stood at rest and Mbuno would need to rest prone.

Pero wondered if Mbuno had ever slept with a herd before. How did that work? Nancy filmed Mbuno eating a banana, sharing it with the mtoto, peel and all.

Nancy asked Akale, "How long till sunset?"

Akale responded, "Less than a half hour."

Pero said, "It'll be a long night. Please get the warriors and women sorted out. They, too, need their rest. Tomorrow will be a long and difficult day." Akale, to his credit, only nodded and went to deal with the tribespeople. He sent the first six home with half the women, told the night warriors to be ready, and finally, told the day warriors who had walked with them to sleep as soon as possible.

Pero was ill at ease. Something was worrying him. Something he had forgotten. He pulled out an MRE for Nancy and himself and settled down to wait for sunset. Where they were sitting, on the grassy bank of the Omo River, birds dipped in and out of reeds and a small egret fished, possibly for frogs. As the light faded to anticipated black, the moon not yet showing over the mountains to the east, the last rays of the setting sun cast beams turning the small clouds crimson. Pero watched the curtain of light recede with a feeling of uncertainty. In the middle of this wilderness, he thought, *Has anything changed for millennia? Are we forcing change too fast?* He shook his head to clear his thoughts to more pressing matters, like watching Mbuno in case the elephants moved too suddenly and stepped on him. All too soon for Pero's comfort, the darkness fully descended and he could no longer see his friend.

Nancy touched Pero's shoulder to reassure herself that he had not moved, seeking comfort in joint presence as the tree hyrax started their raucous calls. To add to the nighttime cacophony, carabid beetles roam at night and crawl all over anything alive looking for a quick meal. When brushed off, especially in urgency, they emit a ratchet sound like a small rattlesnake.

In a natural world so utterly devoid of artificial light, the light from the stars and moon, if there is one, allows the human eye to see much more clearly than many would have thought. Pero and Nancy both reveled in the star-lit clarity. The Southern Cross hung nearly overhead so close to the equator. As the moon rose, still in crescent form, its reflected light was almost too intense. Pero was glad he could still see the herd and Mbuno. The herd was hardly moving but soon began feeding on the reeds along the bank.

The night light was, in Nancy's camera-astute perspective, romantic and foreboding at the same time. Suddenly, all tranquility was destroyed. When there's a flash of light from a fire, even fire miles and miles away, the disturbance of the night sky and pitch darkness is brushed away, leaving shadows that should not exist. Light beams that seem unnatural radiated across the flat plains and river.

Akale was the first to stand and register the fire in the distance. He called out to Pero and Nancy. She raised and turned her camera on, using the telephoto zoom to try and determine where the fire was. "I can't tell where it is or what's burning, but the flames are high. It's a big fire."

Akale looked sullen. "It is my bēti." Pero only nodded. There was no other structure large enough, no village hut, no pile of wood—nothing large enough to cause a fire that could be seen miles away as the crow flies, except for the ranger's home.

"Sorry, Akale." It was then Pero realized what he had forgotten—the Land Rover. It was parked by the river outside the Suri village. The poachers must have gone there and realized whose vehicle it was and went back to the ranger's bēti. But why torch it? he thought rhetorically. Pero knew why and so did Akale. To send a message. They were coming for him. Soon, first light, in the morning. Akale was now undoubtedly a target.

Through the night, the six warriors kept guard. The fire did not concern them, and Akale chose not to explain the significance as they might worry about their village. Pero asked Akale to make sure they watched the river in case bad men came that way. The warriors divided their forces, three looping ahead of the elephant herd and three stationing themselves by the riverbank. The other six warriors slept, ready to wake and assist against an attack if necessary. Pero saw Akale check his revolver twice.

It was risky, Pero knew that, but he needed to talk to Mbuno. He didn't want to call out—sound carries, and besides the elephant needed tranquility. So Pero crawled the yards to Mbuno who, of course, knew he was coming. "My brother, you even make noise on your belly," Mbuno whispered it with a slight chuckle.

Pero spoke close to Mbuno's ear, "We've posted three men ahead of you in case the Somalis come down along the river from the north. That leaves three here guarding the riverbank. The others sleep but will wake if called." Mbuno nodded. "The fire . . ."

"The bēti, I see it."

"Yes, Akale said it had to be that. My mistake, I forgot the Land Rover being left there would tell them, if they came, that the Suri are with us and the ranger." Again Mbuno only nodded. "Thankfully, Joshua and the others got away safely, Nancy said so. She checked."

"What is worrying you, my brother?"

"As soon as we turn into the valley leading into the mountains, if we can turn the herd, I want to send all the tribespeople home." He paused to see if Mbuno agreed or disagreed. Mbuno said nothing. "I can carry at least one bundle of bananas, maybe two, Nancy and Akale one each. You'll need one to turn them. That will have to do, I can't risk these Suri being cut down by AK-47s. We know they'll be coming after us, we need to let them get clear."

Mbuno's voice was barely a whisper, "It is as I want too. But we must let them make their plan. Suri have honor." There was nothing to be said; Mbuno's logic was, as always, perfect. Pero's Western desire and Mbuno's passion to protect meant nothing compared to what the Suri tribe would insist on for their honor and that Mbuno would respect, no matter the consequences. Pero patted his brother on the shoulder and crawled back to Nancy.

Pero slept fitfully but when he woke, minutes before the sun's rays peeked over the mountains to their east, he was surprised at how well he felt. Self-assessment was one of his strengths, so he questioned why he should wake feeling rested and ready. It did not take him long to realize that there were no nagging doubts about what he had forgotten. All was in play then. Light would bring the enemy, light would start events they had planned for. All Pero had to do is keep alert and ready.

First daylight allowed him and Nancy to assess where they were, where the warriors were. Akale, a few yards away, looked dead tired, dozing while sitting cross-legged, his revolver in hand. Pero called his name softly. Akale's head rose from slumber. "Ah, I was sleeping, sorry."

Pero smiled. "Brave of you to stay on guard all night." Then Pero had a thought, but first he needed to talk with the lead warrior. "Akale, let's talk to the warrior who's in charge. Can you get him to come over?"

Akale whistled and three heads turned. Akale pointed to one

and motioned him over. They spoke for a few seconds and the warrior went off and woke one of the six warriors who then joined Akale and Pero. Nancy started taping, careful not to lift the lens to her eye, she appeared to be doing something but was, in effect, shooting from a crouch.

Pero told Akale his plan. Akale kept nodding, finally saying, "I agree, it is right." He spoke to the two warriors who both immediately disagreed. Pero expected that, saying to Akale, "Tell them I understand Suri honor. It is great honor and I respect that. But the rest of the women need to go home, to be safe. We need to escort them home safely. Six"—Pero pointed at the night team—"can take them home safely and"—he pointed to the leader of the day team—"six can stay with us to uphold Suri honor."

Akale took a few minutes to explain. Some arguing ensued, a firm discussion between the two warrior leaders as well, but in the end, Pero's decision was logical and held firm. Pero added, "And, Akale, I need you to go with them; you need to get safely to authority and report what has happened." Pero reached into his backpack and pulled out the letter from the prime minister and gave it to Akale. "Use this, get help for the Suri and your people. This letter will ensure that you can get police and military help." Pero took out a pen and wrote on the backside. "Call this number if you cannot get the prime minister's people to listen. Tell them I demand help. Use that word, 'demand.' Understood?"

Akale didn't want to leave, that was clear, but given the new responsibility Pero had thrust on him, he had no choice. He was thinking all the while. "I will walk the women along the river, but stay on this side until we come to the village. We will try and stay out of sight. Then, if the Land Rover is burned"—he thought the poachers might have destroyed it as well—"I will get two men to walk with me to my bēti. Behind Joshua's house, he has a motorbike. I will go to Key Afer, there is a telephone there . . ." Pero guessed it was the same one Nancy had used. "And I will do as you say." There was pride in his voice, quickly replaced with anger, "I will get help to kill these evil men."

Pero wanted to make sure Akale stayed focused. "Remember, step by step. First get these women safe, then make sure the Suri village is safe as well. Then get to Key Afer however you can. Once you call in help, stay and protect the Suri village."

"And you?"

Pero assured him they were sticking to plan. Akale had one last item. He undid the gun belt and holster and handed it to Pero. "You must take this. Only four bullets." Pero wanted to refuse but saw Akale's logic. He strapped it on and thanked him.

There was no time to lose. In the dim early morning light, Pero urged Akale and the night watch warriors to leave with the women quickly. Akale assured Pero that when the three up ahead returned, they would do so immediately. Pero wished them a safe trek home and turned to help Nancy with her banana sling. He put two on his own back along with the backpack. Nancy helped him get adjusted. It was a heavy load, but Pero was determined to manage. That left one bunch for Mbuno's morning needs. A warrior picked it up and brazenly walked it over to within ten yards of Mbuno, who motioned for him to put it down.

The six day-watch warriors were prepared and patient awaiting Mbuno's signal to get moving, each standing on one leg, the other naked foot perched over a knee, the donga acting as a balance. With a free hand, each ate strips of jerky taken from the rolled cloth held by string around their waists.

On Mbuno's signal, all stood ready for the move on. Mbuno picked up the banana bundle and walked into the herd. Pero guessed he would be doing his belching humming. The herd let him pass, trunks exploring the smells coming from the cloth bundle, a mixture of human sweat and delicious bananas. Confused, they recoiled. Mbuno reached in and snapped off a small banana, slipping it to the mtoto who gleefully took the treat. Mbuno looked down at the mtoto's wound, which seemed dry and clean. *Good, it will get better*, he thought.

Reaching the far side of the herd, Mbuno whistled so that the leader would know he was there. He dropped a banana and the mtoto followed. The leader quickly passed the mtoto, side-swiping it with his trunk to make the point, and calmly walked up to Mbuno, who rewarded him with a banana. Peel and all went straight into the gaping mouth. Up ahead, Mbuno could see the returning three warriors who'd kept vigil all night. Spotting Mbuno, they waved, clearly indicating there was nothing ahead that they could see. They stayed off to the side, away from the river, waiting for the herd to pass. When Pero came up to them, he motioned them to go back, pointing to the four men and three women standing together a few hundred yards behind. The men understood and trotted off.

Now, they were on their own, down to just six warriors, Nancy, Pero, and Mbuno, a herd of eleven elephants and one mtoto, along with a bunch of bananas as enticement. Reading the map as he walked, Pero could see the hillside contours off to their east matching the survey map Akale had in his bēti that Pero had marked on his travel map.

The warrior leader came up to Pero and spoke. Pero did not understand a word, of course, but the hand gestures meant the leader wanted three men—he pointed them out—to leap-frog Mbuno and the herd, thereby protecting the front. The remaining three warriors would stay with them. Each man was extremely thin, wiry, and eager. They had adjusted their body paint on waking, scraping this or that off, spitting on the white chalk designs and elongating some, turning others. Pero had no idea what all the signs meant but the overall effect was dramatic and imposing. He was grateful for the men's presence as was Nancy. Their bravery was infectious. He waved them on.

In under an hour, they could be in the valley, but it was a peaceful hour they would not have. Nancy's sharp ears heard an engine approach. Soon, its throaty sound reverberated and was heard by all. It came up from the south along the river. Although Pero could not yet see it, he was sure it wasn't the ranger's Land Rover. Its revving was too high for a diesel and it was too throaty to be a normal car or truck. Pero called out, "Take cover!" He was sure Mbuno could hear him.

Pero pointed to the three warriors and motioned them to hide behind bushes and to take Nancy with them. Pero quickly dropped the two banana bundles in a dip, keeping his backpack on, and he walked patiently ahead, wanting those in the vehicle to see a man calmly following an elephant herd on foot. Pero made sure he took off his hat so his white neck skin showed.

Around the bend of the river, an off-road tubular frame vehicle came charging up, huge treaded tires spitting mud.

The elephants spooked and ran ahead.

Pero turned toward the intruder, acting surprised. He held up a hand. The balloon tires rotated to a stop and two men got out. One was visibly Pokot, although he had a sidearm, which Pero found unusual. Pokot were traditional Kenyan tribesmen who would, given a chance, carry a rifle, any rifle, but a sidearm is a mzungu's weapon, a white man's status symbol. Pero recognized the holster of the sidearm was new, the pistol grip black, possibly a Beretta. The driver of the off-road vehicle motioned to the Pokot not to draw his firearm. He walked to the front of the vehicle and calmly sat on the front bumper. His body language was disarming. It was meant to be.

Pero played along, saying, "Hey, you guys have frightened the elephants I was following."

The driver brushed off some mud from his camouflage jacket casually. His English was clipped British and yet still carried an Arab accent, "What you doing here?"

"I am on a foot safari. Who are you and what do you want?"

"You are on my land, that is who I am. I rule this land, and you are trespassing. You will leave." The threat was clear. The man looked at Pero's old gun, still in its holster. "If you have no permit for that, you will give it to me." He still had not risen from sitting on the front bumper. His manner was confident and assured.

Pero decided to take a more provocative posture, playing the ugly American tourist who believes the world is his playground. "That's not going to happen. Show me your papers and authority and we can discuss this. I'm an American and you have no authority over me."

The man glanced at the Pokot who drew and raised his gun, pointing it at Pero. The Arab calmly said, "You had a chance . . ." He rose. "Now, you will put your hands up and do everything I say or Nicholas will shoot you."

CHAPTER 6

MAKE THE TURN BUT KEEP A REAR GUARD

Pero could not hear the Suri warriors move although he saw their speed and stealth out of the corner of his eye. He struggled to keep his eyes focused on the Arab. Out of nowhere, a donga came crashing down on the Pokot's wrist, shattering it instantly. A second warrior on the opposite side of the vehicle hit the Arab across the shoulder blades. The Arab crumpled to the ground on his knees and passed out with his face in the dirt. *It looks like he's praying to Allah*, Pero thought, *but the idiot is pointing north.*

The Pokot on his knees was holding his shattered wrist when two of the Suri men began beating him, literally to death. It took only six blows. They rounded on the unconscious Arab and hit him while Pero yelled and waved for them to stop.

Mbuno came at a run and used Suri words to make them stop hitting the man again. The Arab was out cold but breathing. The second blow rose in a red welt on the Arab's neck that could have been fatal. If that cracked the neck vertebrae . . .

Mbuno took charge. He pointed at the dead Pokot and had the men drag him into the water. First, they removed the pistol and gave it to Pero. It was indeed a 9 mm Beretta, fully loaded. Pero went over to the vehicle and looked inside. There were no papers, no ID of any kind. He found a small box of ammo for the pistol. There was a kerosene can and a petrol can. Either could have been used to make a fire.

Pero went over to the Arab. He pushed him over and searched him. The man was still unconscious but breathing, however shallowly. Pero pulled ID papers from pockets that matched the ones he had retrieved two days before—Was it only two days ago? Three?—different name, same "The Youth" company. And there was a crude map someone had drawn, showing the river, bends in the river, and, marked with an X in a circle, what was probably their base camp. The valley Pero was planning to have Mbuno lead the elephants was not marked, only hills were marked there. On the back of the map were pencil stripes, four to a set with a diagonal line indicating a count of five. So far, there were three sets of five and a single stripe. Pero assumed these were elephant kills.

Pero asked Mbuno, "What are we going to do with him?"

"Let us wake him." Mbuno reached into the vehicle and pulled out a water sack, canvas-covered, like camel travelers used. He pulled the cork and dumped water on the Arab's face.

The man sputtered and on the second dousing, his eyes opened, "Ma . . . min ant?" Pero told him to speak English if he wanted to live. The man tried to sit up and cried out in pain. "'Linaa muta'alimun. La 'astatie al'iistiqaz." Pero reminded him to speak English. "I am hurt. It is very bad. I cannot get up."

"Then stay down. Give me your name."

Lying on his side, the man mumbled something and spat. Pero pulled out the man's ID and permit, showed it to him, and told him to try again or Pero would have them hit him again, pointing out the Suri warrior and his donga. The man spoke, his breath shallow, "Akim Moustafe."

"That's right." Pero compared the permit papers. "Now tell me the name of your boss." The man was silent. His neck hurt too much for him to shake his head, but his refusal was clear. Pero pointed to the man's shin and motioned to the Suri warrior to hit there, holding his own hands out and motioning for the hit to be gentle. He didn't want to break the man's leg. The thwack was, nevertheless, hard and fast. The man screamed in pain. Pero continued, "Now, let's have the name of your boss. So far, you threatened to kill me, you had your man aim to shoot me, so you may guess I am in no mood to listen to nonsense or prevarication. That too tough a word for you? Prevarication means lying, which will waste my time. Don't do that again or I'll have him break one bone at a time and leave you naked for the jackals to finish the job tonight. Your choice."

Mbuno looked at Pero, wondering how much of the fury Pero was displaying was real and how much was show. Pero knew Mbuno would be wondering if, indeed, he could kill this man so easily, so Pero quickly said, "Susanna is pregnant, I will be a father, he tried to ruin Susanna's life." Mbuno understood. The rage was real even if he also knew Pero was not and could not be a cold-blooded killer.

The Arab on the ground, however, was convinced his life was forfeit and dishonorable and so he must do anything to survive. It was an inevitable decision for a previously coolheaded bully who was used to commanding. His authority was stripped away along with any pride or self-esteem he had. He began to weep. Not from the pain but from the utter degradation of who he had believed he was. He began to talk, in lengthy sentences, telling his life's story, how he became part of the Youth—he called it by the real name al-Shabaab—how proud he was to be gathering funds for their global campaign to spread Islamic law like wildfire. He named his boss as "the great Rahman Qamaan." He used the word *jihad* several times, even referring to himself in the British vernacular of jihadist. He said all this in between sobs, his reality crumbling away, his future now defunct, his passage into Jannah all but doomed.

Pero turned to Nancy. "Getting all this?" She nodded. "Good, let me know when you need a new chip." He turned to the prostrate Arab. "Now, Akim Moustafe, can you move yet? Can you sit up?" No one tried to help him. Pushing with his arms, he barely rose to sitting, legs splayed, back up against the bumper. "Good, now, Akim, the next part you may not like very much. We have a choice, to leave you here dead"—the man sobbed some more—"or to leave you here as a prisoner of the Suri, the one who hit you with his donga. You may think that is not so bad until you remember how much that donga hurt when he did not even break your leg."

Akim responded, "I am dead anyway; when Rahman Qamaan knows I am missing, he will find me and kill me." He had a moment of bravery, adding, "And you all too . . ."

Pero calmly said, "That's hardly likely—for any of that. You'll be put in prison for decades and grow old there. Your family will be purged, no doubt by the Somali government to appease the Ethiopian government who will, rightly, see your efforts as promoting more insurgence emanating from Somalia against Ethiopia. As for Rahman Qamaan . . . we'll find him and bring him to justice as well." Pero paused. "Get the picture? So what's it to be? Prisoner or death?"

Akim gave a small sob and lowered his head. Out tumbled the words, "I am a prisoner, liusaeidni Allah." Pero assumed he was asking Allah for help. He would need it.

It took Pero and Mbuno a few minutes to explain to the lead warrior what they wanted to do. In the vehicle, they found some rope and they trussed the Arab man up so he could not move. Two warriors dragged him into the bushes. Mbuno made them understand that they were to wait—he pointed at the sky, tracing the passage arc of the sun twice—two days before going home. The warrior understood. Pero asked Mbuno if they should leave two men, not just one, and Mbuno agreed.

A dilemma occurred to Pero when he looked at the vehicle. How could they hide that thing? Even if pushed into the bushes, it would be visible. It was Nancy who had the answer, "Drive it away, over there, on the other side." She pointed across the river to the thicker forest. Pero agreed and within a half hour, he returned back across the river shallows and then trotted back to rejoin the herd, which Mbuno had already gotten moving.

Pero grabbed his two banana bundles, loaded himself up, and walked to catch up to Nancy. What Pero didn't want to tell her was that the Pokot's body was already downstream by the shallows being fought over by a pair of very large crocs.

A few more bananas from Mbuno and the herd followed. It wasn't as if they were tame; Mbuno knew that and had to be constantly watchful. They were more puzzled by this strange ape who could mimic their sounds, an ape who had special treats for them, and presumably—given that their leader had been slaughtered days before—their untested new leader was grateful for direction.

The problem came when Mbuno wanted them to turn to the east, toward the beginning of the valley. That was not their migration route. Elephants as an animal and a species have generational memory. The migration route along the Omo River was one they had used for perhaps thousands of years. Here they were being told, coaxed, bribed to turn away from that route and follow this strange ape. The new leader refused, ears flapping in annoyance. Mbuno hand signaled back to Pero, who went in a semicircle around the herd to join him fifty yards in front of the pack. Mbuno explained the problem and the two men discussed a solution.

"They need to be frightened again, they need to want to follow me."

Pero understood the logic. Mbuno's stomach sounds and humming might not be effective in persuading them. Pero had to show them their old way was dangerous and that Mbuno's way forward was safe.

"Mbuno, take one of these bundles"—he passed the bundle of bananas—"and go that way." He pointed east. "And lay a trail. I'll go to those bushes there with one warrior, you take two ahead with you"—he pointed at a dense Commiphora bush on the side of the Omo—"and I'll fire the gun a few times. That should spook them, and in these valleys, the sound shouldn't travel."

"Ndiyo, but we do not want them turning around. Nancy would be trampled."

"Okay, I'll go back there and tell the Suri men to shout and yell when I fire the gun. Give me fifteen to twenty minutes. We'll give it a go." Mbuno agreed. Pero took the semicircle route back to Nancy downstream of the herd and explained.

Nancy wanted to film the herd's reaction. She looked about for a higher vantage point, one that could also keep her safe. An old abandoned termite mound was solid enough and one of the Suri warriors helped her climb. "Okay, Pero. This'll do."

Pero spent several minutes explaining and positioning the Suri men. Akale's gun he pulled from the holster was an old, noisy Webley. He held it up, said "Bang, bang," and waved his arms pretending to be shooing the elephants inland. Then he tried to tell the men to yell when he would fire by saying, "Bang," then pointing at one man, opening his mouth, and mimicking yelling. He repeated this each time and finally, it seemed the two men understood. At least he hoped so. Mbuno would explain to the two with him.

After his trot with one of the Suri in the semicircle around the elephants again, he waved to Mbuno, already hundreds of yards inland, and got a return signal. Pero hoped Mbuno meant go ahead. Pero ducked into the Commiphora bush, pulling the warrior with him, and waited, counting slowly to one hundred. He peeked through the branches and saw that the mtoto had already moved inland to get the first banana . . . he pulled the old pistol and fired two shots, watching the elephants' reaction. They were spooked. Then he heard yelling, Nancy's voice and the other warrior's carrying as well from south of the herd. With nowhere to go except to follow the mtoto, the herd turned and the mother of the mtoto was first, finally followed by the new leader who glanced about wondering if it was a trap. The rest followed and they all began running.

Elephants running are deceptive. If you watch their feet, the pace seems like a quick walk. When you measure the distance covered, you soon realize that they're doing over twenty miles per hour. With two feet always on the ground, it's not really a run, like a horse, but the speed and power are there. Any bushes in their way were flattened. The dust cloud from shuffling feet disguised the herd as they approached Mbuno. Pero was frightened he had overdone the shooting. Maybe one shot would have been enough . . . Of course, Pero realized he had fired half of Akale's big caliber .45 bullets. The weapon was almost useless. Watching the herd, hoping to catch sight of Mbuno, he stuffed the revolver into his backpack and slipped the Beretta 9 mm in its holster.

Nancy and the one remaining Suri warrior caught up, walked up the river, and Nancy called out. Emerging from the bush,

Pero asked Nancy if she was okay to carry on. She responded, "If Mbuno is, then yes. Good footage." The Suri and the two of them stared at the elephant dust cloud now a quarter mile away. Without taking her eyes off the cloud, Nancy filled Pero in, "The Arab back there jumped every time you fired that gun, muttering the name Rahman Qamaan . . . I think he thought there was a shootout. I think he's more frightened of this Qamaan than any of us."

Pero nodded. "Yeah, well, he may be right. And now that we've made that much noise and there are elephant tracks to follow, they might attack us from the rear again. Damn."

Nancy shook her head. "Nope, I don't think so, not yet. Remember, Qamaan's got his man back there, the overconfident type, patrolling. He'll think it was his man doing the shooting. By the time he investigates, we can be miles ahead. Let's get going. Okay?" She lifted the camera in her right hand, made an adjustment, and started walking. Pero motioned to the warriors to follow. Nancy set the pace, an easy trot. Pero spent much of the first mile watching to the rear.

It was three hours later when the rising valley opened up to them to their north, just past Labuko. Labuko was a small settlement of a few huts and dirt pathways a mile or more south of them. The new valley was nothing special. Narrow at first, perhaps only a half mile in width, with a small stream flowing downhill toward the Labuko settlement. The stream was almost dry, puddled here and there, and would be until the rains came, then it would become a torrent across the whole valley. Pero looked for what he termed as high-tide marks on the rock wall to his left and spotted a line below which there were no bushes.

Through the afternoon cloud of flies, his eyes spotted the movement of lesser kudu on the west wall, above the rocks at the bottom of the hillside. What gave the four animals away were their movements of black twisted horns against the tan dried vegetation. The bodies' gray and white stripes matched the vegetation perfectly. Lesser kudu are forest antelope and Pero was surprised to see them on the valley floor with little in the way of trees. He looked higher up on his left and only saw the same scrub bushes before the top, which seemed denuded. Looking to the east, on this right, he saw the forest line fifty feet up the valley wall. No doubt the kudu were waiting for them to pass, before regaining the safety of the forest.

Up ahead, the elephant herd changed direction, across the streambed. There was no haste, but their change in direction was puzzling to Pero. When he reached the crossing point, he saw why. A herd of a dozen giant eland were standing in the water, drinking. The elephants gave them a wide berth. Pero had never been that close to eland before. Taller than a steer, with long sharp horns, the tan-sided eland is a powerful animal of more than twelve hundred pounds. Two of the herd watched Nancy, Pero, and the Suri pass while the others drank. Pero made sure they followed at the same pace as the elephants, clearly demonstrating their passivity and union with the beasts they were following. The eland let them go, necks raised in watchful observance.

With only one bunch of bananas left, weighing him down by the mile, Pero hoped that the pace Mbuno was setting would meet the elephants' needs and keep them acquiescent. That agreement was in no way certain. Mbuno must, by now, be exhausted humming and belching, Pero thought. Pero looked over at Nancy and saw she was still taping the eland they were passing. Suddenly, coming off the eastern slope, a herd of perhaps twenty Grévy's zebras came cascading down to the water source.

Pero was startled at how big they were. Perhaps half the size of the eland, they were much stockier and more muscled than the plains zebras he had seen on safari. Grévy were rare, he knew, but he hadn't realized how unique they were. He pointed them out to Nancy and told her what they were. Nancy called for a new chip for the camera and continued taping.

The day wore on. Pero was aware his stomach was growling. Nancy shot him a glance, adding, "For god's sake, eat something." She was annoyed his stomach might be heard in her taping. Instead of a banana—worried they would need every one for the elephants—he stopped and reached into his pack for an MRE, which he opened and handed half to Nancy. He began walking again, eating as he went. Nancy thanked him saying, "Yeah, me too." She looked about. "This place is a paradise." She suddenly pointed off to her right. About two hundred yards away, running up the valley was a small herd of perhaps fifty animals that looked like antelope, maybe a couple of hundred pounds each, curved horns on heads with long faces. The hides were tan to darker brown, but the hind thigh and legs were black gray. They were moving at a very fast pace. "What are those?"

Pero didn't know. He'd never seen or filmed them before. He turned to the warrior and said, pointing, "Antelope?"

The warrior made a disapproving face and said, "Toe-pi." And he used his donga as a spear, pretending to want to hunt them. He rubbed his stomach. Apparently, toe-pi were good eating, even for an agrarian tribe.

Pero thought about that and wondered if the word was *topi*. Nancy was right, in any event, this valley was paradise and untraveled by the tourist trade. Much of East Africa was that way, if you had the right guide and were prepared to get out of tourist areas to experience the incredible beauty and bounty.

Walking in the elephants' footsteps, there was no danger of animal or reptile underfoot, although the elephant dung was to be avoided, if only to leave the weaverbirds undigested fibers to scavenge and the dung beetles alone to do their jobs. In a lull in the shooting, Pero explained to Nancy that the elephants eat seeds from all the plants they consume and eventually drop seeds across all the migratory routes, replanting the wild. Hearing that, Nancy made a point of taking close-ups of the dung beetles moving, rolling round balls, dropping them into animal holes, no doubt to plant some future crops. The fungus that would grow underground would feed the beetles, the seeds would grow later using the manure as fertilizer. "I love this complete circle of nature, here in one small dung ball . . . amazing!" Nancy was enthralled.

As the valley rose, there was a flatter place, and there the water pooled into a pond filled with reeds. Mbuno stopped and sat. A herd of gazelles paid him no heed as they took their daily drink. Except in the dry season, gazelles rarely went to water. They replenished their water needs feeding at dawn when the grass was covered in dew.

The elephants, not knowing where they were, wanted to go on. The leader tried to move Mbuno. Mbuno folded his arms and sat still, being pushed on his side like a ball. The mtoto reached into the shallow water and plucked a reed, tasting it. It must have been good because soon the herd was attacking the reed bed with alacrity. The gazelles fled the commotion of the elephants. Pero hoped the elephants were there for the night. He needn't have worried; Mbuno had the same thought.

With two warriors in tow, Mbuno joined the other two Suri, Pero, and Nancy at the rear. He pointed up the west wall of the valley, about ten feet up the side, where there was a small ledge. Just above the ledge, smaller trees grew, mostly young, stilted mahogany, increasing in size as they marched up the hillside. "We camp there; they"—he pointed at the herd—"will stay here for the night." To the Suri he said, "Come!"

They all climbed to the small ridge and everyone dropped packs and whatever they were carrying.

Mbuno looked down the valley back toward Labuko . . . "I cannot see Labuko, we are far enough. I can see if anyone comes." He took a warrior who had walked with Pero and Nancy aside. Using the few words Akale had taught him, he said, pointing at the ground then the man, "Sleep . . ." Next he pointed at the sun, motioning its path to fall in the west. He repeated, "Sleep. Wake, protect." The man said, "Sisi," which Pero took as a yes and seemed to settle down, uppermost on the ledge, near the trees, and assumed a fetal sleeping position. Within moments— Pero was amazed—the man seemed fast asleep.

Mbuno manhandled one of the other warriors, positioning him to look down the valley. Another he positioned looking up the valley. The third he positioned to watch the valley floor. Satisfied, he said to Pero, "You have food, yes?" Pero had already taken out an MRE for Mbuno, and another one for himself and Nancy to share. Taking out the Katadyn filter, Pero went back to the small stream and pumped until he had a half liter of clean water. Mbuno drank it in one go. Pero repeated the process for Nancy and himself, in between chewing the MRE meal.

Checking the Beretta was loaded and full, Pero made sure the safety was on. He showed it to Mbuno and reminded him to take it if he needed it. Mbuno declined. With Mbuno's permission, Pero found a mossy spot to lie down on and tried to slip off to sleep. Pero wanted to review the day with Mbuno and see if changes in their plan needed to be made, but right then, for both men and Nancy, rest was more important while the Suri men could keep watch. *I am not as young as I once was, these ten-plus mile days are harder than ever . . .* and he was soon asleep.

It was the lions that woke them in the dead of night. The elephants were not worried by them, as a small trumpeting sound from the leader told the lions to stay away. But the sound woke the team on the ledge above.

In the moonlight, the three lionesses passed, at great speed, only four or five yards away uphill of their ledge, chasing the kudu through the saplings. One lesser kudu was brought down about six hundred yards away, turning and trying to flee downhill. The kill was swift and silent, choking off the kudu's air and suffocating the animal. Nancy, taping, whispered, "Not sure if this night filter chip is working, maybe we can fix it in post." She meant postproduction. The arrival of the male lion, calmly walking uphill from the valley floor, claiming his prize of the liver and choice meat, should have frightened anyone being that close. Mbuno knew better. The elephants were their protection. His confidence in their safety inspired the Suri, including the one woken at dusk on night sentry, to stand and observe that which normally would have them retreating. Still, their guardian Suri friends edged closer to Mbuno, assuming it was his magic with animals that kept them safe.

Just before dawn, the top of the hills to the west began to glow. The full sun would be up in under a half hour, slowly making its way down and exposing the valley floor. Pero calmly watched from the ledge at the advancing glow of sunrise, knowing that as it finally touched on the stream below they would be off. He could see that the elephants were still feeding. They seemed in no hurry to march on. Pero looked at the last bundle of bananas he was to carry up the valley and hoped that they would suffice for Mbuno's needs. In checking the backpack, he came across the Yaesu walkie-talkie, VHF only. He looked it over. Made for the Russian market, it had a small battery indicator when he switched it on. Full charge. Static crackled and he turned the volume knob all the way down. The Cyrillic lettering told him nothing useful. Turning it over, two apparent frequencies were written on a piece of paper, clear-taped to the battery box. Pero assumed they were in meters: eight point two and six point five. As a mental exercise, his brain was automatically searching for a hidden connection . . . searching to remember something so esoteric as the conversion of radio frequencies. Years ago, he had memorized the Kenya Wilson Airport frequency—118.1 MHz. *Of course*, he thought, *just my luck, damn Yaesu for not using megahertz. Gotta figure this out. . . .*

Pero always had a reliable memory and right then he was struggling to remember the conversion of megahertz to meters. Since he was a kid he remembered many conversion formulas. An inch was 2.54 centimeters, Fahrenheit to Centigrade subtract 32 divide by 9 multiply by 5, miles per hour to kilometers per hour divide by 5 multiply by 8, and so on. He took out a pen and turned the map over. Mbuno scuttled over and asked if he could help. Nancy leaned back and said, "I'll help too. What's up?"

Pero looked at the handwritten numbers again, showing them both. "If you had a walkie-talkie out here, you'd have your base's frequency and you'd have a frequency for another team or teams in the field. I'm assuming these two numbers"—he pointed the pen at them—"are the same: two Somali shufti contacts. But I need to try and reach ATC in Kenya." He pointed to the top of the west hill. "If that's high enough, I might be able to talk to them. They're on 118.1 MHz, but this thing is in meters." He tapped the display screen. "I have to make the conversion. I know it's in here somewhere"—he tapped his head. "All I remember is that it had a trick." He meant the conversion wasn't a simple multiplication or division. He pondered, scribbling on the backside of the map.

Nancy leaned over his shoulder and looked at what he was writing. Nancy was, by trade, an engineer for Sony, a television camera operator and repair expert. In short, she was scientifically trained. She saw Pero's mistake. "Isn't it an inverse ratio? Frequency numbers go up in megahertz and meter measurements go down?"

"Well done, Nancy . . ." Her clue helped Pero remember the formula. "Megahertz equals roughly three hundred divided by meters. It's a little smaller number than three hundred, but we'll get close enough, with using three hundred. I think it's two hundred ninety-nine, but three hundred will do." He did the calculation again, "So, one one eight point one equals three hundred divided by x . . ." He wrote the numbers quickly. "So x equals three hundred divided by one one eight point one equals . . . two point five four meters, or thereabouts." He tapped the unit's frequency down button on the unit and saw the number change to read 2.54 "This should be Kenya air traffic control at Wilson Airport. If we're lucky." He smiled at his friends.

Mbuno looked pleased as well. "Ndiyo, you must try." Mbuno looked down at the herd in the early morning light. They were still happily feeding. "When they drink, then they will want to move. We must be ready." Pero nodded, descended the hill, crossed the valley floor, and started the climb to the top of the west hill as fast as he could.

Ten leg-pumping minutes later, Pero stood at the top, only to be faced with a view of hills stretching all the way west, some much taller. VHF radios are line of sight only . . . He looked south and saw a hill range there, too, perhaps not as tall. He tried the radio, going up and down one or two stops. Nothing, no noise, nothing. He checked the numbers on the back and pushed the button back to 8.2 Nothing. He tried 6.5 and there was traffic, Arabic it sounded, well, almost Arabic. Somali! Pero corrected himself. The traffic was one voice, one tone, repeating a phrase. He listened intently, then heard a clue, "Akim, kaalay, soo sheeg." Then just, "Kaalay, soo sheeg . . ." repeated again and again. Pero guessed they were calling for Akim to respond. But Akim was currently bound and held by the two Suri warriors back at the river.

A familiar sound reached down from the sky and made Pero look up. Four strong contrails from a jet that was streaking across the sky, heading south. Quickly Pero pushed the buttons back to 2.54 meters and listened. Nothing. He pressed send and called, "Mayday, Mayday, can anyone read this?"

The radio crackled to life, with a clipped British accent, "Roger that, this is BA flight 65, what is your position?"

Pero, who had thought this out beforehand as he climbed the hillside, replied, "BA 65, this is Pero Baltazar on the ground near the Omo River in Ethiopia. We are being pursued by Somali terrorists led by Rahman Qamaan, confirm Romeo alpha hotel mike alpha November, then Quebec alpha mike alpha alpha November. Four dead already, heavily armed terrorists. Request assistance. Contact this number Nairobi, urgent . . ." and he gave Tone Bowman's number.

"You say you're Pero Baltazar, confirm."

"Affirmative."

"Terrorist is Rahman Qamaan, confirm." And the pilot spelled it out again, "Romeo alpha hotel mike alpha November and Quebec alpha mike alpha alpha November."

"Affirmative."

"Contact emergency number in Nairobi is zero two zero tree sixer sixer two zero one niner. Confirm."

"Affirmative, Tone Bowman will summon authorities." Pero got out the map, "As near as I can tell we're moving north on foot from five point three latitude, thirty-six point three longitude."

"Got that five point tree latitude, thirty-sixer point tree longitude." There was a pause. "We're losing you . . ." Pero looked up and saw that the jet had moved well south. The voice broke up but Pero heard, "We're on . . . radio . . . obi now. Good . . . uck. BA . . . out."

"Thank you, BA 65." Pero had taken a chance there would be pilots on the way to Nairobi already setting the next frequency for Wilson Airport, Nairobi ATC as they crossed from Ethiopia into Kenya airspace. He felt elated that it had worked out. *But will anyone reach us in time before we bring the elephants down again to the river?* Like the letter to the prime minister, or a fish-monger remembering to make a call, or Akale reaching that phone, or an aircraft message that may fall on deaf ears, Pero worried any help would probably arrive too late.

When the elephants decided to move, it took several bananas, broken up into smaller morsels to stretch out their supply, to coax them to continue uphill. As these elephants were not mountain elephant, normally they would never climb. Even if Mbuno and Pero knew that the valley had a side valley coming up in under three miles that would lead downhill to the river, the herd would not understand climbing away from the river. For the elephants, the way ahead seemed a climb to nowhere familiar and they were reluctant. Mbuno turned them and coaxed them on. Once they got moving, they seemed resigned.

Mbuno watched as the morning sun heated the atmosphere. In East Africa, clouds—often called thunder-bumpers—formed all the way up to forty thousand feet. Looking like mushrooms with a dense top, these towering columns held some of the most dangerous winds, tons of moisture, and, if you flew into them, hailstones that could—and did—wreck the largest of aircraft foolish enough to tempt fate. That morning, Mbuno watched warily as the clouds domed quickly and grew to enormous size. In the valley itself, no clouds formed yet, but on either side of the valley, especially to the west over what was the Omo River valley, huge clouds were forming.

Thunder-bumpers heralded the beginning of the rainy season. Mbuno had stationed three Suri warriors, the ones who had a good night's sleep, to precede him by at least a mile as scouts up ahead. They readily agreed, sensing that danger could require their stealth and dongas before long. The men were under no illusion that the mission was not still extremely dangerous.

Mbuno explained to the remaining last warrior that he had to walk with Nancy but walk behind her only. That way, he was not in her camera shot. Pero brought up the rear, gun ready if needed, fully aware that an attack could catch up to them at any moment.

A loud thunderclap behind them made all of them turn to look, including a few of the elephants. Way down at the beginning of the valley, clouds had settled over the river and where the valley began near Labuko. The thunderclap heralded rain and downpours. The full torrent of the rainy season was coming soon and in earnest. Pero asked Nancy to zoom in on the valley entrance.

"Nothing there, Pero, just black from a downburst . . . it's raining hard, dense."

Pero felt relieved. "If they don't know which way we went, if they try and follow, the rain will wipe out any tracks in minutes." Nancy agreed. It was good news.

When they reached the top of the valley, a cliff face three hundred yards ahead halted all progress. It had now begun to drizzle in the valley. The elephants were happy for the light rain, but the cliff face seemed to concern them, halting progress. Mbuno knew the rocky and steep valley wall on the left had to have a gap for them to follow—the map said so—a gap that would lead them into the side valley and back down to the Omo, but in the drizzle he couldn't see it.

Nor could he see the Suri warriors.

Suddenly, lightning cracked overhead to the north of them, somewhere past the cliff face. Thunder followed in under two seconds. The rain downpour was now close, very close. In the position they were in, a sudden downpour could cause a flash flood, certainly sweeping the men and woman away instantly. Mbuno was about to call for an emergency climb off the valley floor when the Suri suddenly appeared as if from nowhere. They appeared to run straight out of the west wall.

CHAPTER 7

MSIMU WA MVUA HUANZA—RAINY SEASON STARTS

They were smiling and waving Mbuno on. The rain that fell over and past the cliff came in torrents and started to cascade down the cliff face. Thunder rocked the valley. The elephant were getting panicked. Mbuno called back for Pero and the bananas. Pero dropped his backpack and ran to the west wall carrying the bananas, around the herd, and found Mbuno. "Is there a way out, or is it all cliff now?" Neither man could see much through the torrential rain.

Mbuno pointed at the Suri warriors, just barely visible now. "Two are there." He pointed into the dense mist and rain. "We must go now." He grabbed the bananas and fed one quickly to the mtoto who immediately followed. This time, the leader also followed and was about to stop Mbuno when he, too, received a banana with Mbuno careening ahead on the slippery grass and mud toward the last place he saw the warriors.

The valley exit was an optical illusion. The cliff and rocks on the west wall matched the look of the cliff face at the head of the valley, but once you got up to them, the gap revealed itself. The ground there was steeply ravined, but there was twenty feet at the left of the ravine forming a single track heading west. If an elephant were to slip into the ravine, it was only four or five feet to the bottom, a bottom that was rapidly filling with moving water. Mbuno wondered if an elephant fell, if they could get it out.

Pero wasted no time. He ran back along the west valley wall, picked up his backpack, and rejoined the Suri and Nancy. He explained, using hand gestures, where they were going. Nancy was already taping the receding elephants who seemed to disappear into a solid wall. As the humans walked to follow, they dangerously swung right a little to get a better angle for Nancy to film the elephants entering the side valley. The warrior wanted them to hurry. He kept saying something neither understood. He pointed at the north cliff face and urged them to hurry away, follow the elephant herd, and not film. He pushed the camera down, pointing ahead.

Pero looked up and saw what frightened him. The rain had begun in more earnest over the top of the cliff and the water cascading down the cliff resembled more of a waterfall now than an overflow. "Nancy, we have to hurry, the valley above must be a catchment that empties here, down the cliff face. We have to get out of this tight valley right now." As he said that, a wave burst over the cliff face and thundered on the ground below.

Thankfully, Nancy had begun to run, the warrior at her side. Pero headed to the nearest high point. The rushing water moved rocks and debris where he had stood. Flash floods are always faster than imagined and Pero knew the danger was real. He climbed higher. Nancy and the warrior made it safely to the gap, which was slightly uphill of the torrent and were safe, following the elephants. Pero was cut off from the valley exit.

There's no way out of this but up and over, he thought. So he climbed the hill's slight cliff face to the sloping hill above, keeping the rock gap on his right. The hill was steep but he knew he could manage—in the dry it would be easy. In the rain, any slip would result in a slide into the rocks and the gap. Pero placed his feet carefully, concentrating on a safe arrival into the new valley cut.

As he passed the headland, he could see the elephants, already a few hundred feet below his position. They were making good time and the valley, although narrow, seemed reasonably inclined. Down the middle of the new valley was a waterway cut, already filling but in no danger to flood. The rain was still pounding them all, but the new valley seemed small enough, with good drainage. It would not act as a water basin at the bottom.

As suddenly as it had begun, the rain stopped as the thunder-bumper moved to the east. The sun broke through. Unlike nontropical areas, monsoon rain came and went like an on-off switch. Once the mist lifted, Pero could see all the way down the valley. A family of giraffes casually ambled up the opposing hillside to the tree line into a stand of mimosa and acacia, no doubt looking for dinner.

They were only about ten or twelve miles to the Omo River by his estimation. Pero reached into his backpack for his binoculars. He scanned the descending path the elephants were on and saw nothing. As far as he could tell, it would indeed take them back to the river where they had to turn the herd north, away from where Akale had estimated the shufti encampment was situated.

The hill Pero was on seemed to follow the new valley, gently sloping at the same rate until it ended near the river. He remembered his original training, when he first volunteered to assist the State Department and CIA as a runner: When in doubt, take the high ground. After the Lockerbie disaster that killed his wife Addiena, he'd wanted to do something to help oppose terrorist movements. All he did for the State Department and the CIA was act as an extra set of eyes. When he was in an airport, they might ask him to see if he could spot a woman or a man they were tracking. Or they would give him something to carry in all his TV equipment that an agent in the field needed, like a satellite phone or papers. Those days felt like a lifetime ago, but here he was, instinctively obeying his original training to keep to the high ground. Observation was key to any operative, even the lowliest runner. From where Pero was, he could see the elephants proceeding happily now that the rain had halted. Mbuno was walking with the mtoto who was sniffing him up and down. No doubt hoping for more bananas, thought Pero. When Mbuno looks up, I'll wave and make it clear I'm okay. He had decided to stay up on the hillside.

Twelve miles in a day is reasonable for trained men. For Pero, after the fifteen they had already completed in the past days, not including their first three days on foot, Pero knew twelve in a day was simply beyond his capability. From his vantage point, all along the march slightly downhill toward the Omo River, he kept watch on Mbuno, Nancy, and the Suri men. The elephants were moving happily enough, halting here and there, grabbing tufts of grass from the green valley. Ordinarily, Pero would sit and picnic overlooking such a perfect and idyllic vista in East Africa. But Mbuno was setting a pace that caused Pero to worry his brother wanted to make it all the way to the river in that same day.

* * *

By midafternoon, Pero knew he was flagging. He raised his binoculars and looked at Nancy. She seemed to sense him looking and peered up into the lens. She waggled her hand telling Pero she, too, was beginning to have difficulty with the ordeal.

Pero couldn't yell down to Mbuno, it was too far. Every once in a while, he saw Mbuno looking up but before Pero could try and make hand gestures to tell him to stop, Mbuno looked away as the elephants surrounded him, which meant he needed to focus in case they accidentally trampled him. Of course, Pero eventually realized what Mbuno was doing: he was waiting for a signal from Pero. So Pero sat and waited for Mbuno to look up. A sitting Pero would tell Mbuno it was time to stop and talk.

Some while later, Mbuno climbed the hillside to confer and collect an MRE for himself and Nancy. A Suri warrior came with him, busily eating a strip of what looked like more dried meat. Mbuno seemed exhausted. "Pero, my brother, why did you not stop before?"

"I was waiting for your command." He handed Mbuno the binoculars, then opened his MRE and began to chew. Mbuno scanned the lower valley and the river, just visible. Pero continued, "How much farther? Can we rest here tonight?"

"Yes, there is water, and the elephants also want to rest." Mbuno returned the binoculars, quickly took out his knife, and threw it. It struck a snake perhaps attracted by the smell of food. He retrieved his knife from the still-writhing reptile, sliced off the snake's head, and slit it from top to bottom. Peeling the skin as he talked, "There is grass, not very much, but they seem happy to wait here. Some may try the smaller trees. In the morning, we need to move fast at the river and turn them north." He threw the snakeskin a few yards away, holding the quivering snake carcass in his left hand. The Suri retrieved the skin, rolled it up, and put it in his waist bandanna. "Then," Mbuno continued, smiling at the warrior, giving him permission to not waste the skin, "we need a plan for the shufti."

Pero knew that was still Mbuno's end goal. For Pero, if they could get the elephants and his friends to safety, he'd be happy enough. But he knew Mbuno needed to stop the poaching. It was his tribal ethic. Being happy enough had never really been a standard for Pero as well. It was why he had made the radio call. To lighten the mood, he looked at the bloody snake carcass. "And I suppose you're going to make Nancy eat that for dinner?"

"Miss Nancy does not eat snake? It is very good. Fresh." He held it up for inspection. Pero was sure he saw a Suri warrior lick his lips. Mbuno and Pero looked down the hill at Nancy and her Suri warriors.

Mbuno was, like many guides, an excellent mimic. With an impish grin, Mbuno's voice changed to Pero's and suggested, "Try it, Mbuno, it is only sushi eel. You'll like it." Changing back to his own voice, "Is that not what you said once in Nairobi? Ah yes, the very bad not cooked eel. Let us see if Nancy likes this raw."

Pero responded with, "Idiot." Mbuno smiled and walked down the hill, no doubt to share his prize in peace with the Suri.

Alone again, with the binoculars, Pero scanned the lower valley and a little to the south along what he could see of the meandering river. Nothing seemed to be moving, no fires, no vehicles—so far.

Pero knew help would probably not arrive quickly—or even at all—and yet he felt he needed to try to stop the Somali. For Pero, they represented the evil that was infecting all of Africa. He rightly saw them as dangerous, violent men intent on power and control who stopped at nothing. The word *terrorist* had a different meaning for Pero from the evening news definition meant to titillate viewers in America. Pero knew that, in reality, every terrorist meant to inflict terror, not merely win a battle or establish a caliphate. Pero didn't want to live in a world where terror was accepted, where fear was commonplace.

The glow of Pero's watch told him it was after two a.m. when the buzzing sound woke him. He recognized that sound, it was unmistakable and completely foreign to this part of the world. A high-speed turboprop of very small size made that noise. Pero looked up and saw nothing. The stars were hidden by high clouds and not a glint of starlight peeked through. The sound passed overhead again, going from west to east at speed, almost silent but, to Pero, a ray of hope.

Quickly he opened his backpack and turned the walkie-talkie on, selecting the Kenya air traffic control frequency again. He keyed the send button and said, "Baltazar, over." For a moment nothing, then the buzzing appeared overhead but higher and higher and seeming to be circling. The walkie-talkie crackled, "AFRICOM over." Pero knew AFRICOM. They were the cavalry; the US Central African Command operated out of Germany and controlled tens of thousands of African-friendly troops, mostly Ugandans. AFRICOM's role was to keep the peace and thwart terrorism. Pero was ecstatic that AFRICOM had arrived, even if only in the form of a UAV, an unmanned aerial vehicle. Pero thought, Probably a Reaper, wonder if it's armed.

The walkie-talkie crackled, "Send for twenty seconds." Pero understood, they needed to pinpoint his position, so he recited "Mary had a little lamb . . ." The Reaper flew overhead, perhaps ten thousand feet higher than his position atop the hill. It was circling, getting multiple plots. "Located. State condition."

Pero wasn't worried the VHF signal would reach down to the Omo River and any possible encampment. First, there were hills in the way and, second, he moved back to a rock pile putting the rocks between himself and the river. He keyed the send button. "Baltazar plus Mbuno, plus Nancy Breiton, plus four Suri warriors on foot safari. Ran into elephant poachers, three— two Pokot, one Somali—now deceased. Two others, one Pokot and one Somali, tracked us yesterday and one is deceased, one captive twenty or more miles south of here, held by two Suri warriors. Identities . . ." Pero used his penlight, carefully shielded, to illuminate the papers he had, reading everything that was on them. He finished with, "The company for the meat license is the Youth Company. Translates as al-Shabaab. Again, three Pokot dead, one Somali dead, one Somali captured. Leader is Rahman Qamaan, believed to be ten miles below us or more along the river. Has an encampment, vehicles, refrigeration truck, maybe more capability." He meant weapons. He released the send lever.

"Hold." Pero waited, listening, volume turned down and pressed the speaker to his ear. "Await instructions." Again Pero waited. "Await instructions." Pero suddenly remembered they always wanted confirmation of a given command. He clicked the send lever twice and waited. A moment later, "Tews here; remember me, son?"

"Yes, sir." General Tews was head of AFRICOM and had spoken to Pero at the end of the last ordeal in Tanzania. Tews had a Texas twang when he spoke.

"Well, you're dropped in it again. Lewis is not pleased. Our problem is, the name you gave? That last name?" The radio went silent. Pero clicked twice. "Good, well, we need to talk to him, real talk, son. We'll be joining you in forty-eight hours . . ."

Pero tried to cut him off, but the general couldn't hear what Pero was saying while the general was also sending. Pero had to wait. Releasing the send lever, the rest of the general's sentence drifted down, meaningless, ". . . and we'll extract then."

Pero quickly hit send. "Tews, sir"—he was careful not to say "General" Tews, even if the transmission would hardly be over-heard—"we're only six to seven hours on a march to the river tomorrow a.m. Unavoidable. Elephants won't be held here. They want to return to their migration route. We will be at the river by noon."

"Elephants? What the hell are you talking about, son?"

"We're walking, escorting a herd of elephants past the shufti encampment and turning them north on their migratory route. We can expect trouble either from behind or on arrival at the river or shortly after." Pero didn't want to explain that once the elephants got away—if they got clean away—Mbuno would no doubt still form an attack plan on the shufti poachers. If the AFRICOM troops wanted Qamaan alive two days later, that might prove impossible.

The general immediately understood. "No, son, here's an order. We want that man alive. Stay put, we'll extract you and deal with the issue."

Pero smiled, understanding the general's frustration. "Tews, sir, I understand I do, but we cannot leave the elephants unpro-tected, we will be escorting them, and—here's the really bad news—Mbuno is quite capable of inflicting damage without caring about capturing someone if he is in a fight."

"Well, son, you think you gotta do what you gotta do, I can't order you, learned that last time. But I want to use an expression you'll be familiar with. Delta delta Oscar orders you to assist or else." The voice went silent.

Pero had to think. "Please stand by." He heard two clicks. DO stood for the CIA Directorate of Operations. DDO was the director of the Directorate of Operations. Charles Lewis had been newly appointed as the DDO. For Lewis, his old controller, to issue an order with "or else" attached meant this

Qamaan was much more important than elephants. Pero also knew Mbuno would never care about that if it risked sacrificing the herd. Thinking quickly, Pero asked, "You got this drone here quickly, can you send us some reinforcements? We'll guide and assist DDO's requirements. But we will not sacrifice the herd."

After perhaps five minutes, the general was back. "Four hours, inbound, two to assist"—he paused for effect. "Your location." Angrily adding, "Confirm you will damn well wait." He meant wait or else.

Pero responded, "Yes, sir, affirmative. Thank you." There was no further transmission except for the sound of the UAV leaving the area and heading south. Pero looked up, saw the wing lights flick on and off twice as a farewell signal, and then it was lost. The night was again silent and dark. Pero looked down the hill, wondering if he could somehow tell Mbuno. He didn't dare use the penlight to illuminate the way, that was risking too much on such a dark night. He needn't have worried. First, a ground squirrel ran over his legs in a panic to evade Mbuno just behind.

Mbuno so surprised Pero he nearly jumped out of his skin. "For god's sake, Mbuno, whistle or something."

"You were speaking. Who?" Pero told him what General Tews had said. Pero knew Mbuno would understand a direct order from the CIA even if he had no intention of obeying it, unless he could. "Who is coming and how?"

"He didn't say. I asked for help and he said he was sending two. Two what? I don't know. Assume soldiers. Two to arrive how? I don't know. I suspect a drop, parachute drop. Here." And Pero emphasized, "We have to await their arrival, four hours. He said they were inbound. That's one hell of a scramble. This man, Rahman Qamaan, must be really important—they want him captured."

Mbuno spat out, "Wazo mbaya . . ." and continued muttering to himself as he went back down the hillside.

Pero was awake with first glowing light, wanting to see and possibly assist the incoming force, however they were going to arrive. He kept looking up, trying to spot a parachute or perhaps a helicopter. What he had not expected were two men hiking up the backside of the hillside he was camped on. Dressed in full camouflage, head to toe, they were also heavily padded out with bulging pockets, heavy backpacks front and rear, full face covers, and tight-fitting helmets with visors and what looked like a video camera stuck to the top.

Pero looked for insignia, something that would identify them. Seeing none, he pulled the pistol and pointed it at them. "Identify yourself."

The first man showed a palm, carefully moved the hand to a breast pocket, and extracted a small satellite phone. Pero recognized it from previous adventures. The man raised the antenna, pushed the speaker button, and handed it to Pero saying nothing. Pero pushed three fives and waited. He didn't have to wait long. Director Lewis' voice came in loud and clear, "Baltazar, I thought I told you that you were no longer working for us. What have you gotten yourself into this time?"

Pero responded sarcastically, "Hello, Charles, so nice to hear from you."

"Okay, you done?" Pero looked at the two men who could plainly hear. They showed no expression through their face masks. "Tell me exactly what the hell's going on and who is with you and why." Before Pero could respond, Lewis added, "And the letter to the prime minister was cute, our ambassador in Addis is not pleased, but your old friend Pontnoire cleared that up for you. As for . . ." He asked someone a question, mouthpiece covered. Pero heard a muffled "yes, that's the name" then Lewis went on, ". . . as for Akale, whoever that is, he rose all sorts of people in Nairobi on the phone yesterday; you know perfectly well Bowman is not to be involved in your escapades there either. Anyway, they have all been calling my private number and the whole department wanted to know why we hadn't simply refused to help."

Pero interjected, feeling angrier by the minute, "Yeah, and then a name Rahman Qamaan made you come scurrying out of your den to issue me orders, as if I had to take your orders. Before I hang up on you, tell me who these two gentlemen are and what do you want them to do?"

Lewis' voice came across loud and clear, "Pero, for god's sake, this is way bigger than you can handle. Let me take control, please."

When Lewis resorted to calling Pero by his first name, Pero knew something was serious. "Okay, Charles, sorry. I'm exhausted and there is something way too desperate going on here for simple poaching. Look, we came across elephants being poached, one already had been. Mbuno, well, you know Mbuno, he couldn't tolerate that so he"—Pero paused looking at the two men—"so he dealt with the three men there. One was a Somali, two were Pokot, armed with AK-47s. I took all the papers, you know that. Akale is the ranger working for APN; we got him to move family and nearby rangers out of the region once we found out it wasn't a simple poaching gang of three, but an operation here. The local park ranger confirms they've lost twenty thousand plus elephants here only in the past ten years or so. Do the math . . ."

Lewis knew Pero well. "You did the math, you always do. What's it come to?"

"Over four and a half billion dollars." Lewis did not respond.

Pero continued, "And that's calculating ivory tusks averaging one hundred and fifty pounds not the usual two to two hundred fifty pounds." Pero waited, Lewis said nothing. Pero continued, "Okay, I agree my numbers are high because that's the wholesale price of ivory in China and the Far East, but if these guys have an operation that's making half that over the past, say, ten years, that's still over two hundred million a year out of this region. Add in the Somali connection, along with their damn company name, something huge is happening here."

Lewis was calm. "And what do you think that is?"

"Don't get clever, Charles, you were the one who stopped the blood diamond routes. You know how huge sums of money can destabilize whole regions. And these guys are openly calling themselves the Youth; good god, how blatant can you get?"

Lewis calmly asked, "And how do you think they are shipping those tusks?"

It was a question Pero had not contemplated. Then he knew what General Tews and Lewis needed. "You want to ask Rahman Qamaan, right?"

"Bingo." Lewis talked to someone close by. It was too quiet for Pero to hear. He came back on. "Yes, okay. Pero let me introduce you. The fellows listening?" Pero said they were. "First is Sergeant Adam Gonzales of the US Army Ranger Corps." The soldier saluted, then pulled off his helmet and face mask. Older than Pero thought he would be, maybe midforties, clean-shaven, heavily lined face. "The other man you may know. He works for me. He pushed us for this little mission, seems his girlfriend is with you."

Taking off his helmet and pulling his face cover off, Bob Hines smiled at Pero. Pero grabbed him and hugged. Bob laughed. "If I'd known I'd be this welcome, I'd have taken this crazy walking safari with you." Bob looked down the hill over Pero's shoulder. "Nancy down there?"

Pero put his hands on Bob's shoulders, pushed him back, and asked, "I thought you went to Pennsylvania to see your folks."

"I did, but that guy . . ." He nodded at the phone.

Lewis cut in, "Yeah, yeah, we hired him. Sort of freelance. He landed yesterday in Nairobi, on his way, he claimed, to propose to Nancy Breiton. You've been playing cupid, Pero. Anyway, Adam Gonzales is an instructor, working off the *Lincoln* flattop, training noncoms in defusing new IUD types we found in Afghanistan. Only man we had nearby. Had the two of them outfit and zip up to you."

"How'd they get here? I never saw a plane."

Sergeant Gonzales answered, "Osprey, dropped two miles away." He showed his arm where a flexible GPS readout was blinking. "This is you here, we simply walked over."

Lewis cut in, "Now, Pero, listen up. We need to see that operation, we need to catch this Rahman Qamaan—his name keeps popping up in ISIS and al-Shabaab intel by the way—but most important, someone is handling freight and money. We need to find out who, where, and cut them off." Pero knew money was funding terrorism all over the world. Cut off the money supply, and terrorists' capabilities were manageable. Lewis continued, "Pero, something is wrong. Rahman Qamaan is way too high up the leadership structure to be in Ethiopia simply handling tusks."

"Akale questioned the Suri warriors we have here and also reported his own findings—you know Addis never gives him police or military support, right? Anyway, Akale confirmed there's a camp of the poachers just outside the park boundaries, down the hill from us here, hit the river, and turn south. How many are there, and what they're doing, I'm not sure. They have a refrigerated truck, necessary for meat supply, not for tusks. Two guys chased us in an off-road cage-type thing. You know, kind of like a dune buggy on steroids. The Pokot man the Suri killed, but I made them take the Somali prisoner. They're down there, near the river, waiting for us." Pero calculated. "Well, today's the last day I said to hold him. I think they'd just as soon kill him. Maybe not. Maybe they'll take him back to their village."

"Give the phone to Gonzales. Off speaker." Pero handed it over.

Gonzalez listened for a minute and responded, "Roger that." And the satellite radio was turned off. He pulled a second satellite phone from his pocket and handed it to Pero. "He wants you to have this."

As Gonzales was putting his face mask and helmet on, Pero held his sleeve. "You cannot leave until you meet Mbuno and Nancy and the Suri," he said as he pointed downhill. "Mbuno may mistake you for an enemy and we'd lose you."

Gonzales snorted; his training and abilities would, he was sure, overcome any local. Bob grabbed Gonzales' sleeve, "No, man, listen. Mbuno is the finest, quickest fighter I have ever seen." He stressed the word again, "Ever." Gonzales' eyes looked from Pero to Bob Hines and down the hill at the elephants. He simply nodded and started to walk down. Pero and Bob quickly caught up.

Pero whistled in the early morning light, just to make sure everybody knew he was coming down. He picked his way around rocks and bushes and eventually came to Mbuno and Nancy eating, sitting next to a natural rock indentation filled with clear water. The Suri warriors were standing guard on the herd, looking like photographic pastoral Africans, or so it seemed to Pero.

When Nancy saw Bob, she cried out and rushed to him, throwing herself into his arms and then they kissed. Pero and

Mbuno exchanged wry looks of amusement. Pero introduced Mbuno to Sergeant Gonzales. When the lovers disengaged, he introduced the sergeant to Nancy as well.

Mbuno wanted to know, somewhat angry, "Two are here, as you said. What do they want?"

Bob kneeled in front of Mbuno and responded, "Look, I'm sorry, Mbuno, there's a man in the poachers' camp called Rahman Qamaan. He's an evil man, with al-Shabaab and ISIS. Maybe even al-Qaida. Sergeant Gonzales and I have a job to do. We're supposed to capture him, then call for a pickup and take him away for questioning."

Mbuno looked at Pero. "Do you agree with this?" Pero nodded. "It is important, brother?" Pero nodded again. "Will he be interrogated?" Mbuno knew the right word. "Like they do at the Norfolk?" He meant the Norfolk Hotel in Nairobi. The building next door housed the secret service of Kenya and the basement torture sounds often escaped to the street above, terrorizing passersby.

Pero responded, "Hell, I don't know, but I suspect so, yes."

"Wazo mbaya; this is a bad idea. To capture a man, a fighting man, puts you in more danger. To kill is faster and more uhakika zaidi," more sure, "but to capture a man you may have to . . ." Mbuno was trying to find the right words. "Pero, when we fight the Mau Mau, we never try to take a man, it is too dangerous."

"Yes, but, Mbuno, you knew who the Mau Mau leader was; he later became the president. You didn't need to question anyone."

"Ndiyo, the Mau Mau leader was still a bad man. Especially his wife, Mama Ngina, who sold much ivory." He spat, then paused and thought out loud, "If I had been asked to capture a Mau Mau, I would have done it with this . . ." He patted the small leather pouch on his waist belt. Resolved, he said to Sergeant Gonzales, "I can try."

Bob said, "Hell, Mbuno, I saw what your poison powders can do, but we had the drop on those Boko Haram guys. This Somali is a real fighter, professional, more dangerous."

"I would prefer he does not live, but we will try," Mbuno countered, then asked Gonzales, "Can you promise that if I do not succeed?"

Gonzales understood Mbuno meant the man should die. The sergeant had served in what the army termed backwater countries most of his professional life. He had long since lost any Western trappings of the niceties of fair trials and imprisonment for truly evil people. If he could, yes, he'd follow orders and capture evildoers. Military foes, certainly. Terrorists? Hardly. His immediate trust in this little man before him locked and loaded in his mind.

The army Ranger took off his helmet, face mask, and gloves and extended his arm to Mbuno, sealing the deal in a mutual arm grip.

Mbuno stood. "Good, hebu kuanza kutembea." Let us start walking. He marched off and went directly to the herd. The elephants parted, allowing him the lead. The three men and Nancy immediately followed, slowly, waving to the Suri warriors they were on the go.

Gonzales looked at Bob as he put on his face mask and helmet. "You weren't kidding about him . . ." Bob, all during the Osprey flight up from Kenya, had told Gonzales tales of the mzee he so revered.

The Suri warriors proceeded ahead down the valley, keeping to the valley walls in case they needed to duck for cover.

Halfway down the remainder of the valley, the elephant leader raised his trunk and sampled the rising mist coming from the Omo River below. It was familiar, familiar enough to encourage and hasten their stride. A few moments later, Mbuno was being pressured to move faster. He resisted, turning to face the leader and belch-hum as loud as he could. The herd stopped.

Mbuno turned and set a slow pace. He looked back at the three men following and motioned in the air twice and then made a sweeping gesture. Pero said, "He wants two of us to circle ahead. I am sure that means you, Bob, and Sergeant Gonzales."

Gonzales agreed, adding, "Sarge is good enough." And he and Bob set off at an amazingly quick pace, following the Suri warriors' method, dodging from rock pile to rock pile, bush to bush, until they were a half mile ahead. There the Suri didn't want Gonzalez to pass, but, looking back to Mbuno for guidance, the two warriors saw Mbuno wave him on and they let him proceed.

Bob and the sergeant discussed possibilities as they advanced, always watching for any movement or opposition. Both were expert, and yet Bob knew that the sergeant would likely outpace and outobserve him because of his years of in-country experience. When they reached the last two hundred yards from what Bob assumed was the riverbank area, Gonzales halted them behind a pile of fist-size rocks, clearly placed there by man, not nature. He put his back to the pile, patted the ground next to him, and whispered, "We need eyes."

Bob sat, nodded, extracted a small handheld video screen, extended the antenna, and keyed the voice command, "Eyes, our location, three klicks." Both men watched the screen. The down-signal was yellow, green, and red in patches. The yellow was the course of the river, the green where they were sitting, and, a little to the south of their position, next to the yellow stripe of the river, a large red area that extended most of the way to the edge of the screen. Bob keyed send again. "Eyes, our location, four klicks." Moments later the screen showed more territory and the red patch was defined, showing the end of the red area. Bob said to Gonzales, "As a camp, that's two kilometers wide. That's an awfully large camp." He was worried about how many Somali or Pokot might be there. "See down the center, the road heading south, but why does it stop?"

The sergeant nodded. "Find out. Change to synthetic."

Bob keyed send and said, "Eyes SAR, same four klicks." SAR was the military acronym for synthetic aperture radar. Penetrating targets, SAR could let you see beyond trees, beyond roofs, into the ground up to thirty feet.

The screen changed. Colors changed and showed six structures, some long and narrow nearest the river, two square buildings all placed at the hillside of the encampment next to the road running north to south. The same road that seemed to end almost immediately after it left the camp. There were twelve smaller objects, which Bob pointed at, asking "Trucks?"

The sergeant nodded. "Some, yes. Switch to ISAR." Bob called it in. The newest technology ISAR, short for inverse synthetic aperture radar, allowed watching for movement, not taking a static radar image. When the ISAR image appeared, after two fretful minutes, the screen went to black and white with white dots showing movement in real time. The herd and the crew could be seen to their west and, alarmingly, two trucks were proceeding slowly from the Somali encampment north along the Omo River toward the place where the elephants would join up with their migratory route.

As he was folding the antenna and pocketing the screen, Bob wanted to warn Mbuno. Gonzales looked at him, shook his head, pulled the satellite phone from his pocket, and dialed 555, heard a response, "Warn your man, enemy coming upriver. Two trucks. Out." Then the sergeant got to his feet, moved his SR-25 weapon, commonly called a Stoner rifle, from his backpack to the front, checked the ammo clip, and made sure Bob was doing the same with his M4 carbine. The two men moved quickly down the valley to ambush the trucks if necessary.

Still up valley, Pero's pocket buzzed. Quizzically he pulled out the satellite phone and answered, "Didn't know this was on. Who's calling?"

A female voice responded, "Warning from Gonzales, two trucks coming upriver." And the line went dead. Pero put the phone away. He called over to Nancy and told her to stay close to the Suri warrior walking with them. "Whatever you do, do not go down the valley without your man." Nancy nodded. Pero took off running, his heavy backpack swaying.

CHAPTER 8

NJIA YA UHAMIAJI IMEPATIKANA TENA—MIGRATION ROUTE FOUND AGAIN

Pero had to hope, that was all, he just had to hope. He thought, *Elephants are smart, they'd seen me for days, they'll* know *I mean no harm.* Smart though they are, the idea of a heavily laden human walking up to the rear of the herd and then trying to walk through them was not to be tolerated. They didn't mean Pero any harm, they just wanted to stop him. One trunk sent Pero flying flat on his back, the backpack cushioning his fall. The elephant, a young male, came quickly over, leaned his head on Pero's chest, and started to crush him.

Mbuno had seen or perhaps felt the commotion behind him. He ran through the herd, belching-humming all the way, gasping, taking in large stomachs of air. He reached Pero just in time.

Pero had felt the ribs about to break, he had felt the blood pulsing in his ears as pressure built up. On the verge of passing out, the pressure suddenly receded and he only heard Mbuno talking. Pero couldn't see at all or hear clearly. The blood pressure had impaired both senses. As one eye started to clear and focus, he saw Mbuno looking down, hum-belching into his face, checking for vital signs, elephants all around. Moments later, the other eye kicked in and the rumbling in his ears diminished. He looked at Mbuno and said, "Sorry, two trucks, Somalis coming our way. Leave me, save the herd."

Mbuno patted him on the shoulder, rose, turned to face the inquisitive herd, and urged them forward. Passing the mtoto, he took the small trunk in his hand and using a swaying action like the mother, lead the baby down the hill as close to the north side as possible. Mbuno was in a hurry. He reached the hiding place of the Suri guards and urged them north, upriver, motioning them to run. They understood and took off in the direction he pointed. Once they reached the north rim, they crouched behind rocks and waited.

The herd, now allowed to run toward their familiar river, were more than happy to comply. Soon it was a race, the Suri warriors in the lead, being caught by the elephants, and, bit by bit, Mbuno was passed and took up a rear position, urging the less swift to keep on.

The rust-colored, soot-laden river was more swollen than they had seen it days before, but not yet swollen to flooding by monsoons, which would soon arrive. The elephant herd followed upstream keeping up a speedy pace even though they had no idea of the danger they could be in. Once he saw they were proceeding without his urging, Mbuno turned, resumed his hunting run, and went directly south. Four or five hundred yards down the river, he spotted the backs of Bob and Gonzales behind a stand of Commiphora bushes behind a pile of rocks. He joined them saying, "You rest on an ancestor, this is a grave of a chief. Good protection."

None of them looked at one another, eyes being intent on spotting trucks they knew were coming north, but Bob responded with, "Thanks, Chief," and patted the stones.

Pero, Nancy, and Nancy's Suri warrior came breathlessly up from behind and Gonzales told them to lie down. Pero still wasn't feeling well. His ribs were painful. The Suri warrior turned to face upriver and imitated the screech of the golden eagle three times. As the crew waited, Mbuno and the warrior both kept a lookout for the three Suri warriors from upstream to rejoin them. The call was meant for them.

The first truck appeared at the same time the three warriors broke cover. The canvas-backed, heavy-duty truck had been slowly following tracks along the riverbank, about a hundred yards inland from the water's edge. Seeing the Suri men, the truck veered and bumped over uneven ground toward the men. Stoically, the warriors continued walking down the river near the bank, paying the truck no attention, but watching for anyone getting out.

The Suri warrior with the crew in the bushes seemed unperturbed. Pero asked, "Mbuno, ask him why the men aren't running, can you?"

Mbuno shook his head and instead said, "I will tell him danger."

Using the Suri words Akale had taught him, Mbuno said danger and run a few times. Each time the warrior with them smiled and shook his head. Gonzales wanted to start firing, but Mbuno told him to wait. The truck reached a point near the three men. A man on the passenger side got out of the cab. He talked to the unarmed Suri warriors and they paid him no attention, keeping on walking. That put the truck in a tough position as the men had walked past the back end of the truck going downriver. The truck had to back up or turn around. The man got back in. As the truck reversed to begin making a three-point turn, the open canvas back allowed Gonzales and the team to see inside. Both benches were full of men.

Pero ducked down and said, "There's plenty of firepower there."

The second truck appeared, smaller and with a steel box with a refrigerator unit near the top. It stopped when it saw the first truck turning.

Gonzales whispered to Bob, who agreed and said, "Mbuno, you watch that big truck, we'll deal with that one over there." Both men went crawling to the south to get behind the second, smaller truck. The sergeant assumed Mbuno would stay put. Bob looked back, a worried look on his face. He saw Mbuno take some powder out of his leather pouch. Turning to resume crawling, Bob had a grin on his face.

Pero pulled out the pistol, determined to be ready. Mbuno looked at Pero's hand and instead held out his hand. Pero gave him the gun. Mbuno hid it in his waistband under his shirt. Whispering, Mbuno said, "Keep down, keep Nancy safe." He looked at the Suri warrior and motioned him to follow.

Walking casually, the two Africans emerged from the bushes and ambled toward the other three Suri warriors, as if they had planned to meet up. Mbuno carried no weapon the men in the large truck could see, and the Suri only had their walking sticks, their donga. The two groups of Suri men and Mbuno waved at each other, seemingly relaxed. The canvas-backed truck had turned around and was belching diesel fumes catching up to them. Coming to a halt, the same man who had gotten down before alighted from the front cab and called out something and the men from the back began to dismount. There were eight Pokot in all. Two of them looked to be in their early teens. Only two elder Pokots carried weapons. They held them casually, perhaps not sure how to use them in a fight.

Meanwhile, Bob and Gonzales approached the stopped reefer truck from behind, unseen. There was a steel door at the rear. Bob placed his ear on the door, heard nothing, and gave Gonzales a thumbs-up. Gonzales knew that the wing mirrors would show their arrival creeping up the sides of the reefer truck. He waited until he knew whoever was inside the driver's cab watched the other truck intently.

On foot, the man from the bigger truck, clearly in charge, wearing camouflage clothing, pistol at his hip, walked over to the gathering as Suri and Mbuno began greeting each other. The man had no reason to fear them. They did not flee, merely demonstrated disdain. He would be used to that from local tribesmen. That's why he hired Pokot from farther south. Mbuno had evaluated all this. Just as he had assessed that the man would not understand the puff of powder Mbuno blew at him, so fast that no one else could have seen it from the bigger truck.

However, the men in the reefer had seen Mbuno's strange move, and Bob heard their exclamations of surprise and anger as the man in camouflage collapsed. The reefer truck's passenger raised an AK-47 as Gonzales, already at the door, fired his SIG Sauer silenced pistol through the window. The Pokot mercenary was dead, instantly. The driver turned to look, unaware of his door opening; Bob pulled him to the ground and cracked him in the head with the M4 rifle.

The driver of the larger truck, along with the eight Pokot, suddenly realized they were in an ambush. The driver gave no commands, just opened the door, jumped out, and began to run. There was nowhere to run. Mbuno yelled, in Suri, "No kill," as the fastest Suri warrior lit out after him. The Suri warriors began beating the eight other Pokot with their donga, causing the men to scream and fall down begging for mercy. The two armed men dropped their AK-47s immediately. They had not been carrying them to fight with, just to slaughter elephants.

That left the driver of the truck who had fled. When the warrior caught up to him, a quick slash with the donga to his thigh brought the man down. He raised his hands pleading. The warrior looked down, looked back at Mbuno who was calling out, "No kill," then placed a foot on the man's chest and posed, his donga held like a walking staff. Soon after, he dragged his captive, limping, to the pile of other captives.

The nine Pokot sat together, not saying anything. The beating had stopped. The reefer driver Bob had hit in the head moaned but remained conscious. Mbuno crouched down in front of all the Pokot who sat near the fallen body of the leader in camouflage, clearly Arab and not Ethiopian, probably Somali. Mbuno spat at the unconscious man, his spittle landing on the man's forehead, a huge sign of disrespect and fearlessness as he intended. The Pokot, rubbing bruises caused by the donga, cowered lower and lower.

Mbuno's voice was angry. "Ikiwa nitawaachia hapa, wengine hawa watawaua nyote." If I leave you here, these others will kill you. He continued, seeing his words land with impact on the men who knew their lives were held by a thin thread, "Kama ingekuwa mimi, ningewasaidia wao. Nawachukia Pokot bila heshima." If it were me, I would help them. We hate all dishonorable Pokot.

Not a man protested. Their heads hung low. Mbuno pointed to the two youngest and asked, "Kwa nini kuondoka nyumbani?" Why did you leave home?

The boys struggled to get the courage to respond. Finally, the eldest boy said respectfully, "Sisi ni pole mzee, sisi walikuwa kuuzwa. Waliilipa wazazi wetu." Mbuno translated for Pero and Nancy who came up to join them, "They said they are sorry. They were sold. The parents got money."

Pero and Nancy, who was again taping, were shocked. Mbuno continued, "More probably they had a choice: take a few shillings or be killed." Mbuno pointed to the driver who had run away, asking, "Yeye ni nani?" Who is he?

The boy answered again, "Mjomba." An uncle.

Mbuno began to see a pattern, asking, "Je, unaweza kunipa majina ya kila mtu hapa, na kabila lao?" Can you give me the names of everyone here and their tribe?

The boy said he could. For a few moments, he called each man by name, pointing, stating their tribal affiliation, and, if possible, their relation to the other men. The older men never told him to stop. They were so frightened, the peacefulness of Mbuno's question allowed them to begin to believe, just a little, that they might live.

The boy volunteered, and all the men instantly agreed, that they hated doing what they were doing and wanted to go home.

Mbuno walked a few steps away. Gonzales, face still covered, pointed his gun at the now fully assembled Pokot and the unconscious Somali. He made a point of cocking his rifle for effect. The men shrunk down as far as they could. Mbuno said to Pero, while Nancy kept taping, "They are all from the same two Pokot villages near Lomut. It is a poor region. They were forced to come."

Pero asked, "What do you want to do with them? We can't simply leave them here."

"Yes, we can. The shallows there . . ." Mbuno indicated the river where the water was only three feet deep or so. "They can cross with the Suri, who can take them back. Captives. When we finish with the shufti"—he looked at the comatose man as well as the reefer driver Bob had put out of commission—"we can go back and get them. Take them home."

Overhearing this, Bob calmly said, "Pero, why not make a call? They owe you a favor."

Extracting the phone, Pero looked at it with a degree of hatred. Such phones had gotten him into and out of trouble, but it was never without risk—risk to all around him. Resigned to the inevitable, he agreed, "Okay, let's try." He pushed 555. The voice responded and he said, "Baltazar, need to talk to Lewis."

"Stand by." Pero clicked twice. An eagle flew close by, screeching. Pero looked up in surprise. He was watching, trying to determine which type of eagle it was, when the phone made a noise.

Lewis was back on. "Are you there? What is it? Do you know what time it is?" Pero said nothing, concentrating on watching the eagle pass from view. Collecting his thoughts. After a pause, Lewis repeated, "Okay, I'm here, what?"

Pero counted the men into the phone, "Let me see, eight Pokot, recently disarmed, also an unconscious man who seems to be the leader and one driver with a lump on his head, both probably Somali. Plus one . . ." Still on open mike, he asked Mbuno, "What's the other driver, the one who ran from the big truck? Pokot or something else?"

Mbuno asked the boy. He confirmed it was a Pokot who had come with the shufti to take them.

A veteran then, thought Pero, saying, "So, we've got ten Pokot, wait, sorry; one is dead, your man's doing . . . that makes nine. One is a veteran Pokot, a driver, who helped kidnap and hire them to do the dirty work—so, yeah, nine living Pokot. Remember, all of them are illegal here. Plus the one Somali driver captured and another unconscious Somali. All told, besides the Somalis, we have one dead Pokot, a living Pokot driver, who appears to be a collaborator, and eight living terrified, coerced Pokot tribesmen; the Pokot are to be guarded by four Suri warriors who will escort them all back to the Suri village on the banks of the Omo. You can collect the Pokot there"—he paused—"and take the eight home safely, understand, Lewis? Eight safely home."

Gonzales laughed, never taking his eyes or muzzle off the captives. Lewis responded with a curt, "Affirmative. Okay, okay, only eight home." Lewis had understood that the ninth, the Pokot driver, could be taken for questioning. "What about the Somali men?"

"Okay, great. But that's a complication." Using one hand to hold the phone's speaker button, Pero flipped over the shufti Mbuno had blown the powder on and went through his outside jacket pockets. "Driver's license and permit to hunt in Ethiopia. I can't tell who signed the permit, it may be a fake. So, we have here one a Yusuf Liban, resident Mogadishu, yet born in Salah in Oman." Pero dug deeper in the man's clothing, probing, searching one-handed. He found a wallet deep inside the jacket, in a concealed zipper compartment. "Hello! Charles, you'll love this, one guy's got an Omani passport, real name Mohammed bin-Liban, age thirty-five, passport issued two years ago or a little more. The visas and entry stamps in his passport are as follows, India in and out, Oman, loads of those." Pero was flipping pages. "Somalia, loads of those, then Yemen twice, both in and out last year and"—turning a last page—"Hello again! A little piece of paper with a temporary visa taped in for . . ." Pero paused for effect, "Iran."

Pero looked at Mbuno, Nancy, Bob, and Gonzales, saying as much to them as into the phone's open speaker, "What the hell have we got here, Charles? That's the terrorist manifest for cargo and travel all in one passport. The only thing that's missing is North Korea for Christ's sake."

A different voice responded, "Take him and the other Somali."

Pero asked, "Seriously, you want us to take them, somewhere? Where would you suggest, Charles?"

Mbuno suggested, "The unconscious Somali will sleep another day or more." Pero knew the powder was potent but not normally that potent.

Gonzales asked, "What's in that powder, anyway?" Mbuno started to tell him that because the powder had gone in the man's eyes and nose, and because he had inhaled it so deeply . . .

Pero cut their discussion off. "Look, guys, we can't leave him here and these guys," indicating the Suri, "they can't carry him and the other guy . . ."

Nancy, ever practical, asked, "Does the reefer truck have a locking door?"

Pero told Charles. "Call you back." And he hung up.

It took them a half hour to move the reefer truck, deep into the dense cover of a stand of ficus trees a few hundred yards away. The truck was invisible from the riverbank. As they were emerging from the ficus forest, the rains came again and even their recent tracks were covered. In the truck they had found two gasoline cans, which they emptied and filled with river water. They had put the two cans uncapped with the sleeping Somali/Omani as well as the one Bob knocked on the head in the reefer truck and wired the door locked. The reefer back was not ventilated except to the cab in front via a small six-inch sliding hatch. Opening the truck's side windows, only one of which worked all the way, they allowed enough fresh air to keep the men alive. Pero called and told Charles where they left the truck and Gonzales confirmed the GPS coordinates off his sleeve display. Charles said, "Pickup, twenty-four hours."

Then it was time to get the Suri moving. The sergeant and Bob escorted them all to the other side of the river. The Pokot had completely surrendered. After a thorough body search, Mbuno made them understand that if they behaved and caused no trouble, the Suri would turn them over to the police who would take them home. In explaining all this, he reminded them never to trust the veteran Pokot. If they did, that man and all of them would be killed. Either by the Suri or by men who would go to their village and seek them and their families out. Pero pointed at Gonzales to effectively frighten them.

Even as they crossed the shallow river, it was clear the eight men were shunning the veteran Pokot driver who was tapped, every once and a while, not too lightly with one of the Suri's donga. Even Pero understood the Suri commands. Like the order to a recalcitrant donkey, the Suri warrior was ordering the captive onward in no uncertain terms.

When the Suri and their captives turned south then west, Pero, Mbuno, and Nancy all waved to them and yelled goodbye across the river. The men called back, animal calls from some of them, clearly in a good mood to be going home. Pero watched to see the men lead the queue deep into the woods, taking a shorter route to home and avoiding the possibility of anyone in the encampment two kilometers away spotting them.

Pero was sorry to see them go. They were brave and fast. Lord, they are fast with those donga!

Looking north, Mbuno had been sorry to see the elephants go, yet pleased they were on their safe migration route.

Nancy was happy that Bob had been there to see the elephants continue to migrate. As a couple, they had, once again, been a part of something wonderful. It proudly encouraged her to cope with what she felt sure was to come next. She said to Bob, "I really wish the world was as peaceful as those elephants." Bob had nothing to say. She knew he agreed absolutely.

Bob had wished she had left with the Suri. However, Bob was no fool. Nancy would have been angry at the very suggestion.

"Sarge, you want to outline any plan you have?" Pero asked.

Gonzales removed his helmet and face mask. He put the mask in a deep trouser pocket, extracted a stick of black face paint, and striped his cheeks as he talked. "We scanned—satellite images—the compound. It's not what we expected. There are four long huts, some trucks, and maybe something smaller like an ATV, can't tell. Down the middle of the compound, there's a road but it doesn't connect up here or down south. Alongside the road are two square buildings. Bob and I will do a recce and report back. If we're going to do anything before the teams arrive"—he meant reinforcements planned for the next day—"we can discuss that when we know what we're up against."

Pero's mind had been playing its usual tricks. While he was occupied on one series of events, the back of his brain, as he always called it, was calculating away. He had an idea and wanted Gonzales to consider it. "A road? Really? How wide?"

Gonzales looked at Bob, who pulled the screen out and thumbed through the memory, pulling up the SAR image. He pushed a few buttons and a grid was laid over the projected image. Bob counted off grid lines. "Each square is a hundred meters, the road? Say a width of fifty meters, maybe less."

Pero had that feeling his subconscious guess was right. "And how long?" Pero, watching Bob, started nodding, encouraging Bob's evaluation.

Bob measured, then said, "Maybe two kilometers . . ." The penny dropped. "A runway."

Pero smiled. Lewis had agreed with Pero's assessment of the kill volume of ivory, but how was that tonnage of tusks leaving? Any trip over land would be easy to apprehend and a barge downriver to Lake Rudolf would never go anywhere over shallow rapids. Pero's logic? It had to be by air. As soon as Gonzales mentioned a road, Pero suspected a runway, especially in East Africa where bush pilots flew in and landed in the smallest open fields. Make a two-kilometer road, clearing any trees and bushes and you have a runway, a long runway suitable for a heavy load for a long rolling takeoff.

Gonzales pulled out his satellite phone, clicked buttons, and spoke, "Review SAR again, last SAR this location shows two klick road—may be a runway." Gonzales asked for someone to review satellite scanning for the past week to see if anything took off or landed there. Pero was sure they would have to fly in and out, regularly. The volume they were handling was just too large.

Gonzales told Pero, Nancy, and Mbuno to wait by the chief's grave, which gave them protection from anyone traveling up the river, while he and Bob went off scouting. Pero was glad of the rest. His ribs were painful. From the first aid pack, he took out ibuprofen and swallowed two. Mbuno watched and avoided asking questions.

The two military men, trained and professional, covered the distance to observe the encampment slightly uphill of the enemy compound in under an hour. At the lower end of a mahogany wood on the hillside, leafberry trees hosted a band of de Brazza's monkeys, small creatures with black fur and white markings. Bob and Gonzales stationed themselves while the monkeys watched nervously. Both men had binoculars, both men listened to earphones attached to a small monodirectional microphone situated in the center of the binoculars. The monkeys chattered and Bob found them quite talkative. Such regular sounds of nature gave the men cover. If the monkeys stopped chattering, there could be danger. As lookouts, monkeys were useful.

The men's narrow-focus microphones eared through the dim light. They listened to doors being slammed, machinery running, and something heavy being loaded, but nothing very informative.

Bob had immediately assessed the compound below. It was effectively in a hollow. Unless you came around a bend in the river coming from the south, you would never see it. He looked north and realized that the river bent west and the hillside would, once again, hide the campsite unless you were almost on top of it. Bob said to Gonzales, "Pero said that the park guy, Akale Hassan, said there was no traffic downriver this time of year, still too shallow for boats. So they don't need to post lookouts looking upriver."

"Or maybe the men they lost cut their manpower. Let's hope so. Pero and Mbuno accounted for the first three, and then two more, and then we accounted for twelve. So they're down by four Somalis and thirteen Pokot, right?" Bob nodded. "Let's see what they have down there." Gonzalez started to creep down the hill.

Not more than ten seconds later, they heard the wheezing cough of an engine. A plane's engine. A few moments later, there was a second cough and a second engine came to life. Closer now, they could see the square buildings. They were definitely aircraft hangars. Two hangars of corrugated metal, sporting very old rust and bad paint jobs. Bob trained his binos and said, "The hangars are new, but they've been painted to look like they're rusting and old." He swept his view either side. "No sign of anyone moving. The plane is running engines in the hangar." Bob wondered why.

Gonzales looked up as a plane buzzed overhead coming from the north and proceeding south.

Minutes before, back at the chief's grave site, Pero had tuned in the walkie-talkie. He set the frequency to the number that had traffic before. Somali traffic. As a plane approached their position from the north, the radio crackled into life, "Addullah wacaya. Addullah wacaya. Soo gal." The message was repeated. Pero and Mbuno listened closely. A response, sounding clear and possibly very near, "Saldhig halkan. Ogolaanshaha dhul."

Pero sat back. He asked Mbuno if he understood any of that. Mbuno hadn't. Nancy drew a blank as well. Quickly, Pero pulled the satellite phone from his pocket and pressed 555 and told them to listen and translate. The plane circled over the hillside they sat below. "Saldhig halkan. Wadada cad ayaa cad. Diyaar u noqo inaad baxdo." The answer came in English, "Roger. Landing now." A moment later came a completely different voice, "Aamusnaanta. Dhul. Aamus." After that, radio silence and the plane's engines seemed to change pitch and faded past the forest.

Pero was just about to speak to the satellite phone when a new engine sound grew louder and louder. Moments later, the same plane flew perilously close to the ground above their heads, slowly gaining altitude using the open river valley going north. Pero guessed, and said out loud, "Christ, they're struggling to gain altitude, maybe thirty feet per second." He watched as the plane disappeared up the valley of the river. Not two minutes later, as he and Mbuno were waiting for a translation, the same plane—Pero was sure it was the same Skyvan—passed overhead heading south, its turboprops at full throttle, still struggling to gain altitude.

Pero sat back on his rear, dumbfounded. The phone was speaking, "Baltazar, can you copy?" He apologized and said he could. The voice said, "The first message was: Base here. Runway clear. Be ready to leave. The second message was emphatic: Silence, Land, Shut Up. Do you copy?"

"Yes. Please get Lewis." Lewis came on. "Charles, I know how they're doing this. A plane that just took off over my head, it will be almost the only plane in this region. Get the tail number and the transponder squawk frequency and radio call sign they're using. It's loaded with ivory. They have two identical planes— Short Skyvans. The old model, I think it's the 330 or 360? You know, the one with the flat fuselage panels and twin tails. The twin tails and flat sides give it away. So, get this, one flies over, lands, just as the identical plane—same markings, everything— takes off. Only the plane taking off is loaded with ivory. So where the first flight came from, they did a preinspection for Kenya or maybe Somali customs, probably as a mail carrier or something. No one will search an older Skyvan—especially if they're precleared. They can land anywhere. These two are painted gray, with red markings and white numbers. One flew right over our heads."

Lewis affirmed he got the info and warned Pero to stay out of danger.

"Yeah, well, that's all well and fine." Then Pero thought of something. "Charles, those planes are turboprops. They burn kerosene, there's no fuel storage here . . ." He paused, thinking, "Oh god, I get it. The one landing had a belly tank, and so did the one that flew off. You know you can unfuel those or just transfer fuel in flight. Nobody questions you if you want to fully fuel a plane out here, you know that. Anyway, plane one comes in, unloads or transfers the kerosene into his own tanks ready for the next flight. The belly tank is now light and empty. They load up the Ivory waiting for plane two to reappear, fuel heavy, of course. Then, presto, plane two drops below radar—if anyone was watching, which I doubt in this region—and then plane one pops back up. Same transponder squawk, same tail numbers, and call sign. It's a doppelgänger trick. Neat too."

An explosion coming from downriver cut the call short.

* * *

Mbuno was the first down the valley. He was in his hunting run, crouched low. Pero and Nancy followed, keeping eyes on Mbuno as long as they could. When the two cleared the forest edge, the runway was on their right, and, half a kilometer ahead, all four long huts were on fire, four or five men were running, some on fire, clothes burning. Out of the closest of the hangars, a plane's engines roared and a plane emerged turning south to reach the end of the runway.

Pero called out, "Bob! Gonzales! Stop the plane." Pero was certain this was an escape plan. Pero called out again and got no response. He extracted the phone and told them to tell Gonzales the plane was planning to escape, it would turn at the end of the runway. Its takeoff would be south to north, into the light breeze.

He needn't have bothered yelling. Shots rang out and the plane swerved dramatically left off the runway. Seeing impact was imminent, the engines cut before it impacted the second hangar. The Skyvan came to a stop, its propellers spinning down. The fuselage was tilted strangely to the left. Pero looked and spotted that the left undercarriage tire was shredded, shot out.

The thin skin of the plane echoed with the sound of boots running. The aft ramp plopped down and three men emerged, two holding up their hands. The third carried a pistol in his left hand. Pero could just make out Gonzales next to the first hangar's corner as he yelled, "Drop it or you will be killed." The man spun around to see who was yelling, raising his pistol. A pilot in uniform, he raised his gun looking for a target. Three silent puffs of dirt kicked up at his feet and he dropped the weapon. "Sit down," came the command. The man sat, telling the two men, both dressed in mechanic's overalls to also sit.

Bob emerged from behind the second hangar and looked down at the men, carbine aimed with intent. "Hands on head, now!" They did as they were told. Gonzales ran off to the huts and the burning men.

Mbuno was already at the second hut looking down at three men lying flat on their stomachs. Gonzales heard the end of a command Mbuno made and went in search of stragglers. Mbuno told him to stay, explaining that there were only these three and the other two. He pointed to two bodies, burned to death. Mbuno added, his voice showing utter disgust, "Walikuwa trapped, kufungwa katika. Ilikuwa ni bomu la moto."

Gonzales stopped and asked Mbuno to explain.

"I said they were trapped, locked in. It was a fire bomb." Mbuno asked one of the captives who had locked them in.

The Swahili response from the Pokot man closest to Mbuno was clear. Mbuno translated, "They say that their boss, Rahman, that man you name Rahman Qamaan I think, told them to wait inside and locked the door. They had food and then the fire came." Mbuno turned his back on the men, addressing Gonzales who was keeping his gun trained on them. "They are only butchers. See their shirts. They are Pokot." He told the men to stand and ushered them back toward the plane. The pilot and two non-Pokot were still on their knees, hands on top of their heads. Bob was still guarding them. Mbuno asked the three Pokot he brought over, "Huyo ndiye bwana Rahman?" Which one is the boss Rahman? All three shook their heads and said he was not there.

Mbuno was furious. Pero saw his expression and realized the dead men, still smoldering across the runway, deeply offended Mbuno's sense of right and wrong. Taking his binoculars, Pero scanned the smoldering huts. In the center of one was a blackened pile of what could only be elephant tusks. Tusks don't burn. Pero had seen Kenya demonstrate this before, burning tusks in a false drive to stop poaching, but it was, in reality, a money-raising scheme worldwide. The tons of ivory Kenya destroyed only raised the price of ivory—especially for the hundreds of tons of ivory Mama Ngina had in her warehouse in Mombasa.

He watched as Mbuno went over to the man in a pilot's uniform, pulled him upright, and walked him a few yards away, motioning to Pero to follow. Gonzales was puzzled, about to intervene but Bob stopped him. "Been here before; trust them, they'll find out what we need to know. Besides, you don't want to get in Mbuno's way; he's really angry."

As a pilot over East Africa, the pilot had to speak English but Mbuno quickly assessed that the man was likely to be Arab and unlikely to speak Swahili. To Pero he said, "Wewe kuuliza. Mimi kuhakikisha Yeye anasema ukweli." You ask. I make sure he tells truth.

Pero responded, "Ndiyo." He turned to the pilot, "Stay standing." Calmly adding, "Your name, please?" No response. Pero took a step closer, "Look. Listen. Answer truthfully, and without hesitation, or I will simply turn you over to my friend here. He's an elephant hunter. He knows how to skin an elephant. I'll ask him to start skinning your arm, then a leg, until you will tell me everything. And if not, we'll leave you, stripped naked, facedown, never to see Jannah." Heaven. "When we're through, there will be no aljana," paradise, "for you, when we steal your true faith. You'll be dead and eaten by hyena, faithless, an Allah deserter, before tomorrow's sunrise." He saw his words sink in. "It's up to you." The man's eyes were huge, terrified, but he said nothing, shaking his head. "Okay, if that's what you want." He looked at Mbuno, "Mbuno, please start with his arm, the left one, I can see he's left-handed . . ." Mbuno drew his small knife and advanced.

The man crumbled to the ground, holding up his hands, pleading, "I was hired, I fly, that is all. I don't know what we're carrying, I don't know who these men are . . ." His arms tried to stave off an advancing Mbuno.

Pero responded, "Bad call on your part to lie."

Mbuno's blade moved so fast, the pilot couldn't withdraw his arm fast enough. The slash was along the forearm, maybe four inches long and two inches wide but only skin deep. The skin was curled up, blood oozing. The pilot looked at his peeled arm then screamed and fainted. Pero kicked him in the side and slapped his face. "Wake up, it is not over. So far you have lied. Let's have it all now, one question at a time." While Pero talked down at him, he rifled the man's pockets and pulled out a wallet, work papers, and wads of money, all Ethiopian birr and Somali shillings. Pero looked at the pictured Somali camels again and shook his head. He put the money on the dirt and ground the Somali bills into the earth, making sure the pilot watched.

After a thorough body search, Pero had more than a handful of papers. "Well, Mr."—he looked at the name on the flying permit—"Juma Addullah, if that's your name, oh no, wait there's another, your passport, this one from Yemen . . . Hassan d'Houti. Let's assume that's your real name and, before I ask Mbuno to keep cutting"—the pilot grabbed his arm, folding the flap of skin back along the arm—"my first question is, Where were you going, exactly?"

Mbuno sheathed his knife and Pero questioned the now totally cooperative man for fifteen minutes. In the end, they marched him back to the other prisoners where Bob had taken them, into the hangar to a locked storeroom. After searching everyone, Bob made the men empty everything from the store-room and then used it as a jail, door open, gun at the ready. Pero pushed the pilot into the room. He was still terrified.

CHAPTER 9

FIKIO HALIJULIKANI— DESTINATION UNKNOWN

Pero needed to discuss everything with Mbuno, Nancy, Bob, and Gonzales. But then who would guard the prisoners? Mbuno solved the problem. He went to the open door and saw there was no window. The room was dank and hot. He drew some powder from his pouch and blew it off his palm into the room and shut the door behind him, holding his breath. There were muffled sounds and, moments later, silence. Again Mbuno held his breath and entered. Everyone was out cold, lying on one another. He checked eyelids and touched eyeballs. No one flinched or moved. He exited the room and closed the door. Taking a lung of fresh air, he said, "They will sleep, maybe one hour or two."

Gonzales had to remember to close his mouth. He had opened it in shock, thinking, *What is that stuff?*

Pero thanked Mbuno and suggested they all inspect the plane while they talked. Nancy was first into the fresh air. She went up the Skyvan's ramp at the rear and looked at the few boxes of cargo. "Nothing special here, just some supplies, mainly food. Maybe never unloaded. Cans, beans, soda bottles, orange Fanta bottles, some batteries." She moved to the cockpit. She came back with an aviator's map case. "Only this, Pero. Wanna have a look?" Pero nodded and eagerly opened it. It held the usual East Africa Jeppesen maps showing airports, landing fields, frequencies, all a pilot's usual needs. The maps for the Omo River encampment were not marked, but that map was well creased and refolded several times. The crease was dirt-stained. He looked for another map showing signs of similar use. The only one he found, placed back in numerical order, was for eastern Kenya, carefully folded to place Dadaab in the middle. He kept that information to himself.

Gonzales sat in the pilot's seat and flicked switches, calling back, "Got their squawk frequency . . ." He tapped the transponder. "And here's their call sign." He pointed to the radio call sign, etched into a Formica tag, glued to the instrument panel just like every other small aircraft with multiple pilots. Using the phone as a message board, he entered the numbers and ran out of the plane to get a clear signal to the satellite, pushed send, and followed up with a call. Pero left him to report in.

Message sent, Gonzales turned to Pero and asked, "What did you learn?"

Pero needed to know. "Can you fly this thing?"

"Not with my training, no."

Pero debriefed the sergeant on what he had learned. "Two planes, bought from a Channel Islands charter company in the UK, identical models. Everything as we worked out. The two guys with him are technicians they hired some time ago. He's done twenty flights, the other plane is on the twenty-first. Planes need servicing. Each time they carry two tons of trunks.

PETER RIVA

I work that out to be thirty tusks, fifteen pairs. Value? About ten mil, in dollars. Each flight."

"Jee-sus, Pero, you're kidding, right?" Bob was startled.

"Nope, and I'm rounding down. Forty-one flights and they've shipped over four hundred million out of here." Pero knew what was coming next, "And, yes, the destination is Somalia. Hosingow to be exact, just past Amuma in Kenya, on the border. That's all he knows. Makes sense they haven't told the pilot the value or end purchaser. It's all al-Shabaab. His damn permit to operate in Ethiopian airspace says the same Youth company and the pilot's ticket is BS by the way." Pero handed the papers to Gonzales. "This whole operation is al-Shabaab. He was told to land and depart. My guess? They know they're exposed here and shut down. They were bugging out before they ran into us." Pero pointed at the burning huts.

Sergeant Gonzales was impressed. "I've got to call this in; well done, you two." He looked and nodded at Mbuno, thanking him for intervening. He went away from the crew and called the additional information in.

Pero turned to Bob, Nancy, and Mbuno. "So, friends, we're done here, right? Bob, can you and Gonzales await the incoming assistance—tomorrow, right?" Bob nodded, looking skeptical. "And, Nancy, I'd say we have enough footage for now, do you agree?" She, too, nodded, wondering where Pero was going with all this. "My feeling is that I would like to go home to Susanna and I am sure Mbuno would like to see Niamba as well. So are we agreed?"

Mbuno said nothing, his face tight, eyes focused on the burnt ivory pile. Bob looked at Pero, put his arm around Nancy, and looked down at her. "Nancy, I guess you know, I want to marry you and we should have no secrets." Nancy looked pleased. "So I cannot pretend that anything I just heard

166

was not total BS." He looked at Pero. "What are you planning, man?"

Pero's eyes flicked left and Bob saw what Pero was looking at. A set of replacement Skyvan wheels and tires were stacked next to the hangar.

As usual with one of Pero's plans, Mbuno thought, always someone has to agree. That someone was, for now, Gonzales. Pero walked off with the sergeant and the two engaged in a lengthy discussion.

Gonzales was not amused at Pero's suggestion. Pero was trying to win with logic. "Look, you admitted you can't fly that plane. Of the people here, only I can, I think. I'll take the pilot with me if that makes you more confident . . ."

The sergeant was neither convinced in the end goal, nor the flying. "I don't care if you can fly that piece of junk. You're not pursuing the other plane. You have no idea where it went and as soon as I radio in that you're airborne"—he waved the satellite phone in Pero's face—"they're not going to help you either."

Pero pretended defeat. "I know that. Lewis made that plain as day." Pero shrugged and pressed his argument. "Look, we have a woman—"

Gonzales interrupted, "Pull the other one, she's more capable than you. Cooler headed too."

"Yeah, well, maybe . . . but she can't fly and she deserves to go home. So do I and so does Mbuno. Your people are arriving, when?"

Gonzales checked the message board on his phone. "ETA under five hours."

"Well, in five hours you will have all the help you need and surely even you agree you can hold that bunch." Pero pointed at the hangar where the prisoners were. "Isn't that right?" Pero saw the sergeant's demeanor was softening. "Look, I promise we'll fly to Wilson Airport, the small airfield for Nairobi. We'll leave the plane there as evidence. You can ask Sheryl at Mara Airways, I promise to leave it there. Sheryl runs the place."

Gonzales gave a small head nod. "I have to get an okay." Pero agreed and the sergeant's satellite phone was used to confirm arrival of his support one more time. He added, "One service-able Skyvan plane plan to depart for Wilson Airport with three aboard . . ."

Pero interrupted him, "Four."

The sergeant assumed Pero meant the captured pilot. "Correction, four. Plane to be left at Mara Airways, Wilson Airport. Confirm acceptable."

The answer was, "Get Baltazar." Pero took the receiver, holding it tight to his ear, and said he was on the line. Pero's ruse had not worked. Lewis was hardly fooled and already angry. "What are you doing?"

Pero kept his voice calm and explained again exactly as he had to the sergeant, that it was time to go home and the plane was serviceable, adding, "Your troops are on the way, why not let us get the hell out of harm's way for once?"

The new ruse was, as Pero desperately hoped it would be, too big a temptation for Lewis. "Give the phone to the sergeant." Pero did. "Speaker on." Gonzales pushed the button. "One aircraft, change squawk to . . ." Lewis asked someone they couldn't hear respond and came back on, "Change squawk to 7777. That'll tell us who you are and we'll tell Kenya ATC that you're US military." Squawk 7777 is the international code for military interception. "I warn you, change that code and we'll give the order to shoot the plane down, confirm? Sergeant, you get this?" The sergeant said he did. Pero thanked Lewis, sincerely. Yet he knew the risk he was taking—it could be the last nice conversation they would ever have.

With every one of the prisoners still unconscious, it took Pero, Bob, and Nancy twenty minutes to find tools, remove the damaged wheel, and replace it. Gonzales and Mbuno went through the charred remains of the long huts and carefully searched the other hangar for any paperwork. All they found were the charred remains of two more bodies and tons of tusks in the huts and a paper-burning barrel out the other hangar's back door. Both men came back to help with the changing of the plane's wheel. Neither spoke of what they had found.

After the plane was jacked up, Pero spent ten minutes sitting in the Skyvan's pilot's seat, familiarizing himself with the controls. He opened the flight manual—every airplane carries one—and went over, then rehearsed, start procedures for the Turbomeca Astazou turboprop engines. Pero made a mental pattern of which activation came first. Some were familiar; others, particularly the flight controls for the turboprops, were not at all similar to a piston engine. For starters, they need to run with revs almost full-on, have to remember that. Prop pitch controls only, not throttle after we're airborne. Gotta keep them spinning in case we need thrust.

The plane was retrofitted with onboard batteries to start the left engine. Once that was running, the power needs for the right engine were easier. If the batteries failed, Pero was sure the hangar would have a power cart to connect with. Since the engines had recently run, and run hard, he had confidence the onboard batteries would be charged, the engines still warm.

The left seat cushion was yellow with a yoke steering column that could be pulled back into an indented seat cutout if necessary. Pero again looked over all the controls, instruments, radio, and transponder placement and rehearsed controlling the plane. The Short company, builder of the plane, was British and consequently everything was where it should be. Pero felt confident he could get the plane off the ground, navigate, and, with a little luck, land. What he was really worried about were thunderclouds, which he knew he had to avoid en route, and the need to fly at altitude—with part of the flight likely at night. Turboprops worked better above six thousand feet. One of the instrument panel gauges, left engine temperature, was taped over, a mechanic's sign that it was inoperable. As it had a duplicate on the copilot's side, Pero decided not to pay it any attention. The trim tab operation worried him. The flaps he knew he could handle because there were markings on the flaps' wheel for takeoff and landing positions.

However, he knew the trim might be an issue with the plane empty. Or full. Maintaining an operational center of gravity with such a short, stubby plane was harder than people imagined. If the trim tabs weren't set just right, the plane could pitch up and be uncontrollable. If the trim tabs were set for nose down, the plane would plunge, finally invert, and crash. Pero read the manual, read the trim tabs' number settings, and determined they were set about neutral. He decided to only adjust them in level flight after takeoff.

Knowing their takeoff weight would be well below maximum, no tusks and no twenty passengers that the plane could hold if it still had seats, the runway was certainly long enough and the engines had seemed ready to pull steadily. There was still enough daylight to take off in, but landing might be in the dark, not something Pero was looking forward to. Landing gear is fixed, nonretractable, so that's not a problem, he thought. This is one stubby, short, boxy plane with two big engines. Might be hard to handle at low altitude.

Mbuno walked up the ramp and went to stand behind Pero. "You can fly this, yes?" Pero explained he was sure he could take off, not so sure about landing. "You can land, a small crash,

yes?" Pero again agreed that was possible. "Then we go ufua-
tiliaji wanyama."

Pero recognized the words for vermin and tracking. Turning
to face Mbuno, Pero asked, "You sure?"

"Ndiyo. They must be stopped. You must fly."

Shaking his head to dispel qualms despite Mbuno's assertive-
ness, Pero got up from the pilot's seat and walked back to see
Bob tightening down the last bolt on the new wheel.

Bob, sweating from the effort, said, "The pressure in this new
one seems higher than the other side, so be careful taxiing." Bob
looked into Pero's eyes, adding, "With whoever you've got on
board." Still kneeling next to the new wheel, Bob raised a hand.
Gonzales, back from inspecting the hangar, helped him up.

Pero explained, "Sarge got the okay for four to travel." Pero
then waved all the crew together. "Let's push her back and
turn her back toward the south end of the runway. I'll run the
engines up and then load people in. I'll taxi all the way down
there"—he pointed south—"then turn and take off this way." He
pointed north. "Then I'll bank going back south and proceed
into Kenya." His explanation was factual if not complete.

Gonzales added, "You're going to Wilson Airport, right?"
Pero nodded. "So how are you going to fly with that pilot and
keep him guarded?"

It was Nancy who responded. Nancy was determined and
strong-willed. "He's not. I've seen him leave out details before.
Four to go? You mean you, Mbuno, me, and Bob, right?"

Gonzales was instantly furious, reaching for his satellite
phone. Nancy had spoiled his plan. Pero felt guilty putting her
in that position. He held up his hands in surrender. "Please,
Sarge, hear me out, okay? I need Bob. Then if you want to call,
I'll not stop you."

"You have two minutes."

"Okay, let me get something." Pero went back into the plane and emerged with the two Jeppesen maps. Taking his time, way more than two minutes, he explained what he had deduced, where the other plane went. "Look, the pilot said the end destination for the tusks was in Somalia, a small village called Hosingow. That's where they hired him. That's only a hundred kilometers from Dadaab"—he pointed at the Jeppesen map— "here. The UNHCR has a serious refugee camp there, well, three actually, all close to each other. The UNHCR office is at Alinjugur, here, see? All Somalis who are fleeing the fighting with Ethiopia all along the northern and west border of Somalia. Maybe two hundred thousand refugees are camped there, in several campsites. You think some are maybe al-Shabaab?" Bob's and Gonzales' faces showed they accepted that. "Damn right. The place will be riddled with crooks, scoundrels, terrorists. It is why Kenya and AFRICOM guard the camp on the west and south sides, the sides where they worry if people get out, they will infiltrate Kenya and cause more mayhem. The whole area is scrub desert. Easy to spot anyone trying to walk south or west. To the east and north, there is only desert. Remember the three attackers in the shopping mall in Nairobi? All three came from a camp there. UNHCR is not the police and two hundred thousand or more people are impossible to watch twenty-four seven." Pero dropped the last clue, tapping his knuckles on the open Jeppesen map. "And this"—he pointed at the flight case— "is the only other map in the case that was folded just so, so that Dadaab was dead center."

Gonzales and Bob said together, "And?"

"And Mbuno and I will land there and see who comes out to greet us. Assuming Qamaan was on the other plane, he will land there soon and he will know the other plane, this one, was supposed to come after. Remember the translation? Be ready to leave? The sooner we're in the air, the better. They would be expecting this plane to follow."

Gonzales, satellite phone in hand, squinted his eyes watching Pero's face. His anger subsided. He then looked at Bob. "You okay with this?"

Bob thought it through, out loud, "One, if Pero's right and they do welcome this plane landing, we'll know who and where. Two, they may not know we've infiltrated their base. Yes, they burned it down, but only their pilot would fly and know where to fly, right? With the two mechanics, which I am sure they'd like to have back. Pero could radio and say he had mechanical issues that he had to fix, that's the delay. It's plausible. Three, if this plane doesn't show up, al-Shabaab will decamp Dadaab and blend into the countryside. Think about it, over two hundred thousand people, all terrified of al-Shabaab. We'll never find them. We'll never know who, or how." Gonzales was nodding acceptance of all Bob laid out. Bob continued, "And there's another point, the other plane was heavily loaded with tusks. That will take time to unload and move. They won't leave the tusks, no way. Too much money. We may be able to see where, who, and how they are doing that."

Gonzales had to admit the logic was sound. What was never going to happen under his watch was to allow Bob or these civilians to disobey orders. Pero saw the resolve on the sergeant's face, even as he saw the sergeant agreed with all Bob explained. Pero let out a huge sigh and calmly said, "Let's call Lewis." He pulled his satellite phone out of his pocket and made the call.

Later, airborne, Nancy raised her voice to be heard over the roar of the engines. "I thought Lewis would kill you. He may later anyway. I get it you have called in every favor he owed you, but what's the deal with asking Blackbridge, and who the hell is he?"

Bob, sitting in the right seat, helping with controls when Pero told him what to do, responded, "Seems like Pero has higher contacts than Lewis."

Nancy answered, "Yes, well, on speakerphone I would say the only bridge Pero was referring to was the one he burned with Lewis."

As the plane droned on at eight thousand feet, the transponder squawking four sevens, the radio tuned to 118.1 for Nairobi ATC, Pero felt soon he would have to explain. They were coming up on a course correction. He called ATC on the radio using the plane's call sign and affirming they were squawking four sevens. ATC confirmed they saw him. Pero keyed the mike, "Roger, Nairobi, planning to turn, now coming up on Loiyangalani, new heading one thirty-five heading south, end destination Dadaab Airstrip." ATC told him to proceed. Pero moved the rudder pedals and yoke slightly and the plane banked left on the new heading. Pero was watching the instruments, especially the artificial horizon, not out of the windscreen. Bob was spotting out the front for any air traffic or obstacles. Pero was worried he'd miss something vital or become disoriented unless he kept his eyes on critical instruments. It was easy to become unbalanced in the air, even on a sunny day. So far, they'd only had to dodge two thunderclouds. Pero informed the crew, "We're doing a little more than one forty-five knots, say two hundred seventy kilometers an hour, and have about seven hundred kilometers to go, so figure about two and a half hours, give or take."

Nancy wasn't distracted and prodded the conversation, "This Blackbridge, Pero?"

He gave in. "There was a US ambassador on a flight to Berlin a few years back, where I met Susanna. . . . Anyway, his name is Pontnoire. He owes me a favor, he promised. I made Lewis speak with him."

Bob responded, "Wow, clever code name for the guy who's running for president! Pont and noir, bridge and black. You're calling in that big a favor? Lewis must be seriously pissed at you now." Pero only nodded. What worried him was that he knew Lewis would be calling Susanna right about then, making sure she knew it wasn't Lewis' doing. Lewis was more afraid of Susanna than angry at Pero. The only thing that frightened Pero more than al-Shabaab was losing the love or respect of Susanna, and Lewis knew that. It was Lewis' payback.

Pero looked back into the open cabin behind them. Mbuno was lying down, fast asleep, his head resting on Bob's military backpack. He had covered himself in the frigid cabin with one of their sleeping bags. Since they had boarded, Mbuno had been uncharacteristically silent, only telling Pero once again before takeoff, "You fly, we go." The resolve in Mbuno's voice was acid, cold steel.

Night came sooner than Pero wanted. It took him a while to find the cabin lights as well as the navigation lights on the wings and tail. Bob flew the plane, holding it level, while Pero had to look up the instrument and lighting controls in the manual. Nancy's only sarcastic comment was, "You sure you can land this thing? Do we even have landing lights?" Pero's brow creased further as he flipped pages and looked up where the landing light switch was.

He clicked the landing lights on and off, seeing the telltale glow off the landing strut out his side window. Bob confirmed he could see the ones on the right side as well.

Since taking off, Pero had told Bob and Nancy everything he was doing. "Okay, we're getting close. I do not know if they have runway lights. Nancy, pull that Dadaab Jeppesen map out and read me a frequency that should be there, alongside the runway."

"It says one one two point zero megahertz."

Pero turned the radio from 118.1 to 112.0. Putting the mike into his jacket breast pocket, he keyed the mike through the cloth, "Dadaab tower, this is . . ." and he went through the usual call signs, asking them for permission to land, and for light assist as they were a few miles out.

Dadaab tower acknowledged him, saying they were receiving him only two by five. The muffled sound of his shirt pocket was working as intended. Dadaab tower added, "We were told to expect your arrival an hour ago, in daylight."

"Sorry, Dadaab, we had mechanical problems and Yusuf Liban was late." Pero knew that other ears could be—likely should be—listening. If they understood that Yusuf Liban, the prisoner currently in the back of the reefer truck, had made it back to camp, they should be pleased he was on the plane. It might make them come to them, once landed. If Pero got the plane down safely.

Another voice came on, "Dhul iyo sug. Ikke la flyet."

Dadaab tower cut in, "Burn barrels positioned only on south end of airstrip being lit now. Land one three right." Pero looked at Bob, Bob shrugged. It was then Pero realized the flaw in his plan. The pilot of the plane would have made the approach and landing at Dadaab twenty times. He would know the runway, the layout. And it was likely he would call the landing party beforehand. Pero knew nothing about where they were going to land except what the map told him. One three right meant one hundred thirty degrees, landing from the right, basically going northward.

However, hearing the new voice also told Nancy that they were probably walking into a trap. "The other voice, he used Somali, right? Sounding like it. There is no way someone would use Somali unless they know this is their plane and that you've not followed protocol. Damn, they've assumed their pilot is still flying and they are telling him something in case he's flying under duress." She paused to think. "I think I heard *dool eeyo soog*. And then *icky la flyette*. That sound right?"

Bob asked Pero for the satellite phone. He extended the antenna, cracked his side window, and pushed 555, got a response. He asked, "Translation think Somali, *dool eeyo soog. Icky la flyette*."

"Stand by." A moment later, "Land and wait. Do not depart plane."

Nancy said, "That's an order to stay put."

Pero agreed. Asking Bob to hold the plane steady, Pero looked at the map more carefully. Dadaab was four hundred meters above sea level. The whole region was flat and had no hills or mountains and, as Pero remembered, no trees anywhere as the refugees had cut them all down for firewood to cook with. The runway ran from the northwest to the southeast. But for them, landing would have to be from southeast to northwest. Lighting barrels only at the southeast start of the runway. The northern end abutted the A3 highway where the terminal hut was. "Let's get down to fifteen hundred feet and see something. I've got control, Bob." He pushed the column forward and descended, watching the altimeter unwind. At fifteen hundred feet, he called out, "Nancy, Bob, eyes, please." He called back, "Hey, Mbuno, could use your eyes up here."

Below them, it was Bob who first spotted lights. "Cars, there off to the right, headlights." Pero knew it had to be the A3 main road. He banked right and then left lining up the plane with the direction of the road, all the while slowing the plane down to eighty knots. Frightened about stalling, he remembered the manual. The Skyvan's stall speed at low altitude was sixty knots. Everyone peered out the windscreen. Then they flew over a car going southwest right under them, then they passed two cars going northeast. The A3 was straight and led directly to a sharp left turn, the flight path indicated on the Jeppesen map to land at Dadaab.

Mbuno pointed. "Fire, there." Two to four miles ahead there was a small straight line of fires parallel to their flight path. Pero saw them and reduced speed to sixty knots and lowered the flaps to the indicated "landing" position. The plane pitched nose down and Pero compensated. He gave a little more bite to the propellers. Sweat was running down his neck.

Pero called out, "I see the runway end, those fires tell me where the runway starts. Everyone get buckled in. Now." He flicked on the landing lights. He still saw nothing. Being disoriented at night was the most dangerous condition for pilots. Pero kept his eyes on the altimeter, the artificial horizon to make sure he kept the wings level and, every second or so, looked out forward, hoping to see something identifiable.

Pero slowly banked the lumbering Skyvan toward the fires and dropped altitude as close to the ground as he dared. When fires disappeared under the nose of the Skyvan he kept inching down, down until he could just make out the ground color difference with the night sky. He knew he had two kilometers of runway. . . . Then, much too suddenly, the ground was illuminated and seemed to be coming up at him with too much speed. He pulled the yoke back too fast but, sensibly, at the same time, changed the prop pitches to neutral. The engines revved to their red lines. The boxy Skyvan lost all forward drive, stalled, and dropped the last eight feet onto the packed earth airstrip. The impact sheered the main landing gear off. The flat bottom of the Skyvan started to skid. The plane settled onto the dirt, sliding, the skin of the plane emitting terrible screeching sounds, and then the fuselage turned to spin slowly counterclockwise. Pero desperately cut the engines and flipped off every switch he could reach and awaited impact with anything that could be in their way. The noise from the floor was deafening. Impact would come at any moment.

Then nothing happened. The spinning slowed then stopped. The wings rocked once or twice and then silence took over punctuated only by the creaking metal of the floor of the fuselage unbuckling itself. From the rear of the plane, Pero heard Nancy calling out gleefully to be safely down, "It felt like the Flintstones. The floor was rippling under my feet!"

Mbuno lit a flashlight. His command was urgent, "We move, now." Pero knew he was right. Unbuckling, he moved toward the back of the plane where Bob, headband light switched on, had already opened the right-side passenger door. Mbuno helped Pero with his backpack and Bob first loaded Nancy's and then his own pack, armed his carbine, jumped from the plane, and stood guard. Pero was the last one out, closing the door. In the starlight, Mbuno commanded, "We move, this way." He set off at a fast pace toward the side of the runway using the dark far side of the plane to shield their presence from the Dadaab tower building on the other side. The plane had come to rest on the left of the runway strip, less than fifty yards from the end and two hundred yards from the two hangars and Dadaab tower hut.

Immediately where the airstrip ended, short scrub began, not more than six inches tall. There was nowhere to hide except flat on their stomachs.

There was no one coming. After two minutes, Bob could see no lights coming on, no movement, he affixed a nightscope to his helmet and scanned the airport. He whispered, "A plane comes in, crashes, and no one cares?" He peered toward the tower hut. "There's movement there."

As his eyes grew accustomed to the darkness, Mbuno watched for signs of any movement. Pero and Nancy saw nothing. Mbuno whispered, "I hear a door close." He tilted his head. "I will go see." He rose to a crouching position and began to run away from the plane. Pero lost sight of him in the darkness.

Bob moved over to Pero and asked, "Where's he gone?" Pero explained Mbuno had heard a door close, and then they all heard the sound of a car's engine starting.

Lights came on behind the tower hut, and in seconds a car emerged and immediately turned to advance on the Skyvan. Two men in UN uniforms got out of the Toyota Land Cruiser and approached the plane. One said something to the other and he went around the tail toward the door calling out, "Hello, in the plane, anyone hurt?" The other man came around and they opened the door. One went inside, the other watching from the doorway, ready to assist. Pero heard the creaking of the Skyvan floor as the man walked up and back down, pausing at the door, saying, "Ingen her. Hvor går de?" Pero recognized Norwegian or maybe Swedish. He whispered it to Bob and Nancy. The three of them lay prone, grateful for the dim light as the two men looked all around, turning this way and that, seeing nothing. "Hvem det enn er, han er igjen. La oss kalle dette inn."

Pero understood that well enough; they wanted to call the mystery crash in. The two men went over to their Land Cruiser and, reaching through the open window, took a mike out and radioed in. What they said was unintelligible but clearly, they were reporting not finding anything. Pero saw the man use his flashlight on the tail's lettering and then read the plane's identification into the radio. The response from the car radio was surprisingly in English, "Okay, I'll call that in. Whoever flew that plane is around somewhere. We'll make a search in the morning if they simply don't walk to find you. Leave all the lights on, to show them where to go. Return to base. Over." The two men, taking another look around and calling out, "Hello? Are you all right? We come to help!," gave up and got into the Land Cruiser and drove away, back around the tower hut. Moments later all the exterior sodium lights came on, showing the main parking apron. A small Beechcraft was parked there but no other Skyvan.

Bob asked, "Now what? No welcoming committee from the bad guys? No idea where we are and those two were officials were UN, not al-Shabaab."

Pero didn't have an answer. He asked Bob if his night vision could spot Mbuno or anything. Bob went to his knees and scanned all the way around. Lying back down, he lifted the scope off his eyes and reported he could see nothing moving. "Two hangars, one with a light inside, maybe. The other has all its doors open, empty, and no light." The tower hut was still lit and Bob said he could see one of the men pass in front of a window.

Pero asked, "See Mbuno?"

He needn't have asked. Mbuno rejoined them from behind, startling Nancy who reached for her knife before realizing who it was. Mbuno said, "Sorry, Miss Nancy. There are men in there." He pointed to something neither Pero nor Nancy could see but Bob knew to be the hangar with lights. "I counted three, maybe more." Mbuno took hold of Bob's sleeve. "You and me, now. Pero, Nancy wait." Mbuno, still holding Bob's sleeve, began his running crouch across the airstrip toward the hangar.

When they reached the side of the hangar, Mbuno walked the two around to the south and saw a door ajar, light peeking out. Mbuno pointed Bob at the door and gave him a little shove away from the doorframe. "Not go in. Wait." Mbuno sprinted back the other way, circling the hangar. Bob stood guard next to the door, waiting for someone to be flushed out—if he had understood Mbuno's plan correctly.

Someone inside yelled, another crash, someone swearing and then screaming in pain. A man appeared in the doorframe, backing out, holding a sawed-off shotgun. Before he could fire, Bob knocked him out with his carbine.

Stepping silently into the doorway, his eyes took a moment to adjust. He saw Mbuno holding a man upright using him as a shield. A man was yelling at Mbuno. The man Mbuno held up was not conscious. Mbuno was looking at something to Bob's left, something he could not see. Bob put the carbine around the edge of the door, blindly pointing at whatever Mbuno was watching, and fired two rounds. Whoever was there fired three times back in Bob's direction, splintering the doorframe as Bob ducked.

Dropping his human shield, Mbuno moved swiftly and reached the shooter before he could fire again. There was a small scream and then silence. Bob entered the room to see Mbuno standing over the man he had killed. Bob asked, grateful for Mbuno's speed, but nonetheless he had to ask, "Is that the man we want?"

Mbuno shook his head. "These are workers, Somali wanyama. They were weighing those." In the dim light, Mbuno pointed across the hangar floor to a large pile of what looked initially like firewood. Tusks. Next to the pile were twelve pairs of tusks, tagged, laid out on the concrete floor, each twin snuggled next to its corresponding match. Behind the pile of tusks was the matching Skyvan.

Hearing movement behind him, Bob turned, carbine ready, only to see the man he had knocked out twitching a leg. Bob went outside, grabbed the man's collar, and dragged him back into the building. He dropped him next to the dead man while

Mbuno dragged over the man he had used as a shield and added to the body count. Bob asked, "Dead or asleep?" Mbuno explained it could be either but soon they would know if he died. He said he was sorry for using too much powder. Bob said, "It's okay; we can wake this one and question him."

Next to the man Bob had shot at was a canvas satchel. Seeing it, he told Mbuno to stay back. Bob knelt and carefully peered inside. "It's a bomb, there's no timer I can see, probably a delay fuse. Let's stay away."

Mbuno asked Bob to use his special night vision and get Nancy and Pero. Mbuno would keep guard. When Pero and Nancy got to the hangar, Mbuno was reaching into the elephant pile, fingers stroking the tusks, muttering prayers that his wife, Niamba, had taught him. From the pile he picked up a small tusk, not more than thirty pounds in weight and, lowering his head, began to weep. Not for himself, not just for these elephants who were not ready to pass on, but for Africa that was being destroyed.

Pero went over and tried to console him. An angry Nancy looked at the bodies, assumed they were all dead, and said, "Good riddance to bad rubbish." Bob explained one still lived and they wanted to question him. Nancy said, "Just make sure it's painful. For what they have done"—she looked at the pile of tusks—"they deserve no pity." Bob's heart swelled, his need to protect her rising. He was seriously worried by Nancy's reaction to death and wondered, *Has she seen too much death now?*

Pero found a sink. He filled a bucket with water and doused the unconscious man. Under questioning by Mbuno, he responded in poor Swahili and said he worked at the airport. He was a Somali, from the Ifo refugee camp nearby. This was his night job, to feed his family. Bob waved the man's sawed-off shotgun in front of the man's eyes and Mbuno told him a real worker does not need a weapon. The worker explained that people had tried to steal the man's tusks before and he was told he had to stop thieves. Then he asked, "Je, wewe ni wezi?" Are you thieves? He looked confused.

CHAPTER 10

UFUATILIAJI WANYAMA— TRACKING VERMIN

Pero responded with, "Je! Wewe ni sehemu ya al-Shabaab?" Are you al-Shabaab? The man, sitting on the concrete, tried to squirm away, terror in his eyes. He said, again and again, that he wasn't, he had nothing to do with al-Shabaab, he didn't know any al-Shabaab, he was just a worker with family at Ifo camp. Pero switched to English, "You know what, chum? If you hadn't said you didn't know any al-Shabaab, you might have gotten away with it. But that's a lie. Everyone in these camps knows someone who is al-Shabaab. And most people working at airfields speak a little English." Pero saw that the man understood, so he pressed him with a name and looked at his eyes for a reaction. "Where is Rahman Qamaan?"

Before the man said anything, Mbuno said, "He knows." Looking at the man's eyes, Pero was sure as well. The man still said nothing.

Bob intervened. "Okay, he speaks English. Or understands it. Let's try this." Bob looked at Mbuno. "Let me take him outside and question him and then we'll go get his family, especially the wife and daughter, or boy, whatever." Nancy stiffened, looked shocked, but Mbuno immediately agreed.

Pero thought it might work and enthusiastically added that, "The guy might also have parents in the camp." Bob nodded at the suggestion. The three men all agreed that the interrogation would include the man's entire family.

The man did not agree. He knew then he would have to tell them everything. As his head was still hurting, he threw up, splashing one of the dead, and collapsed into a fetal position. As he started praying to Allah, Pero started with, "I know, we'll put him in the plane and set fire to it. With him and his family inside."

The praying stopped. In a sobbing whisper, the worker said, "They go Hosingow. They have truck."

Pero asked, "Is Rahman Qamaan in the truck?" The man didn't answer right away, his eyes darting for an escape. "Is Rahman Qamaan in the truck?" Pero picked him up by the front of his shirt, yelling at him, "Tell me now or we'll tell everyone you work for the UN police." As a stooge, the Somali's life would be minutes long in the camp. He would know that. And his family would be penniless and ostracized. He started to weep. Pero pressed him for an answer. "When did they leave? How long ago? Was Qamaan in the truck?"

"Qamaan talked on radio. Then he took truck and left."

Pero looked at Mbuno and Bob. It was Nancy who responded, "Told you that radio call didn't work."

Mbuno quietly said, "We go now. Capture him."

Bob had another idea. Pero agreed with Bob's plan with one proviso. As Mbuno gingerly carried the satchel bomb back to the Skyvan, Pero asked Bob to give him five minutes once they got to the plane to see if he could steal a car. If they were going to chase Qamaan, they needed something faster than a truck. Grunting with the load of a body over his shoulder, Bob said, "All right." Pero picked up the other body. Mbuno had made sure the men were, indeed, both dead.

The worker, holding his head, was set on a metal chair in the hangar and then tied up like a Thanksgiving turkey. Nancy guarded him, hunting knife visible. There was nothing genteel about her demeanor. She talked to him, asking questions. The man remained talkative and seemed to be trying to be helpful. He wasn't. Nancy was simply passing the time. She did learn that the man who shot at Bob intended to blow up the plane. What was more interesting was that the hangar's Skyvan had been refueled. She also learned where the battery cart was. Just in case.

Out on the end of the runway, after placing the two men in the crashed Skyvan, Bob aimed his headlamp to illuminate the satchel bomb's mechanism for Mbuno, then said, "It's simple, you pull this cord and you have a minute, probably less. Saw similar devices in Iraq years ago. Gonzales is the expert, wish he were here. It's nasty." The fuel left in the wing tanks dripped on the dirt. Bob looked at Pero and his watch. "Okay, get going, five minutes then boom."

Pero sprinted over to the Dadaab tower hut. The two UNHCR Land Cruisers were unlocked. Pero entered one, pulled down the visor, and the keys dropped on the driver's seat. He checked the lights were off, inserted the key, and read the fuel gauge. The first car was half full. Both had long-range HF radios and whip antennas ten feet high. The second was three-quarters full but with the key in, the radio sprang to life and the end of a transmission came through, the volume loud in the stillness of the night, ". . . patch Two R and three F are on their way. HQ has been advised. Confirm plane down, no pilot or passengers seen. You will advise if they turn up. Over." Pero turned the key off and pocketed the second Land Cruiser's keys. Putting the first keys back in place, he reached under the dash and pulled the wires to the HF radio, breaking a few in the process, and then hid from sight.

When the plane exploded, even though he was behind the hut, the illumination of the second and third wing tank explosions lit the sky everywhere. The very ground rocked. The two UN men came bursting out the back door and got into the second Land Cruiser. No keys, they yelled at each other in blame, then dashed to the other vehicle, started it, and drove off. Pero went inside. On a table was an HF station. Quickly, Pero disconnected the antenna lead and cut the thick coaxial cord with his pocketknife. He tucked the cord behind the table.

Outside, he started the second Land Cruiser and, lights out, drove carefully back to the hangar and Nancy. Parking by the side door, he turned off the engine and lights and waited. Moments later, Bob and Mbuno reappeared. Bob relieved Nancy at guard duty and asked, "What now? What do we do with him?"

Pero answered, "We take him into the desert and drop him. Make it a half day's walk for him back to Ifo. If he makes it, his family will see him again. If not, he'll feed the vultures." Pero knew the man understood.

Mbuno hurried everyone into the Land Cruiser; the prisoner still tied up was dumped into the back with a mouth gag. Mbuno started the engine and drove back around the hanger toward the perimeter gate to the airstrip, only then turning on the headlights. The gate was open. He drove straight through onto the A3 main road access ramp and stopped. He glanced at Pero in the passenger seat. "Where now?"

The Land Cruiser was equipped with satellite GPS tracking mapping. Pero told Mbuno to turn left. "Look for a sign to the Hagadera Refugee Camp about four miles away—it's the road to Amuma. We've got to go through there . . ." Pero pulled the Jeppesen map from his jacket side pocket. "Yeah, the road goes past the Hagadera camp and Alinjugur and then on to the border with Somalia at Amuma . . . Then it's another forty miles to Hosingow."

From the back seat Bob said, "I've got to call this in. Any objections?"

Pero immediately agreed.

When they turned onto the road to Amuma, Bob's call connected, the antenna sticking out the partially opened window. After reporting in, Bob said, "Yes, we're all here, plus one prisoner." He listened. "No, not that prisoner. We're on the way to see if we can catch him." Bob listened, responding, "Okay." He pushed a button. "You're on speaker." He leaned forward and placed the phone as near as he could to Pero and Mbuno while still sticking part of the antenna out of the window. Pero pointed up at the sunroof, opening it enough for the antenna to point into the night sky. Bob nodded as the phone carried Lewis' voice loud and clear.

"Well, Baltazar, you're alive and you haven't gotten your friends killed. That's something."

Pero laughed. "Hey, any landing you can walk away from is a good landing, right?"

"Not funny." Lewis coughed. "I need some sleep. Look, where the hell are you going?"

"Somalia if we have to. We're chasing Qamaan, he's in a truck. We're in a stolen UNHCR Land Cruiser doing"—he looked over at the speedometer—". . . nice, Mbuno, fastest I've seen you go . . . We're doing a hundred and twenty kilometers an hour on a dirt road. Soon we'll pass the UNHCR HQ in Alinjugur, then straight on to Amuma and the border. Unless we catch the truck first."

"And if you catch the truck, how do you plan to stop a truck? Look, Baltazar, leave this to us, we'll get him eventually."

Mbuno answered for them all, "No. We chase now, take now."

Lewis offered nothing. A moment later he said, "Off speaker, ears only." He was asking for Bob, no doubt, giving his private instructions. When Bob disconnected, he said to Nancy, "I guess I'm fired already. He thinks I'm too reckless." He looked at Pero. "Thinks you're taking an unnecessary risk. Wants me to stop you. I didn't tell him that I wasn't going to do that. He's angry. Nothing I can do about that."

Mbuno, driving as fast as he dared go, drove right past the UNHCR HQ buildings, flags flying, men standing sentry. The guards watched the white UNHCR Land Cruiser disappear down the road, wondering what was going on. In these areas, no team went out in one vehicle alone. This was al-Shabaab territory and a Land Cruiser was a prize they would eagerly pursue. The HF radio sprang to life, call signs, reports of a stolen Land Cruiser, and then HQ sounding an alert for security to pursue if at all possible. Mbuno paid no attention and depressed the pedal farther. Pero looked at the speedometer again, one hundred and forty. At that speed, the gravel in the road caused the tires to dance on marbles. Mbuno, always the top safari driver, kept them straight.

Halfway to Amuma, Mbuno said, "We drop him now." He stopped the car and Bob got out, pulled the prisoner from the car, cut the ropes binding him, removed the gag, handed him a water bottle found in the car, and told him to start walking. Bob still carried his carbine. The man had the good sense not to complain or make comments. With Bob back in the vehicle,

Mbuno sped up again and the chase was on. They careened left and right through Amuma, headlights catching the town's only tree outside the painted wall proclaiming Amuma Primary School, and carried on into the dead of night on a single-track road heading straight for Somalia.

Pero wished the moon would come up, thinking, *Only six miles to go . . .* The prospect of entering Somalia frightened him. With reason. Pero and Mbuno were known to have thwarted al-Shabaab before. They would be a prize if caught by the terrorists.

In the dead of night, reaction times are everything. Toyota Land Cruisers are reliable, well-equipped vehicles for Kenya. Fast, with good headlights, solid brakes, and comfortable seats, Nancy and Bob were buckled in on the back seat, confident Mbuno could handle the drive down even a single-track road. Of course, even in the wide arid vistas there in East Kenya, in a near desert, wildebeest herds sometimes need to cross. Seeing the road as a possible obstacle like a river, a herd now approached at a swift run.

Wildebeest travel in herds of upwards of three hundred. Once they start to cross the road in a stampede, you have to wait or they will slam into your vehicle in anger, delaying your journey as you watch their horns permanently disable your suspension. Mbuno knew this and instead of waiting or trying to push his way through, he turned the Land Cruiser away from the direction they were heading, engaged low gear, and simply drove around them. Four minutes later, he regained the dirt road, if it could be called a road, and pressed on.

The al-Shabaab truck driver had not been as alert as Mbuno. When they came upon the truck a mile later, it lay on its side off the left side of the road, wildebeest dead in front and on the road, a man sitting on top with a pistol. He waved at the Land Cruiser to stop, threatening to fire. Mbuno stopped short, asking Bob,

"Please shoot this man." Bob stood through the open sunroof and, exposing the man in the headlights of the Land Cruiser, aimed his carbine, and pulled the trigger. The man fell to the ground. Engaging low gear, Mbuno quickly drove off road and around the truck, all the way around. No one else came out to challenge them. He stopped the car. Pero and Bob got out, flashlight and headlight on, and quickly scouted the truck and contents. The back was stuffed with tusks, each with labels and Arabic writing.

Walking back to the car, Pero called out to Mbuno, "Where are you?"

He answered, some distance off, along the road, "Tracks, they are walking."

Bob asked, "How far to the border?" Pero estimated another four miles at most. Bob's enthusiasm was evident. "Then let's go get them!"

Everyone piled back into the truck. Nancy asked, not really wanting to know the answer, "The truck was full of more tusks?" Pero said it was. Nancy mumbled something about savages and looked out the window, her body stiff and trembling slightly.

Mbuno focused on the chase. "We must catch them, soon." Every once in a while, Mbuno would slow down, lean out the window, and look for tracks, "Footprints. Two men, walking." And he'd press on, albeit at a much slower pace.

What Pero had not expected two miles shy of the border was a helicopter blocking the road, its landing lights and searchlight snapped on. Lots of nonsense is rumored about helicopters threatening cars. If in flight, one touch of a car and a helicopter will crash. Parked in the middle of the road, all the Land Cruiser had to do was drive around. What prevented them from doing so were two men with blue UN helmets with M16 rifles pointed at them. Pero said, "Wait here; Bob stay hidden, in case."

Pero got down from the Land Cruiser and raised his hands. "Thank god we've found you. They blew up our plane, we had to get away." He turned back to the Land Cruiser, keeping his hands in the air, calling out, "Nancy, it's okay, please come and talk with these men."

One of the two lowered his rifle while the other kept it trained on Pero. Nancy went up and introduced herself, "Nancy Breiton, American."

Pero did the same. He offered his hand, the UN soldier stepped back, saying, "Stand there. What about the driver?"

Pero said, "Oh, that's just Mbuno, my Kenya scout, we let him drive, he knows the roads better than we do."

A speaker behind the helicopter lights said, "Passports."

"Okay, okay," Pero answered. "I have mine and she has hers in the truck. I can get them."

The disembodied voice said, "No. You stay, hands up. She goes to get them." Nancy went and did as she was told, whispering to Bob, lying in the footwell of the back seat, that she was all right. She pulled Pero's plastic bag and hers out from their packs and took them to the men. One of the two soldiers took them back to the helicopter. Pero could not see past the bright lights. He couldn't tell what type of helicopter it was nor its size. All he saw were the drooping blades, lazily oscillating over the soldiers' helmets.

The voice came back. "You wait, stand still." There was a nervousness in the voice that made the soldiers straighten up and keep sharp aim. A few tense moments later, the brightest lights were extinguished and the voice said, "Baltazar, come forward." Pero did as he was told.

Once he walked, arms up, past the soldiers, Pero could see the helicopter was camouflaged for desert warfare. He didn't recognize the type. It had a narrow glass cockpit, left-side-only pilot chair, and the canopy side window was open. The pilot held out Pero's and Nancy's passports. "I was told to return these to you with a message. We're to airlift you back to Dadaab where you are to wait."

As Pero's eyes grew accustomed to the reduced glare, he saw the German flag on the pilot's uniform. "And what are we supposed to do there while our quarry gets away?" The pilot had no answer. Of course, Pero knew that, but Pero was hoping he could get the pilot to make a radio call. "Can you ask General Tews of AFRICOM if he wants Rahman Qamaan or not, please?"

The pilot, behind his visor, smiled (sarcastically?), answering, "Ja, sure, I'll call him—"

Pero cut him off. "Well, just who are you talking to? I need to ask General Tews about Rahman Qamaan who's just a mile or maybe less, just ahead of us, on foot. You guys want him or not? Before he reaches the border?"

The pilot saw that Pero was serious. He radioed that the subject was requesting a patch to General Tews at AFRICOM about some guy called Rahman Qamaan. He heard a response through his headset and said, "Ja, I know, but he asked." He listened some more and simply said, "Sorry, orders. You will be returned to Dadaab immediate."

Pero sloped his shoulders and seemed resigned. "Well, how many can you put into your small helicopter?"

"We can take the three of you."

This time, it was Pero's turn to smile. "Well, the joke's on you. We're four." Pero turned and called, "Hey, Bob, come on out but leave the weapons there, okay?" Bob's head popped up, he raised his arms. The two soldiers pointed their rifles at him as he slowly went to where Pero was talking to the pilot. Bob handed over his ID. The pilot inspected it and radioed it in.

Waiting for a reply, Pero said to Bob, "Seems we're going back. I feel really bad about the Land Cruiser though. Leaving it here, it'll be in al-Shabaab's hands within a few hours. Still, we tried, right?" Bob said nothing. Pero pretended to have a thought and walked over to the soldiers who were standing at ease, wondering what was next. "Hey, you two wouldn't mind driving the Land Cruiser back to Dadaab for us, would you? That way, the copter can take us four and our gear." Pero spun to face the pilot. "That'll work, won't it?"

The pilot radioed the question in, received a reply, and responded, "Roger that." He looked at Pero. "Okay, I'm to take you four and the UN soldiers will drive the Land Cruiser back. No one here travels alone. They'll rendezvous with the two UNHCR vehicles coming down the road to make a convoy." He paused, looking at Pero, raising his visor. "Those are my orders and, Herr Baltazar, they are also your orders. Will you comply?"

"Come with you? Of course, happy to." He told Bob to go and get his supplies, but be sure to leave the carbine and Bob's sidearm in the Land Cruiser so they would have no weapons on the helicopter. While he said that, he reminded Bob that the Beretta was in Pero's pack, "Be sure and leave that with them, too, okay? Just bring me the satchel with the first aid kit, the camera chips, and my satellite phone. Oh, and Nancy's camera equipment as well. She won't want to leave any of that behind." Pero called over to Mbuno, "Hey, Mbuno, leave the vehicle and come over here. We're going back to Dadaab." Mbuno got out and slowly ambled over to Pero, standing slightly behind him, acting the servant.

Pero, feeling more in control, asked the pilot his name, learned it was Stefan, and introduced everyone, leaving Mbuno for last. The pilot told them to get aboard and strap in. There were two bench seats, one facing aft. Mbuno and Nancy took the rear seats, facing forward. The space for the copilot's seat was used for storage, so they put their backpacks and gear there. Bob got on, sitting next to Pero, and handed him the satchel Pero had asked for. Pero motioned for everybody to buckle in and then he slid the door shut. When they were ready, Pero turned and said to the pilot over his right shoulder, "All set, Stefan!" The turbine whined into operation, and the blades started rotating, eventually getting faster until the rhythm settled into a reassuring sensation of power. Nancy and Mbuno watched the Land Cruiser lights come back on and then it backed away and began to make a U-turn, going back to Dadaab.

Pero estimated that they had maybe ten minutes left.

Pero had always liked helicopters. Particularly, he liked that they could be made to land anywhere. As they lifted off, Mbuno and Bob saw that Pero reached into his satchel for Akale's ancient Webley pistol that had only two bullets left.

Nancy was shocked to see Pero pull the pistol, turn around, and tap the muzzle on the pilot's head. The pilot turned and stared into the barrel. "Scheisse . . ." was all he said.

Pero gave the command as loud as he could. "Turn around, make speed, head for the border. Do not cross. Hover, turn your searchlights on, and travel back along the road toward Dadaab." The pilot started to ask why, but Pero cut him off. "The less you know, the better. Look, we are going back to Dadaab, I promise; we've just lost something on the road and we've come a long way to pick it up. Okay with you?" Pero waited but the pilot didn't answer. Pero tapped the helmet again. "Don't be a hero, it's only two miles back and two miles more after that. Ten minutes tops. And hurry."

The pilot gave in. The copter spun around, Pero leaned farther over the pilot's shoulder and checked the compass heading. "We're heading due east, that's good. Watch for the border . . ."

Like most of East Africa, there is nothing marking a border. There are no fences, no border huts on tiny dirt tracks that often predate even the Roman or Egyptian eras. Pero knew the pilot would be familiar with the exact coordinates of the border if only to make sure he never crossed it. As the GPS on the dashboard read -0.34 and 40.99, Pero knew they had arrived. The Jeppesen map had warned so in bold letters, "War Zone."

The pilot hovered. Doing as he was told, he rotated, pointed back at the dirt road, and turned on all the lights. Pero yelled, "In the next two miles, Mbuno will see the man we want and we'll land, capture him, and then we'll all go home to Dadaab. That agreed?" The pilot nodded but mumbled something Pero couldn't catch. Pero yelled again, "And keep your finger off the transmit button, got it?" Again the slight nod from the pilot.

Mbuno and Bob slid the side door open and Mbuno, holding the seat belt strap in his left hand, leaned out and watched below.

Slowly then, they started forward, maybe doing twenty miles an hour.

Spotting a man, or even two men, walking in the desert is nearly impossible. Qamaan didn't need to walk the road, he could walk anywhere. As long as he crossed into Somalia, he would be safe. Time was critical. Pero needed to spot their prey before they deviated from the road too far to be spotted. And of course, the chances of seeing someone from a noisy machine with all those lights on was less than ideal. All the men had to do was drop, cover themselves with sand, and wait for the helicopter to pass overhead.

On his own, Pero knew he would never spot them. For Bob, sitting across from Mbuno, it seemed a fruitless venture. Even for the scout, seeing hiding figures at night would be next to impossible.

But Mbuno was not looking for the men. He was looking for tracks. And he found them. He yelled, "Stop!" And Pero told the pilot to hover. Mbuno pointed off to the south, "There, two tracks, fresh. Follow, tafadhali." Pero told the pilot where to fly, slowly. Under a minute later, Mbuno again said, "Stop!" The copter hovered. "Now down, tafadhali." When they were four feet off the soft sand, Mbuno jumped. Pero told the pilot not to move but hover.

Sand was kicking up and the pilot said, "I don't want to suck that sand in, I'll hover at ten meters." And the helicopter rose. As it did so, the lights caught three figures engaged in a fight. One man dropped and then another. Mbuno turned and waved.

Pero said, "There's our passenger pickup." The pilot nodded. He advanced the helicopter forward until it was almost over Mbuno. The scout shielded his eyes from the sand. The pilot settled the craft, keeping the blades slowly rotating and the turbine engaged. Bob jumped down and helped Mbuno strip one man, checking for papers. Then they went through all the other man's papers. Bob held what looked like a passport up to the helicopter's searchlight beam to be able to read. He looked into the lights and gave a thumbs-up, then placed both hands together in mock prayer and put them next to his ear, the international gesture for sleeping.

Mbuno and Bob sat the man upright, picked up what looked like a child's schoolbag, and dragged it all to the copter. Pero and Nancy helped pull the body into the space between the bench seats, both then putting their feet on him. Mbuno got back in, Pero asked, "You hurt?"

Mbuno grinned. "He is too slow."

"And the other guy?"

Bob answered, "Didn't make it, one small cut and he's dead." Pero knew that meant Mbuno was using his tribal powder on his knife that, once in the bloodstream, kills instantly. Mbuno handed Pero the passport. Pero opened it, saw Qamaan's name and photo, looked down at the sleeping visage for a match, and nodded. He slid the door shut.

The copter was revved up. Pero asked the pilot to go home, politely. He still had to shout to be heard. He reached over the pilot's shoulder after they lifted off and handed him the Webley, yelling, "Only two bullets left, not sure they would fire anyway."

Bob's headlight was on. He was reading papers. He exclaimed loudly, "Pero, you better have a look at this," and handed Pero a small sheaf of papers. Taking out his penlight from the first aid kit, Pero scanned the papers. It was a list of names and amounts. Some of the names were world-famous. Pero leaned back, realizing that this would blow up internationally in a hurry. Some of the people he read on the list were at a G6 meeting with presidents and world leaders. And yet, there, on the list, were the fifty or more names with amounts. Pero wondered, *Owed or paid?*

Realizing the papers were dynamite, and dangerous for the four of them, Pero looked at Nancy, Mbuno, and Bob, saying, loudly, "We never saw these. No papers, nothing. They can have him, but not these papers. We need to decide what to do much later. Together. Agreed?"

Nancy said she didn't understand, so Pero handed her the papers and his flashlight. She and Mbuno looked at the list. Even in the dim light of the helicopter cabin, Pero thought Nancy's tanned skin turned white. Mbuno's face showed no expression except for the eyes. They narrowed and almost closed, such was the hatred of what he read.

Bob refused to take the papers back, so Pero rolled them up and pushed them into his backpack inside the Katadyn water filter bottle. He had to hide them in plain sight for he was now convinced they would be searched. He leaned forward and said to Nancy, "Start taping, him, me, you, Bob, and Mbuno. Even Stefan the pilot when we land. Make it a celebration. I'll cover our actions, saying I was doing what General Tews commanded me to do. And he did, remember? He insisted they wanted this man. We did what he asked. Period. No more, no less." All three nodded. "Right. Now, Mbuno, you captured Qamaan, so you have to hand over what you found. Bob, do you have the passport, and is there anything else?" Bob showed various papers, receipts, fuel charges, plane stubs, all stuffed into the kid's schoolbag. "Okay, say the truth. We found this bag with him. The passport he had on him. Hand it all over. I am damn sure by the time we land, there will be plenty of military to welcome us back. They'll search everything. They wanted him so badly, not only because he was a terrorist, but because he was the moneyman. We *must*," he stressed, "really we *must* know nothing."

Mbuno shook his head. "We know he killed ndovu. It is enough." Pero and Nancy nodded.

Bob folded his arms and leaned back. "As I said, my guess is I'm already fired. I'll hang around and see where this goes but for damn sure I don't want anyone to get away with this." Mbuno patted Bob's knee. Nancy leaned forward and put her hand on Bob's cheek.

The helicopter droned on. Pero dozed a little, more aware of the fatigue of the past few days. His ribs were still hurting if he slouched, so he kept sitting bolt upright. When the pitch of the blades changed, he woke momentarily wondering where he was. He looked at his companions and called out, "We ready?" All three gave him a thumbs-up. "Okay then, we're happy, we caught the bastard!"

Nancy responded, "Camera, lights, action!" She held up the little video recorder.

The colonel waiting for the helicopter's blades to slow was in no mood for congratulations in the dead of night. Nancy got off first along with Mbuno, then Pero, and finally Bob. The four of them stood blocking the helicopter doorway. Bob was ordered to stand behind the colonel, leaving the three facing an irate commander and his troops, all heavily armed. The pilot shut down all the systems, deplaned, and was told to rejoin his forces. Pero looked and saw a small group of German uniforms waiting somewhat anxiously off to one side.

Pero raised his hand and extended it. "Pero Baltazar, nice to meet you."

The colonel almost spat out his reply, "You won't be . . ." He turned and started to walk away.

Casually, Pero asked, "What? You don't want our present?" The colonel turned to face Pero. Nancy's hand moved to capture the scene as surreptitiously as she could. Pero, Nancy, and Mbuno stepped aside, allowing the body in the plane to become visible. Mbuno reached into his trouser pocket and took out Qamaan's passport, tendering it to the colonel.

The colonel took a step forward and took the passport, opened it, and read the name. Cool as could be, he looked into the copter and matched the image and the man. He stepped back. Pero wondered what would be coming next. It wasn't what he expected. The colonel said, "Arrest them all." He turned and pointed at Bob, "Including him!" Then he indicated Qamaan. "And him, the sleeping one." Men immediately grabbed their arms and stood waiting for the next command. Qamaan was dropped onto a stretcher. "Take these four to the hangar, they have explaining to do. Take that man to the hospital in my chopper. Search their belongings."

Once in the hangar, Pero looked and saw that there was no sign of tusks or any blood on the floor. The place had been sanitized. The second Skyvan was still there. Four chairs had been placed in a row and the four of them were told to sit, under armed guard.

The colonel came in and ordered four men to patrol outside. "I want total privacy, understood?" The men ran to obey. Once the door closed, the colonel took a deep breath and advanced to Pero. "Sorry about that. I'm Colonel Morgan. We need to cover your operation. If we're going to get Qamaan to reveal all, people have to think you're being blamed. Sorry but it's necessary. You're antipoaching activities only caught a poacher, that's the story."

Mbuno said, "Yes, it is true."

The colonel looked at Mbuno and said, "Stick to that. Don't ever deviate or you'll become a target." He looked at all of them. "And that goes for all of you. I was told, let's just say, ordered, to make sure you got that message. For your own safety, no one knows your names, no one knows who the antipoachers were, and no one knows Qamaan is alive except you four outside of my forces. Agreed?"

All four agreed immediately. Pero didn't want to give the impression they'd rehearsed their reactions, so he turned to his friends and said, "Look, guys, I've been here before. When Lewis says he'll keep you out of it, he can and does. Let's let them do their job. We've done ours."

The colonel responded, "Nice speech. I hope you mean it. As for Director Lewis, he has a score to settle with you that you won't enjoy. I'll leave that for him, but let me give you a bit of advice. You kicked a hornets' nest and people you could rely on before are swarming mad."

Mbuno asked, "Where are the tusks?"

The colonel asked, "What tusks? There never were any tusks here in a refugee settlement area. Understood?" Pero looked at Mbuno and shook his head secretly. Mbuno's tension seemed to ebb. He said nothing. The colonel turned to his lieutenant. "George, these folks need food, water, and sleep. See that they get it, and tomorrow"—he turned to the four—"that there Skyvan will be all yours to keep. We'll loan you a real pilot." He frowned at Pero. "One way only. Where's it to?"

Nancy broke. She stood, her face flushed, the camera in her right hand panning the room. "That will about do for this adventure. My maybe fiancé comes to the rescue, we chase a terrorist and stop poachers. Get threatened by our military and then get given a tub of a crappy plane—only because they want it gone, I assume. Well, I am hungry, dirty, have been bitten by thousands of mosquitoes and want to sleep for a week. Then I want to edit my elephant film, that's all." She looked at Bob. "You going to propose properly anytime soon?" Bob stood and hugged her. She went on, "Yes, well, that's nice but that's not enough, yet." She addressed the colonel, her voice rigid with sarcasm, "Can we please get moving here?"

The colonel responded by turning on his heel and ordering the lieutenant to "Deal with them." He slammed the door behind him as he exited the hangar.

The lieutenant smiled broadly at Nancy and said, "Yes, ma'am. Right away, ma'am."

Somehow, all four had a good night's sleep. Short but solid. The cots were canvas, their military sleeping bags kept out the cool night air, water was provided for washing, and, much to Pero's surprise, the hangar had a real bathroom complete with shower. Where they got the water from in this desert area, he had no idea. The food was a disappointment, MRE rations in self-heat cans. At least they were better than the peanut butter ones they had used along the Omo River.

Before dinner, Pero asked if he could call his wife to assure her he was safe. The lieutenant told him that he couldn't but that Mrs. Baltazar had been informed Baltazar was returning the next day. Questions Pero had for the lieutenant about Akale, the Suri, and the prisoners they left behind and, especially, the whereabouts of Sergeant Gonzales went unanswered. Taking Pero aside away from the other three guests, as he called them, the lieutenant advised, "Forget all that, get away from here and don't stir things up. At least for now. When they're ready, they'll fill you in. Maybe." Pero knew that "they" meant people like Lewis and nodded in agreement. He had known that would be their official position, but it would have been imprudent not to ask as a normal person would.

A suspicion that he wasn't acting normal could lead the four of them into hotter water. Pero, Bob, Nancy, and Mbuno had no intention of forgetting anyone. At the earliest opportunity, Pero knew they all planned on checking everyone and everything.

CHAPTER 11

DADAAB AIRSTRIP

After breakfast, their gear was given back to them and, under the lieutenant's watchful eye, Pero verified that the film microchips were all still in their waterproof case. He told Nancy the memory cards, the chips, were safe and sound. Nancy was relieved.

The Skyvan was rolled out onto the apron shortly after breakfast and some soldiers helped prepare the interior. From somewhere, four seats had been found and were bolted to the floor runners built into the airframe.

Pero and Bob walked into the sunshine. The airstrip was busy. There were three helicopters, all German, a C-130 Hercules of US command, likely AFRICOM, and three smaller planes, all single prop, two of which had UNHCR logos on the tail. There was no sign of or any evidence that the previous night ever happened. No burn patch, no debris, nothing. Pero pointed to the tower hut and there were two Land Cruisers parked, exactly as Pero had found them the night before. Bob's comment made Pero laugh. "Were we even here?"

Two pilots showed up later that morning. Neither was wearing any military insignia but their papers seemed to satisfy the lieutenant. They said they were hired by UNHCR to prep and fly the Skyvan. Watching their professional approach in checking the Skyvan properly, Pero guessed that they were Arab originally, judging from their clipped dialect as they talked to each other. Pero went over to discuss the handling, warning them it had a habit of pitching up quickly as well as stalling when you got down to sixty knots. Both men made no comment on Pero's flight or his advice. They asked no questions and didn't care about his warnings. Finally, as Pero peppered them with questions, one said, "We will fly safely, sir," and made no further comment. Pero turned and left them alone, smiling. He had learned what he needed to know.

When the military covers its tracks, or in this case Pero's tracks, it is consistent that everyone in contact with Pero have nothing to say, nothing to respond to. In short, Pero didn't exist in that place, at that time. Never was there, didn't belong there, was leaving—and when he left, there would be the same amount of evidence that Pero was ever in Dadaab as there was of the pile of tusks in the hangar.

Not there. Weren't there. All gone.

In a sense, this was fine with Pero. Of course, the urge to see if the Katadyn filter had been discovered was like an itch he couldn't scratch—along with a dozen mosquito bumps he could—and did—scratch. He desperately wanted to know the papers were still rolled up in there, but he was acutely aware that everything the four of them did for that day, at least, was being carefully watched. Those papers were critical for what would come next and he knew, if not him, then Bob and Nancy, and especially Mbuno, would be determined to have a next phase, a resolution, and a reckoning.

Pero sipped a cup of hot chai, tea brewed with milk and sugar, looking out over the airport where military personnel were servicing planes, running engines, and thought, *This ain't over, not by a long chalk.* The chai was almost as satisfying as were his scheming thoughts. *Mbuno is right, someone has to stop this slaughter.*

As the Skyvan was rolled farther out onto a taxiway and the fuel truck came to replenish tanks, Pero, Bob, and Nancy watched the airport activity. The military presence was impressive, if not a sure demonstration of a cover-up. The Hercules C-130 had high-sided, covered pallets loaded and then took off. Not twenty minutes later another C-130 touched down, the reverse pitch of the turboprops stopping the plane in under a half mile. The aft ramp lowered and two Humvees rolled out along with another twenty or so troops. Without taking his eyes off the spectacle and military buildup, Pero asked Bob, "They fire you, or are they just avoiding you?"

"No one is saying. They've taken all my gear." He meant military gear. "I've been told to expect a call at ten hundred Zulu." Bob indicated the satellite phone, looked at his watch, and showed it to Pero. It was eleven o'clock local time. "Two hours to go."

Pero, his teacup at his lips said almost silently, "Want to work for me?"

Bob's head didn't move from the military scene in front of him, "Thought you'd never ask." And nodded. Next to him, joined at the hip, Nancy squeezed his arm to show she agreed.

Mbuno walked over, eating, unimpressed with the bread and jam. His face had a scowl and he was looking at the slice of bread, one bite missing, and shaking his head. "If they feed this to the people in the camp, they will want to go far away." Pero responded that maybe that was the idea.

Off to the east of their position, a convoy of six UNHCR Land Cruisers and one larger vehicle with a mounted turret gun advanced toward the airport entrance. All had their headlights on. Three had flashing blue and red lights on the roof. A siren wailed. At the airport entrance, the convoy was stopped by military personnel. Pero watched as the US soldier acting as gate guard saluted and then pointed to the hangar where the team stood. Pero said, "Company coming. Let me speak to them. Mbuno, disappear, please." Mbuno nodded and went back to the food table. He understood that trouble could be brewing and that Pero was better able to deal with whatever UN politics might arise.

Mbuno wasn't confident, not for a moment, that they were out of danger. There was too much corruption around poaching and the revenue it brought. If the tusks had not been taken away, he might have confidence that someone wanted to stop the slaughter by keeping the evidence where it was, tying people and events together for a thorough investigation. Taking the tons of hangar tusks away only told him that the mzungus were more interested in appearing clean than actually cleaning anything.

Pero started a conversation about fishing in Lake Rudolf with Nancy. She caught on and asked Pero to describe how the natives caught fish. Although she had seen native fishing before, Pero was grateful she was playing along. Bob, puzzled, looked down at Nancy. She gave him a cold stare. It was enough to warn him.

Four men, all armed and in UN uniforms, walked into the hangar through the side door. They were followed by two civilians who waited at the doorway. The uniformed men inspected the hangar, saw Pero, Nancy, and Bob standing in the open hangar doors facing the runway, chatting. One pointed and gave an all-clear. The man and woman in street clothes walked over to the trio and introduced themselves. The man was first, "I am Commissioner Sing of the UNHCR, in control of the refugee camps at Dadaab and this is Undersecretary Chang, my superior." The way he said superior, bowing his head as he did so, reminded Pero of other Chinese diplomats he had met, always deferring to superior authority. Pero knew that undersecretary at the UN meant second-in-command, the secretary being the head of a division. The secretary of the UNHCR was also an undersecretary of the UN as a whole. Pero knew the UN system well. The woman was second-in-command of one of twelve undersecretaries-generals of the entire UN, worldwide.

Pero extended his hand to the undersecretary of the UNHCR and said, "It is an honor, Madam Undersecretary."

She responded, "Please call me Mrs. Chang." Pero said he'd be honored, again. Mrs. Chang got to the point quickly, way too quickly for Asian etiquette. But, Pero reminded himself, *She doesn't know I am familiar with Asian etiquette; to her I'm just an American.* Her voice carried the quiet authority of someone used to saying things once and being obeyed. "The poachers, shufti as we believe they are called here, have been stopped. We are pleased. Their presence here is terminated, further activities prevented. AFRICOM officials have assured us of their cooperation in this matter. The matter is closed."

All the time she was speaking, Pero was thinking as fast as he could. He needed to have the right response. He sensed that Mrs. Chang's presence went way beyond a cover-up. *She knows the soldiers have cleaned everything up. So why is she here? If we simply acquiesce, then she'll know we're lying and intend to pursue this further. Why is she here?* Pero needed more time, so he answered with a partial truth, "We had to stop them, they were slaughtering elephants and we were making a documentary about migrating elephants when we accidentally stumbled onto them. As for the rest? Well, it just seemed wrong to let them get away."

Her eyes narrowed. "Your determination to come all the way here and then chase the leader is, of course, unusual but commendable. We would say way outside of normal expectation." She was sizing up Pero.

Pero noticed that she never referred to herself, except with the royal "we."

To avoid looking too interested in a follow-up response from Pero, she turned to Nancy. "And what a terrible ordeal for you, my dear. We understand you were forced to come along with these two gentlemen. We are so pleased you are safe and remain so."

The whip at the end of the sentence was clear, Nancy's safety needed to *remain so.*

Mrs. Chang continued, next looking at Bob. "We understand you were brought in to help safeguard these people. It is a pity you became involved, but we are happy that task is over." She paused, looked from one face to another. "We are pleased you are safe and we are pleased to arrange your leaving and hope you return to your filmmaking and leave this matter to us."

Pero understood perfectly. "Yes, Madam Undersecretary." Pero did not address her as Mrs. Chang, determined to formalize the conversation and appear subservient. "That's all we want, to return to our documentary and get away from all this." Pero waved an arm to indicate all the military activity.

Mrs. Chang formed a frozen grin, held a gaze with Pero for a few seconds too long, then nodded, and turned to leave. Commissioner Sing added, "See that you do. Our crew will take you back to Lake Turkana." He swiveled and followed her back to the UN soldiers who escorted her back to her Land Cruiser. Pero, Nancy, and Bob watched as their blue and red lights lit up, the siren started, and the cars made a sweeping circle to point back out the gate of the airport. They were gone in a cloud of dust and sand.

Pero was deeply troubled. *She knows we're going to Lake Rudolf.*

Mbuno walked over and simply said, "She is a mamba. Most dangerous." Pero, long since used to Mbuno's habit of equating humans to animals to better predict their behavior, felt a shiver up his spine. Black mambas are Africa's most deadly snakes, always unpredictable and usually lethal. Mamba have been known to kill large animals to wait to feed on the scavengers that appear on the corpse.

Pero looked at the two pilots prepping the plane. The words *unpredictable* and *Lake Turkana* inundated his thoughts. Saying, "Everyone, stay here, get ready to leave; now, Bob, give me the phone," Pero went in urgent search of the lieutenant.

Finding him in the tower hut, Pero asked if they could speak outside. Aware that it was unlikely that the lieutenant would know what could possibly be underlying Pero's concern, Pero had to tread carefully. "Hey, Lieutenant, is it possible we could change our plans?" The lieutenant asked why and to what. "Well, I know this may sound weird, but Nancy is terrified after I crashed the Skyvan yesterday and as we're going to Nairobi, anyway, I was wondering if you have people going there, or maybe you can loan us a car? I promise we'll turn it in . . ."

"No can do. Orders. You are taking the Skyvan to Wilson Airport, we arranged local pilots from the UNHCR." Pero felt the chill up his spine again. *The lieutenant thinks we're going to Wilson Airport, but Mrs. Chang clearly said Lake Turkana.* The lieutenant continued, apologizing, "Sorry, I can't change the orders."

Pero was getting desperate. "Well, if I make a call"—he pulled out the satellite phone—"and you get a new order, would that be okay?" The lieutenant nodded, his face concerned now that something else was wrong. Pero connected, dialing 555 and asking for Lewis. Not on speaker, Pero started to plead his case. "Hi, Charles . . ." Lewis was so angry he would not respond except to acknowledge he was listening. Pero continued, "It's been a hell of an ordeal and Nancy really doesn't want to fly in that god-awful Skyvan again."

Lewis confirmed he knew Pero had crashed the last one, adding, "Pity it didn't kill you. Only you."

Pero laughed. "I know you don't mean that. Anyway, would it be okay if you could ask General Tews to tell this nice lieutenant here to either drive us to Nairobi or loan us a car so we can?"

Lewis responded, "What are you playing at? Your wife is in Loiyangalani, that's where you are going."

"Of course, of course, Nairobi it is. Have to be, we will do as you say. Nairobi or nothing. Nice and safe, no danger, Interconti for us all. Is that okay?" Pero used the shorthand for the Intercontinental Hotel in Nairobi. Lewis would have to know something was wrong if Pero wasn't going to join his pregnant wife at the Oasis Lodge near the lake.

Lewis' voice got serious. "Danger threat? Give me a number one to ten."

"Oh, it's already ten here or past that. I want to make sure Susanna is there at the Interconti when we arrive. We could drive to Nairobi by nightfall."

"Stand by."

Pero looked at the lieutenant and said, innocently, "He told me to stand by." And shrugged his shoulders. The lieutenant seemed patient enough, awaiting the outcome.

Lewis came back on. "Patching." Pero heard a series of clicks. "General, danger imminent, need evac four to Nairobi. Orders for your team in . . . where are you, Pero?"

"Dadaab airstrip."

"Right. General, can you give them a vehicle or safely get them in a military transport to anywhere but not there asap?"

General Tews' Texas twang came through clear and loud, "Baltazar. In trouble again, son? Well, tell me who you have there to speak to."

Not disconnecting, Pero asked, "Lieutenant, can you tell him your name? I have General Tews, AFRICOM, here asking." And he handed the phone to the lieutenant.

All Pero heard was the lieutenant saying a yes sir and no sir, then adding, "Lieutenant George Thomas, sir; Colonel Morgan is away presently, and, yes, we have a C-130 ready to go." A few more yes sirs and he handed the phone back to Pero, saying, "Oh, great."

Pero listened as General Tews was finishing explaining to Lewis, ". . . are now that lieutenant's sole responsibility. I told him to get them out of there now, no delay. Priority one. That do?" Lewis thanked him, said "out," and the line went dead—for Pero as well.

Pero put the phone back in his pocket and the lieutenant looked into Pero's eyes. "Something's not right here, but you have two minutes to get on board that." He pointed at the C-130. "Sit down, shut up, and we'll get you out of here. Next stop, Mombasa. From there we'll arrange transport—"

Pero stopped him. "Mombasa will do; we'll take it from there." He took the lieutenant by the arm, "And you might, once we sprint for the plane, watch those two"—he nodded at the Skyvan—"as I suspect their job was to lose us somewhere. Permanently."

The lieutenant's eyes grew larger. He looked over at the Skyvan, being loaded with what appeared to be two duffel bags and the lieutenant wondered out loud, "Saw them take their gear on board earlier, and everything was inspected; wonder what's in those bags?" Well trained, expert at his job, George turned to Pero and issued a command, "Grab your gear, get on the plane now." Saying that, the lieutenant sprinted to the C-130 and climbed the ramp.

Before Pero even got back to the hangar, the C-130 engines were starting up.

Mbuno saw Pero's haste, as Pero told everyone to get onto the C-130 right away. Nancy started to ask why but Bob knew something was wrong as the C-130 crew member at the foot of the rear ramp was waving at them to hurry. Bob grabbed her arm, Pero's backpack, and went into a headlong rush to get aboard. All four ran across the apron and as Pero's foot hit the ramp, he felt the winch starting to lift. Outside the plane, watching the ramp rise, the lieutenant was taking no chances. A final salute and the hatch closed as the C-130 started to move.

Safely up the slowly closing ramp, Pero turned to a window to watch the Skyvan. The two pilots were running to the beat-up car they had arrived in, abandoning the Skyvan and their intent.

Pero knew then that Mrs. Chang would be hunting the four of them in both Mombasa and Nairobi. Nowhere would be safe.

The two-hour flight to Mombasa was proceeding in a noisy if uneventful way. The crewmen and one crewwoman could not have been more helpful. It was clear to the crew that the four passengers were VIPs, sufficiently important to warrant departing under an emergency order, reaffirmed by AFRICOM once airborne, telling them where to park once they got to Mombasa's Moi International Airport where the US and several other countries maintained secure facilities. The C-130 was to park directly in a hangar, wait until the doors were closed, and then allow the passengers to disembark.

Halfway to Mombasa, a crew member came to get Pero. The noise inside the C-130 was so intense that Pero and his companions had not been able to converse, except for Pero to yell, "I'll explain when we land."

The crewwoman pulled Pero's sleeve and yelled into his ear, "Flight deck, sir." Pero followed.

Behind a bulkhead, thickly padded on the outside with insulation, the cockpit was relatively silent except for the drone of the four turboprops. The copilot was flying, the pilot swiveled in his seat and addressed Pero. "They want to talk to you in"—he looked at his watch—"three minutes. I'll patch it through when they do." He pointed at a Clark headset on the bulkhead next to Pero, then to the jump seat. Pero lifted the headset and put it on. He lowered the jump seat, sat, and nodded to the pilot who asked, "You hear me okay?" Pero said he did. "We're about forty minutes out from Mombasa, I'll patch you in when they call."

Pero sat there looking at the beauty of the land they were flying over. The route the pilot had taken was from Dadaab directly to the coast and then followed the coastline to Mombasa. Pero knew they had already passed Lamu, one of the most beautiful places in Kenya founded by Arab traders millennia ago. Then, soon, they'd come up on Malindi, a famed resort with crystal blue waters, and wonderful coral formations teeming with tropical fish. Minutes after, they would descend slowly into Mombasa, an ancient seaport, possibly created by the Egyptians thousands of years before. Pero looked at the altimeter. It read only eight thousand feet. The pilot saw Pero reading the dial and commented, "Nice day for flying, thought we'd take the scenic route."

Pero responded, "It's always so beautiful." The pilot nodded.

Pero heard the call sign and then the pilot confirmed reception and passed the call to Pero saying, "Your ears only, we're out." He flicked switches in the center console and Pero heard Lewis' voice clearly.

Lewis was still angry. "Okay, Baltazar, damn you, what's this all about?"

"I have one question for you. How did Mrs. Chang, undersecretary-general of the UNHCR, know we were going to Lake Rudolf?"

"Who's Mrs. Chang again?"

"Look it up, Charles. Listen, two things. Maybe three . . . One, this very powerful woman and her sidekick showed up, they're in charge of the Dadaab complexes for the UNHCR, and they told me we were going to Lake Turkana, not the older name, Lake Rudolf, that I always use. That tells me someone was looking it up, so she must have been told we were going to the Oasis Lodge. How would she know that, Charles? How?" Pero was angry, wondering if Lewis' office had a leak. "Two, she made very subtle threats for Nancy's safety and berated me for going, as she put it, outside of normal expectation. Charles, why would she have any expectation unless she was being informed by you or someone in your damn office what we were doing? Only you, me, and Gonzales knew where we were going. Or so I thought. Who did you tell?" Pero was building a head of steam. "And last, Charles, either she, or her sidekick, one Commissioner Sing, were calmly arranging to kill all four of us. This flight prevented that, I am damn sure of it." Pero waited for a response. After a few moments, he asked, "You there, Charles?"

"Stand by," not Lewis' voice commanded.

Lewis came back on, his voice business-like and monotone. Pero knew that was a bad sign, something either went horribly wrong or was about to. "That lieutenant you were talking to? Seems he inspected the Skyvan after you left. Found parachutes and a delayed fuse bomb. He just escaped with his life. The two pilots must have set it before they left. Spoke to a colonel in charge there. They found the pilots' bodies in a burned-out car in a ditch alongside the road. IDs as Somali from Camp Ifo. They're evacing the lieutenant to Nairobi hospital now, prognosis good, some burns, nothing life-threatening. Wait, more coming in." There was a pause. Pero assumed, actually hoped he was right to assume, that the plane communication was military, no doubt a secure line, UHF, probably a satellite bounce. The signal was crystal clear. Pero also hoped it was scrambled.

Lewis clicked back on. "Okay, Commissioner Sing was found dead in a tent behind the latrines in one of the camps. Undersecretary Chang is nowhere to be found. They are conducting a search."

Pero added, "Somalia is only twenty miles away. She's probably there. Follow the money, Charles."

"We would if there was any trace. Rahman Qamaan died suddenly this morning."

"Don't tell me; he was under UNHCR guard, right?"

"Stop guessing, Baltazar. I'll tell you what you need to know." Pero heard his sigh even on the UHF radio bounce through a satellite twenty-five thousand miles up. The sigh was a sure sign Lewis was giving in. "Okay, okay. He remained unconscious until this morning—from whatever you gave him, I understand. Pakistani doctors, part of UNHRC, were tending to him when he became conscious—and died in their small hospital. They say he was poisoned. There's a UNHCR request sent to Kenyan authorities for the arrest of all four of you."

Pero thought, *Perfect.*

Lewis continued, "We quashed that the moment the plane blew up. We're not that stupid."

Pero wanted to scream, Yes you are! You leaked to someone! Instead, he kept quiet. His mind was spinning. Before he felt they were under imminent threat from Mrs. Chang or, more likely, Commissioner Sing. Now he knew it was worse than that. Mrs. Chang was cleaning her tracks. And those tracks would likely include the four of them. Mrs. Chang would leave no stone unturned to find them, eliminate them, and—Pero thought about the documents they should still have hidden in the Katadyn filter—make sure Pero and his team did not have any papers, anything financial from the al-Shabaab accountant and strong-arm poaching head, Qamaan. Pero asked, "This is important, Charles. Important, do you copy?" He said he did. "Charles, you need to find out if anyone, and I mean anyone, talked to Qamaan before he supposedly died. Our lives hang in the balance."

"We will do that. Why do you need to know?" Pero was silent. Lewis tried again, "Baltazar, respond, why do you need to know?"

Pero responded calmly with, "When I see you face-to-face, I'll tell you. Not until then." Pero thought quickly, What would Mbuno do, where would be safe?

Lewis interjected, "Flight Loyangalani departing with Susanna aboard in a few minutes, seems there was a tourist charter plane there making deliveries. She will rendezvous at Intercontinental Hotel."

"Charles, thank you for that." A thought clicked in Pero's memory. "Now, seriously, remember years ago I told you about a mountain rhino safari Mbuno did for an American client, name of Grimaldi? Call Tone or Grimaldi and ask him where that was. We'll meet you—and only you—there."

"What's this about, Pero?"

"A list. The whole thing is about a list. I cannot tell you more now. Get moving. It's that important. Over and out." Pero took off the headset, thanked the pilot, and made his way back into the plane.

In the main cargo space, there were too many crewmen around and, besides, he'd have to shout to explain. He gave a thumbs-up to Nancy and Bob. Mbuno wasn't fooled, his eyes focused on Pero's backpack. Both men knew their future prospects lay in that Katadyn filter if the papers were still there. *No, they would be*, Pero thought. *If they'd found them, they wouldn't be bothering with us.* Pero looked at Mbuno and made a little wave as if to say it was okay. Mbuno would have to take it on trust.

The C-130 made a straight-in approach at Mombasa and then a long taxi to the US military secure section of the airport. On the back of an old Jeep, the "Follow Me" sign was illuminated and guided the plane, outboard engines cut, straight into a vast hangar. Once in, the inboard engines were cut and the crew member told the four, "Please wait, I'll lower the ramp when I get an okay." She was listening to orders on her headset. A moment later, "Okay, we're set to go." The ramp started to descend, so Pero and the team gathered their possessions and walked down the lowering ramp into the empty hangar. Pero asked a soldier where the restrooms were and got directions. Pero suggested to his three companions that they make use of them before the next leg of their journey. Puzzled, the three agreed and all four walked to the toilets. Nancy went into the women's and the three went into the men's.

Bob started, "Okay, Pero, what the hell gives?"

Pero was quick, "Bob, the Skyvan was blown up. We were supposed to die. Go tell Nancy, help her—it'll be another shock—and then have her come in here so we can talk." Bob turned and left.

Mbuno nodded his head and said one word, "Mamba."

Pero nodded and went into a toilet cubicle and locked the door. Working quickly he checked the filter contents and got out his Leica camera.

Minutes later, Pero and Mbuno waited for Bob and Nancy. As Nancy came in she asked, "Really? They wanted to blow us up? In the air? What about the two pilots?"

"Seems they had parachutes. Anyway, they're dead, found at the side of the road." Pero could see the impact of his words. Bob protectively hugged Nancy while Nancy just looked angry. Pero continued, "The little guy, Commissioner Sing? Dead. Undersecretary Chang is missing. My guess? Somalia already." He let them digest that, adding, "Qamaan died this morning. Apparently woke up and then died. My guess is that Chang came to see us to determine if we had any paperwork. Qamaan may have told her what he was carrying. The mistake I made was not throwing the kid's schoolbag away. The only reason he would be carrying it was for something important. What was left inside—receipts and notes and a map—was not important enough to carry when he was on foot. That's my mistake . . ."

Bob interrupted him, "You couldn't have known Pero."

"Doesn't matter who's to blame, it was a tell. It tells them we took something out. The US military searched our effects, remember? They found nothing. Either there was nothing or we hid it so well the military search missed it. Chang couldn't take that chance. She knew there had to be something simply because Qamaan carried that damn schoolbag. And he may have told her. We have to assume he told her, right?"

Mbuno nodded at the logic. He put a hand on Pero's shoulder. "Brother, it does not matter. It is there. Ndiyo, I think you are right." He tapped the backpack that lay at their feet. "Now, we have to go. Where do we go?"

"First we need something very public. I say let's fly back to Nairobi, first class, and use the first-class waiting lounge to make calls." Everyone agreed.

Bob added, "We do not need the backpack. Put the filter in your first-aid bag and we will have no luggage for the plane." Pero did as suggested, resisting opening the tube again to show them it was safe.

Mbuno needed them all to feel less nervous in case they were being watched. He looked at them, commanding, "We are happy, we are here. We are coming back from safari, we only are people at the end of a safari." And he led them out of the toilet and, finding a soldier, managed to hitch them a ride over to the main terminal.

Moi International Airport has two floors, with check-in and departure on the upper floor. Pero used his American Express card to buy four one-way first-class tickets to Nairobi, apologized for their rough appearance and sweaty clothes, explaining they had just completed a two-week walking safari. The first-class waiting room attendant understood completely, especially when Pero gave him two twenty-dollar bills as a tip. Pero asked for a phone for Kenya calls and the attendant showed him to a row of three of them saying, "Please, be our guest." Then he walked away.

Pero called Tone Bowman first, at home. Tone was happy to hear from Pero and said Pero's wife had also called, something about emergency bookings at Interconti. Tone had already arranged for four rooms. Quickly, Pero told Tone what else he needed. An ex-military man approaching seventy, Tone had lost none of his efficiency. He replied to Pero's requests, "Consider it all done, old boy. Meet you at the Interconti." He hung up.

Listening in, Bob was impressed. "He's still a good man to know, Pero." Pero agreed. Bob added, "You know, I missed my call, the incoming one, while we were airborne. Think I should call in?" Pero shook his head. Bob agreed. "They can't fire me if I don't speak to them." He looked at Pero intently. "You serious about that job?"

"If you want it, yes."

"Taping? Something less risky?" Pero smiled at Bob and nodded. "Okay then, let's see if we can get there from here." Bob knew they were on the run, it was that obvious. Standing next to him, Nancy said nothing, but the look on her face was not one of fear but pent-up anger. Bob looked at her and asked, "Nancy, you okay?"

Her voice lowered, she hissed, "Don't ask if I'm okay. No, I am not okay. People are dying, getting killed, they try and kill us and you ask if I'm okay? No, I'm not, but that doesn't mean I'm giving in. Whatever we need to do to get these bastards, we need to do." She rounded on Pero. "You get that, right? You're a producer, as Heep, your partner says. So produce this damn mess and get it sorted out." Pero said he would try his best. Nancy merely nodded.

Mbuno, watching this interplay, added, "I will need to go home to Giraffe Manor." Pero knew it was not simply to see his wife, Niamba, who lived in their small home there. Pero had seen Mbuno fingering his almost empty leather pouch. Mbuno was preparing for what was to come.

Mbuno also explained to Pero, "I need to call the dukka," shop, "near my village and have them get Ube to join us." Pero nodded toward the phone bank.

Mbuno sat at the phone desk and dialed. When it answered, he asked for and then said "Jambo bwana Singh," hello to Mr. Singh. "Huyu ni Mbuno. Naweza kukuuliza msaada?" This is

Mbuno, can you help me? Mr. Singh on the line said he could. Mbuno continued, "Ni muhimu zaidi kwamba mwanangu, Uburu, ndio Ube, aje kwenye Hoteli ya Intercontinental mara moja. Je! Unaweza kuendesha gari kwenda kijijini na kumwambia?" It is most important that my son, Uburu, yes, Ube, come to the Intercontinental Hotel immediately. Can you drive to the village and tell him? Mbuno listened and signed off with, "Asante, Bwana Singh, hiyo inasaidia sana. Tafadhali mwambie ni ya haraka." Thank you, Mr. Singh, that is most helpful. Please tell him it is urgent.

Pero understood enough Swahili to know that Mbuno was calling reinforcements in the person of his son, Ube, a premier scout and completely capable fighter, if need be. Bob heard the name and asked, "Calling for Ube to join us?" Pero nodded. Bob was happy at the prospect, looking down at Nancy and saying, "Ube's coming. Good to have him back with us." Ube, Bob, and Nancy had formed a bond after the last safari in Tanzania and the troubles they had faced together.

The group's flight to Nairobi was called an hour later and the four walked to the plane, settled in their seats, and, for the one-hour flight, ate a snack meal and dozed. On landing, they left the plane, skipped baggage claim because they had nothing in the hold, and went outside. Mbuno talked to two or three drivers all touting for business with their minivan taxis, found one who was not Kikuyu—a tribe he never trusted—assured him they were paying in dollars, and told him where to drive. Once on the highway into town, Mbuno changed where they were going. He made the man cut through Nairobi Wildlife Park for which Pero paid the entry fee in dollars. Then Mbuno directed the driver along park roads, past giraffes, warthogs, a lion on a carcass—all things tourists loved to see—without stopping; they went out the Langata Gate, turned left toward Langata, and followed road signs to Giraffe Manor. Mbuno told the driver to wait outside the main gate. He then left the car and sprinted downhill toward the small cottage he and his wife, Niamba, lived in.

Mbuno had been banished from his village after defying the tribal chief's orders and opposing Niamba's brother's plan to illegally secure the future for the Liangulu people as poachers. Niamba's brother pretended to be working for the park people but was, in fact, helping an elephant poaching gang just outside Tsavo National Park. The elephant raid was a trap by political forces in the government to outlaw all the Liangulu tribe as poachers, kick them off their land, and build more tourist facilities, further lining the pockets of corrupt politicians. Mbuno had prevented the raid, killing Niamba's brother in the process, and rescuing Ube who had been stabbed by his father for being disloyal.

Although the Liangulu tribe recognized that Mbuno had saved them, tribal law had to apply. Mbuno had disobeyed his chief and was banished. Niamba, the tribal liabon, went with him. People in the safari industry recognized Mbuno's extraordinary actions in saving his tribe and, through a rich American donor, Harry Grimaldi, secured a small cottage on the Giraffe Manor estate on the hillsides of Langata for them to live in for life. Niamba had never ever had running water, let alone hot water. She always marveled at her husband's status being so respected.

Mbuno rushed into their home, hugged his wife, and while he was opening the leather pouch, asking her to replenish the powder, he told her all that had happened. Halfway through, Niamba told him to sit and wait. He explained friends were waiting in a car. She glared at him and he sat. Niamba took out her enkidong gourd, laid out her hide with painted symbols, and cast stones. She asked, "Mwanamke, yeye ni kabila gani?" The woman, what tribe is she?

"Yeye sio Mwafrika. Yeye ni Mchina." She is not African. She is Chinese.

CHAPTER 12

KUFUATILIA HUANZA—THE CHASE BEGINS

Niamba threw the stones. She removed several, absentmindedly putting them back in the gourd. She looked puzzled. Mbuno had never seen her look puzzled with a reading. He waited. A few moments later Niamba said, "Yeye yuko mbali sana. Yuko hapa. Hapa, karibu. Lakini pia mbali sana." She is far away. She is here. Here, nearby. But also far away. "Sijui jinsi anaweza kuwa katika maeneo mawili." I do not know how she can be in two places.

The reading over, she put her gourd and hide away. She handed Mbuno the refilled small leather sack, hugged her husband, and pushed him toward the door, "Ube itasaidia." Ube will help.

As he ascended the hillside to the main gate, Mbuno thought, *I did not tell her Ube was coming; she knew.* And he smiled at her extraordinary abilities that always gave him such pride being married to such a great liabon. Mbuno climbed back into the cab and nodded to Pero. Pero told the driver to go down the Langata Road and on to the Intercontinental Hotel. Bob and Nancy sat tight together saying nothing; Pero watched familiar houses, the Langata Police Station, and several new bars pass the window. Rain began to fall, light at first, promising the beginning of the rainy season for Nairobi. Pero thought, *Those poor people in Kibera in their makeshift houses are about to be flooded out again.* And he shook his head. He had sought to protect the slum area just outside Nairobi once—had succeeded with Mbuno—but, always a man of conscience, wished he could do more. *Another day, Pero, another day, concentrate . . .* In his head, his thoughts sounded like his father's voice when he was a teen.

As the car pulled up at the Interconti, the portico shielded the car and the alighting passengers from the downpour. Kamal, the doorman, recognized Pero and saluted. Pero patted him on the shoulder. "Hi, Kamal. Mr. Janardan around? I'll need rooms." Mr. Janardan was the undermanager of the hotel and a longtime friend of Pero and his taping crews.

Kamal helped Nancy from the back seat and replied, "Oh no, Mr. Baltazar, sir, but Bwana Bowman is here with your memsaab. He has arranged your accommodation. Everything is most perfect, sir. He told me to watch for you." Nancy thanked him for the assist and he said, "Pleasure, madam." He asked if there was luggage and was surprised there was none.

Pero put him at ease. "Luggage will come later, maybe tomorrow. Not to worry. A good bath and time with my wife will make our stay perfect. Again, thank you, Kamal." With that the four walked into the lobby where two underdoormen were waiting, one handing Pero four keys, saying, "Bwana Bowman is waiting in your suite, sir." He indicated the correct room key. "This one, sir." Pero thanked him and the four piled into the elevator. Pero scanned the lobby. Aside from the usual tourists and two foreign dignitaries with their secretaries, nothing seemed out of the ordinary. Pero hoped no one could know they were in Nairobi. The leak of their previous destination, the Oasis in Loyangalani, revealed by Commissioner Sing, still had him worried.

In the elevator, Pero distributed keys, handing Nancy her own. Nancy gave it back and took Bob's arm. Pero simply smiled.

On the fourth floor, Pero and Mbuno found Tone Bowman waiting in the Baltazars' suite, dozing in an armchair. Nancy and Bob stood near the entrance, not sure if they were coming in or going to their room. Susanna came out of the bedroom and ran to her husband. Quietly, her cheek on his chest, she said, "Ah, meine dummer Mann, again you come back as you promised." She stepped back and examined him. "No leeches this time, yes?" He told her none. "Ah so, and what are these?" She examined the welts on his arms. He explained the Omo River valley had the largest and hungriest mosquitoes he had ever come across. Susanne told him to go wash. She turned to Mbuno and hugged him. "My brother, you are well?" Mbuno admitted he was, but hungry. "We will fix that." She tapped the leg of the armchair and Tone startled awake. "Tone, sorry to wake you, but we need food for these four, I think, and toast and honey as well." Mbuno smiled and gave Susanna another hug.

Susanna, in complete command, turned her attention to Nancy and then Bob. "So, have you asked her yet?"

Nancy responded, "He keeps assuming it is a done deal . . . I, on the other hand, am waiting . . ."

Susanna was having none of that. "Well, then, take your room key, go have a shower together." She poked Bob in the chest with her index finger. "And you will ask her immediately, understand?" Bob started laughing, sputtering that he had tried. . . . "Not try." She called over to her husband, washing his hands, "What is that silly movie you like, Pero? *Space War* or something . . ." He called back that it was *Star Wars*. She said to Bob, "Ah, yes, as that little green man says, Not Try, Do!"

Bob, still chuckling, shook the room key brass tag, turned to Nancy, and said, "Sorry, let's do as she says and I'll see if I can get this right."

Nancy smiled, responding, "I'll see that you do." She hugged Susanna. "Men are clueless, aren't they?" Laughing, Bob and Nancy went to find their room. Drying his hands, Pero had nothing to add, so he asked Mbuno, "Half an hour, here?"

Mbuno said, "Ndiyo." And left for his room.

Tone Bowman hung up the phone and said, "Food, twenty to twenty-five minutes."

Pero came back into the room and enveloped his wife. "You okay, honey? I am sorry to bring more stress, especially . . ." He looked down at her belly.

Susanna patted her baby's womb. "Ach, this little one had better get used to it now." She looked up into her husband's eyes. "You didn't do anything to start this, you are fixing it, yes?" Pero nodded. "Gut, so we are safe here and we will all fix it together, nicht wahr?" Pero knew better than to disagree with his wife. He kissed her once, hard.

Tone settled back into the armchair, swiveled it to face Pero and Susanna who then sat on the couch, and, in a kind, fatherly way said, "I've been awake for almost two days now, thanks to phone calls from all and sundry. Now, Pero, what's all this about?"

Looking at Susanna and Tone, Pero took a deep breath. "I'll show you footage when Nancy is up to it, but here's what happened . . ." For the next fifteen minutes, Pero recounted everything.

PETER RIVA

Pero was relating his meeting with Mrs. Chang and the threats from Commissioner Sing, when Tone held up a hand, shaking his head. "That doesn't make sense. Mrs. Chang is my neighbor. Nice lady. She has twenty-four-hour Securicor guards. Normally, she is in New York at UN HQ but when she comes to inspect the UNHCR wallahs." Tone used the Indian slang for businesspeople. "She has that nice place two doors down from mine. She overlooks the valley. Million-dollar palace."

Pero asked, "You know her well?"

Tone nodded. "Fairly. Dinner once or twice a year. Cocktail circuit and the Muthaiga Club." The Muthaiga Country Club was the oldest colonial-times club in East Africa. "Not very social perhaps, earnest type, dedicated to her work, but never missed a bridge game when she was in town." Tone pondered for a moment. "Actually, last week someone from UNHCR came up our road and the Securicor johnnies wouldn't let the car in. The visitors saw me walking the dog and asked if something was wrong since they had a morning appointment with her and she hadn't shown up at the offices." He paused. "I had no idea what to suggest and they drove off."

Pero felt it didn't make sense. The woman he met, the under-secretary of the UNHCR, was hardly the type Pero could imagine being social at the Muthaiga Country Club. Mrs. Chang was business, all business. And her cohort, Commissioner Sing, was unmistakably bad news.

And now dead, he remembered. Pero continued explaining. After he had explained the C-130 switch and then the bomb in the Skyvan and the two dead refugee pilots, he finished with, "Sing they found, dead behind a refugee camp latrine. Chang has disappeared, suspected into Somalia."

Tone was incredulous. Susanne, nodding, narrowed her eyes and asked her husband, her gaze locked on his eyes, "And why

230

are you worried? What are you running from?" She knew her husband all too well.

Pero reached into his small canvas bag and took out the Katadyn filter unit. He unscrewed the base and pulled out the roll of papers. "Rahman Qamaan was carrying these. We liberated them." Tone reached for them. "No, Tone, I cannot let you know who's on this list. Your life could easily be forfeit if anyone found out you read it. Bob, Nancy, Mbuno, and I went through this list and, I can tell you, it is a death warrant for anyone who knows what names are on it."

Tone lowered his hand to his lap. "Well then, tell me what the list is, if not who's on it."

Pero paused, wondering how far to go. "I can tell you this. I spotted three of the names that were at the last financial meeting of heads of state in Davos. No one on this list is not powerful and connected. The list has accounting numbers, next to each name. It is either a list of debts or a list of payments made. Lewis and General Tews wanted Rahman Qamaan badly for questioning. Our guess is that Rahman was the accountant for al-Shabaab for their fundraising by selling tusks."

"Bloody hell. That's what we've all been looking for. Catching poachers in the field is one thing, knowing who's paying for the damn things, we've never cracked that. The parks' people and every animal rights' johnnie here will want that list."

Susanne interrupted, "But you know the real buyers . . . the Chinese take all the ivory they can get. They are the end users. The World Wildlife Fund people are always trying to stop the Chinese ivory trade."

Tone shook his head. "That's true, but they never get whole tusks. If you have the whole tusk, it is worth much, much more than the small items they carve for rich families in Shanghai. To sell a whole tusk, you can triple the price per pound."

Pero did the mental math again and explained, "I calculated that they've taken about two hundred million dollars out of Ethiopia each year for the past ten years. But I was calculating at wholesale prices in China. I have no idea what a real tusk is worth."

Tone did. "If you can get a pair, large or small . . ." He paused. "Look, even a small pair is worth over fifty thousand dollars."

Pero remembered that all the tusks in the hangar were tagged and arranged in pairs. "Tone, they were tagging and selling pairs. We saw them laid out on a hangar floor. Only pairs. They'd fly them from the slaughter camp next to the Omo River to Dadaab and then drive them into Somalia and who knows where after that."

Tone stood and looked out the window at the pool below. "It doesn't matter, chum. A container, a freighter, anything disappearing into Somalia reemerges across the world." He looked down at Pero and Susanna. "Any of those names from Saudi Arabia?" Pero nodded. "Biggest numbers? My guess? Kuwait, Iraq, and Iran. How about Brunei? Those are my suspects." Pero nodded again, twice. Tone shook his head. "Coupled names and money? Death warrant list, I see. People who believe they are above the law." He clapped his hands. "So, what do you want to do?"

Pero shrugged. "Honestly, I have no idea. I've told Lewis I will see him, in person, deep in the forest on the Matthews Range—you know the Grimaldi safari Mbuno did, the one everyone knows about? I thought there was the safest. I want no other witnesses." He looked at Susanna. "Honestly, I want to stop them, and you know I get too damn nosy when it comes to figuring out the people and power play. Last time, I nearly got the whole of Africa in an uproar. I don't want to take that risk again. These people"—he tapped the papers—"rule most of the world." He shook his head, suddenly feeling tired. "But, Tone, Mbuno will not stop until he's broken this poaching ring. And I cannot ask him to do it on his own. That's why I asked Lewis to show up."

Tone faced the window with his back to the couple. "Yes, I see that. Lewis confirmed he's arriving tomorrow, early. I'm making safari arrangements, his orders." He turned around. "Let's get Mbuno in here . . ."

Susanna added, "And Bob and Nancy . . . let's eat and talk."

On cue, there was a knock at their suite door and Pero let two waiters bring in two rolling tables with food. He went across the hall and tapped on the other rooms. Mbuno opened his door and came out with Ube, his son. Pero hugged Ube and then realized he would have to tell the story all over again. He looked at Mbuno and then Ube, realizing Mbuno had already told Ube all he knew. Ube patted Pero's shoulder. "We will find them and we will stop them." His youthful confidence made Pero smile. *Cavalry to the rescue.* Nancy and Bob joined them, hugs all around and they went to eat.

Pero's thoughts invaded every second while they ate. Nancy brought her camera and the chips—running early sequences for Bob, Susanna, Tone, and Ube. Pero concentrated on eating, Susanna watching him carefully out of the corner of her eye. Pero was deep in thought.

Mbuno listened to Nancy's descriptions but said nothing. He was mindlessly staring out the window at the pool, four floors below, watching the bathers enjoying the crystal-clear water. Pero stood next to him, his face also blank.

Once the videos were over, Tone, Susanna, Bob, and Nancy began to throw out ideas and plot different courses of action, none of which matched reality nor, Pero felt, anything that was worth the risk of their lives. Pero was deep in his own thoughts,

We have to do something, anything, and yet somehow stop this blowing the world apart. The list is evidence, deadly evidence. And then, suddenly, he thought of the only way out.

Pero turned and held up his hand, calling for silence. "There's only one way out of this. I will call Mrs. Chang and offer to return the list to her superior." Everyone except Mbuno protested. The objections were based on the assumption that that would allow more poaching. Pero waited until their arguments petered out. "Look, she knows we have the list. It wasn't on Rahman. He was probably questioned before they killed him. He would have told them that he had the list in the schoolbag. What I think we need to do is to have me tell her that I alone have the list. And that I'll return it to her boss for a cash payment. I'll sell it back to them. They're crooks, they'll assume I am a crook too."

Tone asked, "But what about the names on the list? Are they all to go unpunished?"

Pero faced Tone Bowman, ex-white hunter, dedicated naturalist, and safari outfitter. "Tone, do you really think the world order will allow the global economy and power structure to be upended? To allow the removal of all the oil suppliers, all the princes, kings, presidents, and captains of global companies? To allow them all to be arrested, to be labeled contributors to the poaching epidemic here? Get real, even if we shared this list with the media and it was published everywhere in the world, and every citizen saw the list . . . it would be branded as fake, a forgery. If it were believed, whole world orders could crumble. Even governments against poaching won't allow that. People get killed for less." Pero paused, seeing the accusatory faces of his friends. Then he went on, "Look, and even worse . . . if it were believed . . . if it were believed and acted upon, economies would topple, industry would falter. It would cause a global downturn. People would lose their jobs, economies would take years to recover. In the end, yes, some people would die but never the really rich and powerful. No, as usual, it would be the innocent people, the poorest people. We drove past the Kibera slum on the way here; those people already at the sharp end of survival won't stand a chance. Across the world, the poorest will lose the most." Pero's voice was beseeching, "We can't allow that, it is too big a risk."

Mbuno put a hand on Pero's shoulder. "But we must stop the poaching."

Pero nodded, finally able to set things right. "Of course, that has to be our goal. Mrs. Chang and her organization have to pay the price, agreed, they have to be stopped. But beyond that? We need to lose this list in a way they can believe. They must feel they are safe or none of us will ever be."

Mbuno muttered, "Pembe. Kwa nini watu wanataka pembe za ndovu?" Ivory. Why do people want ivory?

Pero understood, but it was Tone who answered, "For thousands of years, ivory has been as valuable as gold and precious stones. Before plastics, you could carve things that would last for centuries—strong yet light. Nowadays? It's purely a status symbol. And a pair of tusks shows both how rich you are as well as how powerful . . . everyone knows ivory tusks are poached. If you display them, you're saying you're above the law and can't be touched." He turned to Pero. "That about right?"

Pero agreed, explaining that was why the list of the people who were really above the law was so dangerous.

Mbuno only wanted to know if Pero had a plan.

"Yes, I think I do. We need to raid Mrs. Chang's home. I need to get inside and await her return, because, if my hunch is right, she's going to return as if nothing happened. She's got full diplomatic immunity. No one in Kenya will stop her, even if General Tews wants to apprehend her. She can use her diplomatic immunity to avoid any arrest, I'm pretty sure. If I can see her face-to-face, then I can make her my offer. In her own house, she won't worry about surveillance, she won't worry about talking." Pero asked Tone, "Got any idea how we can break in?"

Tone laughed. "Well, if it's a raid you want, let's plan a diversion to get those Securicor guards busy so you can slip in." He thought for a moment. "You know, there's a new house going in opposite her place on Dik Dik Lane. Our properties are on Lamwia Road, but the new construction is on Dik Dik Lane at the back of hers. Maybe the workers could have an accident with a runaway bulldozer or maybe a fire?"

Mbuno was decisive. "Early morning, tomorrow. Pero and I will break in." He looked at Tone. "You can arrange for this?" Tone nodded.

Bob asked, "What do you want me to do?"

Pero was icy calm when he said it, "Call Lewis; they'll patch you through to the plane he'll be traveling on, tell him everything on the secure satellite phone. Tell him you have not seen anything on the list—Bob, that's critical, for your own safety—but tell him that we're breaking into Mrs. Chang's house tomorrow morning to sell it back." Pero paused, wanting to make sure Bob understood. He pleaded, "But, Bob, to your dying day"—he turned to Nancy as well—"you two never tell anyone you saw that list. Forget you saw it, forget it even exists. If anyone asks, tell them I took it before you could read it. Okay?"

Pero's tone frightened the ex-Marine and his future bride sufficiently that they both agreed. Pero wasn't worried about Mbuno telling anyone and, besides, Pero knew that if Mbuno ever came across anyone on that list, he would know what to do. Mbuno's sense of honor was beyond Pero's control, of that he was certain.

Pero took the papers and rolled them back into the Katadyn

filter tube and handed it to Mbuno. "Can you find someplace safe for this?"

Mbuno suggested Ube that take it and put it in a bank vault at the Standard Chartered Bank immediately. Pero agreed and Ube took the Katadyn filter and left the room saying, "I need to get there before they close. I will be back soon."

Once that was settled, Susanna rose and said, "Then I better get the Silke Wire ready, because if you think you're going to speak to that woman without all of us hearing, you have another thing coming."

Susanna was a sound technician who constantly amazed her producer husband. She was the inventor of the Silke Wire, named after her deceased mother who had secretly recorded her al-Qaeda captors' dialogue when she was held for ransom; Susanna's invention was genius. A thin wire that could be sewn into fabric, acted as both microphone and antenna. The transmitter and proprietary coding hardware were smaller than a matchbox and easily disguised. Pero and his video crew had used it several times already to great effect. The sound quality was perfect and the transmission distance was over three hundred feet.

After Susanna's pronouncement, Tone Bowman immediately ordered up changes of clothing from a local safari outfitter for the four, which were delivered to the hotel in short order. While the others rested in their rooms, Susanna finished sewing the antenna into a new jacket for Pero before dinner. They tested it and were both professionally satisfied. While they worked, helping to take their mind off the danger the morning could bring, they again talked of her pregnancy and, especially, where they might want to live. As newlyweds always on the go taping, neither Susanna's home in Munich, Germany, nor Pero's in Manhattan had been visited yet as a couple. Susanna broke the ice by explaining, "We need a new place, one that is ours. In a place we can trust."

While walking with the elephants, Pero had had pondering time, as he called it. He'd mentally toyed with the idea of their child being born in New York, selling his apartment, and perhaps buying a house in Upstate New York where they could have animals and grow vegetables. He had wondered if Susanna would like that. Now, he realized that the word *trust* that Susanna had used had serious significance for them both. Trust didn't mean being in hiding or off the grid; it meant being able to live openly in a safe place. They'd been chased, they'd been threatened, and they survived. Pero, too, was feeling he needed to live somewhere they could be safe, a place of trust while trying to enjoy a normal life.

Sensing her husband's thought processes, Susanna remarked, "Loyangalani would be great for a long stay, but not to bring up a child. Nairobi, and most of East Africa, is changing too fast to be safe; I feel there is civil unease here now." Pero nodded in agreement. She went on, "Munich is safe, but I don't want to live there anymore." She paused. "Is there somewhere you want to live, somewhere you loved as a child?"

Susanna had, of course, nailed down the thought process correctly. Pero's mind went to his childhood, to boarding school, to Switzerland. "I always loved Saanen in Switzerland." Susanna studied his face, touched his cheek. Pero admitted, "It's a place where everything works, where people treat you as equals, and yet you're at the center of Europe for culture, travel, and . . ." He paused. "I trust the Swiss."

Susanna smiled. "When this is over, let's go visit." Pero agreed.

As agreed earlier in the day, the team of seven met over dinner, served in Susanna's suite. They went over details, laughing at

Tone's explanation of the diversion he had planned. "Bulldozers will run over anything . . . we'll pull the brake pin so it'll be impossible to stop. We'll simply aim the Komatsu bulldozer at the Securicor hut and flatten it. It moves slowly so no one should get hurt, but the patrolling dogs will get out, and that'll keep the handlers busy. And if they don't get it stopped before it reaches the front gates, they'll be flattened and then on to the main road . . . traffic will be a mess." Tone was smiling, showing his prankster side.

Mbuno wanted to know if they should follow the bulldozer.

"Yes and no." Tone explained, "The bulldozer will break through the bougainvillea fence—there's chain-link fence in the middle—then proceed directly at the Securicor hut. The guards will be raising all sorts of hell by that time, trying to shut it down." He chuckled. "Such a pity the bulldozer cabin door also locks shut when the door is closed. Our man, the driver, will be screaming for their help to get the door open. The dogs will no doubt escape through the broken fence trying to catch the two kids we've hired on dirt bikes—they'll be laughing and shouting by the way, as if they set the bulldozer on its way. So, when all is underway, pick your moment and slip in. Sunrise is at six-thirty tomorrow. The bulldozer normally fires up around then—which seriously annoys all of us living nearby."

Pero thought the plan was fine. Mbuno only added, "Bougainvillea has thorns, you need to be careful, brother." Pero said he would. Mbuno continued, "I am not coming in with you through the fence. I will come and rescue you later if sister Susanna tells me to. She will be listening."

Tone confirmed his garden shed had electricity and was already set up with chairs and a table so Susanna could sit in there with Mbuno. Pero and everyone felt they had planned it as well as could be expected. Pero asked Bob if he had talked to Lewis.

"I have, he'll be here tomorrow. Sometime before noon." Bob looked at Tone. "You've got him a plane, right? To go to the Matthews Range?" Tone said he did. "And you want Ube to take him, right? But why not Nancy and me, too?"

Pero had been thinking about that. If the meeting with Chang went as planned—if there even was a meeting—he would still have to hand over the papers to Chang's boss—if there was a boss. He hadn't told anyone he had doubts about getting to talk to anyone higher than Chang. But once the filter was delivered and payment made, he would need to disappear for a while in the hopes that Chang would either be removed by her boss or, if she was the boss, see that nothing else happened, which would mean Pero kept his word. A place to hide out seemed the only way to ensure they were out of harm's way. And as he thought it through again, he realized Bob and Nancy needed to go along, too, if only to stay out of harm's way. "Tone, is the chartered plane for Lewis and Ube big enough to take Bob and Nancy as well? We'll keep the rooms here, never check out, make the enemy feel we're around somewhere."

Tone explained he could swap planes for one larger, but the rations he'd already sent ahead would need to be increased for a week's stay. Mbuno said, "When Pero and I go, we can take more food." Mbuno looked at Susanna. "Sister, will you stay with Tone Bowman?"

Tone piped up, "We'd be delighted to have you stay." Susanna agreed and Pero could see she was relieved. Being pregnant, air travel did not agree with her, especially if by small bush planes.

Pero stood. "All right then, tomorrow Susanna, Mbuno, and I will be at your house Tone at five, Bob and Nancy will meet Lewis with Ube and go directly to Wilson Airport to get aboard a charter flight to the Matthews Range. We'll do our little diversion, make a promise of an exchange with Chang, and then get to Wilson for a flight." Pero was in action mode. "Sleep, everyone, it'll be a long day tomorrow."

Twenty minutes later, in bed, holding Susanna tight in a darkened bedroom, Pero reminded Susanna how much he loved her, feeling her tears on his arm under her cheek. He consoled her fears. "Sleep, darling, it'll be all right." Moments later, drifting off, a thought of recrimination kept popping up in his head: *Why did I take the damn papers in the first place? The damn way he was carrying them was so obviously a trap.*

Tone Bowman's plan worked exactly as he planned. Perhaps it was a little more chaotic, but Pero didn't have time to watch the spectacle. At that early hour, half the guards were in their underpants running around trying to stop the bulldozer. The two kids on dirt bikes followed the bulldozer onto Mrs. Chang's front lawn, digging deep ruts, yelling and laughing before they turned tail and roared away, dogs and men chasing them. Pero had no trouble slipping by everyone and entering the house, stealthily checking ground floor rooms before he went upstairs.

A woman is different from a man returning home. A woman will usually check her bedroom first. Pero wanted to wait for her there.

What he found startled him.

Handcuffed to the bedframe, half-naked, eyes bulging in terror, an oriental woman lay on soiled sheets. Pero quickly assessed that her one handcuffed wrist allowed her enough movement to reach the camping toilet next to her bed, a glass pitcher of water and a glass tumbler on a nightstand, and a light switch. Her feet were red and open sores were oozing. Quickly Pero went over to her and before she could scream, he placed a hand over her mouth and said, "Friend." To no one in particular, Pero voiced into the Silke Wire, "A woman's here, upstairs bedroom, handcuffed to the bed, been here for days. I have to get her to safety. Mbuno, I need your help."

To the woman, he said, "I'll get you out of here, but please stay quiet. Someone may come up here to check on you. We caused a commotion downstairs . . . they may want to check. I'll hide if they come in. Then we'll get you safely away." He looked into her eyes. "All right?" Under his hand, he felt her chin bob up and down. He took his hand away. "Do you have a name?"

"Chang, I am the undersecretary-general of the UNHCR."

No time for the shock he felt, Pero heard voices outside the bedroom in the hallway, perhaps coming up the stairs. The woman's eyes looked left and Pero followed her line of sight. Moving swiftly, he opened the already ajar door and entered the bathroom. He waited. The voices got louder, a nearby door opened and a man's voice came from inside the bedroom. The man sounded annoyed, responding to someone in the house in a language Pero didn't understand. Another voice told him something and Pero watched, through the crack in the bathroom door, as the man checked every corner of the room, every closet. Pero heard doors opening and being slammed shut.

The woman started to yell at him, "Stay away from me, stay away from me . . ."

The man laughed, sneering in broken English, "Or what, stupid woman? You shut up, I beat you again!" Pero heard the clink of the glass pitcher pouring water into the glass. He moved swiftly, knowing the man's back would be turned away from the bathroom. At over six feet and strong, Pero grabbed the shorter man in a half-nelson hold, closing the man's airway, choking him. The glass tumbler fell to the floor and shattered on the marble tile. Weakly, the man struck Pero on the hip and tried to hit the top of his head a few times before he slumped. Pero kept a tighter hold until he was sure the man was fully unconscious if not dead. The man's face was bearded and definitely not local, but Pero could not place his origin. Quickly, he searched him, finding a Grach 9 mm pistol and a cosh. In an upper breast pocket, he found a key with a tag with calligraphy characters that Pero could not read. He tried the handcuffs with the key, it popped open. Whispering into the Silke Wire, he said, "One man down. Handcuff key worked." He hoped Mbuno had heard.

Pero offered his hand to the woman. "Can you get up? I'll carry you, but I need to know if you are otherwise all right." He was looking at her feet.

She said, "Get me out of here." Then she added quite politely, "Please."

Pero thought, *Now this Mrs. Chang I can see at the Muthaiga Club!* He turned his back on her, sat on the bed edge, and said, "Climb aboard if you can." She did, clumsy to be sure, but determined. Pistol in his right hand, left hand supporting her as a seat, he walked and listened over near the door. What he heard puzzled him; something thudding on the landing floor and then a low humming belching sound.

He flung open the door inward and Mbuno smiled. "We go now, hurry." Stepping over two bodies, Pero noted that these were not Securicor men, but more men who were possibly Arabic. Carrying Mrs. Chang on his back, Pero followed Mbuno down the hall, down the steps, as Mbuno turned toward the back of the house. In the kitchen a track-suited Chinese man was slumped on the kitchen table, blood running from his nose, revolver on the floor. Mbuno paused at the back door, listening as he opened it slowly. He took the gun from Pero and waved them forward.

At a trot, the distance to Dik Dik Lane was only a hundred yards, perhaps the most frightening hundred yards of Pero's life. As they entered the construction site, a Land Rover, engine running, was waiting, back door open. Pero and Mbuno helped the woman in and then climbed in as Tone already had the tires spinning in the soft sand. Pero took off his jacket and wrapped it around the woman covering her near nakedness. Not a shot was fired, no sirens were heard. Tone drove on steadily away from his own house deeper into Langata. Pero asked, "Where are we headed?"

Tone's response was terse, "Niamba."

The woman again introduced herself and said, "I am Mrs. Chang. Nice to see you again, Mr. Bowman. Thank you for rescuing me, but we need to see the police right away."

Tone replied forcibly, "No, madam, we do not. We need to hide and get you medical attention." Pero looked at Mbuno who simply nodded agreement. The Land Rover sped on.

At lower Giraffe Manor, Mbuno got out and went to talk to Niamba who, having heard the Land Rover pull up, had already opened the front door. She pushed past her husband and approached the green Land Rover. "Lady not well." She looked at Pero. "Bring in, tafadhali." Please.

Pero did as he was told, cradling Mrs. Chang and entering their simple cottage. Niamba pointed to the worn leather couch, probably secondhand from the Giraffe Manor hotel, in front of a wood fireplace, embers still radiating heat. Pero eased Mrs. Chang onto the couch, and Niamba took control, feeling the woman's bone structure starting with her head, down her torso, and finally her feet. "Ahya, vidonda hivi ni mbaya." These sores are bad. "Kunipata maji, maji ya moto." Fetch me hot water. Mbuno went to the kitchen. Niamba went into the pantry and they could hear her opening and recapping glass and earthenware jars. Mrs. Chang said nothing, but her eyes were watching every movement, like a bird wondering how or if she could escape.

CHAPTER 13

KUWEKA MTEGO—SETTING THE TRAP

Pero knelt in front of the couch, calmly explaining, "Mrs. Chang, my name is Pero Baltazar." He gestured to the others. "Tone Bowman, who you know is Kenya's premier safari tour operator, then there's Kenya's premier safari guide, Mbuno Waliangulu, and his wife, Niamba, a most experienced native doctor. We went to your house to confront the other Mrs. Chang who threatened us in Dadaab two days ago and tried to kill us by exploding a small plane. We had no idea you were the real Mrs. Chang nor that you had been held prisoner." While Pero worked to calm what he felt was a woman surely on the verge of shock, Niamba approached with clean rags and Mbuno put a bowl of hot water on the floor near the end of the couch. Niamba proceeded to wash Mrs. Chang's feet. Once she was satisfied they were clean, she unwrapped a small piece of paper, took a pinch of mixed quantities and colors of powder, and pressed the mixture into each sore. Mrs. Chang flinched but did not cry out.

Pero knew it must have been painful so he held Mrs. Chang's hand. Her fingers tightened each time Niamba made contact. The soles of one's feet are covered in nerves and hers were surely inflamed and extremely painful

Tone chimed in, "Mrs. Chang, I trust these people with my life. You can speak freely."

Niamba said, "Miguu itakuwa kuponya. Katika siku mbili unaweza kutembea."

Mbuno translated, "The feet will heal. In two days, you may walk."

Mrs. Chang pulled Pero's jacket tighter and calmly responded to Niamba, "Thank you, madam." Her eyes locked on each face, one at a time. "And you, Mr. Bowman. And you, Mr. Baltazar. And you, Mbuno of the Liangulu." Her grasp of the provenance of last names for East African tribal members impressed Pero. "Asante. Most sincerely, I thank you all." Her chin wobbled. "Why was I taken prisoner? Do you know? Is this about the refugees at Dadaab?"

Pero remembered something critical, looked at Tone, and asked, "Did anyone know it was your Land Rover that picked us up?"

Tone smiled and said, "Accidentally happened to wrap the license plates, front and rear, with old rags. My guess is not; all old safari green Land Rovers look the same."

Pero continued, "Good. Are the rest of the plans still underway? Flights to the Matthews?" Tone nodded. "Okay then . . ." And, still on the floor to keep eye level contact with Mrs. Chang, Pero explained everything that had happened to them in the same way he had explained to Tone Bowman, omitting, as before, mention of which names were on the list. He concluded with, "I will not share the names with you, Mrs. Chang, because—and I appreciate that you better than most can understand this—they would not hesitate to kill anyone who saw the list. And I doubt any world government would stop them."

Mrs. Chang looked at Pero. "You realize then, if you admit you read and realize the import of those names, you are signing your own death warrant." She patted Pero's hand. "Your life is surely worth more than that."

Pero had to admit it was. He had hoped to strike a bargain, make a deal in which only he was at risk. In the past, going up against terrorists and misadventures, he had risked others' lives. This time, he was determined to limit the possible casualty to himself alone. "If that had been a real UNHCR Mrs. Chang I was dealing with, I was willing to trade the list for silence, with the papers to be revealed if I died under any circumstances. Or get a deal from her boss, if it came to that. If she even has a boss. Now, frankly, I do not know what to do."

Mrs. Chang nodded. "Yes, I see. But now they know you have rescued me, and there is no guarantee I would be quiet about the identity of that impostor." Pero looked around the room, seeing faces all realizing, perhaps for their first time, that the complexity had grown exponentially.

Pero could only see one way out now, one that amounted to suicide. But first, he had a question for Mrs. Chang. "Do you know who the other woman is? Did you meet her when they captured you?"

Her lower lip quivering, she responded, "A distant cousin. She came to my room to take my clothes. She is part of a triad called Sun Yee On." She seemed to regain strength for a moment. "Sun Yee On are lethal, with half a hundred thousand members around the world. Sun Yee On are led by Ko Chun—a man with considerable political influence in Beijing and Shanghai. Jimmy Huaing from Hong Kong is here in Nairobi. He is a son of the founder of Sun Yee On. At the UNHCR, we have had black-market dealings with the Sun Yee On in Nepal and Tibet. In Nairobi and Dar es Salaam, Jimmy Huaing has been investing in local businesses and making loans to politicians. We have barred him from refugee camps in Uganda."

Tone Bowman piped in, "That little squeak, Jimmy Huaing? He's drunk half the time at the club. Obnoxious twit."

Mrs. Chang narrowed her eyes. "It is an act. In Taiwan, there is still an arrest warrant out for him and his brother after they killed over one hundred of the 14k triad in a weekend slaughter." She looked at Pero. "I do not think you can survive their atten-tion. I am sorry." She paused again, resting her head back down. "Nor will I, I'm afraid."

Niamba had a hot broth on the stove. She poured some into an enamel cup and told Mrs. Chang to drink, slowly. Trying the brew, Mrs. Chang pronounced it delicious and slowly, but steadily, sipped as Pero, Tone, and Mbuno went outside and conferred.

Pero had to put things in order, first things first. Outside the cottage were two three-legged stools and he motioned for Tone and Mbuno to sit while he paced. "Tone, is there any way anyone can associate you with anything that has happened here or before?"

Shaking his head, his voice was confident, "No, I'm pretty sure. Bloody well better not be. Our office arranged your travel, your hotel, all that's normal. No one will recognize the Land Rover and, except for your wife staying with us for now—and no one knows she's there except us—it's simply business as usual for the company." Pero nodded agreement. It sounded logical. Tone continued, "Mbuno, you, Bob, and Nancy are a different matter. They saw you in Dadaab, they know their plot to kill you failed and, if I may say so, they know you. You, Pero, have considerable influence if they know you arranged the C-130. That makes you a significant member of the opposition. Even if the fake Mrs. Chang didn't realize that, her superiors would. And"—his voice lowered to convey his sincerity—"my god, man, you're up against one of the worst Chinese criminal organizations there is." He took a breath. "And that weasel, Jimmy Huaing? He's here and no one knows he's part of . . . what's it called?"

Mbuno replied, "Sun Yee On."

Tone continued, "Right. Sun Yee On. Never heard of them but Mrs. Chang has, and she strikes me as someone who is hardly afraid for no reason."

Pero, taking in all Tone said, felt he had to explain where he felt everything was headed. "Look, maybe we have three options, as I see it. One, we can see this Jimmy Huaing and explain that we didn't know what was going on, hand him the list, and try and assure him we'll keep silent—even with a guarantee that if anything happens to me it can all be revealed. I had hoped that plan could work before, but now I think they will probably simply want to kill everyone before we can make any arrangements. We know they kidnapped and swapped Mrs. Chang, we know way too much about how powerful and resourceful they already are here in Kenya.

"No, they will want to erase everyone before anyone can make plans or reveal anything to the press, police, whomever. And I mean kill us off soon, right now, if they knew where we are.

"So, option two, we can run and see who chases us; that will allow us to know how serious they are. It was why I wanted Lewis to meet and talk, outside of official circles—I figured he could watch us—has the manpower available to watch us and them—and spot them—al-Shabaab—chasing us. Now I see that even that was a bad idea, too simplistic." Pero hesitated, then added, "And we're on a much shorter timeline now."

Tone asked why.

"Originally, I didn't count on such a large opposition in Nairobi, but if a senior Sun Yee On leader is resident here, he'll have hundreds if not thousands of troops he can call on in East Africa right away. I thought we'd have a few days at least. That time frame is gone. Look, we all know the Chinese are expanding everywhere in Africa, especially in East Africa. Have you seen what they're buying up in Tanzania? Almost fifty percent of crops? With the one I choked at Mrs. Chang's and the three Mbuno laid out—dead or otherwise, it doesn't matter—they have people at the ready. And even if they don't have their own people here now, they have hundreds of people who are happy to work for them, financially tied to them. And remember, one of the leaders of the Sun Yee On is right here in Nairobi, so that means they probably have gang members, and a full organization on the ground here in East Africa. We have to assume they do anyway."

Tone and Mbuno both wanted to add something but Pero waved them off. "Let me think out loud here. . . . So, if they wanted, all they have to do is watch Wilson Airport. They can probably recognize Nancy and Bob, so they'll know where they went. If not exactly, at least the region. Right?" Tone and Mbuno reluctantly agreed. "So the only option I can see is to use the only skill we have that is superior to theirs—a skill only we have. We need to lure them into the bush, deep into the bush, and we need to capture Jimmy Huaing."

Mbuno's expression told Pero he was mostly in agreement. However, he stood and revealed his deepest concern, "Black mamba does not look dangerous. It fools you. It cannot be taken. It must be killed."

Tone asked, "You see Jimmy Huaing as a black mamba? I must say that now seems quite accurate given what Mrs. Chang told us." He looked at Pero. "And how do you propose we accomplish this?"

For the next ten minutes, Pero outlined his plan—the only plan he thought could work. Mbuno, as expected, expertly modified it to the terrain of their destination.

Back inside, Pero explained and arranged for Mrs. Chang to stay with Niamba until they returned, explaining it may be three or four days. Mrs. Chang understood that there could be no calls, no communication with anyone until she heard of their safe return. Having been rescued, she understood her silence was critical for their safety. She did want to know what they were going to do, but all Pero would say was, "Mbuno has plans for Jimmy Huaing that you would rather not know about." He left it at that and Mrs. Chang did not press for an answer. These were people who kept her from being killed and she was determined not to risk their safety in return.

Niamba gently patted Mrs. Chang's head as if she were an infant and said, "Mimi kuchukua huduma yake." I will take care of her.

With the women's assurance, the men left the cottage and sped away. Pero removed the Silke Wire and handed it to Tone to return to Susanna. Pero urged Tone to hurry, explaining that with the many forces in opposition, speed was critical. While they drove to Wilson Airport, Pero confirmed his wish that Susanna should stay at the Bowmans.

Tone explained he had already arranged for two armed guards, ex-military experts, to help ensure the safety of his home. Pero told Tone to double that. He was more than ever worried about who they were up against. "Tone, we need them to chase us and not know about you, Susanna, Niamba, or where Mrs. Chang is. Can you make sure of that?"

Tone assured him he could handle his end, adding, "Mind the trap you set gets them and not you." As they pulled up at the south gate to the airport, Pero and Mbuno got out quickly and motioned Tone onward, Pero waving the satellite phone to remind Tone they would be calling.

Wilson Airport is on the western outskirts of Nairobi at an altitude of five thousand feet. Long the exotic safari departure and arrival point, Wilson is steeped in the lore and myths of the greatest white hunterss, their illustrious clients and adventure. Leaving the ground at Wilson always means an adventure is about to begin. It is infectious, permeates even the most experienced scouts and outfitters, and does so not without reason, for a safari in East Africa is always to journey to the edge of civilization, past the rim of the present and into a collective primordial past. In short, to go on safari is to feel alive. This time, the safari was to simply stay alive.

Waiting at Mara Airways was a Cessna T303 twin engine that Sheila at Tone Bowman's Flamingo Tours arranged to have waiting, all day if necessary. Pero casually walked up to Sheryl, the woman who ran Mara Airways, and exchanged greetings as they had long been friends. While Pero went over the manifest of supplies Tone had loaded aboard, Pero asked, "Anyone showing interest in our flight, Sheryl?"

Sheryl admired Pero. She especially revered his heroics during previous escapades of capturing terrorists at the airport. Her reply was terse, showing her concern for her friend, "Two Chinese men in joggers came to ask if your plane was ready and if I knew when you were leaving." Sheryl could see that Pero was instantly worried. "Relax, my friend. Tommy over at Wind Sky had called me to tell me two men asked about a plane ready for you over there too. I told them we had no order from you." It wasn't a lie. Her order would have come from Flamingo Tours. Sheryl was devoutly Christian and could not lie, Pero knew that. "I told them that, anyway, we had no available aircraft even if you wanted to order a plane and that they must have the wrong charter company."

"Did it satisfy them?"

"Yes, I am pretty sure. They immediately left, walking over to Yellow Wings."

Pero thanked her, said a fond goodbye, and walked out to the aircraft to find Mbuno already seated. The pilot welcomed Pero and indicated the right seat, "It's yours, mate. Sheryl said it was okay by company policy." Pero politely declined, wanting to sit and talk with Mbuno.

On the way to the Matthews Range, Mbuno explained to Pero where exactly they were going, "It is the place of the bongo and the forest rhino. They are in the forest all around and on top of the escarpment in the forest. The plane cannot land there. The plane strip is at the bottom. It is a big climb."

"And the campsite?"

"I gave Ube instructions—he has been here before. One maybe two miles into the forest at the top of the escarpment, there is a spring. Water. We will camp there. Ube knows the Samburu people. He told me he would hire two Samburu to help. They may meet us at the strip." Mbuno paused, and asked, "Will you be okay to climb?" He pointed at Pero's rib cage. Pero thought he'd hidden the sore ribs well. He assured Mbuno he could climb. "Good, then we will be like before." He meant on their foot safari along the Omo River. "Walking and sleeping in bags . . ." Mbuno pointed aft in the cabin where Pero saw rolled-up sleeping bags and satchels stuffed with food. Tone Bowman's staff had made great time in preparing for their sudden safari needs.

Pero had never spent much time in the Matthews Range, not to the top of the escarpment anyway. Out there, away from tourist areas, there would be no help from the outside and he wondered about an ambush.

Typically, Mbuno anticipated Pero's next question. "Yes, brother, it is safe, there is only one way up the escarpment. It is a hard climb." Adding, "From the top, one can watch. Watch who comes. They will think we are all on top." Mbuno was preparing the trap. Like most good animal traps, the obvious danger was not the real trap.

Pero, however, was also wondering exactly who they would lure into the trap, and who would show up. By now, Sun Yee On's spies will know we've left Wilson . . .

While the engines droned on, Pero sat in the seat across from Mbuno and spent the time thinking. The identity of the man Mbuno had subdued in the kitchen of Mrs. Chang's home was visually Chinese. That would tie in with the Sun Yee On connection. But Pero was sure the three other men were not typically desert or coastal Arab . . . all were dressed in the same black tracksuits and all wore beards. Their skin color was very dark, almost Middle Eastern. He thought, *Mercenaries?* He shook his head, trying to sort out that image and match a possible origin. If the Sun Yee On are running the poaching ring, is it purely a money exercise or is there something else going on?

Pero asked Mbuno for the gun. Handing it over, Mbuno commented it was Russian. Pero examined the pistol and could see nothing special; handing it back to Mbuno, he said, "You'd better keep this, in case."

Pero brooded. Somalis, poaching for money, for al-Shabaab . . . that was a clear link. But the Chinese helping al-Shabaab? Really? What for? The last thing the Chinese would want was to destabilize East Africa, or Central Africa for that matter. They are doing too much business here to want to change the power structure. The Chinese are against wanton terrorism. In Pero's mind, news reports, and late-night radio listening on world events filtered and replayed themselves in endless loops. And using the refugees from the civil war in Somalia makes sense for al-Shabaab, but no sense whatsoever for a Chinese criminal gang. Pero knew that all the Chinese triads, as the press called them, were into extortion, cargo robbery, graft, casinos, and kidnapping. What use would impoverished, hopeless refugee people be to a triad? And who the hell were those three guards keeping Mrs. Chang prisoner?

Pero, annoyed that he could not see a way through all the conflicting facts alone, realized he needed to talk with Lewis and ask questions only the CIA might have answers to—but that presented other problems. He wasn't sure he could trust the CIA after the leaks in Dadaab. Also, something about the goons—as he started thinking of the men Mbuno and he had tackled—nagged at him. Somehow, he felt the goons might be the key to unlocking an understanding of the mystery facing him. He looked across at Mbuno, and was about to ask Mbuno who he felt the men were when Mbuno locked eyes and simply said, "Brother, we must stop the poaching." Like Pero, Mbuno had been evaluating events and prospects—making his own plans.

The plane adjusted altitude and the pilot called back, "On our way down, landing in ten minutes."

Pero understood Mbuno's linear thinking. Focus on the one thing he could tackle, one thing that needed to be achieved. Stopping the poaching was, of course, the end goal they would all like, but was there something larger here that Pero had also stumbled upon, a thing he needed to address or, perhaps just as important, avoid? His natural curiosity nagging at him, he asked, "Mbuno, do you know who those goons were, the two you took care of outside Mrs. Chang's room?"

"Hawana kuja kutoka Kenya." They do not come from Kenya.

"Were they Somali, do you think?"

"La." The response was negative and assured. Mbuno, over the decades as an expert safari guide, came to know people's nationality with accuracy.

"Do you know what language they were speaking?"

Mbuno frowned. "Nina. Walikuwa wanaongea Kiajemi." I do. They were talking Persian.

Pero's spine stiffened. The plane made a sharp left bank, settled, dropped a few stomach-wrenching yards, and moments later the wheels touched the packed-earth surface of the airstrip.

Pero asked Mbuno, "Kiajemi? Farsi? Are you sure?"

"Walikuwa Kiajemi." They were Persian. Mbuno reached into his shirt, reaching down until he got to the bottom of his shirt tucked tight into the waistband of his trousers and pulled out a small plastic credit card–sized ID and handed it to Pero. Then Mbuno got up and helped the pilot lower the steps, looked out the open doorway, and was greeted by two Samburu trotting over to help. Mbuno descended the steps and directed them to the hatch at the back of the plane, to help unload supplies.

Alone in the plane, Pero stared at the card for moments, seeing the bearded photo of one of the kidnappers on the left side of the card, the Iranian national symbol on the top next to an icon every newspaper in the world often had reason to carry: the Islamic Revolutionary Guard Corps logo. And then, Pero's mind reeling from the evidence in his hand, his eyes focused on an additional icon—that of the Basij—a flying banner of a red ribbon folded on the left, the bottom trailing end forked to represent a serpent's tongue. Pero's blood ran cold. The Basij were the ultra-right-wing enforcers of the IRGC.

If Pero had thought he needed the help of Lewis or General Tews before, he was ever more sure now. And, he knew, matters were quickly becoming urgent, even desperate. Pero had lit the fuse of a bomb by setting up a simple trap. But now the fuse was shorter and the bomb vastly bigger.

Pero remembered an old teacher's explanation, "The Chinese symbol for crisis is danger over opportunity. The trick with any crisis is to make sure the opportunity is greater than the danger."

The two Samburu were decked out in ceremonial garb, usually meant to increase tourist revenue. Earlobes were stretched to hold a small white disc, a silver chain looped from the top of one ear, hanging below the lower lip but above the chin and then on to the top of the other ear. With a single red feather at the back of a tightly woven hairdo, their naked torsos and necks sported elaborate beadwork necklaces of blue, yellow, white, and orange. Known to be among the most handsome of all Kenya's tribes, the tall and fit Samburu were a warring tribe that had, in recent years, adapted to the tourist trade with alacrity. Pero trusted them in that role knowing that Mbuno was revered and vigilant—and they knew it.

Mbuno told Pero, "Ube chose well. These two will help. They are strong." Pero watched as the two men took on all the cargo as if it were nothing. Calling out "Ayahee" to the escarpment face, a response drifted across from the forest at the base of the escarpment matching their call and the two men set out to the cliff face. Pero thanked the pilot and dispatched him home, assuring him the satellite phone could call for a return ride when wanted. Pero and Mbuno watched as the pilot buttoned up the twin-engine plane, started both engines, powered to the end of the strip, roared back toward them, and took off, waggling the wings until he was almost out of sight in the clouds.

Clouds that were gathering, ominous and tall.

Pero walked toward the escarpment and the beginning of the path that led up the face. At the bottom of the path, before the long climb, a familiar voice came from the forest, "Pero, is that you?" Lewis emerged from the dense brush and extended a hand. Nancy, Bob, and Ube appeared behind him. "Hell of a place you chose here." Lewis was panting. "You do know I'm not a field agent, right?"

Pero greeted them all, then let Lewis talk for what seemed like tens of minutes but was probably only five. Everything Lewis said or complained about made no difference to Pero now. Everything that Lewis thought he knew was wrong; poaching, fundraising for al-Shabaab, Somali insurrection—none of those mattered as much as Pero's thoughts and evaluation, which were much clearer now.

This wasn't about al-Shabaab arming their troops. This was geopolitics on a powder keg scale. When Lewis seemed to be winding down, Pero simply asked, "When you use your phone—is there anyone listening in and taking it all down?" Lewis confirmed there was. Pero commanded, "Let's get set up, and then I'll explain."

In Pero's mind, there remained the nagging question: Who told Mrs. Chang and Commissioner Sing that Pero and his team were going to the Oasis? Until he knew the answer to that, no one was to be trusted unless they were face-to-face, phones off.

Looking up, the climb was steeper and more narrow than Pero thought at first glimpse. Near the top, the path narrowed to only the width of one shoe so you had to place a foot and then place the next foot in front of the first carefully so as not to overbalance. Like a tightrope walk, a fall could be fatal.

The Samburu would have no difficulty, nor, of course, would Nancy, Lewis, Ube, or Bob. Pero was, once more, acutely aware that his broad shoulders and increased size compared to those men would put him at a disadvantage.

In any event, he and Mbuno had no intention of climbing until the trap was sprung.

Mbuno was pointing the way up and explaining to everyone that one man on top, looking down, can stop anyone trying to climb. Pero told Lewis, Nancy, Bob, and Ube that in a few minutes they all needed to climb. The two Samburu were asked to make the climb right away and wait at the top with the gear.

Mbuno reminded Pero that soon rain would be coming.

Pero added to Ube, "Later, when you're on top, set up camp under cover, no fire, one man looking down with"—he motioned to Mbuno—"a gun. Okay?" Mbuno handed the gun to Ube, showing him how the safety worked. Watching the exchange, Lewis' expression was, suddenly, less friendly and beginning to be concerned.

Lewis was, gray hair and all, tall, trim, and not yet showing his age. Pero regretted having to make him climb, but he immediately dispelled any sympathy knowing this was the only way he could trust an open and frank discussion and still keep Lewis out of harm's way. Pero shook Lewis' hand and said, "Whatever you think, throw it all out. What we have to tell you, show you, will change everything. I need you to know the truth so that if we don't make it, you can take the next steps."

Lewis started to protest, but Pero patted Lewis' arm and, motioning to Mbuno, urged them to leave the escarpment bottom and go deeper into the forest. Pero stopped all conversation until they could all sit together. "I need us all to hear at the same time. Patience, please."

A clearing appeared in the forest. Mbuno said, "This is the place where I saw okapi many years ago. They will not come near now because we are here, but we must watch for the rhino as they do not like intruders."

Nancy asked, "If they come here, what do we do?"

Mbuno explained, "You can climb a tree, rhinos do not climb. But you must not make noise. Rhino do not see very well, but they have very good ears." Lewis wanted to talk, but Pero told him to wait. Lewis, not accustomed to being told what to do, looked angry. Pero apologized, explaining he had to be sure.

"Sure of what?" Lewis asked.

"Ears. Ours, listening. All radios, and phones, off. Right?"

Pero asked everyone to sit. They arranged themselves in a semicircle, open end facing the path back to the airstrip. Pero started in.

"Everything we thought is wrong. The list? It has to be a plant, meant to be captured and released to the press, to get the world's police involved. Are the names on the list accurate? I have no idea. But the list is a weapon."

Lewis had no idea what Pero was talking about, nor did the team.

Pero took out his Leica, scrolled to the first image of the list, handed the camera to Lewis, then said, "We took this list off Rahman Qamaan who was preparing it, guarding it with his life. Or so he thought." Bob and Nancy were appalled that Pero should show the list. They reminded him no one should see the list, discuss it, it was too dangerous, and, anyway, when did he photograph it? Pero nodded, explained his bathroom photography in Mombasa, and agreed, "Yes, it is dangerous, but not in the way we thought. Look, if you were al-Shabaab, why would you keep a list of names and amounts?" Lewis was scrolling through the names, muttering oaths to himself. "Names and amounts that were paid to your criminal organization? Why would you keep their names and what they paid? Makes no sense. If you were going to blackmail them, perhaps, but some of those names are from Kuwait, Iraq, Syria, Saudi Arabia, Djibouti, the UAE, and so on—all countries that sometimes secretly fund al-Shabaab. Would you keep a list of your friends' purchases for blackmail? Nope. So why? Is it to see who your best customers are to sell them more merchandise? Sure, but you would never want to compromise your customers' names with money already paid. So the list is what it is, a list of names of the richest, most powerful people around the world, from the sultan of Brunei to the president of Russia, from some of the richest Americans to presidents in Argentina and Peru. How many names, Lewis?"

Lewis looked up from the camera screen. "Over a hundred."

"And each of them is a world leader, right?" Lewis agreed. "So the only purpose I can see for this list is to destabilize the world by shaming and prosecuting all these world leaders."

Lewis asked, "Why would al-Shabaab want to do that? Some of these names are their allies. That's throwing out the babies with the bathwater."

Pero had thought of that. "Right, and remember, they were taking two hundred million a year out in cold hard cash from selling the ivory, every year, for ten years at least. If they were selling matched pairs of tusks, even more. So, if they kill off their clients, their funding disappears from every source." He paused. "So, al-Shabaab had no interest in making a list unless they were made to, convinced to make it, paid to make it." A good storyteller, he paused for effect. "I am sure it's a fake list, given to them."

Nancy piped up, "Pero, this is too damn confusing. They were poachers, keeping money records, isn't that plain enough?"

Pero shook his head. "Yeah, that's what it was designed to look like. Taking it off an al-Shabaab would prove authenticity. But, Nancy, Rahman Qamaan was a thug, a strongman, keeping the poaching going. Why would he be there with a list like this? Their accountant? Nonsense." He turned to Lewis, forcibly quizzing him, "Charles, you asked and General Tews leaned on us to let Gonzales and Bob here capture Rahman, right? You already knew the man was there and you thought he was their accountant, kinda like Al Capone's accountant, right?" Lewis agreed it was the intel they received. "And can I assume that intel came from one source, the same source who you kept informed that we would be leaving for the Oasis? Right?"

Lewis squirmed and did not reply.

Pero lost his temper. "Charles, I'll throw you and the whole bunch of idiots you work for off that cliff if you don't respond. It's our lives at stake and you bungled it." Pero picked up the phone and continued, "Or I'll call Pontnoire and tell him all this, if you like. Him I trust. You? Not so much right now."

Lewis crumbled. "Okay, okay. We have a source. Been in the agency for over ten years. Inherited from the previous director. That intel has always been good. Terrorist traffic, solid, reliable tips . . . and this time it was that a senior financial man for al-Shabaab and al-Qaida was checking or closing down a poaching operation near the Omo River in southern Ethiopia. Then you"—he looked at Pero, Nancy, and Mbuno in turn— "you three stumbled on their operation and panicked them. When they panicked, we thought we were going to lose them or at least that Qamaan guy."

Pero took a wild leap and asked, "This trusted—obviously not to be trusted—source . . . he doesn't happen to be ex-Iranian by any chance?" Lewis' head shot up, his eyes wide. Pero continued, "It fits."

Lewis was dumbfounded and started to babble questions, at one point saying it wasn't a man but a woman, ex-wife of a general . . . Pero immediately interrupted, "Husband wasn't high up in the Basij by any chance?"

Lewis fell back on his rear on the soft earth, hands wiping the sweat off his face. His astonishment was evident. Sitting up straight, he asked, "How did you put this together?" Then, looking dejected, Lewis said, "Sorry, she knows I'm here. She's working from my office."

Pero replied, "Charles, it's okay, we can use this. Give me your phone number, I'll need to call you if we're separated—without anyone in DC hearing." Satellite phone to satellite phone was not scrambled, but Pero wasn't worried about anyone listening in locally, just those listening in at CIA HQ.

Bob was still fuming and angrily answered for Nancy and himself, "Hey, Mr. Lewis, I quit. Can't work for rank amateurs." He turned to Pero, smiling, "What's the plan, video man? I'm ready and able; let's stop these bastards."

Lewis, realizing that Pero had more answers, pleadingly asked, "Can you please fully explain, Pero?"

And so Pero did. He explained that the list was meant to be captured in Dadaab by the forces someone ordered there, probably UNHCR Mrs. Chang who was, after all, not the real Mrs. Chang. He told the story of Mbuno's rescue of the real Mrs. Chang, Mbuno explained it was Pero who carried the woman. Pero explained that the fake Mrs. Chang worked for Sun Yee On, probably only reporting to Jimmy Huaing in Nairobi, a son of the founder of Sun Yee On. Sun Yee On may or may not be involved, but Jimmy Huaing was clearly in charge of the operation in Kenya since the guards holding the real Mrs. Chang were Basij. Only someone in charge of the Sun Yee On could have made such a hiring decision. He threw down the ID card Mbuno had liberated.

Lewis picked the card up. If he could turn whiter, he would have vanished.

Pero continued, "On the plane, I was thinking, what do all the names on the list have in common? They are all in the oil business or people who deal with oil cartels to the exclusion of the world's number one embargoed oil producer: Iran. If all these companies and countries' leaders fall out of public favor, Iran may fall back into favor." He paused, seeing that argument was weak and no one's face showed they believed that either. "Yes, I thought that was weak as well. But add in the al-Shabaab element and you get civil unrest in Somalia. What would happen if Somalia fell into the wrong hands again? It's on the brink as we all know. What if the Chinese propped up that new government or what if al-Shabaab made a guarantee to the Chinese, the ones they think they're legitimately working with, and in return for the money they'll need, agreed to throttle the oil coming around the Horn of Africa through the Gulf of Aden? And what if the Chinese get to build a naval or airbase in Somalia? Maybe on one of the uninhabited islands off the coast? Smack-dab in the middle of the shipping lanes? China could be a player in energy delivery worldwide."

CHAPTER 14

NGUVU KUBWA—AN OVERWHELMING FORCE

Everyone was silent until Mbuno spoke up, "It is still the poaching, it must stop."

Pero agreed, adding, "Yes, brother, we can stop them, but if we do not stop the Chinese expansion, tomorrow they can fund hundreds of poaching gangs all across Africa and we can't stop all of them." Pero pled his case. "If Sun Yee On are involved—and with the sale of ivory into China, they are likely to be and have been for decades—maybe someone in Beijing agreed to let al-Shabaab and Sun Yee On continue ivory trading if they did Beijing a favor. And it's a huge favor. Beijing needs Iran's oil, they get it cheap across their common border, I read about that in a UN report of sanctions being flouted." He took a breath, his brain spewing out connections and possibilities. "So, Beijing allows Sun Yee On to continue ivory trading, but above all Beijing wants to be an oil cartel player; getting access to Somalia and access to the Indian Ocean for their navy is one hell of a trade-off for allowing al-Shabaab to keep their ivory money. And it makes sense that Iran supplies serious muscle to make the coup in Somalia happen and stick."

Pero, stopping to think, allowed Mbuno to interject, "The mamba always has a nest for breeding, it is best we kill all the mamba before they spread." No one was sure just what nest Mbuno was talking about.

Lewis didn't understand the reference to something called mamba but knew he had to act and act fast. "Pero, I need to call DC and start the capture of that damn woman."

"Oh no, Charles, we need her." Pero shook his head. "Wait a moment." A thought popped into his head. "There is no way China would want to help the creation of an Islamic nation under al-Shabaab. Allow Sun Yee On to destabilize a pro-Western government, that I can see; bring chaos, yes. Get access to more oil from Iran, also yes. But fund al-Shabaab to create another Islamic nation? Maybe, if the end prize were great enough. Something permanent. The only prize worthwhile for China would be in the Gulf of Aden, a seaport, something like that. The Basij and Iran would support it, because what can block ships can also allow ships to slip through, breaking the Iran embargo. Even a potential blockade . . ." Halting his explanation, Pero raised a hand. "Socotra Island! In the damn middle of the Gulf of Aden. There are atolls near there." He looked at Lewis. "Aren't the Chinese building naval bases on atolls in the China Sea? They know how and can do it here."

Lewis agreed, revealing, "They have a flotilla of navy dredgers and construction ships moored off Karachi in Pakistan. We've been tracking them for months. They seem to be harbored there for repairs. That's what they claim."

Pero was, frankly, amazed at the puzzle they were uncovering. "It all fits, the whole damn thing fits. Somalia and Yemen have been disputing the ownership of those islands. I think there are four or five of them if I remember correctly. In any dispute, the Chinese can simply annex what they want. And Yemen is still in civil war, hardly likely to oppose anyone." He paced and now became apologetic. "Damn, this is huge. I've gotten us all into a mess. We're up against Sun Yee On, the Basij, Beijing, and, never least, al-Shabaab."

Mbuno added, "If we stop the poaching, they all stop; their nest will die."

Pero responded, "Let's hope so, but for now we need to prepare for what's coming. So, Lewis, when you get up top, call your office. Make no mention of the Basij but explain that we've uncovered a double cross by the Sun Yee On to grab not only the al-Shabaab money but also to set up a new puppet Somali government. And pass the word that when there is one, just like in the gambling and crime-ridden Macao, they'll make more money. Tell your office Beijing has made a deal with Sun Yee On's Huaing for a new Macao in Somalia. New Somalia equals no religion, definitely no Islam, loads of tourism and gambling. Everything an Islamic state like Iran would hate. Let her feed that back to the religious nuts in the Basij in Tehran."

Lewis agreed that should both get the Basij out of the picture and set them against Jimmy Huaing in a hurry. Pero then suggested he tell his office that the list was discovered by a maid at the Interconti working for the Israeli Mossad. That would kill the list's usefulness. Again Lewis agreed, adding, "You sure you don't want my job?"

Pero let that slide, continuing, "The way I see it, there are two possibilities here. Jimmy Huaing either is already acting on his own or soon will be. Maybe he's breaking away from the Sun Yee On even though his father founded it—and by the way, why wasn't he made head? That might be a motive. Can you find out, Charles? Anyway, I'm not sure about that, but if Jimmy Huaing comes for us, then we'll have a better idea if this is a Chinese operation, a Sun Yee On operation, or a solo venture. But the moment your mole tells the Basij that an Islamic state is not in the cards, you can be sure he won't arrive with Iranians."

Lewis thought and replied, "I'm not so sure Beijing knows anything. Jimmy Huaing may want to pull off a coup with the help of the Basij and simply up his status with Beijing and the Sun Yee On, later on, delivering a coup on a platter. Frankly, he won't come alone, if he personally comes at all."

"Okay, there's that possibility," Pero said, then quickly added, "So also make sure you tell them that you're on top of the escarpment, looking down on the airstrip, awaiting Sun Yee On arrival."

Bob asked, "What's next?" And answered it himself, "We see who turns up."

Mbuno looked up. "Ndege ni kutua." A plane is landing.

Pero turned his head skyward. Raindrops hit his eyes. He wasn't sure he was ready for the rain. But before everyone got to the path up the escarpment the skies opened and the downpour began. Mbuno looked up and predicted it would last the rest of the day and night. Monsoons had arrived.

Urging them to climb quickly, Pero put Nancy, Lewis, and Ube up the path first, with Bob covering the rear. He assured them he and Mbuno would follow later. It was a white lie, but the sound of an incoming plane spurred them on and before the plane touched down, the four had made the climb to the top. Pero yelled up and reminded Nancy to film everything. She waved back down.

Pero thought, *With this rain now, I doubt I would want to climb in any event.*

He and Mbuno never had any intention of making the climb.

Pero could not recognize the type of twin-engined plane they saw land. Markings were tail number and camouflage paint only. The registration number began with 5H so Pero guessed it came from Tanzania. It handled the short runway easily since it was turning back to the staging area before even running out of airstrip. When the door opened, Pero counted only eight men disembark. Four wore military camouflage gear.

They split into two groups. Pero watched one of the military men speak into a phone or walkie-talkie. Within seconds, he became animated, yelling at the four nonmilitary types. Some pushing began and the man with the phone ordered the four military men back onto the plane. Immediately, the plane revved up, taxied to the end of the runway, and departed. The other four men moved to the end of the airstrip, out of gun range from the escarpment, and squatted, waiting.

Pero called Lewis and asked if he had reached his office. He explained he had and Pero told him what happened, adding, "My guess is the four and the plane, from Tanzania, were all Basij. They're gone, leaving behind four who are presumably Sun Yee On." He had Lewis pass the phone to Nancy, asking, "Nancy, can you see anything? Zoom in . . ."

"A couple of them have looked up, seem to be estimating the path up. I assume you wanted them to know we're here . . . Chinese faces, all of them . . . no rifles, just sidearms that I can see. One's using binoculars."

A few minutes later, a second plane approached. Pero strained to see through the rain what type and capacity. A Cessna Caravan, a single-engine turboprop, swooped over their heads, circling the forest. After two sweeps of the escarpment, the plane lined up on the airstrip below and made a gentle landing in the pouring rain, tires splashing through the puddles. Two people got out, a man and a woman. The four waiting men trotted to join them.

Pero called Lewis' phone again and asked if Nancy could zoom in again. She gave a running commentary. "Hello, Mrs. Chang is the woman, I'd know that woman anywhere. She's seen us with her binos. The guy she's with is wearing a safari suit, like he came from an office somewhere."

Mbuno commented, "They are making camp."

Pero sat on a log near the edge of the forest, mumbling to himself and Nancy on the phone. "Now that Mrs. Chang's cover is blown, why aren't they attacking, starting the climb? They must know the real Mrs. Chang told us about Sun Yee On. And they have to assume we have satellite phones or at least cell phones."

Nancy responded, "Maybe they want to keep us up here. What was it you said? They want the list found—they must still assume we have it here—and if that Mrs. Chang has convinced someone in authority that we're a poaching gang and that they have us cornered . . ."

It was as Mbuno had planned, they had set up a perfect trap for themselves—if they were on top of the escarpment. What Huaing and Mrs. Chang had not counted on were the bush skills of East Africa's premier scout and ex-elephant hunter waiting in the forest.

What Pero had not counted on was that Jimmy Huaing had called the police to arrest a poaching gang. Lewis got phone confirmation that Kenya's Anti-Poaching Rangers, Team Lioness, were on the way.

A common problem for tourist visitors in East Africa is a lack of Western efficiency. Huaing may have called in the police, but the police would take time, maybe a day, to show up in so remote a location. Pero and Mbuno, down below, and Ube, Bob, and

Nancy, up the escarpment, were on watch, taking turns. They observed the four men and the two Sun Yee On leaders set up a small campsite. From the Cessna Caravan, the men unloaded supplies and soon had a fire going, despite the rain, using jet fuel drained from the Cessna's wing tank to kindle a blaze.

On the phone, Bob commented, "Well, my guess is they know the police are coming but not when. Not tonight anyway."

Mbuno smiled. Nighttime tracking was his specialty.

Lewis had news. "Passed on all you requested. No feedback yet. Put a call into General Tews, secure line not through the office. Tews reports that the last tusk haul was found in an abandoned truck south of Dadaab. Evidence of a struggle, no body or person found. Your doing?" Pero assured him he hadn't done it and avoided telling him Bob had shot the driver. Lewis continued, "The truck had a small metal lockbox. Stuffed with banknotes and checking account books for Nairobi. We opened the accounts. We found huge sums being laundered through two Chinese shipping companies. Also, there's a shipping company linked to Sun Yee On leaving Mogadishu tied into the affair. Their whole operation is busted. Tews has taken charge with Army Intel, leaving us out of it." He meant leaving the CIA out of it. Pero wanted to know what Tews thought of the Gulf of Aden scenario Pero had imagined. Lewis chuckled, imitating Tews' Texas accent, and responded, "Damn son of a female dog, that fellow's got a sick mind. We'll check on that, right away."

Somehow, knowing that General Tews and AFRICOM were in charge of the destruction of such geopolitical altering schemes gave Pero confidence. He told Lewis so, aware that it carried a rebuke for the CIA in the process. Lewis told Pero to take it easy, there was still a night of danger for them all to face.

What Lewis could not know, but Bob was sure to explain, was that Mbuno would, from that moment forward, be in charge of the mamba nest below. Mbuno's capability had to be witnessed to be understood and Pero knew he would be taking Mbuno's orders, gratefully, for what was to come.

Night fell. Mbuno disappeared. Pero had not anticipated that.

Pero spent over an hour watching, peering through the darkness and rain trying to see. It's hard for people not accustomed to the bush to understand that tropical cloud cover plus determined rainfall, especially at night, results in absolute darkness and human isolation. Not even nighttime animals venture out in those conditions. All the senses are affected. No sight, smell swamped by the misty damp earth vapors filling the nose, hearing diminished as the solid rain breaks apart sound waves. Even touch was unreliable, as everything is soaked through and through and either resembles wet cloth or sticky mud. As for taste, open your mouth and the flavor of dust-impregnated water obliterates any individual flavor.

Pero had experienced that isolation before, but the absence of Mbuno while they needed to watch the completely invisible Sun Yee On crew, was unnerving. An hour into his vigil, there was a small tug of his sleeve. Pero startled, turned, and bumped into Mbuno's arm. "Sorry, you startled me."

"It is good. Now we go. They are moving."

Holding Pero's sleeve, Mbuno walked Pero forward, out of the cover of the last trees, onto the airstrip apron. Pero still could not see a thing. He asked Mbuno to stop, asking, "How can you know where we are going?"

"I saw the land before. I remember."

"You remember?"

"Ndiyo. Kutembea." Yes, walk.

They continued, Pero following the tug on his sleeve as they made their way up the airstrip. The ground was level and

Mbuno's footsteps were sure and unhesitating until they reached what Pero felt must be near the end, then Mbuno turned left, off the airstrip, and whispered, "Lift up your feet."

Pero then took shorter steps, each time lifting his foot anticipating rocks or fallen branches or trees. At one point, Mbuno moved swiftly to the right and then back left, around some unseen obstacle. After a few minutes, he pulled Pero's sleeve down and they squatted. Ears pricking, straining all his senses for any indication of what was before them, or for that matter behind them, Pero was acutely aware that they were in the middle of a wild area, in the middle of the night, in a downpour, completely unprotected. Of course, his worry passed since he knew Mbuno, more than any other person he had ever known, was a master in this element. It gave Pero the confidence and courage he had momentarily lacked.

Whispering directly into his ear, Mbuno gave instructions, "Do not move. Brother, stay here." Pero nodded. Mbuno disappeared. Moments later there was gunfire. Pero thought he saw a flash of a gun very close by. Then all went silent.

A woman's voice yelled, "Nǐ zài kāi shénme qiāng?" She repeated it. Pero heard part of a response but didn't know what was said. The woman's voice was near, very, very near.

Once again, Pero jumped as Mbuno tugged at his sleeve. Whispering into Pero's ear, he said, "Kytambaa . . ." Crawl. Pero did as he was told and Mbuno tugged his sleeve for a few yards. Pero felt something near his face and reached out, gingerly. It was nylon. Mbuno tapped Pero's ear. Pero understood, inched up, and put his ear near the tent nylon, listening. Two people were having a discussion, a heated discussion. The man's voice was pleading, the woman furious.

Pero recognized the fake Mrs. Chang's voice. "Nǐ shībàile. Méiyǒu gèng duō de zhēnglùn. Míngtiān wǒmen líkāi, nín shōushí zhège làntānzi."

The response was in English, the man's voice desperate, his accent Chinese, "I did what you asked, I set it all up."

Her voice had a finality, "You failed, Huaing. Enough."

Pero then knew who Huaing's boss was. The fake Mrs. Chang was higher up in Sun Yee On than he was. Mbuno tugged at Pero's sleeve and they crawled back for maybe twenty yards.

Whispering in each other's ears, Pero explained who the top mamba was. Mbuno agreed. Mbuno told Pero that the nest needed to be cleaned. Pero agreed but wondered what Lewis and General Tews would give to capture that woman. Mbuno knew Pero well enough to need to dispel any such foolishness, saying, "They do not leave here, brother." There was a determination Pero could not disregard. He owed Mbuno that.

Pero asked, "What now? How do you want to deal with them? Remember, if the rain stops tomorrow, the police may come and they will escape."

Mbuno simply said, "Wait here."

Twenty minutes later, Mbuno returned and handed Pero a pistol, safety catch on, Pero felt the steel and surmised it was likely a 9 mm Glock. He whispered, "Now there are only two watu wa Kichina." Two Chinese men. "I will take care of them . . ."

At that moment, a single gunshot came from very near the place where Pero was sure they'd found the tent. Then the woman's voice yelled, "Dào wǒ zhèlǐ lái. Huáng sǐle, bǎohù wǒ."

Pero heard Huaing's name clearly.

Mbuno tugged Pero's sleeve and they crawled toward the tent and then off to the left. Moments later, a campfire exploded in flame, the smell of kerosene reaching Pero's nostrils. It illuminated the tent walls where Pero and Mbuno crouched. Mbuno took out his knife and made a slit to peer into the tent and saw

Mrs. Chang and two men talking and gesticulating. Mbuno moved aside and Pero peeked in. From the gestures, Pero was sure the two men were expressing they had no idea where the other men were.

On the floor of the tent, next to a fold-out cot, lay the body of Jimmy Huaing still oozing blood from a head wound. In Mrs. Chang's hand, a pistol caught the flickering light from the campfire. As Pero watched, one of the men went off to their left and she called after him. When he returned, he was dragging a body by one arm. Mrs. Chang kneeled and examined the man. She was puzzled, there seemed to be no wound, she opened his tracksuit and felt for something. The two men with her stood to military attention. Pero motioned to Mbuno to look.

The woman stood and looked about, trying to see through the curtain of rain. She issued an order, "Yǒurén zhèyàng zuòle. Zhǎodào tāmen." The men looked at each other, drawing their pistols, and each went slowly into the rain, away from the fire, on the hunt.

Mbuno put his mouth close to Pero's ear and whispered, "I will get them. You get her." Pero nodded but felt less confident. The woman was holding a pistol—a pistol she knew how to use—and Pero had no weapon. It was Mbuno's thought as well as he passed his small, very sharp knife to Pero. Mbuno rose and went into his hunting crouch run and disappeared.

Watching through the tiny slit in the tent, Pero saw the woman reach for a small satchel and a flashlight. She shouldered the satchel, lit the light, and turned toward the fire blazing, now slowly dying in the rain, beyond. Pero moved, by feel, around the tent, intent on following her.

The flashlight illuminated the ground, inches in front of her steps as she made her way to the end of the airstrip and the parked Cessna Caravan.

The rain let up suddenly, with only a fine drizzle still falling. Pero looked up and saw the clouds thinning and moonlight creeping through as a glow.

At the rear of the cabin, she rotated the door handle and opened the door, allowing the fold-down steps to drop. She climbed up and walked down the narrow space between the seats to the front, settling in the copilot's chair. She reached for the radio controls.

Pero had to move quickly, afraid she might see, even though the moonlight was very faint.

Like most aircraft in East Africa, the Cessna had two antennas, one VHF and one UHF. The UHF antenna was always longer and as aft of the plane as possible, to get better reception for long-distance communication. UHF was the over-the-horizon radio, critical for use in such vast areas.

By the tail, Pero reached up high, took out Mbuno's sharp knife and cut through the vinyl sleeve then slipped the blade between the spring outer coil of the antenna. The knife, ultra-sharp, cut the wire in the center. Pero was lowering his hand when her voice said, "Keep your hand up, and the other one. You moved the plane, that was a mistake." Pero raised his left hand and turned to face Mrs. Chang aiming a pistol at him. She shone the flashlight on his face.

"Well, madam, whoever you are, care to tell me your name?"

She recognized him but showed no surprise. "I have no urge to tell you anything, Mr. Baltazar. Sit down." Pero looked at the mud at his feet. She waved the pistol and he sat. "You may be most useful to me. It seems it is time to leave and I need a pilot." Pero started to deny he could fly the Cessna. "Please, let's not try such stupid games. You flew the Skyvan, although you crashed it, albeit somewhat safely, so you can fly this single." She meant single engine.

Pero marveled at her perfect English. "Madam Whoever, what makes you think I can or want to?" And, from his seated position, he asked, "I can't keep on calling you madam, want to give me something to call you? We all know you're not Mrs. Chang."

"You may call me Zi Mao. Now, get up and familiarize yourself with the aircraft and prepare to take us away from here."

Pero knew it was fruitless to resist. First, there was the gun; second, she was clearly competent with the pistol, having killed Huaing, and that gave him an idea. Slowly he rose, hands aloft, and walked to the stairs. He climbed aboard and walked up the aisle, with her following, pistol at the ready. She lifted the steps, closed the aft door, and locked it, all done one-handed while she kept the gun pointed at him. As he settled in the pilot's chair he asked, "Why did you have to shoot Huaing? He was your pilot, yes?"

"He became expendable, as you may be. But you ruined my chance to call for my backup transportation, so you'll have to do. Make ready. We are leaving."

Pero put a shocked look on his face. "In this rain? Are you crazy? We'll never make the end of the runway!" He waved an arm forward as if demonstrating the futility of such a rash decision.

Zi Mao was unimpressed. "It does not matter what you think. We will fly, we will crash, it makes little difference. But we will not be here."

Pero understood. In a few hours, it would be morning and she wanted to be long gone before authorities arrived, authorities no doubt Huaing had arranged. He decided to test the theory. Slowly reaching for the plane's manual, he said, "I have to check the starting procedure. Every one of these planes' engines are different." He buried his nose in the book, asking, "It was Huaing's idea to bring the cops, was it?"

"Yes."

"Pretty stupid of him." Pero thought out loud, and then the penny dropped, "Ah, he didn't know who was here, did he? He thought it was just us documentary makers, right? He didn't know who is really here. No way the authorities would believe him over our man."

Sitting in the first row of seats in the cabin, pistol unwavering on her target, she responded, "Clever of you. He thought he had it all planned out. Little boy wanting to take over his father's legacy—and then gambled and was bound to lose. I was only here to try and sort out his mess. Those al-Shabaab idiots were careless in using the refugees at Dadaab, especially the Ifo camp. Too many spies, too many ears. Too many bribes to keep it all quiet."

Pero reached the point of starting the engine. "Are we waiting for your colleagues?"

"I told you before, do not try and be clever. Start and leave." Pero knew then that she had calculated there were more people working with Pero in the darkness of night. "If they survive, they will understand my safety is more important. If they do not, it is of no consequence." The woman was cold-blooded, as cold-blooded as any Pero ever had the misfortune to meet. He started the turbine and waited until the dials all read within limits and asked when she wanted to depart. "Now, immediately."

Pero turned on all the landing lights, showing the strip before him.

The packed earth airstrip was slippery but not yet feet deep in mud. Pero knew that even a day later and this airstrip would never allow a takeoff. He explained, "There's no wind, but I want to go to the end of the runway and come back down this way, that way, if the climbing rate is slow, I won't hit the escarpment."

"Do what is necessary."

As Pero taxied down the airstrip, he worked the steering and rudder pedals, fighting the plane's tendency to skid and side-slip. "You know, these may be your very last moments on earth, Zi Mao. I am hardly a good enough pilot to pull this off." The plane suddenly veered left and Pero had to fight to get it back to the centerline. "See, and at a good speed this will be even more dangerous. You sure you want to try this?"

"Proceed. That is an order."

Another thought occurred and in his mindless fear for what he was about to attempt, Pero blurted out, "Oh, I get it. You're not with Sun Yee On, you're MSS, aren't you?" The MSS were the Ministry of State Security, the CIA of China. He glanced at her face and saw recognition. "You were sent to see if Sun Yee On's boy was likely to deliver on his promise, right?"

Zi Mao said nothing. Pero had reached the end of the airstrip and carefully swiveled the plane around, skidding sharply to the left. He placed the over-the-shoulder harness on while wondering if the undercarriage would sheer off on such lateral pressure. It held, somehow, and he thanked the people who built the Caravan, *like a truck, reliable.*

Using the time before what he was sure was going to be an early demise, he asked, "So you have to be a colonel or higher, yes? Your cousin, the real Mrs. Chang, remembered you. She was pissed you stole her clothes." He locked the brakes and asked once again, "You still sure about this?" The airstrip lay straight ahead of them, partially illuminated by the plane's landing lights. The rain started again, building in earnest. He tightened his seat belt as hard as he could and then turned the flaps to twenty degrees. He could not read the setting for the flaps in the manual and was guessing.

"I am sure, Mr. Baltazar. Proceed." Cold sweat dripped down

his back. Reaching to the center console, he inched the throttle forward until the engine was screaming. They did not move. "Why aren't we moving, Mr. Baltazar? I would just as soon kill you here and now."

He looked back at her, reaching for the propeller pitch at the same time, pushing it all the way forward and releasing the brakes at the same time. The powerful turbine and Hartzell blades bit the air and the plane shot forward. For all her composure, Zi Mao was startled and gripped the handrest. The gun wavered but came back on target.

At ninety knots, the twenty degrees of flaps did their trick and the plane leaped into the air. Pero reached down and reduced the flaps, allowing the blades to continue pulling as strongly as possible. The engine, a powerful jet turbine, whined in slight agony.

Their climb rate was a thousand feet per minute and they were shooting up at a steep angle. Pero watched the speed indicator and pulled the yoke closer to his chest, causing the plane to slow but continue to climb at a steeper angle. Pero thought, *In about a minute, we'll stall, and that will be that.*

Zi Mao ordered, "You will fly south-southeast and when you reach the coast I will tell you where to land."

The stall warning buzzer kicked in. Pero appeared panicked, yelling, "What the hell is that? What do I do?"

Zi Mao looked about anxiously. "Give me the book!"

As he passed it back to her, Pero pushed the column forward with his left hand and then turned the yoke sharply to the right while pushing on the right pedal. The Cessna inverted and, strapped in, Pero flew the plane upside down, then pulled the column back putting the plane into a steep dive.

Zi Mao had bounced off the roof of the cockpit, dropping the gun in her attempt to cushion the blow, and then she careened forward into the back of the copilot's chair. Once she reached that point, Pero pushed the column forward and Zi Mao pounced back and crashed into the first row of seats, Pero pulled the column, then pushed it again . . . again and again, until the weightless form of Zi Mao was a completely inert bundle at the back of the cabin.

Carefully, slowly, with trial and error, Pero righted the plane, trimmed the forward speed to under a hundred twenty knots, searched for, found, and set the autopilot. Unstrapping, he calmly walked back, picked up the gun, and went to inspect Zi Mao. He felt for a pulse and found none. Not sure, he lifted her and strapped her into a rear seat, borrowing a cargo strap to circle the seat and running the strap through her open mouth. The smell of her bowels evacuating finally convinced him she was dead.

He stopped to collect her satchel and put in in the copilot's seat. His eyes narrowed as he thought, *Lewis will want what's in there . . .*

Returned to the pilot's chair, Pero dialed up 118.1 MHz, Kenya Air Traffic Control—*Funny, I'll never forget that number now*—keyed the microphone, and called, "Mayday, Mayday, this is Cessna Caravan . . ." He read the call sign off the Formica tag glued to the dashboard, spun the transponder numbers. "This is a hijacked charter plane. I'm squawking 7777 and requesting guidance to return to Nairobi, Wilson Airport. Hijacker dead."

Within seconds, especially after he said there had been a hijack and a person was dead aboard, Nairobi scrambled two Tigers out of Moi Airbase in Eastleigh, Nairobi, and Pero awaited their arrival while he answered questions as briefly as possible. He gave heading, his ability to fly level, his unfamiliarity with the Caravan, which he had never flown, and his desire to have some help with landing procedures. It was when he was asked his name that matters escalated. After that, only one authoritarian voice talked to him, on a different frequency and he was told to not say anything unless asked. He was assured the police would be awaiting his arrival.

If he got down in one piece.

And he almost did. The approach was textbook, in the pouring rain, with one of the Tigers in full stall mode riding alongside. The landing gear was inspected visually by the Tiger and pronounced intact. Pero had been a little worried after that last airstrip skid, but it would hold. The problem with his landing was that he so wanted the flight to end that he cut the engine speed instead of the propeller pitch and the plane floated a little far and, suddenly, Pero saw the end of the runway looming, even with the brakes full on. Without power, even changing the pitch of the blades to reverse, seemed to have little effect. Sure enough, the Cessna ran off the asphalt onto the grass, skidded, dipped a wing, spun around just as Pero had done in Dadaab, and then the right landing gear finally quit.

CHAPTER 15

YOTE NI VIZURI KWAMBA MWISHO, KWAMBA NI YA KUTOSHA—ALL'S WELL THAT ENDS, THAT IS ENOUGH

Emergency services were quick. Pero was dizzy as he reached across to the bag on the copilot's seat. When the emergency people came aboard, they found him in the pilot's seat, clutching a personal bag as he merely pointed at Zi Mao in the back. The stink was getting bad, one of the firemen commented.

A police van pulled alongside and a burly man came up the steps to arrest Pero, telling everyone to stay away "While I do my duty."

Gibson Nabana, Pero's friend, sergeant of the Langata Police Station said, quietly, "I was told to arrest you and take you away from here." Pero nodded in agreement and handed him the Glock pistol. Gibson marched Pero off the plane and into the police van.

Once they were on their way, Pero asked, "Where to, Gibson?"

Gibson laughed. "Beer later, my friend. Now my captain wants to talk with you. Where are the other people you left with?"

It took three days, a full day after the downpours stopped, to get to the Matthews Range airstrip and pick up the rest of the team. There were exactly five people there. There never was any sight or mention of two missing Chinese. Nor of four other Chinese. Nor of any person shot in a tent. It seems the wildlife in that region had their own ideas.

Mbuno had collected their ID cards and gave them all to Lewis. When picked up, Lewis simply showed his diplomatic papers and the Kenya authorities, investigating the death of the Chinese woman hijacker, were forced not to search or question him. Lewis took up residence at the US Embassy while he worked with local operatives to seek out and destroy what was left of the al-Shabaab poaching operation and to clean house concerning any evidence that Pero, Nancy, Bob, Mbuno, or Ube were there at all, ever.

Turns out, the official record showed they never were.

The Kenya authorities were most helpful when Lewis' operatives were able to identify the Chinese shipping containers in Mombasa stuffed with tusks. The president of Kenya had another televised tusk-burning ceremony and celebrated his genius in stopping poaching, "And making Kenya the safe haven for African elephants!"

Mbuno attended, incognito, and wept at the loss of the heirs.

Niamba and Mrs. Chang had become fast friends. Her feet had healed, as promised, and she invited Niamba and Mbuno to a weekend at the beach, to a luxury hotel as her guest. Niamba asked, "Will there be fish?" Assured there would, for Niamba loved fresh, salty fish, the couple joined Mrs. Chang and a few of her colleagues. The weekend stretched a few more days for Niamba and Mbuno, both relaxing after the ordeal. On the third day, Mbuno asked Niamba how she had known, with the enki-dong, that there were two Mrs. Changs. Her look of derision silenced him. He smiled and so again acknowledged that her abilities were always, and would always be, greater than his. She made him order her fish for dinner, once more.

Bob and Nancy left for Pero's apartment in New York. As a wedding gift, he arranged for them to get married at the Church of the Heavenly Rest on Fifth Avenue and take a two-week paid leave, honeymooning, using his apartment. He called friends and also arranged theater and museum passes for all the best shows. He owed them that.

Lewis returned to DC and, on arriving, promptly resigned and, within a week, joined the presidential election campaign as an intelligence adviser to Ambassador Pontnoire who was, increasingly, looking like the favorite. No doubt Lewis brought Pontnoire up to speed. It helped that Pero eventually sent Lewis and Pontnoire the satchel and cell phone he had liberated from Zi Mao. The intel would help oppose the plans of the Chinese Ministry of State Security, plans a new administration now had evidence to confront them with.

Pero and Susanne took up residence at the Interconti. Tone Bowman, Mbuno, Niamba, and Ube came to visit unan-nounced from time to time—always warmly welcomed. Their discussions mostly centered on the happy demise of a major poaching syndicate that no one else knew they played a hand in destroying. They had a right to be proud.

More to Pero's liking, everyone felt enough was enough. Once again, he longed for a normal life as a producer and, looking at his wife, the joy of being married and an expectant father.

About two weeks after they'd settled into relaxing at the

Interconti, Pero and Susanna, Mbuno and Niamba were having lunch by the pool when Mr. Janardan, the undermanager, came up to their table. Politely he asked, "Mr. Baltazar, sir, we do appreciate your custom, but would you happen to have any idea how long you will be staying, sir?" In a hurry to make sure he was not hinting Pero should leave, he added, "You are most welcome to stay forever, sir, but it would help us to plan other reservations."

The forever part intrigued Pero. He looked at Susanna, wondering if she agreed. She knew his mind. She smiled up at the undermanager and explained for them both, "Another week, no more, Mr. Janardan. You are most kind to ask."

The matter was said with finality, so Pero merely nodded adding, "Oh, okay."

Susanna added, "We're off to the Oasis in Loyangalani for a week—no more—with our friends." She indicated Mbuno and Niamba.

Niamba added, "Wanaume hawa wana kazi. Hakuna likizo tena."

Mbuno translated, "Men have work. No more vacation."

Smiling and nodding, Susanna weighed in, "Yes, so, after the Oasis, it is back to work for my husband, no more holidays." She turned to look at Pero. "Right?"

What else could he say? Pero smiled, thanking Mr. Janardan who walked backward, gave a small bow, smiled, then turned and went away still smiling. Pero was his favorite guest.

Almost asking himself, Pero muttered, "So is everyone going to boss me around from now on?"

"Ach, yes, mein dummer Mann, someone has to. You always get into trouble."

Mbuno looked at Niamba, who nodded. Mbuno added, "Niamba can throw the enkidong later, and then you will have a more safe plan. One you have to follow, brother. It is best you know who is in real command." Niamba, understanding, tried to look smug. Susanna gave Pero a stern look but couldn't hold it long.

Then all three burst out laughing at him.

Pero put his head in his hands and, joining their merriment, asked, "What the heck has happened to my life?"

ABOUT THE AUTHOR

Peter Riva has traveled extensively throughout Africa, Asia, and Europe, spending many months spanning thirty years with legendary guides for East African adventurers. He created the *Wild Things* television series in 1995 and has worked for more than forty years as a literary agent. Riva writes science fiction and African adventure books, including the Mbuno & Pero thrillers. He lives in Gila, New Mexico.

THE MBUNO & PERO THRILLERS

FROM OPEN ROAD MEDIA

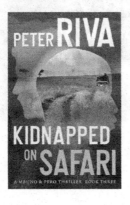

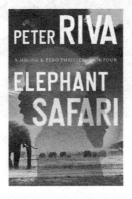

OPEN ROAD

INTEGRATED MEDIA

OPEN ROAD

INTEGRATED MEDIA

Find a full list of our authors and
titles at www.openroadmedia.com

FOLLOW US
@OpenRoadMedia